Charles Ives

The Isles of Summer

Nassau and the Bahamas

Charles Ives

The Isles of Summer
Nassau and the Bahamas

ISBN/EAN: 9783337406851

Printed in Europe, USA, Canada, Australia, Japan

Cover: Foto ©Andreas Hilbeck / pixelio.de

More available books at **www.hansebooks.com**

View from high ground back of Nassau.

THE ISLES OF SUMMER;

OR

Nassau and the Bahamas.

"A listless climate that, where, sooth to say,
No living wight could work, nor cared even to play."
Thompson's Castle of Indolence.

Illustrated Edition.

By CHARLES IVES, M. A.,

A MEMBER OF THE NEW HAVEN BAR.

➤ ● ◄

NEW HAVEN, CONN.:
PUBLISHED BY THE AUTHOR.
1880.

Hoggson & Robinson, Printers,
New Haven.

E. B. Sheldon & Co., Electrotypers,
New Haven.

TO HIS WIFE,

Catharine M. Osborn Ives,

THE COMPANION OF HIS TRAVELS,

WHO GREATLY INCREASED THE PLEASURES TO WHICH

NEW SCENES GAVE BIRTH,

ENCOURAGED AND AIDED HIM IN HIS LITERARY LABORS,

AND HELPED TO INSPIRE HIS BEST THOUGHTS,

THIS BOOK IS AFFECTIONATELY DEDICATED,

BY ITS AUTHOR.

PREFACE.

In offering this book to the reading public the author of the ISLES OF SUMMER is not unmindful of the maxim that "silence is golden." But silence is often a grave mistake, and may be a crime. The gift of speech has rendered possible the intellectual development which distinguishes the human race. The different stages in the progress and perfection of language are the tide marks of civilization. Take from man the power to express his thoughts, and you degrade him to a beast. There is a time to speak and a time to abstain from speaking. More than golden are those gems of thought which inspired genius has in by-gone times wedded to imperishable language and given as a rich legacy to the ages. But he is a wise man who knows how properly and when to address the great public and challenge its attention. The loud din of a garrulity stale and insipid, is ever mingled with the elevated and ennobling notes of inspired voices. Many of the utterances that evidence man's divine origin, to which the Present listens, broke the stillness of dim and distant ages in the morning of civilization, while the genius of each succeeding age has imparted to the literary air vibrations of its own, that mingle with those of the past, and a great tide of melody that never ebbs, rolls grandly down to our own times.

It would seem to be sufficient for the Present to sit at the footstool of the Past and listen. The public ear is not only filled but trained, educated and critical, so that a new voice has no more chance of being heard, than a little ripple of attracting attention when ocean's great heart throbs with the quickening breath of a hurricane. A new book by a new author is like a new leaf amid the evergreen and varied foliage of a tropical forest. When one unknown to fame, takes his first born literary child in manuscript sheets to any of the notable publishers in either of our great cities, the cordiality with which he is received is like that with which a tramp is welcomed at the front door of a palatial dwelling. The chance that the latter is an angel in disguise, is considered equal to the probability that the former is inspired. In many cases, probably in most, the publisher is too busy to even look at the literary bant-ling, although, for aught he knows, it is a little, live, genuine literary Moses, nestled among the reeds and bulrushes of the river of immortality.

It sometimes happens that in the firmament of letters, brilliant with the light of stars unfading and quenchless, great intellectual luminaries appear unheralded,

> " Whose sudden visitations daze the world,
> And flash like lightning; while they leave behind
> A voice that in the distance, far away,
> Wakens the slumbering ages,"

and, as publisher's are not infallible, and do not by intuition know every thing, it has occasionally happened that they have found out, when it was too late, that they have ignorantly confounded these celestial wanderers with the countless fire-flies that rise from literary meadows, and disappear with the warm summer night that gave them birth and made their short-lived existence possible.

Publishers are book-brokers, or middle men, who bring producers and consumers together. They are the merchants of literature, and merely dispose of the brain crop. Generally indemnified against loss, theirs is the lion's share of the profits when profits are realized. Authors, even the most successful, receive but a very small percentage of the profits realized from the sale of their works. Great publishing houses accumulate great fortunes; while great authors die poor, and leave to their families only a brilliant and enduring name, which is impotent to keep the wolf of hunger from their doors. But publishers are to authors a convenience if not a necessity. They supply the wings which are required to enable a new candidate for literary honors to ascend sufficiently high in the world of letters to be seen. As notable publishers have at times fastened to dead weights, they have become exceedingly incredulous and cautious, and look with great suspicion upon all who have not demonstrated their ability to float and fly in the upper air of popular favor. As doorkeepers they guard the entrance of that great stage upon which the new author must stand in order to be widely known, but they are so chary of their favors that only an occasional novice is allowed to tread the boards, and take his chance of being hissed or applauded by the great public whose attention he presumes to challenge.

As the author of the ISLES OF SUMMER was well aware of these facts, and had no standing place in the great world of letters, why did he not continue to devote himself exclusively to the law? Why did he presume to write a book, and having written it, fossilize it with type, and coffin it in gilded covers?

These questions are legitimate, and they shall be honestly and frankly answered.

While treading the deck of a New York and Savannah steamer, after having been a day or two at sea, and while gazing with a pleasing awe upon an ocean mysterious, restless and sky-bound, he heard, like the author of Revelation, a voice saying unto him "*Write!*" and without pausing to think or inquire whether the injunction came from heaven or elsewhere, he obeyed with alacrity. It did not appear to be a matter of choice, but of uncontrolable necessity. He had taken with him neither ink nor paper, but the ship's purser kindly provided him with both and with a seat at his table. When the author's pen was fairly started, it was like the artificial leg which an ingenious German invented—it could not be stopped; so he continued to write as he traveled, and to travel as he wrote, and this volume is the result.

Visiting for the first time "the home of summer and the sun," the author was constantly surprised and charmed with new phases of that wondrous beauty which ever, in the vicinity of the tropics, rests like an atmosphere upon sea and land. His nerves were soothed and quieted by a climate which the Gulf Stream and trade-winds delightfully tempered and medicated. Lulled, soothed, and pleased by such novel surroundings, it was a relief to the mind to give expression to its agreeable sensations, and shed some of its thoughts. To gratify and amuse his friends at home, many of his impressions and pen-pictures were forwarded for publication in the New Haven *Journal and Courier*. They met with unexpected favor, and if his vanity had not, as he trusts, departed with his youth, he would have been proud, as he certainly was gratified at the warm, hearty and general commendation with which his published letters were received. Much enlarged, and to some extent re-written, they are now issued in book-form at the request, frequently and urgently expressed, of many of the readers of his newspaper communications. The author has the more readily yielded to these requests because he believes his book will meet an unsupplied want, there being no work in the market which gives the information it contains. A literary tent has only at long intervals been pitched for a few days upon the Bahamas, and the coral isles have yielded to letters very meagre though valuable harvests. Enjoying to some extent the fruits of the labors of others, the author has also cropped new fields, and while he has not exhausted or very much impaired the fertility of the soil, he trusts his book will not only minister to the pleasure but be of some practical value to those of his fellow citizens who, for any reason, desire to avoid the severity of the weather at the north during the winter and early spring months. It is but a chance seedling, but valuable fruit is sometimes found upon trees by the wayside and in hedge-rows which no professional pomologist has planted. If in the fruit gardens of literature the ISLES OF SUMMER shall take root and flourish in the warm sun of popular favor, its author will be gratified; and he believes he will not be greatly troubled should it be consigned as rubbish to the brush-heap—

> 'For he wrote not for money, nor for praise,
> Nor to be called a wit, nor to wear bays."

He seems to himself not so much an actor as a spectator having little interest in the result. The freedom of his will has in this matter, to a large degree, been dominated and controlled by circumstances. The movements of the pen which recorded his thoughts seem like yesterday's heart-beats—they left so little impression upon mind and memory.

Seven of the wood cut illustrations in this book, being those which in the table of illustrations are numbered respectively 4, 5, 7, 10, 11, 13 and 14, are by permission of C. H. Mallory and Company of New York, the proprietors of the steamship line now running between New York, Nassau and Matanzas, copied from an illustrated pamphlet which they have printed for the benefit of the patrons of their line. The other wood engravings have been made for this work and are with two exceptions from photographs taken in Nassau by Mr. J. F. Coonley of New York. The lithographic plates are from drawings made by Mr. J. H. Emerton of New Haven, and are mostly from specimens which the author's wife collected in the Bahamas. The author takes pleasure in acknowledging his indebtedness to Prof. A. E. Verrill, of the Sheffield Scientific School, for valuable suggestions and for the scientific names of the specimens in natural history pictured upon the lithographic plates

IVESTON, near New Haven, Ct.

December 13, A. D., 1880.

CONTENTS.

ILLUSTRATIONS.

WOOD ENGRAVINGS.

LITHOGRAPHS.

CHARLESTON
SAVANNAH
77
73
ATLANTIC
OCEAN
FERNANDINA
St JOHNS RIVER
JACKSONVILLE
St AUGUSTINE
FLORIDA
C. CANNAVERAL
STRAIT of FLORIDA
G. BAHAMA
ABACO
N.E. PROVIDENCE CHAN.
NASSAU
NEW PROVIDENCE
BAHAMA Is
S. SALVADOR
WATLING
Gt BAHAMA BANK
C. SABLE
KEY WEST
TORTUGAS
FLORIDA REEFS
CARDENAS
MATANZAS
HAVANA
CUBA
Trinidad
JAMAICA

CHAPTER I.

> "The sails were filled, and fair the light winds blew,
> As pleased to waft him from his native land."—BYRON.

NATURE's special favorites are the birds. With the speed of the wind, and a flight almost as noiseless, they ever follow Summer where she leads, bask in her sunlight, and repose in her grateful shadows. As Winter, snow-clad and frozen, advances or retreats, they follow in his footsteps, and sport in the forests of verdure, and in the fields and bowers of bloom, that soon clothe his track of desolation with wondrous beauty.

What nature denied, man has acquired for himself—a speed superior to that of the birds and outstripping the wind. His thoughts travel with the lightning, and, practically, space is almost annihilated by his steam chariots upon iron roads.

Science, meanwhile, has explored and mapped the great ocean world, sounded its profoundest depths, discovered and described its shoals and rocks and winding shores, and, wedded to mechanical ingenuity, has enabled man, in the glowing language of the east, to "take the wings of the morning and fly to the uttermost parts of the earth."

13

Hence, after the dwellers in the north have each in his generation for untold thousands of years been snow-bound and ice-anchored, their descendants in our day are able at winter's approach, to migrate with the birds, and thus secure perfect exemption from its discomforts. To many, suffering from disease, or with blood which age has made sluggish, this is a great boon.

In the winter of 1879, and again in 1880, the author influenced mainly by sanitary considerations, fled from frost to the islands of unending summer, spending sometime in Florida when going and returning in 1879, and again on his way home in 1880. The knowledge he was thus enabled to acquire, is in part contained in these pages. Most of his notes upon Florida may perhaps form the ground work of a future volume.

On a clear morning in January, A. D. 1879, the author looked out of his office window upon New Haven's beautiful "Green," and saw its noble elms in their maturity, lifting their long bare brown arms towards heaven as if in supplication, while a white and beautiful carpet of snow revealed the shadows and reflected the sunlight. Three days afterwards, he sat upon the deck of an ocean steamer, in a pleasant summer atmosphere, within one hundred and fifty miles of the city of Savannah, with nothing in view but the blue dome of the sky, the restless ocean waves, and some daring sea birds which hovered high in air above the steamer's foaming track, and watched with their telescopic eyes, and waited for their share of the noon-day meal. The contrast was most striking; the change from a life of care and of continued moil and toil, to a state of calm and peaceful rest, was as agreeable as it was marked and sudden. But life is full of startling and unexpected contrasts. There is seemingly no stability but instability, nothing constant but unrest. Change itself becomes changeless in its unvarying mutability.

Friday has acquired a bad name, especially among those who have their "home upon the rolling deep." But for the author, it had no terrors—particularly as he never made it a matter of conscience to keep its fasts or to diet exclusively upon its fish. He did not therefore hesitate to take passage on board the steamer Elm City for New York, on Friday evening, the 17th of January, A. D. 1879. Never in summer did he more comfortably pass over Long Island Sound, or awaken after it feeling more invigorated and refreshed. A short while previous the little light snowflakes had noiselessly fallen upon the great city of New York, effectually barricaded its immense net work of streets and avenues, and more effectually held it in subjection than could a great and powerful army with banners. With a feeling of great relief we soon exchanged its dirty and slippery sidewalks for the busy deck and luxurious saloons of the screw steamer City of Savannah, a floating palace of the sea.

At about half-past three o'clock, P. M., on Saturday, the 18th of January, we left pier No. 43, North River, steamed down the harbor of New York, between the pleasant but then cold shores of Long Island and New Jersey, into the broad Atlantic, and fancied its gentle, murmuring, dancing and slightly foam-crested waves gave us a friendly greeting, and as warm a welcome as was possible at that frigid season of the year.

At the mention of a winter's voyage, before a blazing fire or near a comfortable steam radiator, one involuntarily shudders, shivers and recoils. But had we not just got to the end of a long series of storms, and fierce, cold winds? Had not the wind god of winter exhausted himself, and would he not now stop to take breath? We thought so, and soon found that we were right. Saturday afternoon and night the Atlantic was in one of its mildest moods. Sunday the wind took us directly aft, rounded out our foresail, foretopsail and foregallant sail, billowed the water's

surface just enough with snow-white crests to please the eye, but
not enough to awaken feelings of danger even in timid minds.
The clouds gradually thickened overhead, a few snowflakes with
seeming reluctance noiselessly descended, and were instantly lost
in the mysterious depths of the ocean—for a snowflake and a
steamship are alike insignificant so far as old ocean is concerned.
Soon we experienced the pleasure of seeing, what is not very often
witnessed, a heavy snow storm off the capes of Virginia, and it
seemed so queer to see the snow fall hour after hour and leave
not a trace behind. No rocks, no shrubs, no evergreen trees
were glorified by it, but ocean, with cold indifference, received
this gift from heaven unmoved and unaffected. Earth may well
welcome the snow storm which protects and saves its priceless
floral treasures, but what is the use of wasting snow storms upon
the ocean?

At half-past six o'clock on the evening of January 19th, the
snow storm being over, we saw at a distance of some fifteen miles,
the revolving light of Hatteras. Can it be, we inwardly exclaimed, that this is the place that navigators of the sea would
be so glad to avoid ; the home of the strongest and most fitful
winds, and of wildest storms; a place loved only by wreckers?
Our steamship still spread her sails to the wind, and her rocking
was so gentle that not a passenger's seat was empty at the supper
table. It was not long before spittoons commenced a game of
ten-pins upon the floor of the main saloon, the wind howled and
hissed at us as it passed; the propeller uttered its cry of alarm,
as, in the rolling and pitching of the vessel, it protruded out of
the water; strong men staggered and reeled, while during the
short momentary intervals of comparative repose, they moved
from one holding-on place to another: the ladies sought refuge in
their state-rooms, and, devoutly thankful that he had not broken
any of his or his fellow-passengers' bones, the author soon fol-

Screw Steamer City of Savannah.

lowed their good example. We were steaming away from Hatteras, when the demon of the stormy cape sent some of his specimen blasts after us. Our captain deemed it best to "lie to" awhile until that "little spell of weather" was over.

During the night nearly all the passengers were more or less sick, and the cold was sufficient to freeze water on the deck of the steamer from stem to stern. The next day the weather was all that could be desired; the atmosphere calm, agreeably cool and bracing, while the sea was as smooth, quiet and peaceful, as if it had not yet been awakened from a night of profound repose and quiet sleep.

The "City of Savannah" is one of a line of steamers built and owned by the Georgia Central Railroad Company, for the transportation of passengers and freight between Savannah and New York. At an expense of one million of dollars—being one-fifth of its capital—it secured the building at Chester. Penn., of four steamers, named respectively, the "City of Macon," the "City of Columbus," the "Gate City," and the "City of Savannah." They are all substantially alike, and the last was placed upon the line in the summer or fall of 1878, and the first about a year previous.

Our steamer was almost a novice upon the ocean. A few months before in the State of Pennsylvania, and from the west bank of the river Delaware, it first took to the water. Yet how grandly, with an air of conscious power, it made its way over the pathless, fathomless and boundless sea! When no land-marks are seen upon the horizon's verge, and no guiding stars in the sky, it still speeds confidently and unerringly on its way over the trackless wilderness of water.

Born to an inheritance of labor, the author experienced a new sensation—he had nothing to do. He determined therefore to make the acquaintance of the ship, and thus utilize some of his leisure hours. No expense was apparently spared to make it in all respects first-class, and in it are embodied the latest and best improvements and appliances of marine architecture.

The length of the Savannah, measuring fifteen feet from the water line, is 260 feet; its length over all is 275 feet. It is 38 feet 6 inches beam molded. Her depth from base line to tip of spar deck is 26 feet 10 inches; depth of hold 24 feet; total depth below spar deck 75 feet. Her registered tonnage is 2,092 $\frac{84}{100}$ tons. She can carry at one time 4,000 bales of cotton. She has three decks besides the hurricane deck. The spar deck is entirely of iron; the main deck is partly of iron, and the deck frames are all of iron. She was at first brig-rigged, and could spread 5,000 yards of canvass; but the spars on the mainmast have been taken down, as it was found that they were not needed, so that now her rigging is that of a hermaphrodite brig.

The dining saloon is located aft the main hatch on the main deck, and is 50 feet by 29 feet at a distance of 30 feet from the main stairway. Aft of and near the dining saloon, is the main saloon with rows of state-rooms; each state-room is elegantly and conveniently fitted up, and has a window looking out upon the ocean. A small saloon over the dining saloon is called "social hall," and being so fortunate as to have a room which opened into this "hall," the author is able to testify that "social hall" is decidedly the best part of the ship. There is another saloon with state-rooms aft the main hatch, but it is much less desirable than the other two.

The saloons are elaborately and most beautifully finished with the choicest woods that money could secure. The natural grain has been preserved and the polished surfaces are as hard and smooth as glass. Cherry, mahogany, black walnut, bird's eye maple, tulip wood and amaranth are so combined as to produce the best esthetic effect, and one never tires looking at and studying them.

Each state-room is provided with roomy berths, first-class spring matrasses, and patent wash slabs and bowls, with convenient fixtures,—the latter superior to any we had ever seen. Stationary chairs, with revolving backs, along the dining tables are a very desirable improvement.

The engines of this great steamship are a credit to the age in which we live. As tide-marks of intellectual development and monuments of man's dominion over matter and over the hidden and latent forces of nature, they far transcend the pyramids that have excited the wonder and admiration of the world for thousands of years. While propelling us through the ocean at the rate of thirteen miles an hour with a 1,650 horse power, there was almost no noise, and every part is so perfectly adjusted that the motion of the vessel was as gentle as the rocking of a cradle—indeed, more so, for the author found no more difficulty in writing at a table in the purser's room, within six feet of the engines, than he would at a table in any private house.

Her boilers, tubular cylindrical, are four in number, each 12 feet 8 inches in diameter, and 10 feet 6 inches in length. The working pressure is 80 pounds to the square inch. The stroke of the pistons is 54 inches.

The ship has a patent condenser of 3,000 feet condensing surface, by means of which her supply of Croton water taken in at New York is vaporized and condensed constantly during the voyage, thus avoiding the necessity to a great extent of using sea water, and making a very great saving of the boilers, fuel, and labor.

The propeller has a diameter of 14 feet 3 inches, and it makes 70 revolutions per minute. It is of the Hirsch patent, and has four blades, which are so fastened that they can be removed when necessary.

It is interesting to see in how many ways steam power is brought into requisition to save labor on this ship. Two donkey engines are used for clearing the bilge and for some other purposes; three or four for loading and unloading cargoes; one for the anchor and the sails; one in part for supplying water closets with water; one for operating a steam steering apparatus; one for operating a newly devised governor, which so controls and governs the propeller that it cannot make more than a certain number of revolutions per minute. This last takes the place of a man who had formerly to devote all his time to this work.

These engines are in addition to the main engine for pumping out the ship. There are six water tight iron compartments in the ship, and if one should be stove in or should spring a leak from any cause, the others would float her while the great circulating pump of the condenser would be brought into requisition, whose power to discharge water is very great.

The crew number forty-seven, and the monthly pay-roll is about $2,000. The powerful and complicated machine requires constant watchfulness and the greatest care. To lubricate it one and one-half barrels of oil are used every trip. The average consumption of coal is 130 tons for a round trip. The average length of the voyage is from fifty-five to sixty hours. The Savannah has once gone from dock to dock in fifty-two hours and thirty minutes.

The regular sea route from New York to Savannah is not through any part of the Gulf Stream, that immense river of warm water, a thousand times larger than the Mississippi, which flows in a cold water bed, and helps to temper the severity of the frigid and frozen North; but between that great and, as yet, inexplicable phenomenon of the ocean, and its beautifully winding western shore, our steamer grandly plowed its way. Like the "shining shore" of the "better land," we well knew, that although invisible to our material eyes, it was near at hand. This passing in a few hours from ice-bridged rivers with snow-enshrouded banks to fields of perennial green, so forcibly symbolizes man's passage over the river of death, that the author sometimes more than half believed that he had indeed made the journey to that mystic realm between which and earth the travel is all one way.

We approached the bar off the mouth of the Savannah river in the morning twilight of January 21st, passing quite a number of ships at anchor in the offing. From prudential reasons our captain so timed the steamship's progress that we crossed the bar at high tide. As we entered the river, we turned to waft upon the mild and gentle air a silent but heartfelt blessing to old ocean for having treated us so well during our voyage, and we inwardly hoped that nothing in the future would occur to make us like each other less.

The color of the waters of the Savannah river closely resembles that of a New Haven mud-puddle, and after leaving our New York steamer and its excellent Croton water, it was a constant study with us how not to drink it, there being but a small and inadequate supply of condensed water on our next steamer. We approached the city between low sedgy meadows, some of which are utilized for the cultivation of rice. Forts, with their large guns still in sight, and low mud batteries, remain to keep alive the memory of the recent "unpleasantness," while new saw-mills, large lumber yards, spacious warehouses, bales of cotton, barrels of resin and turpentine, twenty-five or thirty first-class ships and three-masted schooners moored to wharves—all a mile below the city and near the eastern terminus of a branch of the Gulf railroad, told of northern capital and enterprise, of the healing and healthy influences of peace, and of a growing feeling of fraternity between those so recently engaged in a life and death struggle for the mastery in the dreadful ordeal of battle on sea and land. Everything was so quiet and peaceful, it was hard to realize that that whole section was so recently a vast military camp, ruled and governed by a despotism such as only war necessitates and breeds. Although defeated, it must be a grateful luxury for the southern people to inhale the glorious air of freedom once more, undisturbed by war's alarms, and battles whose very victories were purchased at a cost of evils only equaled by their defeats.

The few hours that intervened between the arrival of one steamer and the sailing of another, were pleasantly occupied in making a cursory examination of Georgia's principal seaport. It is a city of parks—some twenty or more we believe, in all, great and small, so arranged that some one of them is within easy access of every citizen's dwelling. The avenues, pleasantly shaded, turn every two blocks to the right and left, and surround emerald parks—reminding one of the rivers of Florida, those blue ribbons upon which the jewelled lakes are strung. The largest and most beautiful of the parks upon Bull street, is the "Pulaski." Semi-tropical trees of large size and luxuriant foliage, some festooned and draped in gray moss, gave it a very attractive appearance. A large new park has been laid out and enclosed, adjoining this, called the Pulaski Extension, upon which a large and handsome confederate monument has been erected. We were pleased to see no evidence anywhere of the ruin and waste that so often mark the bloody footsteps of war. Sherman's grand march to the sea rendered the city's surrender without a struggle an inevitable necessity. Its forts and batteries were of no use with a large victorious army entering its back door.

The tourist at Savannah, bound for Florida, can make the journey in a few hours by railroad, or go by either of two lines of ocean steamers, one of which takes the route outside the islands, and the other avoids the hazards of the open sea and the discomforts of sea sickness, by passing between the coast-islands and the mainland. As time was of little consequence to us, we concluded to take the latter.

The people of the north, during the late war, were made acquainted with the fact that the Southern Atlantic States have their sea coast protected by a long succession of islands, between which and the main land steamers of light draft can safely pass along their whole extent, as far south as the mouth of the St. John's in Florida. Batteries, torpedoes, shoals and tortuous and intricate channels protected this portion of the southern seaboard, so that our navy found it impossible to destroy or seriously cripple confederate communication by water along this portion of the coast. One needs to go through these inside channels to fairly comprehend them. We think of the Connecticut coast shielded by Long Island, but along a portion of the coast of Georgia, instead of a Sound thirty miles wide, we have narrow and winding water-ways more like Mill river at the base of East Rock. We took the side-wheel steamer "City of Bridgeton" at Savannah for Jacksonville in Florida—a boat that brought to mind the steamers of the New York and New Haven line "long, long ago." It has since been modernized and very greatly improved, so much so that we recognized this year very little of the old boat except its name, and even that gloried in a sort of new birth.

Following the doublings and sharp curves of the inside route, as we neared the river St. John's the colored man at the wheel required and exercised constant vigilance and the greatest care. Much local knowledge and great practical skill were brought into constant requisition, and only once was the bow of the boat run into the soft bank. The shores of the sedgy marshes were white with extensive beds of oyster shells, while countless beds of small oysters were everywhere to be seen as the tide receded. Occasionally we passed islands rich with tropical vegetation, where nature seemed to be reveling in a perfect wilderness of beauty, and nothing was wanting, unless perhaps an occasional rocky bluff and mountain peak to give more variety and sublimity to the scene. The clear sky and balmy air were in perfect accord with the beautiful panorama that opened constantly before us as we glided over the quiet water. Towards the lower end of this charming route, near the close of day, the whole blue dome of heaven, with all its rich adornment of sunset clouds gorgeously illumined, was more perfectly reflected in the still clear water than the author ever saw it before—save once only on the river St. John's, in the British province of New Brunswick. That surpassed anything of the sort he had ever seen or conceived, and this, on the whole, excelled that, for soon the side-wheels of the boat caused great circling eddies of skies, frescoed and wonderfully and indescribably colored, to follow the steamer, until gradually, as the daylight vanished, this remarkable phenomenon passed away—remaining, however, indelibly pictured upon the memory.

As we neared Fernandina, we passed the Great and Little Cumberland islands. The largest is said to be from twenty-five to thirty miles long, and two to three miles wide. It abounds with game, including hundreds of deer, while fish are very abundant in the surrounding waters.

In full view from Cumberland Sound, which separates it from Fernandina, still stand the roofless and windowless walls of what was once one of the most splendid residences of the Southern States and perhaps of the New World. Deserted by its owner during the war, some miscreant's torch made it a ruin.

This island has a history, and romance and poetry will undoubtedly hereafter draw from it inspiration. It will live in deathless song and enduring story. It lies between the ca. and healthy waters like an island of the blessed, and the soft zephyrs that pass over it, born of the not distant ocean, borrow perfumes from its aromatic trees, its spicy bowers and sweet-scented flowers.

The State of Georgia, as a token of gratitude to General Nathaniel Greene, of revolutionary fame and memory, conveyed to him one-half of the island. He died too soon to derive much benefit from a gift which reflected back a pleasing lustre upon the donors. The General's widow married a wealthy man by the name of Miller, who made the island his home and spent his money most lavishly in erecting a palatial mansion, opening splendid drives, laying out the grounds, and adorning them with all the choice trees and flowers that are found or can be made to live in the vicinity of the tropics.

The place is called "Dungenness." Upon the island are the remains of "Light Horse Harry Lee," one of the heroes of 1776, and the father of General Lee, the Commander-in-Chief of the late Confederate armies. Excursion parties visit Dungenness from Fernandina frequently, and in the future it will no doubt grow in popular favor. We visited the island the present year but defer, for the present, a more particular description of it.

The Bridgeton made a detour for the purpose of stopping at St. Mary, situated near the mouth of the river of that name which constitutes in part the dividing line between Georgia and Florida. In the palmy days of the Georgia planters St. Mary was quite a place of fashionable summer resort, and considerable money was spent upon its docks, avenues, buildings and gardens. But it suffered severely during the war, its docks and warehouses were destroyed, and not much remains to indicate what it has been. Its climate, cooled by the ocean, is said to be very favorable to health.

Our steamer stopped at Fernandina just long enough to enable us to ride through its streets, upon one of which we were pleased

3

to see the recently raised frame for *one* new house, as evidencing
the fact that enterprise is here awakening, though very slowly,
from its long sleep.   We rode a mile over a sandy road through
a thicket of palmettoes and wild vines and bushes, beyond the
"city," to its famous Amelia Beach, which is one of the finest
ocean beaches we have seen.   For eighteen or twenty miles the
white beach of a uniform character extended, the dip being so
gentle that a wide belt was left between the sand hills and low-
water mark, which the incoming ocean tides had pounded and
compacted until but little impression was made upon it by the
hoofs of our horses.   The shoals near the shore caused the waves
to break into stretches of white spray crests, and gave a pleasing
variety to the ocean view.   The gentle waves, as they approached,
rolled up as they reached the shore, and adorned the extreme
edge with a beautiful white border of foam in an unbroken line
of many miles.   The mildness and softness of the air, and the
pleasing and soothing murmur of the water, so gently rolling
in upon the white sand beach, almost as far as the eye could see,
caused us to prolong our stay to the very last minute of our
allotted time.   The hard, smooth beach of Fernandina, with its
unobstructed ocean view on the one side, and sand hills on the
other, as we saw it then, will ever occupy a sunny spot in our
memory.

It was eleven o'clock at night when we reached the Windsor
Hotel, at Jacksonville upon the St. John's river, thankful that
thus far our ocean trip in midwinter had been so extremely pleasant, and that nothing had occurred to give us a moment's uneasiness.   It is true, the same kind Providence would have been over
us had we made our journey by land, but some persons who came
that way, seemed more inclined to the opinion that in the construction and operation of southern railroads some evil genius
had been permitted to have things pretty much his own way.

With the return of prosperity under the banner of peace, improved and more safe communication by rail will follow as a necessary consequence.

After spending a few days in Florida (rendered necessary by the fact that no opportunity existed for sooner continuing our journey) we at last were able to cross over to Nassau on the side wheel steamer Secret. The passage occupied fifty-two hours. She was advertised to make the run in thirty-six hours, but the time was purposely understated in order to make the trip appear more attractive to the seekers of health and pleasure. The Secret was about fifteen years old, English built, sheathed outside with iron and was constructed somewhat after the model of a Connecticut river shad, being very long and very narrow. According to a Jacksonville newspaper, her length was 231 feet, and her breadth 26 feet. She was built for a blockade runner, and was considered a good sea boat. We found her state rooms and berths too small for comfort, and the approaches to the dining saloon long, narrow, unpleasant and unsavory. But we are disposed to apply the bridge rule to steamboats, and to speak well of those which carry us safely.

Before leaving home we doated on the Gulf Stream. It was our ideal salt water, and bore the same relative position to the rest of the ocean world that the Garden of Eden did to all the islands and continents outside. When the fifty separate and distinct persons on as many different occasions asked us if we were not afraid to take an ocean voyage in winter, and more especially when every newspaper was and had for some time been filled with accounts of terrific storms, accompanied by winds before which the strongest ships were like so many egg shells, the ready reply which then so satisfied us seemed to be equally satisfactory to them; "Oh, no; we do not fear or dread it at all, for in thirty hours from New York we will be in the Gulf Stream, where the water, flowing in a stream a thousand times larger than the Mississippi river, from hot equatorial regions, is always warm, and the air, loaded with ozone, saline and other health imparting ingredients, is as warm and pleasant as that which we breathe at our best seaside resorts in summer ; storm-caught and ice-coated vessels run into it to thaw out." But alas! all our ideals vanish into thin air and disappear forever the moment we attempt to seize them with our hands of flesh. The beautiful vision of the Gulf Stream exists for us no more. It will never return. We have been there. We were from eight to ten hours crossing it at an oblique angle. We rolled and tossed "in and over" it to the content of our hearts and the disturbance of our stomachs. As it piled up its huge waves higher than our ship, one after another of the passengers seemed to have "a call" to go somewhere else, and left the deck, first bending over the guard rail, with their faces turned mysteriously towards the angry waters, with an agonized expression, as though they had caught sight of some large sea serpent. One gentleman was asked by an innocent sympathizer if he was sick. The quick and forcible reply seemed to be perfectly satisfactory. "Do you think I am such a d—n fool that I am doing all this for fun?" Having personally paid unwilling tribute to Neptune, we turned our back upon the foam-crested billows and took refuge in our little sardine box below, where, with the port hole closed, we lay above the heaving bosom of this enchanting ocean-river. And now, ever and anon, upon all sorts of occasions, the Gulf Stream, disenchanted, calls up the same memories and fills us with the same feelings of thankfulness and gratitude which Sancho Panza experienced whenever he thought of the blanket in which he was ingloriously tossed in the yard of the Spanish inn. The steamer in which we left New York, had carefully hugged the shores of the Atlantic States and kept out of it, and we skirted the east coast of Florida below Jacksonville for some twenty-eight hours before we turned near Jupiter Light to enter and cross it.

One cannot understand the phrase "A wilderness of waters" until he actually sails day after day with nothing in view but the deep below and the deep above. On the second day out from Jacksonville we first sighted, off our starboard quarter, a faint trace of curling smoke in the distance, and soon, after crossing our bow, a Havanna steamer exchanged flag salutations with the Secret.

The character and disposition of people are often strikingly displayed on shipboard. Some are so kind, so considerate, so mindful of their fellow-voyagers, so forgetful of themselves. Others seem to believe that the world, and all that it contains that is worth having, was made expressly for themselves. They seem lineally descended from the man whose only prayer to God was that He would

> "Bless me and my wife,
> My son John and his wife,
> Us four—and no more!"

And also to be very nearly related to the individual who owned one-half of a negro, and who was accustomed to request the divine blessing for "myself, my wife, and my half of Jake."

A novel sight presented itself as we approached the ship's dock at Nassau. The perfectly clear and transparent water, exquisitely and indescribably colored; the old, weather-worn vessels at anchor; the forts and sea-walls; the white streets and white stone buildings, all of coral limestone, contrasted oddly with the crowds of persons, mostly colored, that filled all the docks, streets and standing places at and near the landing. We were within several rods of the dock when a dozen nearly naked little Africans commenced the sport of diving off the dock into the deep water after the coins which the passengers threw overboard. They seemed to be amphibious and were all expert swimmers. They generally succeeded in securing the much coveted prizes before the latter reached the bottom. But little, in fact no real annoyance, aside from the delay, was experienced from the custom house officials, and we soon found ourselves at home in the Royal Victoria Hotel, one of the finest buildings of the kind in the Western world.

CHAPTER II.

"We sailed the sea, thick sown with clustering isles."—VIRGIL.

"These precious stones set in a silver sea."—SHAKESPEARE.

HAVING determined to visit the Bahamas, the author commenced immediately to brush away the dust which had during a number (please excuse him from not specifying more particularly how many) of decades of years, covered and obliterated the geographical knowledge of his school-boy days. Learning is like wealth—not to have it is less discreditable than unfounded pretensions. His life would have been worth but very little had it then depended upon his ability to accurately locate and particularly describe Nassau and the island of New Providence, or the group of which that island forms a part. Is it too much for him to assume that his ignorance was not exceptional, and that nearly all of his readers can truthfully make a similar confession? Let the favored few who occupy the geographical front seats excuse the author, and grant him their kind indulgence, while, for the benefit of others, he airs a little his recently resurrected, and, to some extent, newly acquired geographical knowledge.

31

It will be seen upon referring to any good map of the West India Islands that an immense number of islands are distributed upon a line over two thousand miles long, which trends south-easterly from a point relatively near the coast of Florida, to the mouth of the Orinoco River in South America. Sprinkled among these are many reefs, thousands of rocks, and little islets which are called by the English keys and by the Spaniards cays. The north-westerly portion of this chain is composed of the Bahama archipelago, and embraces thirty-nine islands, six hundred and sixty-one keys, and two thousand three hundred and eighty-seven rocks.

This Island system constitutes a vast breakwater, and shelters from the winds and waves of the wide and stormy Atlantic, the Caribbean Sea and the Gulf of Mexico, which bodies of water are perfectly land-locked on their other sides. Were the ocean waters drawn off, we should have, in place of this island system, the Bahama and Caribbean mountains, a lofty range, elevated thousands of feet above the neighboring plains and valleys, towering high up in the air as they now do in the water, with large areas of high table land. The location of the islands to the windward of the banks has favored the formation and growth of the latter.

The Bahama group rises out of several submerged tables of a soft calcareous rock, the two largest of which are known respectively as the Great and Little Bahama Banks. The water upon these banks attains a maximum depth of several hundred feet. The Little Bank is the most northerly, and is only seventy miles from the coast of Florida. It embraces a superficial area of 5,560 square miles, including 1,200 square miles of islands, and has a breadth of from thirty-five to sixty miles. Its principal islands are Great and Little Abaco and Grand Bahama. The two former are separated from each other by a narrow channel,

and with their numerous keys extend along the eastern edge of the Little Bahama Bank for nearly a hundred miles. At the southerly extremity of Abaco is the famous "Hole-in-the-Wall" —a large opening through and below the top of a ridge of calcareous rock. Also a light house bearing the same name. A lady informed us that several years since, while sailing past Abaco, she saw the sun at its setting through this "Hole-in-the-Wall," and that the globe of fire, in its setting of rock, left an indelible picture of rare and exquisite beauty upon her memory.

The north-west and north-east Providence Channels separate the Little from the Great Bahama Bank. The distance between the Banks varies from fifteen to forty-five miles.

"The north-east Providence Channel separates Abaco from the island of Eleuthera and the keys on its northern shore, which lie twenty-seven miles to the south-east of the Hole-in-the-Wall."

"The whole of the trade from North America and Europe to the Gulf of Mexico," says Gov. Rawson, "passes by the north of the Bahama Islands. Steamers bound to the south, stem the rapid current of the Florida Channel," between the Banks and Florida. Sailing vessels pass between Abaco and Eleuthera through the Providence Channels, within forty miles of Nassau, into the Gulf of Florida. "All the return-bound trade to the north, whether using steam or sails, passes with the [Gulf] stream through the Florida Channel."

"From Eleuthera follow, in the same direction, south-east and then south, a succession of long narrow islands, viz.:—St. Salvador or Cat Island, Long Island, Ragged Island and its keys. * * * Outside the bank, forty-eight miles east of the south of St. Salvador, lies Watling Island, * * * and twenty-four miles from the north-east end of Long Island lies Rum Key;" between which and the island of St. Salvador, is the small island of Conception.

South-east of Long Island, beyond the Great Bank, and separated from it by a channel twenty-five miles wide, is Crooked Island ; then succeeds Acklin's Island, with a very shallow connecting channel, once reputed fordable in its narrowest part. To the north-east of Crooked Island is Sumona, or Atwood Key. Plana or French keys are east of Acklin's Island. Then successively follow in the same direction (south-east), the Caicos, the Mayaguana and the Turks Islands—the last of this inhabited chain of islands, six hundred miles in extent, which stretch from a point seventy miles from Florida to within a hundred miles of St. Domingo. The Caicos and the Turks Islands once were within the governmental jurisdiction of the Bahamas, but are now politically associated with Jamaica.

Three smaller banks, separated by channels thirty to fifty miles wide, and called respectively Mouchoir, Carré, Silver and Navidad, extend still further to the south-east, for about one hundred and fifty miles.

Nearly in the latitude of the Turks Islands, and from sixty to seventy miles south of Acklin's Island and Mayaguana, are Great and Little Inagua or Heneagua, detached, and some sixty-five miles north of the north-western extremity of St. Domingo. Great Inagua is one of the largest and best of the Bahamas. Exuma, with its extensive chain of keys, lies upon the eastern edge of the Great Bank, and upon the western side of Exuma Sound. This Sound has an average width of forty miles, extends north-westerly about one hundred miles, and breaks the continuity of the Great Bank between St. Salvador and Long Island.

A very deep sound called The Tongue-of-the-Ocean is projected into the Great Bank a distance of one hundred and ten miles. Major General Nelson, R. E., describes it as having the deep blue color of oceanic depths, while "the color of the water

around the islands is usually that of the *aqua-marine* of beryl."
On its western edge, and skirting the Great Bank lies Andros
island, much the largest of the group, being ninety-five miles
long and having a maximum width of thirty-eight miles.

The Berry islands are north-east of Andros; they are arranged
in the form of a crescent. The horns point to the east, and are
separated by a distance of some forty miles. The south-west
shore of Abaco, on the opposite side of the north-west Providence
Channel, is only thirty miles distant from these little islands.

The Biminis are two small islands rendered famous from the
fact that the Fountain of Youth was reported, in the time of
Ponce de Leon, to be located upon one of them. They are
twenty-five miles south of the north-western portion of the
Great Bahama Bank, and are described as "small, pretty and
fertile."

The Santareen and Old Bahama Channels are south of the
Great Bahama Bank. West of the former is situated the Cay
Sal Bank, embracing fourteen hundred and thirty square miles,
including some uninhabited Keys; while south of the latter
channel is the island of Cuba.

Gov. Rawson states that "all the trade from North America
to Cuba, St. Domingo, Jamaica, the Gulf of Honduras, and the
northern coast of South America passes south to the windward
[i. e. east] of the group, and close to the shores of Inagua.
The return trade, and all the European trade from the same
countries passes north, either through the Crooked Island pas-
sages, or the Inagua or Caicos Channels. These islands therefore lie in the track of two great streams of trade, and, at times,
scores of vessels pass daily by the 'Hole-in-the-Wall,' and the
south western point of Inagua."

New Providence, upon which Nassau is situated, is upon the
northern edge of the Great Bahama Bank, fifty miles south-west

of the north-east extremity of the bank, at the eastern entrance of "The Tongue-of-the-Ocean," and is approached through either the north-west or north-east Providence Channels, the former of which connects it with the Florida Gulf and is traversed by the steamers which bring Nassau's winter visitors from the states.

The following table is copied from Gov. Rawson's report :

	Area.		Extreme Length.	Extreme Breadth.	Average Breadth.
	Square Miles.		Miles.	Miles.	Miles.
1. Andros, ...	...	1,600	95	38	22
2. Abaco, Great, ...	680	776	70	17	12
" Little, ...	96		24	5	4
3. Inagua, Great, ...	530	560	34	25	16
" Little, ...	30		8	7	3¾
4. Grand Bahama, ...	..	430	66	11	7
5. Crooked Island, ...	76		19	8	5
6. Acklin's Island ...	120	204	41	10	4
7. Fortune Island, (Long Cay),	8		10	1¼	¾
8. Eleuthera, ...	...	164	57	11	4
Spanish Wells, ...	...	½	...	...	...
9. St. Salvador, ...	...	160	42	14	4
10. Long Island, ...	...	130	60	3½	2¼
11. Exuma, Great and Little, ...	...	110	32	7	2½
12. Mayaguana, ...	...	96	23	6	4
13. New Providence, ...	...	85	19⅜	7	5
14. Watling's Island, ...	...	60	13	6	4½
15. Rum Cay, ...	...	29	9½	5	3
16. Biminis, North, ...	3	8½	3¼	1½	⅓
" South, ...	5½		3¼	1½	1
17. Ragged Island and Cay, ...	...	5	5½	2¾	1½
18. Berry Island, Great, ...	...	4½	6	1⅜	⅛
Harbour Cay, ...					
19. Harbour Island, ...	...	1½	3	⅗	½
Total, ...		4,424			

The foregoing table shows proximately the length, breadth

and size of the principal Bahama islands, exclusive of the keys which cluster around them.

This extensive and singular group of islands, so unlike the New England that the author had left behind him, charmed by its novelty, and elicited enthusiastic admiration.

> "He found in all that met his eyes,
> The freshness of a glad surprise."

They repose in the lap of unending summer. Daring enterprise, resistless courage, and the intense activities of busy human life, do not cross the great ocean river. No blighting and killing frosts are ever found between its eastern margin and the rising sun. To all that we have been accustomed, or ever experienced before, it had been practically the stream of oblivion— the river of death. The ancient seers who saw and pictured heaven dwelt in warm sunny climes. None of the streets of the New Jerusalem which they saw with spiritual vision, were paved with ice or blockaded with snow. We here found the sea so smooth, the wind so mild, the air so agreeably warm, the sky so serene, the clouds so soft and delicately tinted, and our mind and heart were pervaded by such a spirit of resignation, contentment and peace—of love to God and good will towards man— while the past appeared so unreal and dreamy,—we at times were almost ready to believe that our "mortal had put on immortality." But the regular periodic return of hunger, and an appetite that gave a keen relish to the gross food of earth, soon convinced us that we still inhabited our old bodies, and fly-like, adhered to the surface of one of the sun's revolving satelites.

In this new world our curiosity was awakened and greatly stimulated. What part, we inquired, have these immense banks, with their clustered isles played in the world's history? In what manner were they made? How many thousands of years

4

were involved in their construction? What great cosmic and geological truths is this murmuring ocean endeavoring to reveal?

In groping after truth, man passes over the bridge of the known to the dark and shadowy regions of the unknown. Upward he treads the rounds of a ladder bottomed upon earth but lost in impenetrable clouds. Yet, when considered in connection with human insignificance, there is much which man has been enabled to learn, and in no department of human knowledge has greater progress been made than in that of geology, — a science that underlies, and, to some extent, explains the facts of physical geography.

"The Egyptian priests told Herodotus that from the time of their first king, which was eleven thousand and odd years, the sun had four times altered his course; that the sea and the earth did alternately change into one another."* New evidences of some of these changes, clear and indisputable, have been found in our own time and country. Upon the American continent, man walks and works, and muses upon mountains and plains once a portion of the ocean's bed. Vast quantities of the skeletons of "monsters of the deep," and marine fauna, of families and genera and species supposed to be now extinct, are entombed in the profound depths of its rocks. Upon the low, long and narrow islands and keys composing the Bahama Archipelago, in the soft, languid and voluptuous air, we pensively muse above a continent that nature, in one of her sublime convulsions, or by a slow but no less grand process, requiring cycles of time of vast and inconceivable extent for its completion, has buried from human sight in the unfathomable depths of a wild waste of waters. There is something grand and appalling in the chapters of the earth's autobiography as disclosed by its continents and ocean isles. Like the astronomer who discerns and translates for us

----

* Montaigne.

"the thoughts of God in the sky," so the geologist who reads to us from the book of the rocks, seems, like Moses upon Sinai, to commune with Jehovah and to have his lips hallowed with a divine inspiration.

To man's inquiring thought, the ocean responds only in dirge-like harmonies. In its mystic and profound depths, during the long and silent ages, the sea has kept its secrets well. But in our own time—thanks to a Darwin, a Dana, a Marsh, and an Agassiz—the key of the known has unlocked many of the mysteries of the unknown, and in these rocky isles we now behold the head-stones of lands that the sea engulfed!

Prof. Dana, in his work upon Corals and Coral Islands, after alluding to "the northern continental upward movements which introduced the glacial era," and stating that "while the earth's crust was arching upward" at the north, "it may have been bending downward over the vast central area of the great ocean," adds:

"The changes which took place, contemporaneously, in the Atlantic tropics, are very imperfectly recorded. The Bahamas show by their form and position that they cover a submerged land of large area, stretching over six hundred miles from north-west to south-east. The long line of reefs, and the Florida keys, trending far away from Southern Florida, are evidence that this Florida region participated in the downward movement, though to a less extent than the Bahamas. Again, the islands of the West Indies diminish in size to the eastward, being quite small in the long line that looks out upon the broad ocean, just as if the subsidence increased in that direction. Finally, the Atlantic beyond is water only, as if it had been made a blank by the sinking of the lands."

*　　*　　*　　*　　*　　*　　*

"The peninsula of Florida, Cuba and the Bahamas, look, as

they lie together, as if all were once part of a greater Florida or south-eastern prolongation of the continent.   The north-western and south-western trends, characterizing the great features of the American continent, run through the whole like a warp and woof structure, binding them together in one system."

To the author of this book it seems probable, from a simple examination of a good West India map, that the subsidence extended in the same general direction to South America, a distance of some fifteen hundred miles further.   While the crust of the earth was being elevated, depressed and rolled "like a scroll," it would have been a slight matter to have enlarged the area of disturbance to the extent supposed.

In the shallow water, upon the mountain tops, the corals planted their colonies, and these islands, and banks, these coral rocks and coral sands, entirely destitute as they are of primitive or volcanic rocks, and of fossil remains, are their monuments. Geologically speaking the Bahamas are of a very recent age. This is indicated by the fact that their hammocks and woods are almost destitute of soil, yet the growth of coral islands is exceedingly slow.   The coral groves and bowers are individually of small extent, very unlike the "illimitable forests" of the floral world, and the limestone annually secreted seems in quantity relatively insignificant.   The vast areas of coral limestones and of coral sands, are composed only of the detritus, torn, grounded and scattered by an ocean never at rest, and often exhibiting an energy and power almost divine, and of fragments of marine shells broken, pounded and rounded in the same way.   Shells of existing species are found in the rocks, and Charles Burnside, Esq., son of a late Surveyor-general of the Bahamas, informed us that in a Nassau quarry upon his grounds which we visited, a large and perfect egg was taken from the rock at a distance of sixteen feet below the rock's surface.   It is clear that ocean has been and is one of the grinding mills of the gods, and that duration or extent of time is only a conception of man. It is said to require under favorable circumstances a thousand years to make five perpendicular feet of coral limestone, and that coral rock exists in the Pacific ocean two thousand feet thick. In contrast with such almost infinite durations, well may the Chinese philosophers and sages compare the life of man with the little insignificant span of the measuring worm.

The important part taken by the Bahama shell fish in the formation of the banks and rocks of the Bahamas is indicated by their very great abundance. Major-General Nelson states that "at Six Hills (Caicos Group) the mass of Conch Shells (*Strombus gigas*) is so great and sufficiently cemented together as to form not only a rock, but an island several hundred feet in length."

While the highest land in the Bahamas is 230 feet above the sea, generally the hills on the larger islands are much under 100 feet in height, and from 10 to 50 feet on the islets. They abound with "pit holes" and "rock marshes." The water upon the lower flats is brackish and rises and falls, though not contemporaneously with the tide, or at a uniform rate. There are many ordinary and mangrove swamps, small and shallow, more or less connected with the sea. So far as there is any soil it is found in the little pockets in the rocks, and is scant and fertile. There are also large areas of "pine barrens" where the pine and the palm flourish side by side—the north and the south to this extent meeting and mingling harmoniously in the floral world. Lakes of salt or brackish water mirror the heavens and add a new charm to the landscape upon many of the islands. Andrus alone boasts a fresh water lake and a few small out-flowing fresh water streams. The rocks are all calcareous, soft and easily worked below the surface, white and dazzling when first quarried, but they acquire a flinty hardness of surface, and assume a subdued and darker shade (an ashen gray) when exposed to the sun and air.

The Bermuda Islands are closely allied to the Bahamas, having the same formation and being surrounded by coral reefs. They are situated in the same latitude with Charleston, S. C., and are seven hundred and eighty miles distant from Cape Hatteras, and seven hundred miles south-east of New York. Science has discovered, and historical records have furnished most reliable evidence, that this group of coral islands, since their first discovery in the early part of the sixteenth century, have been in a state of subsidence, so that they are now far less extensive than they were between three hundred and four hundred years ago. Prof. Dana says: "Twenty miles to the south-west by west from the Bermudas there are two submerged banks, twenty to forty-seven fathoms under water, showing that the Bermudas are not completely alone, and demonstrating that they cover a summit in a range of heights; and it may have been a long range."

CHAPTER III.

> "This sceptered isle;
> This earth of majesty; this seat of Mars;
> This other Eden—demi-paradise."—SHAKESPEARE.

"The poor contents him with the care of heaven."—POPE.

THE island of New Providence, although small in size and greatly deficient in soil, far transcends in importance all the islands with which it is more immediately associated. Nassau, the Bahama capital, reposes in calm, quiet dignity upon the northern slope of the hill that rises to a height of ninety feet above its northern shore, bathes its feet in the sheltered sea, and lifts its municipal head above the heights that overlook Grant's Town. It is to the entire archipelago what Athens was to Greece and the rising sun to the old Persian fire-worshippers. "Paris is France;"—Nassau is New Providence and the Bahamas. But for its harbor and favorable location, it never would have risen from the rocks, or reposed under the shadows of its tropical and semi-tropical trees. Its superiority as a shelter for ships, caused

43

it to become for these islands the seat and focus of civil, political. ecclesiastical, and military power. Without its geographical and topographical advantages. it is not probable that within its narrow borders a Colonial Governor would ever have had his residence, an Episcopal Bishop his seat, or two companies of her majesty's colored troops their barracks. No old and rusty guns would have given to the crests of its hills a military and warlike aspect; jurisprudence would have sought elsewhere room for her highest courts. and no colonial representatives or lords would have occupied imported high-backed chairs in its legislative halls.

New Providence has an extreme length of about nineteen and three-eights miles from east to west; an extreme width of about seven miles from north to south; an average width of about five miles; and embraces a total area of about eighty-five square miles. From the north shore in front of Nassau, the distance across the island is between five and six miles. With the exception of a very few square miles occupied by Nassau and its suburbs, there is little upon the island except water and wilderness; the former brackish. and throbbing and in some places appearing and disappearing with the long pulsations of the sea's diurnal tides, and the latter, to a large extent, a dense low jungle, with stretches of pitch pine forests rising from a thick undergrowth of scrub palmettoes. all being root-fastened to the rocks and apparently living like Dr. Tanner during his recent forty days' fast, exclusively upon air and water.

The western extremity of New Providence is called Clifton Point, and its eastern extremity, East Point. In a south-westerly direction from Nassau, at a distance of probably seven or eight miles, Lake Killarney is situated —a body of shallow, brackish water nearly three miles in length from east to west, and about two and three-fifth miles in width from north to south.

The Blue Hill range is about seven miles long, and running east and west, separates this lake from Lake Cunningham—a smaller body of shallow water, half a mile wide, and two and two-thirds miles in length from east to west. The negro drivers, by design or ignorance, palm off this lake upon strangers for Killarney—it being nearer and more accessible than the latter. Cunningham, with its little mangrove islands, is well worth visiting, and the drive for a mile or two through the pine woods and scrub pal-mettoes, rendered necessary to reach it, gives one an opportunity to see something of the low, wet, rough, and rocky make up of portions of the island. Wild flowers and palmetto leaves, gath-ered by the wayside, often give a gay and festive appearance to the vehicles of the excursionists upon their return near the close of day or in the edge of the evening. The Blue Hills attain an elevation of 120 feet.

Caves exist in the western extremity of the hill that separates the two lakes, and there is always connected with caverns in the rocks enough of the weird and wild and mysterious to make them objects of interest. We found it so with these. Indeed their proximity to a sea so recently infested by pirates, and their loca-tion upon an island not very long ago in possession of a now vanished race of men, suggest many a question which only the dead can answer. As we followed our dusky guide and passed from one chamber to another over the rocks, disturbing and driving from their dark retreats the bats, it was not difficult to imagine that the ghosts of the cruel and reckless buccaneers, and the shades of the unfortunate and grossly wronged Indians, were peering at us in the darkness and gloom. But after building a fire in the deepest, darkest and most dismal chamber of them all, which was entered through a small opening in a partition of rock, we experienced a feeling of relief, knowing that the elfs of evil vanish with the light.

In quite a number of instances the ceilings of the rocky chambers had partially fallen in, and, through the openings, the roots of wild fig trees had made their way, dropped from ten to twenty feet to the bottom, where, entwined among and running over the rocks, they seemed in the dim light like huge anacondas, whose repose it might be dangerous to disturb.

Catesby, a century ago, in writing in regard to the natural history of the Bahamas, observed, that "many of these islands, particularly Providence, abound with deep caverns containing salt water at their bottoms. These pits, being perpendicular from their surface, are frequently so choked up and obscured by the falling of trees and rubbish, that great caution is required to prevent falling into these 'unfathomable pits' as the inhabitants call them, and it is thought that many men who never returned from hunting have perished in them."

We called the attention of an intelligent native and old resident of Nassau to this passage and he assented to its truth. To this day, the island, though so small, is largely an unknown country to its people. This seems incredible, but it is none the less true. Stimulated by a crisp and frosty air, northern people fit out exploring expeditions to the North Pole and the interior of Africa; but the citizens of Nassau care not to explore the dense jungles that exist a short distance from their doors.

An article appeared in the Nassau *Gazette* a year or two since in which a correspondent describes a natural reservoir of fresh water called "The Mermaid's Pool," or "The Black Water Pool," which seems to resemble the deep caverns or pits to which Catesby refers, except that it is filled with fresh water. This writer states that it is located in the south part of the island of New Providence, about a mile from the shore, near an extensive cocoanut plantation, then belonging to the Hon. J. S. George, a gentleman who is since, we believe, deceased. "It is in a rocky, wooded plain, so perfectly level that it would be difficult for a rabbit to find a hillock sufficiently high for concealment." It is about one hundred and fifty feet in diameter, sixty-five feet in depth, and without banks. The water comes "to the very brim," and it has "a depth of forty feet at the very edge, which is the more remarkable as the adjacent sea is so shallow that it would be necessary to go five miles from the shore or six miles from the pool, before a depth equal to that of the pool is reached." Although a great natural curiosity, and but a few miles from the city, the writer says "it is almost unknown to the people of Nassau." He gives the substance of a wild, romantic legend concerning this "Mermaid's Pool," in which a dusky island princess and a foreign shipwrecked prince act prominent parts. Strange noises are heard there at night, and in the form of a mermaid the princess at times emerges from the dark pool in the dim moonlight, seizes any unfortunate damsel who happens to be in the vicinity, and carries her a prisoner to her watery home in the rock.

The Bahamas yield a "cave earth" composed of phosphates of lime and some ammonia. It is a kind of guano, and has sufficient value as a fertilizer to cause it to be exported to other countries, principally to the United States. The total value of this guano exported has often been about $20,000 a year, at about fifteen dollars a ton. It is not used in the colony.

Nassau is situated in latitude 25° 51' north, and longitude 77° 21' west. The rock upon which it is situated has furnished the materials for the outer-walls of all its public and many of its private buildings. Nature seems to have had regard to the fact that the people who were to live in this enervating air would never voluntarily quarry granite or any similar stone, and therefore she has provided them with a rock that is soft below the surface and easily worked, but hardens when exposed to the air.

Many gardens, orchards, and ornamental grounds are enclosed with high walls made of this rock. These walls are stuccoed, and covered on top with fragments of glass embedded in mortar, all which impresses one with the conviction that petty larceny is an offence not unknown upon this happy and innocent-looking isle.

Very many of the houses have large, heavy blinds on the sides exposed to the street and the sun, which enclose spacious piazzas, and thus secure cool air and seclusion. The blinds, in connection with the garden walls, give them, to northern eyes, something of the appearance of Turkish harems, and the impression is deepened by the additional fact that one seldom gets even a glance at the beautiful ladies who are supposed to occupy these pleasant homes.

We are unable to give accurately the population of Nassau. In 1861, the population of the Bahamas was 35,287, of which number 11,503 were upon the island of New Providence, and, according to Gov. Rawson, "of these, upwards of 10,000 lived in Nassau and its suburbs;" and as Grant's town and Bain's town, two of the suburbs, then contained a population, the first of 2,398 and the second of 1,315, it left only 6,287 for Nassau. The population of the Bahamas in 1871, according to Moseley's Almanac, was 39,162, an increase of a little less than 4,000. If we allow Nassau and its suburbs their proportionate share of this increase (one-third) and add an equal number for the increase since 1871, it will make the present population of Nassau and its suburbs between 12,600 and 12,700. There is, however, nothing to indicate that there has been much addition to the white population of Nassau.

Bay street monopolizes nearly all the business of the city, and is its principal thoroughfare. It skirts the harbor, is shaded by rows of almond trees, stretches east and west for several miles

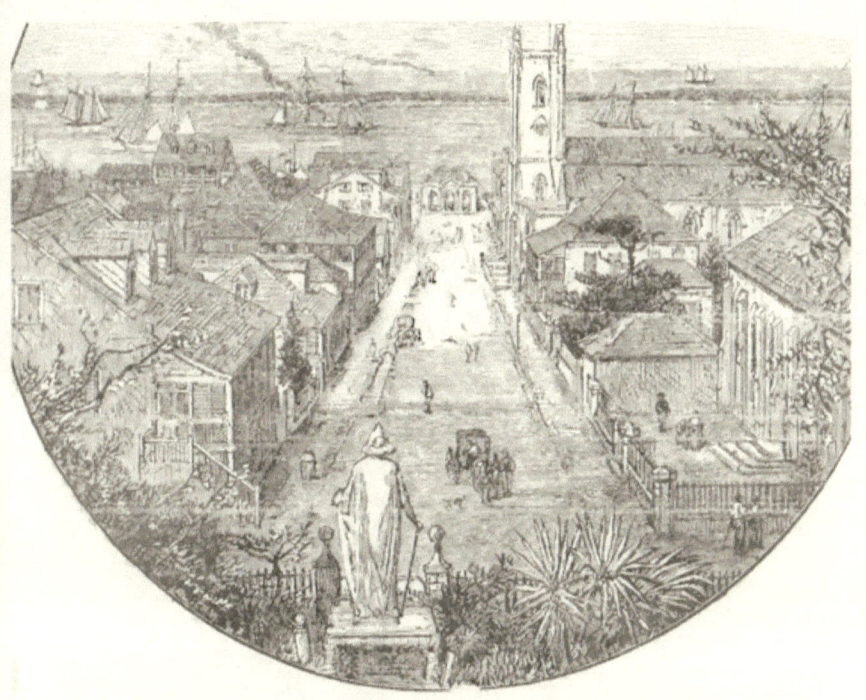

Looking down George st. from the Government House. Statue of Columbus
in the foreground. The Cathedral on the right. The Vendue House
at the foot of the street. The Harbor, Barrier Island,
and Ocean north of the city.

beyond the limits of the city, and is made lively and attractive by trade and travel. The docks and landings, the public market, the stone barracks with their iron framed and stone-paved verandas, Fleming Square and the officers' quarters, the airy uninclosed Vendue House, numerous stores and dwellings, a few small hotels and private boarding houses, the eastern Parade Ground, and an old cemetery still further to the east—all give tone, character and importance to the street, and confer upon it a very great pre-eminence over all the other streets of the city.

For several miles, during all parts of the day, Bay street is thronged with people, almost exclusively colored. Many of them are women and children, merchants in a very small way, bearing their stock in trade upon their heads. Idlers abound. No one is in any hurry. "How are you to-day, massa?"—"God bless you, massa"—"Can't you give me a penny, boss?" are among the common salutations. The elderly colored women, when informed that we feel pretty well to-day, with much gravity of look and a devout expression, ejaculate "Thank God!" and pass along. The diminutive black vocalists remember our interest in their sacred songs, and have another song which they are anxious to sing to us.

Nothing so impressed us with the evident poverty of the colored people of Nassau as a class, and of the difficulty they experience in getting a good and honest living, as the large number of colored women and children to be constantly seen during every business day upon Bay street bearing in their hands, or, (when walking,) upon their heads, their little stocks in trade—here a few pennies worth of candy, and there a little trifle of cake; some with small quantities of peanuts, and others having small supplies of flowers or fruit—the appearance of the latter often suggesting the thought that it had been prematurely picked to meet wants that were pressing, and would not wait. A capital of twenty-five

5

cents appeared amply sufficient to enable most of these street or curb-stone merchants to have a good start in life. The good nature and generosity of the colored people as a class was very marked. They freely gave to each other from their little stores, and never seemed to either fret, fume, worry or hurry. Truly blessed are these destitute children of the sun, for theirs is the kingdom of heaven—if heaven is the state or condition of being contented and happy—or if it is a country where nothing that makes a man rich in this ever enters. It is worth a journey to Nassau to learn the extent of man's artificial wants.

The streets of Nassau are to a large extent made in and upon the surface rock, the paving having been previously done when the shell and coral sands were hardened into stone. By filling up the hollows with broken stone, the roads are easily kept in good repair, as the rains soon dissolve the lime in the rock sufficiently to form a cement which makes all compact and solid. Prisoners in small squads, ornamented and secured by chain and ball, are daily seen working upon the roads—sitting sometimes, while working with their hammers, unshielded from the hot sun, in the dazzling light reflected from the white surface, while the thermometer registers from 140° to 150°.

Sherley street runs next south of and parallel with Bay street, and is the second street in extent and importance. East Hill street runs for a short distance back (south) of the Royal Victoria Hotel. A few cross streets extend southerly from Bay street—most of them but a short distance. The principal of these are: 1st, Market street, leading to Grant's Town, the north terminus of which is at the City Market; 2d, George street, which, commencing at the Vendue House, passes in front of the "Cathedral" or Christ's Church, and extends to the foot of a long flight of steps leading to the Government House or residence

Fort Fincastle.

of the Governor of the colony; 3d, Frederick street, upon which is the Wesleyan Trinity Church, and St. Andrew's Presbyterian Church; 4th, Parliament street, on the east side of which, at its northerly terminus, are the legislative and judicial buildings, while the Victoria Hotel is on the same side at its southerly terminus; 5th, East street, which, passing the hotel, leads to Fort Fincastle, on the crest of the hill.

This fort commands a good view of the ocean and is utilized as a signal station. Whenever any vessel approaches either entrance to the harbor of Nassau, the direction from which it comes and its character are indicated by flags hoisted upon its flag staff. It is a queer looking affair, running at one end to a point, and looking like some old sharp-bowed ante-diluvian water craft, ossified and turned into stone, which from the bottom of the sea had been pushed up into the air and the sun-light when the rock upon which it rests was elevated. Little negro cabins cluster around and cling to its side like so many large barnacles.

SIGNALS UPON FORT FINCASTLE.

Flags at *mast-head* denote the description of approaching vessels.

Small *quarter flags* at the *point* of the *yard arm* indicate the number of approaching vessels. Four halyards attached to the yard arm are thus used;—one on the first halyard signifies *one vessel;* on the second, *two vessels;* and so on.

If more than eight vessels are approaching from one quarter, the *fleet flag* is hoisted at the mast-head, and the quarter flags at the point of the yard arm.

A *Mail Packet Steamer* is indicated by a *Red Pendant* at the yard arm, over the quarter flag.

When the mail steamer anchors, a *Union Jack* is hoisted on

the Public Abutment; when the mails are landed it is hauled down.

A *Red Pendant* is hoisted at the mast-head of the fort when a vessel of war approaches; and should the Union be flying from the fort, the Red Pendant is hoisted under it.

A *Large Union* is hoisted on Sundays, all public days, and whenever the royal standard is unfurled at Government House. It is kept flying, except in bad weather, from eight o'clock A. M. until sunset.

A *Small Union* hoisted at mast-head over the signal which denotes the description of the vessel approaching, indicates that the Governor is on board, and is kept flying until the vessel anchors.   His excellency is evidently the Queen Bee of the little hive.

MAST-HEAD SIGNALS.

Red and yellow (vertical bars), steamer.
Red and white cross, brig.
Red, ship or barque.
White with red cross, brigantine.
Blue with white cross, fore and aft schooner.
Blue, top-sail schooner.
Blue and yellow (horizontal), fleet.
White and blue (horizontal), distress.

YARD ARM SIGNALS--(QUARTER FLAGS.)

Yellow, west.
Blue and yellow (vertical), north-west.
Blue, north.
Blue and red, north-east.
Red, east.

Very near to its north wall a deep cut has been made in the

rock through the hill, as if for the purpose of obstructing by an artificial chasm the approach to the fort by a hostile land force from the north. In this deep gorge there is a long high flight of stone steps, which are dignified by the name of "The Queen's Staircase." It is an interesting spot and much visited.

Back of Nassau, over the hill, towards the west is Delancy's Town—a suburb of the city occupied by colored people ; Grant's Town and Baine's Town lie also back of the city below and beyond the crest of the hill, but are further to the east.

These suburban villages are inhabited largely by manumitted slaves and the descendants of those who have been enfranchised. Some, it is said, still use their native African dialects, and harbor some of their old superstitions. We frequently visited these suburbs, and were always much interested in their teeming population, huddled together around their humble dwellings, sitting upon the rocks, or leaning upon the rude division and front walls of their village lots. With no corroding cares, no troublesome anxieties about to-morrow, and no wants not easily supplied, they seemed more to be envied than many of the tired toilers in colder climes. Excepting the divers, we saw none of the " nearly naked negroes " that others have described. Once while sailing before a good breeze, a boat passed that was sculled by a small boy, whose costume consisted only of a shirt, or, as a lady very forcibly expressed it, " two sheets in the wind, or one flying." His diminutive size, ebony complexion and comical attitude, self-satisfied air and "*ascension* robe," contrasted strikingly with the size of his boat, the dignity and gravity of his passengers, the clear and exquisitely beautiful water, and the green background of Hog Island, whose southern shore he was approaching. But little money is, however, spent for dry goods, and many are barefooted, while the poor apologies for shoes which others have, make it impossible for them to walk except with a noisy, shuffling gait, which equally grates upon the ear and offends the eye of people from the States. Those whom we have seen Sundays have been well and neatly but not expensively dressed.

The streets of these suburbs are narrow and cross each other at right angles. Building lots have been laid out upon them, upon which there is usually a small one-story house, and sometimes two or more, embowered in orange, tamarind, cocoanut, banana, sapodilla and other trees, and with flowering shrubs and vines. Here, as elsewhere generally upon the island, so far as we have seen it, the trees rise up out of the bare and naked rocks. Gov. Rawson in his report for 1864, speaking of this locality, says: " Fruit trees of various kinds are crowded around the dwellings and cottages, growing luxuriantly, but planted without order, unselected, unpruned, and unimproved, often finding a place and nourishment for their roots in crannies and fissures in the rocks into which it would appear impossible for them to penetrate."

One can hardly believe his own eyes in looking at them. The plow and the spade, the harrow and the cultivator, the scythe and the reaper would be as much out of place here as snowballs in a baker's oven. The only implements of husbandry that can be made available are the pick and the crowbar. By prying up the end of a stone, or finding a crevice or making one in the rock, a place is found for slip, root, or seed, and when thus utilized, small rootlets start out, follow all the minute inequalities of the porous limestone, penetrate all the little pockets in the rock, run over and down ledges ten to twenty feet high, searching for fissures and crevices in the hard bottom of stone below, as if guided by intelligence, and impelled onward by a strong and most tenacious love of life, while, at the same time, buds and twigs and stems and branches push upwards, enlarge and multiply, drawing rich supplies of food from a hot sun that warms but never wilts, and from the dews and showers that come down from heaven for their sustenance, until a dense and seemingly impenetrable forest, fast anchored to the rocks, and a wild tangle of vines and bushes, blushing with flowers that perfume the air, cover all the apparent sterility of nature with a beauty which seems like childhood's dreams of fairy land.

The houses of the negroes are built mostly of wood, but some have limestone walls, while the roofs are covered—some with shingles and others with a thatching of palmetto leaves. It is rare to see a house with glass windows—board shutters take the place of sashes, and fire-places and chimneys are unknown. A little fire out doors, for cooking, made of dead wood gathered in the forest or thickets, which is transported in little bundles upon the heads of women and children, is all that is required in this warm climate. The walls are not sheathed or plastered, and the furniture of the houses is of the rudest and most simple kind. The colored people in the day time live out of doors in the open air, so that in riding through these suburbs, the whole population comes under review. Nobody appears to be at work. In sunshine or shadow, having nothing and wanting nothing, taking no thought for to-morrow, they live on like the birds from day to day, not needing to take lessons of the ant nor of any other of the world's greedy and grasping toilers. All are merry, light-hearted and joyous; nobody frets or scolds; not a child cries; and the dogs, crouching beside their indolent masters, are literally too lazy to bark. All the thieving is of the petty kind—it would be too much like work to plan and execute robbery on a large scale—and what is the use of committing burglaries and grand larcenies when a little sugar-cane or a handful of fruit fills to overflowing the measure of their wants! There are no trades-unions, no commercial revulsions, and no strikes for higher wages. No heads ache from the pressing weight of the crowns they wear, and no brains give out in the ceaseless and crazy struggles for wealth and power. Voluptuous idleness is the happy offspring of these charming isles of the sea, where frosts are unknown, and health and happiness float on each passing wave of the soft, perfumed air.

Some of the military officials having very kindly designated a time when they would show the interior of Fort Charlotte, including its extensive subterranean works, to some of the hotel guests, we were enabled through the politeness of Edward N. Shelton, Esq., of Derby, Ct., to participate in the pleasure of the excursion.

This fort, in its completed form, is not a hundred years old, and yet neither history or tradition are able to inform us positively when or by whom its foundations were laid. Mr. Charles Mosely, an old resident of Nassau, long an editor and publisher of one of its newspapers, says in his almanac: "It is *supposed* to have been begun by the Spaniards. It was finished *about* 1790, but the information regarding its history is very meagre and incomplete." Thus the same air that stimulates into rapid and vigorous growth the vegetable world, operates as an opiate upon animal life, puts the Genius of History to sleep, and makes the Present too indolent to prepare and preserve records of the most important passing events.

Fort Charlotte is upon the summit of the hill upon which Nassau, in a state of semi-tropical torpor, reposes. It is west of the city, and commands the principal or west entrance to the harbor. We passed a small open shore battery, and, ascending the hill by a winding roadway, soon reached and crossed a drawbridge over a dry moat, ascended a flight of steps cut in the rock within the fort's walls, to the high rocky table within the ramparts, where we found our military escort waiting to receive and welcome us. We felt no desire to enter the fort as prisoners of

View of a part of Grant's Town.

war, and no ambition to take possession of it for and in the name of the Great Republic, although, if somewhat reduced in size, and safely floated over the ocean, it might add a pleasing interest to some great American Museum or Inter-national Exposition. We were well satisfied to enter it as willing captives of British and Bahama hospitality.

To our civilian eyes its armament did not appear formidable. Its old and rusty ordinance seemed little better than Quaker guns. No doubt, however, they exert as salutary a moral influence upon Nassau's suburban colored inhabitants as would the best rifled and breech-loading peacemakers of modern times.

To us the fort had a special value by reason of the extensive and picturesque views it affords. In front, and far away to the right and left, were the strings of beaded keys with which the shores of New Providence are exquisitely jewelled. Numberless rocks and reefs, lying in ambush in the shallows of the sea, were revealed by the white, foaming breakers that dashed over them. The iris colored and ribboned waters, with their settings of islands and keys, constituted a lovely sun embroidered border for the dark, deep blue dress of the ocean, which, in wide and waving folds, brushed against the sky. Turning to the opposite side, the contrast was most striking. The hill upon which we stood, Prospect Hill to the right, and the Blue Hills in the distance, are densely wooded banks and water sheds of a low, wet wilderness. We were very near to a colonial capital in which we had witnessed, in rather a small way, something of the pride and pomp and glory of this world. From our commanding positions we were able to observe its "back country," and to see no small portion of the island, yet we looked in vain for green pastures and flowery meads, for villages and farm houses, for orchards and gardens. The glassy surface of a small, salt and shallow lake alone broke the continuity of the low, thick, impenetrable

jungle. There was much to please the eye, but not a little of
the beauty was eliminated when we paused to muse and meditate.

Before we had an opportunity to do much of the latter, we
were invited by our military friends to explore that portion of
the fort which exists below the surface, in the very bowels of the
limestone hill. Colored subordinates attended with lanterns,
while the military officials devoted themselves to their guests,
and, with a gallantry characteristic of military men, personally
aided the ladies in treading the dark and dismal corridors, and
exploring the windowless rooms which have been excavated in
the rock. We entered the mouth of a small, round, deep well
hole, and descended a long flight of spiral stairs cut in the rock.
We traversed slowly and carefully in the darkness, one after the
other, the small convolutions of this long, perpendicular, immov-
able, excavated stone cork-screw. Our memory of this artificial
military cave is not clear cut. It partakes somewhat of the darkness of the caverns we explored. The rooms and corridors, with
their sides, and floors, and ceilings of stone, were no doubt made
after some deeply cogitated and wise plan, but the most we rec-
ollect is that they were dark and dismal dungeons. Here and
there we remember to have seen loop holes, through which, from
safe coverts, musketeers might shoot the men who should succeed
in scaling the walls.

If the reader desires, in a cheap and comparatively easy way,
to experience the delightful sensations which a visit to Fort
Charlotte's subterranean rooms is so well calculated to produce,
he has only to go into some large deep cellar and follow a negro
with a lantern for half an hour in the darkness, and his curiosity,
if he is a reasonable man, will be fully gratified.

Not far from our first landing place at the foot of the spiral
stairs, we remember endeavoring to peer into the darkness of a
well hole in the rock which had been sunk to the foundations of

the hill, and to have drank some cool and pleasant-tasted water which was drawn from it.

Nor would we if we could forget "The Queen's Chamber," where, for the first time in our lives, we ate and drank at the expense of the British Government. With cheese and crackers and wine, the darkness was in a measure dispelled, and the representatives of the old and new worlds there assembled, in those artificial Bahama caverns, drove a few nails into the great international Platform of Peace.

After drinking to the health of the British Queen, and to the prosperity and speedy and rapid promotion of the military gentlemen who had so kindly given us their time and attention, we ascended into the sunlight, and soon, resuming our carriages, returned to our hotel.

The military barracks formerly occupied at Nassau an elevated position on the grounds of Fort Charlotte. They were commenced in 1790, and finished in 1794, and cost the home government about $150,000. After being used for between forty and fifty years, they were condemned as unhealthy, and taken down. An obelisque has been erected upon their site, which is utilized as a land-mark by vessels entering the harbor. Some of the Nassau people, we were told, claim that this removal was accomplished under a false pretext; that it was "a put up job;" that the military officers desired to be nearer to Nassau while doomed upon the island of New Providence to play the part of Napoleon Bonaparte at St. Helena. The sickness complained of they allege, was caused by imprudence; some of the soldiers, after spending an evening in the city, were too heavily loaded with liquor to get back to their barracks without lying down to rest and sleep in the damp night air. Hence the fevers from which they suffered. But as the prevailing winds swept over the low wet lands of the island before they reached the old barracks, it is quite probable that, at least during the wet rainy season, they were unhealthy.

Little Fort Montague has been keeping watch and guard at the eastern entrance of Nassau harbor for a little less than a century and a-half. It was finished in 1742. Lieut. Bruce, who planned it, and superintended its construction, had sufficient skill as an engineer, and talent as an author, to ensure its transmission to our own times doubly preserved. Its walls remain intact, and the pen of its engineer secured for it an abiding place in letters.

It is only as a relict and reminder of the by-gones that it has a present value. It is not garrisoned, but its old and rusty guns, in appearance at least, continue to guard Nassau's back door. Although we never entered its walls, it always calls up pleasant memories, as we often passed near it during the forenoon sails and afternoon rides that did so much to fill our cup of pleasure at Nassau.

The Governor of these islands, while we were in Nassau, sent a written message to the Bahama legislative assembly, signed by himself, in which he asked for an appropriation of £50 (about two hundred dollars) to " His Excellency in Council, to cause to be collected and printed the judicial decisions of the Superior Court of this colony during the last quarter of a century." Does this not indicate a great amount of legal business? What an opening exists in this extensive group of islands, keys, rocks, and banks for young and aspiring members of the legal profession! Only £50 wanted to collect and print all the decisions of all the Bahama Superior Courts for twenty-five years! And two dollars will purchase sugar cane enough to support a man and keep him fat and healthy for three months. Observe also how the Governor regards the maxim that " A man cannot expect others to think any better of him than he thinks of himself,"—and styles himself "His Excellency!" The more we study the royal institutions of the Bahamas, the more satisfied we become that our boasted republic is a failure, popular governments a mistake, and that it is about time to give some of our most skillful artists a liberal order for crowns, scepters, thrones, and all the gilded trappings necessary to set up one of those lofty imperial governments which are "ordained of God." Perhaps it may be well to start one first upon the "Thimble Islands," that our people may see with their own eyes how beautifully the thing works.

In a newspaper which is issued there semi-weekly, entitled "The Nassau *Guardian*," &c., we find under date of February 24th, 1879, a letter of welcome to the newly elected Bishop of the diocese from the rector, wardens and vestry of a church upon Harbour Island (one of the Bahamas) upon his first visit to that island, and the bishop's reply. The correspondence has no particular interest to the outside world except as it shows how great, windy titles thrive when transplanted upon these wonderfully productive calcareous rocks. The Harbour Island church officials addressed this successor of poor and humble apostles as follows:

"The Right Reverend Dr. Francis A. Cramer-Roberts, Lord Bishop of Nassau, Reverend Father in God."

The Bishop in his reply concluded as follows:

"Believe me to remain.
"Your affectionate Father in God,
"FRANCIS-NASSAU."

Now if these little rocky isles of the ocean can sport "Fathers in God," "Lord Bishops," and other high ecclesiastical digni-

taries, in addition to a Governor and lords temporal enough to
stock a great empire, isn't it about time for the people of the
states to wake up and do something?   Haven't we all the materials
necessary for the manufacture of whole regiments of "lords
temporal" and "Fathers in God," and why shouldn't we have
our share?

Nassau harbor is about one and one-half miles long, and two-
fifths of a mile wide.   Potter's Key runs mid-way down the harbor from the east, and separates the eastern half into two parts.
The quays and landing places are on the south side of the
harbor, opposite the east end of Hog Island.   The shipping
occupy the south side of the channel, which is separated from
the north side by a bank having fifteen feet of water.   The
ordinary tides rise from two to three feet.   It is not generally
practicable for vessels to enter the harbor from the east which
draw over nine feet of water.

Old wrecks and storm-worn and condemned vessels abound,
and suggest to a stranger Nassau's importance as a seaport.   Her
back door is open only to small vessels, while her front door is
barred.

That the bar at the main entrance to Nassau harbor is often
a very serious obstruction to navigation, is evident from the fact
that the authorities have established the following bar signals:

" If the harbor is approached with a northerly wind, and there
is an uncertainty as to the state of the bar, should it be dangerous to cross, a red flag will be hoisted on the signal staff near the
lighthouse.   *   *   Should it be possible, but too dangerous to
get out, a white flag will be hoisted, and the pilot-boat will be
seen in waiting just within the breakers, showing a flag red and
white horizontally," &c.

The Governor in his report for 1878, stated that in September
of that year, for six successive days, no vessel was able to cross

the bar, on account of the disturbed state of the water, caused
by the high winds and storms which had prevailed outside. Also
that the harbor had not before been thus closed for so long a
period within the memory of the oldest inhabitants. One can
easily understand the danger of crossing at such times who has
watched the high breakers, with foaming crests, leap along the
bar from the back of Hog Island. It is often a pleasant and exciting pastime to approach this bar in a yacht, and watch the
high waves as they approach, getting near enough to them to
realize their power, and be baptised in their spray. How grandly
they approach, with their high and foaming crests, "white as
carded wool," or an Alpine torrent! The waves seem marshalled
for the onset. Like the measured tread of an army, they roll in
upon the honey-combed and trembling isle at short and regular
intervals. Here and there a daring column of assault leaps over
a depression in the rocks, but the main body, baffled in its purpose, rolls and foams along the rocky rim of the shore, envelopes
the lighthouse in a mantle of spray, traverses the whole length
of Nassau bar, and spends itself at last upon the white shore of
Silver Key. Like the heavy roll of distant thunder, but with
more exultant tones, loud voices from the troubled ocean mingle
with the hoarser and louder reverberations that arise from the
long line where sea and shore meet and struggle for the mastery.
Following the first great breaker there is always a second, which
in turn is succeeded by a third, at short and regular intervals.
All travel the same path, and, like swift moving snow-clad railroad trains, glide rapidly across the bar. It was easy to believe
them strange monsters of the sea, they sampled so well its mystery and power.

A short lull occurs after the third breaker, of sufficient length
to enable waiting vessels to cross the bar. This novel race by
high mettled, spray-enveloped ocean steeds, with their long white

foaming trains, always secures a high degree of pleasurable excitement. We always welcomed the showers of glistening pearls that on such occasions greeted, enveloped and followed us, as a holy baptism from Neptune's sacred but unseen altars.

The inscription upon a coraline monument which occupies a conspicuous position upon the sea bank opposite the western or main entrance to the harbor, is strongly suggestive of the danger which attends the crossing of the bar on some occasions. Below the names of five men is the following testimonial.

"Who perished on the bar of Nassau harbor, February 26th, 1861, while gallantly volunteering their services in the effort to save two men belonging to the pilot boat, which had been upset by a heavy sea. This monument is erected by the legislature of the Bahamas, to commemorate their gallant conduct and self-sacrificing heroism."

Thus does this monumental stone serve a double purpose. It honors not only the dead but the living, for the men who, in this substantial manner, recognized the noble virtues that animated and inspired these obscure heroes in humble life, and thus caused them to inculcate a lesson of self-sacrifice to every passer by, at the same time, all unconsciously, provided a memorial of their own justice, goodness and practical wisdom.

On the first day of March, 1879, aided by a good glass, we witnessed a grand and extensive display of breakers from the cupola of the Victoria Hotel. The reefs, rocks, shoals, and outlying keys were all marked and enlivened with the constant dash and play of the foaming breakers. The plucky resistance of Hog Island to the angry and impetuous assaults of the sea, challenged our admiration. The light house, which rises from that island's eastern terminus, a spindle of limestone sixty-eight feet high, had its top obscured with the spray of high breakers that threatened to sweep it into the sea. We could not but muse and

View from Fort Fincastle.

meditate upon the question of its desirableness as a summer residence, with a cyclone outside traveling at the rate of one hundred miles an hour. For we well knew that at times, not only

> "The startled waves leap over it; the storm
> Smites it with all the scourges of the rain,
> But steadily against its solid form
> Press the great shoulders of the hurricane."

As we saw it on that occasion, we realized more than ever before its great importance, and the beneficence of its mission. We seemed to hear its hopeful and inspiring voice above the roar of the angry breakers.

> "'Sail on!' it said, 'sail on, ye stately ships,'
> And with your floating bridge the ocean span,
> Be mine to guard this light from all eclipse,
> Be yours to bring man nearer unto man!"

The Bahamas offer special attractions to the conchologist. Their waters abound with a great variety of handsome shell-fish, and the shells, profusely scattered along the shores of the islands and keys, as the tides ebb, are exquisitely beautiful in form and color. They are mostly small, and so delicate and varied that with them the natives have long been accustomed to make various articles for the adornment of persons and parlors. They display much ingenuity and taste, and are said to be, if not superior, at least unsurpassed in this department of industrial esthetics. Some of the products of their skill, as well as shells that have been simply gathered from the beach and cured, are most always to be found for sale in the court of the hotel. Also delicate ornaments ingeniously made from the small scales of fish.

In this connection, the conchs deserve special notice, as in the

past they furnished to the natives a most important article of
diet, while the conch shells have been in demand in other countries for their beauty, and have also to a considerable extent,
been utilized in the manufacture of various articles of personal
adornment.　The conch also often secretes a pearl of considerable
value.　The exportation of conch shells for five years, from 1856
to 1860 inclusive, aggregated $75,230, and for the next four
years, (during the war of the rebellion), only $15,445.　In the
Governor's report for 1878 no mention is made of this item of
trade, and I infer the value of conchs exported that year must
have been very small.　The conch is obtained by diving, and
sometimes has been found in very extensive beds.　This may be
inferred from a passage on page 204 of McKinnen's Tour, A. D.
1803, in which he says—that the day after they passed Exuma,
they "steered towards a passage named Conch Cut, from a pro-
ligious quantity of conch shells which have been rolled from the
[Great Bahama] bank or adjoining shores, and thrown together
near this narrow pass."　At the time of the American revolution
of 1776, the Bahama people relied far more upon the water than
the land for their support.　Its fruitage of fish and wrecks never
failed.　They had no more occasion than the birds to sow and
reap.　At that time they acquired the sobriquet of Conchs.
A writer from the Bahamas in 1824, states that many persons
of the highest respectability were then distinguished by that
name, and that they appeared to be not very proud of it,—which
is not to be wondered at, as one might be expected to be equally
pleased to be called an oyster or a clam.　The wreckers of Key
West, Fla., whose ancestors came from the Bahamas, are, we are
informed by an old sea captain, to this day also called conchs.
The surfaces of the inner spiral convolutions of the shell of the
conch are highly polished, and have a most beautiful pink color,
which suggested to our mind the inquiry whether the living oc-

cupant of this little but exquisitely furnished tenement is itself
conscious of the gracefulness and beauty of the inner chambers
of the house it occupies upon the submerged shelf of the ocean.

It was a very pleasant surprise to find at Nassau a well selected
Public Library of over seven thousand volumes. It does much
credit to the government which established and sustains it, and
evidences wise statesmanship. Some of the other islands it is
said, are similarly favored. A person, entitled to draw books, is
permitted to take out five volumes at a time—a very liberal number, and probably more than could be allowed if its patrons were
more numerous. Isolated as New Providence is from the great
world beyond the sea, the stranger, with the works of his favorite
authors before him, is lonely no more. He is in the midst of a
congenial world—the great world of letters—and no longer a
stranger in a strange land. His mind is enriched and seeded
with the great thoughts of the world's greatest thinkers, present
and past. Philosophers unlock the secrets of nature, and spread
her most profound and subtle laws at his feet. Romance lays
bare for him the mysteries (to some extent distorted and too
highly colored) of the human heart, and the lights and shadows
of all phases of human life. History, with graphic pen, dipped
alike in truth and fable, portrays the rise, the decadence, and
the fall of states and empires, and points out the deep-seated
causes that make and ruin nations. Divines cluster around him,
and, while some for a greater or less fee permit him to look
through their little pieces of smoked glass at the invisible world,
others, with lips hallowed with celestial fire from God's own
altar, discourse eloquently upon the mysteries of life, death and
immortality. While the poet, in soothing numbers, sings inspired songs, conducts him on fancy's wings through all space,
and opens for him alike grim purgatorial doors and the golden
gates of the celestial city.

Even in the drowsy air of the Bahamas a studious man is not
satisfied or happy if withdrawn entirely from the world of letters.
He must wander at will in what to him is the very garden of the
gods—those literary fields where is found the choicest fruitage
of the most gifted and cultivated minds. In the mild climate of
Italy, the great Cicero found coveted rest and repose, not in listless idleness, but in a change of literary work. Mind, equally
with muscle, is toned up and strengthened by exercise, and soft-
ens in voluptuous repose. The tired intellectual worker who
seeks in Nassau rest, may, therefore, in moderation avail himself
of the benefits of its library. With leisure and a library, his
mind will not become flabby while his body grows fat.

The building used for a library is of octagon form, built of
stone, and was formerly a prison. Each of its eight alcoves has
a window, so that it is well supplied with light and air. Connected with the library there is a newspaper and magazine department, which adds materially to its value. A beginning (a
small nest egg) has also been made for a museum of natural
history.

CHAPTER IV.

The Royal Victoria Hotel.   Scenes daily witnessed in its Court.   Sacred Songs of the Negroes.

> " Whoe'er has traveled life's dull round,
>   Where'er his stages may have been,
> May sigh to think he still has found
>   The warmest welcome at an inn."—SHENSTONE.

THE words above quoted need to be qualified, for a landlord's welcome is purchased by his guest's money, and disappears the moment that gives out.   The destitute traveler is not presumed to be a disguised angel, and the doors of few public or private houses swing open at his approach, except for the purpose of letting the dogs loose on him.   Hotels are not kept for tramps, and the latter receive but a cold welcome even in poor houses which the public maintain in part for their benefit.

We were much pleased with the Royal Victoria Hotel, and received many little attentions and kindnesses at the hands of its proprietor, (Mr. J. M. Morton), which it is a pleasure to acknowledge, but the visitors from the states must remember that Nassau's justly celebrated hostelry is conducted on business principles, and that plenty of money or a good letter of credit is an essential requisite of " the warmest welcome " of which the poet Shenstone sung.

In a subsequent chapter, reference is made to the object for which this hotel was built by the Bahama government, and to the important part it played in the blockade running business

89

during the late American war. It is so essential to the health and comfort of invalids and tourists visiting Nassau, that we add such other facts concerning it as strangers proposing to visit the place will naturally desire to know.

This hotel stands upon high ground, a little below the crest of the hill upon which Nassau is built. Three-fourths of the square enclosed by Sherley, East, East Hill, and Parliament streets, is occupied as a site for the hotel and for hotel purposes. It faces the north, and commands, from all its front windows and piazzas, a very fine view of the harbor, its sheltering island, some neighboring keys, and the out-lying ocean. It overlooks the judicial, legislative and library buildings, and many private buildings with their embowering trees. Its elevation and exposure to the full force of the prevailing winds, secures for it the full benefit of those from the ocean, which, freighted with refreshment and health, seldom cease to blow.

The hotel proper is two hundred feet in length, four stories high, and is well and substantially built of coralline limestone, and is surmounted by an observatory which commands a very extensive and fine view. Piazzas ten feet wide surround each of the three upper stories, upon which the windows, generally reaching to the floor, open; thus furnishing convenient places for promenades and sittings in the outside air, though interfering somewhat at times, with the much to be desired quiet and privacy of the adjacent rooms. Projecting from the center of the building, directly over and of the same size with the main parlor, there is a piazza in the third story, open on the east, north and south sides, which affords an extensive view greatly diversified and charmingly beautiful. Spacious halls extend through the center of each story of the long building, with tiers of rooms upon each side. The old King's College School building constitutes a part of the hotel. It is in a line with the new hotel building, and is connected with it by large heavy blinds. It has stone stuccoed columns in front, its principal rooms are large and well lighted, and admit of more privacy and quiet than most of the rooms in the new building. The dining room occupies all of the first floor north of the central portion of the hotel, and large windows surround it upon three sides. It has three tiers of tables, and is unusually light, airy and pleasant. A refreshing sea-breeze seldom failed to make it agreeably cool in the middle of the hottest days, and in no instance while we were there was it at night too cool or hot for comfort. Hotel parties, and occasional evening entertainments were given in the dining room, and when its walls were adorned with palmetto leaves, and decorated with English and American flags, it did not need the gay dance, sweet music and the landlord's generous and bountiful entertainment to make it attractive even to the mere looker-on.

The parlors are smaller than those of large hotels at the north, but the climate is so mild the parlors are less frequented.

The hotel is neatly furnished and well kept. The meats, many canned vegetables, and the smaller fruits and other supplies for the establishment, are imported from New York. Packed in ice, in large refrigerators, every steamer brings large additions to the landlord's stores. A very superior class of colored waiters, uncommonly intelligent, and efficient, materially add to the comfort and happiness of the guests. A gentleman well qualified to judge in such matters expressed to us the opinion, founded on his personal knowledge, that there is no hotel in the West Indies equal to the Victoria, though some have cost more money.

We were informed by some of the visitors at Nassau, that this fine hotel has not always been well kept, and that its patrons have some times fared badly, and been the victims of extortion. With an incompetent landlord in charge, and no other suitable house to go to, Nassau would be far less desirable as a winter resort than we found it. For the invalid especially a good temporary home is essential to both health and comfort. We remember to have heard only one complaint of its management while we were there, and that was because the breakfast and dinner tables were for only a portion of the season supplied with oranges, many deeming that fruit almost a necessary of life in Florida and the Bahamas.

Bath rooms, supplied with hot and cold water, constitute a part of the establishment, and accommodate those who do not indulge in the luxury of a bath in the sea, there being nothing in the temperature of the air or water to prevent sea bathing at Nassau every day in the year. The price of board is three dollars a day, and while for many it is a large sum to pay, yet persons who had boarded for a while at some of the cheaper houses informed us that they obtained more for their money at the Royal Victoria than any where else. Washing is an extra, the charge being seventy-five cents per dozen.

A small building at the west entrance of the hotel grounds is used as a barber shop, and for drinking and billiard purposes. North of it is the hotel garden.

The court in front of the principal north entrance of the Royal Victoria Hotel is entered on three sides through eight large, high archways, and its ceiling separates it from the main parlor of the hotel, which is projected out from the main building. Being large, airy, and shaded at all times, it is a favorite place of resort by the guests of the house. As a consequence, the colored yachtmen, including the smooth-tongued, experienced and skillful Captain Sampson, and the good-natured, capable, but less showy Captains Johnson and Mitchell, when not on the water, were ever, during the pleasant days, to be seen arranging for marine exploring parties. The varied attractions of the adjacent waters,

The Royal Victoria Hotel.

islands and keys were portrayed with a fervid eloquence which never ceased to interest. Near by were numerous carriages for hire, which were much patronized. This court is also a great bazaar, to which the colored people of all ages and of both sexes who have anything to sell, resort in large numbers to dispose of their wares. Here, therefore, is offered an excellent opportunity to study the products of these rocky islands and of the adjacent waters, which is much improved and enjoyed. Many kinds of fruits, flowers and other vegetable products, corals in great variety, sugar cane and candies, sponges of all sizes and qualities, shells exquisitely shaped and beautifully colored, shell-work of unsurpassed excellence, canes of the orange, lignum vitæ, ebony, satin and other woods, and many other articles make up their stock in trade. Here also the colored boys came to scramble, in the most laughable manner, for pennies, thrown to them for that purpose upon the hard pavements of lime-stone and brick. When down, and struggling for the prize, in a wild tangle of arms and legs, they seemed a hideous, writhing mass of black and ragged reptiles of the most lively kind. When up, with faces beaming with fun and frolic, their eager calls for " massa " to " trow a penny dis way " soon dispelled the delusion. In these contests, as well as on other occasions, their good nature and amiability are pre-eminently exemplified.

For some days after we first arrived at the Royal Victoria, young Africa gave frequent vocal entertainments in the court of the hotel. The voices of some were soft and musical, and they sang the religious songs which they had learned in " the shouting meetings," with perfect abandon, and with a fervor and zeal that glorified their dusky faces, swayed their bodies, and extended down their arms to the tips of their fingers. A *sacred* waltz was sometimes performed by " Sankey" and his cousin, two little dots of children, in the most cunning and comical manner imaginable, while they sang to the rhythm of the dance, "O it will be joy-ful," &c. When the miniature boy and girl near the close sepa-rated a little, alternately approached each other and withdrew, ogling, twisting, bowing and coquetting, while they continued to sing with many repetitions—"Meet to part no more; meet to part no more," the gravity of the audience was sure to give way in laughter and applause.

The songs sung on these occasions probably have never been printed or reduced to writing. Having taken some of them down, we subjoin them for the benefit of those of our readers who may have a curiosity to know something in regard to their character, although the words alone give only a faint representa-tion of their merits when wedded by these uncultured people to music, and sung with a fervid enthusiasm, born of a native love of melody and of genuine devotional feelings. A prominent member of the choir is Charley, the basket boy merchant—a smart, bright, wide-awake little fellow, who ever has a sharp eye to business.

A marked feature in the following was the rendering of the "Oh's," the notes ascending and descending the scale in a very lively manner, and the musical expression and richness of tone added greatly to the effect.

1.

I'd rather pray my life away,
Oh! oh! oh! oh!
Than go to hell and burn away.

CHORUS.

Save me Lord from sinking down,
Oh! oh! oh! oh!
Save me Lord from sinking down.

2.

I had a book—'twas given to me,—
    Save me Lord from sinking down,
In every line was victory.

        CHORUS.

Save me, &c.

3.

I had a book—'twas given to me,—
    In every line was victory;
I had a book—'twas given to me,
    And every line convicted me.

        CHORUS.

Save me, &c.

4.

Satan made a catch at me,
    He miss my soul and he catch my sins.

        CHORUS.

Save me, &c.

WRESTLING WITH THE ANGELS.

Tell me Lord, shall I be there now,
    To sit on Zion's hill;
To wrestle with the angels all night,
    Until the break of day.
I'll wrestle with the angels
    'Till the break of day.

Tell me Lord, shall I be there
    To sit on Zion's hill all night,
And take a wrestle with the angels,
    All night! all night!
      Until the break of day?

O tell me God, shall I be there now,
O tell me God, shall I be there now,
O tell me God, shall I be there now,
    To sit on Zion's hill,
    To wrestle with the angels
        All night! All night!
      Till the break of day.

To an uncultivated, excitable people, strongly imbued with a taste for music, there is something grand and inspiring in the great volumes of melody which issue from the organ, when its keys are skillfully manipulated. Thrilled by the great tidal waves of harmony, no wonder that it serves them as a symbol of the ravishing music with which all the arches and domes of heaven are supposed to resound. Hence the following:

Unbelievers—hear the organ roll!
    Hear the organ roll!
    Hear the organ roll!
Don't you hear the organ roll,
    On Mount Calvary!

    Hear the organ roll!
Street strollers—hear the organ roll
    Hear the organ roll!
    Hear the organ roll!
Don't you hear the organ roll!
    On Mount Calvary!

In the next verse "Rum Drinkers" and afterwards "Backsliders" and others are each in like manner called upon to "Hear the organ roll," and the enthusiasm and power of musical expression of the vocalists seemed to increase until all appeared at last to have reached the very top of Mount Calvary,—a mountain they evidently believe exists somewhere in the happy land which lies just over the river of death.

The following is indicative of the fact that to some extent the negro mind in Nassau has been affected by its contact with Roman Catholicism here, or upon some of the Spanish islands.

Go and carry the news,
Go and carry the news to Mary,
    I'm bound down to Glory!
Go and carry the news to Mary,
Go and carry the news to Mary,
    I'm bound down to glory!

When Satan says I need not fear,
He'll have my soul in the judgment day:
I'd rather pray my life away,
Than go to hell and spend one day;
    Go and carry the news to Mary,
    Go and carry the news to Mary,
        I'm bound down to glory!

Carry the news,
Go and carry the news!
Sister—carry, carry the news!
    I'm bound down to glory.
Go and carry the news!
Go and carry the news!
Go and carry the news!
    I'm bound down to glory!

Here is a sacred song which is particularly adapted to the indolent habits of life of this idle people. A heaven which necessitated labor would have very little attraction for them:

Come along my sister, come along,
Come along my sister, come along,
For the angels say there's nothing to do
    But to ring the charming bell.
We are almost gone, we are almost gone,
    But the angels say there's nothing to do

> But to ring that charming bell.
> Come along my sister, come along,
> For the angels say there's nothing to do
> But to ring that charming bell.

The following little piece is said to have been composed by a colored girl a short time before her death. In the ringing of heaven's bells, the singing of the angels, and mounting the hill of Zion, her vivid imagination anticipated and had a foretaste of the happiness that awaited her in the other world. It certainly produced a cheery, comforting effect when musically and spiritedly rendered by the dusky vocalists:

> The heavenly bells are ringing,
> Archangels singing,
> The heavenly bells are ringing, —
> O rise loving sister,
> Let us go to Zion's hill!
> Let us go to Zion's hill!
> The heavenly bells are ringing,
> Archangels singing,
> The heavenly bells are ringing,
> In the morning.

At last the penny scramblers and the sweet singers of Nassau caused so much noise, and such a disturbance of the quiet which usually prevades these dreamy shores, that a man with a long unsentimental whip was sent, whenever they assembled, to drive them away. Still, however, they occasionally appeared, and, for the base coins of the strangers, exercised those gifts divine, which, like milk in a cocoanut, one, from outward appearance, would never for a moment suppose to exist.

CHAPTER V.

Flora of the Isles of Summer. The Fertilizing Air. Large Trees from Stone Quarries, and upon the Tops of Stone Walls. Trees that will not Die and cannot be Killed. Trees Within Trees. The Monkey Tamarind, the Wild Fig, and the Ceiba or Silk Cotton Trees. Thompson's Folly. Palm Trees—the Cocoanut, the African, the Cabbage and the Palmetto. The India Rubber Tree. The Singing Tree. The Tamarind Trees, and Trees Valuable for Timber, for Dyes, for their Spicy Bark, and for Medicinal Purposes. The Natural more Wonderful than the Supernatural.

> "And all the broad leaves over me
> Clapped their little hands in glee,
> With one continued sound,—
> A slumbrous sound, a sound that brings
> The feeling of a dream."

WHEN visiting for the first time the isles of unending summer, one cannot fail to be deeply impressed by their new, diversified, and curious forms of vegetable life. It matters not that he is not a close observer of nature, or an educated and trained botanist. Perhaps if he were he could not, by reason of his profound technical learning, so well communicate to common minds, the impressions and thoughts which such scenes make and inspire. The learning of some seems to make them useful only to scholars.

Upon the island of New Providence we trod what was to us a new world, and every climbing vine and flowering shrub, and branching tree ministered to our happiness. We seemed to ourselves to be a newly made Adam first introduced to his garden,

79

fortunately relieved, however, from all obligation to "dress and keep it." If we had the learning of an old and experienced botanist, we should have seen too much. As it was, we saw as much as, untrained and unpracticed, we could well master, or describe in a single chapter. A few pen-photographs of some of the more striking floral scenes and pictures which we witnessed, may communicate to our readers something of the interest and pleasure which the reality produced upon the mind of the author.

The first impression was one of astonishment at finding upon such almost naked rocks anything above lichens and the smaller and simpler forms of vegetable life. But nature is never as unjust or partial as she often appears to the casual observer. When she withholds with one hand, she, with the other, is busy dispensing lavishly her gifts. The principle of compensation exists everywhere throughout her wide domain. Human life and human experience teem with evidences of this great and universal truth, while the material world, in all its varied and wondrous forms, is permeated with the same great principle. Upon the Bahama islands it is manifested on every hand. The want of soil to cover the nakedness of the rocks finds material, though not full compensation, in a climate so happily constituted that life exists and thrives largely upon air.

Mr. Charles Burnside (whose kind and obliging attentions we are glad of this opportunity to gratefully acknowledge) took us to the coral limestone quarry upon his premises, to which we have already referred, from which, for a hundred years or more, stone has been taken for building purposes—including stone for the Royal Victoria Hotel. On the floor of that quarry, bottomed upon rock, and upon nothing else, we saw in full and lusty vigor, a wild fig tree, a species of the banyan, which in forty years had attained a great size, its many large branches towering high up in the air with a lateral spread of about eighty feet. It was full of fruit in every stage of development, the ripened figs being of the size of the end of one's little finger, but as perfect in their parts as the larger figs of commerce. Little lizards, like embryo monkeys, were here and there seen through the green foliage, while below, sheep were browsing, and eating the fallen fruit, docile and happy, growing for the shearer their wool, and fattening their carcasses for the butcher. These figs are to the taste sweet and pleasant, and, though so small, their immense number make them valuable. Children eat them, and upon them hogs are fattened. Under this tree, the top of the rocky floor was covered with a net work of its roots, one of which penetrated the cellar of Mr. Burnside, some three hundred feet distant.

We saw two of the same species of banyan tree that had obtained a large growth from seed blown by the wind or deposited by birds on top of a stone wall. This wall was composed of irregular fragments, and was two and a-half feet wide at the top and about four feet high. The seed there germinated, pushed out their little fibrous roots, which crept down each side of the stone wall, and fastened to and extended among the rocks in the fields which the wall in part inclosed. These rootlets enlarged with the growth of the trees, while from the top of the wall stems pushed up into the air. One of the trees had five stems whose diameters varied from six to twelve inches. On the top of a stone wall within the grounds of the Victoria Hotel, there is the stump of a tree a foot in diameter, which unquestionably grew there, as its roots are still seen where they entered and pushed out from among the stones of the wall. Having had some experience in setting out, manuring, watching and watering trees in Connecticut, the pluck, enterprise, persistence and independence of these wild Bahama trees challenged our warmest admiration.

Mr. Burnside also called our attention to a banyan tree upon his grounds near his front gateway, having a spread of about one hundred feet, inside the body of which there is the dead and decayed body of a Pride of India tree.   Mr. Burnside is about thirty-five years of age, and when a boy, as he said, he "often went all through the Pride of India tree, and there was nothing of the banyan tree to be seen."   A banyan seed in some way— perhaps as the result of one of the experiments in raising trees of some bold and intelligent bird—found lodgment where the branches of the old tree diverged from its stem, from ten to fifteen feet from the ground, and, no way dismayed at the dis- couraging prospect, it did not repine at its hard destiny, or arraign the goodness of Providence, but concluded to make a bold and heroic struggle for existence.   Its little, minute fibrous rootlets started out upon a seemingly hopeless mission.   To the Pride of India, with its graceful branches, beautiful foliage, and large and fragrant clusters of flowers, they were like so many gossamer threads.   But the days and months and years rolled on.   The rootlets noiselessly and stealthily passed down upon all sides of the trunk that was giving them a support, fastened into the rocks, and the doom of the Pride of India was forever sealed.   The law of "the survival of the fittest" was exemplified.   The little rootlets around the trunk enlarged into stems, perfectly encircled the old tree with a living wall of a tree of a most rampant habit of growth, and now, only by a close and critical inspection, can a stranger ascertain that this immense banyan tree perfectly encloses the dead body of a victim, whose life it has, anaconda fashion, crushed out.

Mr. C. Waterton in his " Wanderings," states that in Demerara, S. A., the wild fig tree in a similar manner often " rears itself from one of the thick branches of the top of the mora," feeds upon the juices of the latter, and in turn is taken possession of by vines, and doomed to contribute a portion of its juices towards their support and growth, so that "with their usurpation of the resources of the fig tree, and the fig tree of the mora, the mora, unable to support a charge which nature never intended it should, dies under its burden, and then the fig tree and its usurping progeny of vines, receiving no more succor from their late foster parent, drop and perish in their turn." The piratical fig tree we have described appeared to be receiving all its nourishment from the rocks to which its net-work of roots were fastened, and from the air that enveloped its wide spreading and lusty branches. No usurping vines imperilled its life.

In the destructive hurricane of 1866, some six or seven large trees were torn up by the roots in one of Mr. Burnside's lots. One tree which was completely prostrated, still adhered to the rocks by a few of its unsevered roots, and we saw it green and growing still, as if nothing unusual or adverse had happened.

A large Jamaica tamarind tree, four or five feet in diameter at its base, was at the same time also prostrated, and it had thus far resisted all the efforts of the father of Mr. Burnside during his life, and of his son since his death, to kill and get rid of it. Fires were built around it, but it was too full of sap to burn, and the baffled fires went out. They " hacked it " as they had time and opportunity, but the wounds soon healed and were covered with new bark. It was in the way, but they had thus far been unable to wholly abate the nuisance. At one time a large section of the trunk was detached and afterwards removed with very great difficulty by piece-meal. After more than twelve years, some six or seven feet in length of the butt remains. It is fastened to the rocks by a very small number of the old, and by large re-inforcements of new roots, which this butt end of the old trunk has pluckily and persistently formed and tied to the under-lying rocks. Every wound it has during all these years received, has been perfectly healed, and over the whole of the part from which the section was detached—a circle not far from four feet in diameter—a new and healthy bark has grown, while small new sprouts have in different places made their appearance. Such tenacity of life and recuperative energy we had not supposed existed anywhere. Were the climate of the Bahamas as stimulating to mind as it is to matter in some of its forms, its inhabitants would intellectually far excel all other people past or present. Notwithstanding the "never say die" pluck of this memento of the great hurricane of '66, its continuance for many years is also in part traceable to the absence of proper tools and appliances for its removal. The mechanic arts are there still in a state of rude and primitive simplicity. Aside from the building of small vessels of not exceeding a hundred tons, and at rare intervals a new store or dwelling, there is little skilled labor, and an official report states that their only manufactures are ropes, baskets and palmetto hats.

Two or three small sugar mills run by horse power, and a grind stone in the rear of the hotel, rotated by hand, were the only labor-saving machines we saw upon the island. The pine trees are cut down often, and perhaps generally, with long knives. They are not very large, and the swinging of an ax would require too great an exertion in this climate to suit the taste of its amiable, good-natured and politically free negroes.

The Jamaica tamarind tree is sometimes called the Monkey Tamarind, from the fact that occasionally in Jamaica a monkey will insert its paw, when open and extended, through the end of the large, hard, woody pod, which the tree produces, for the purpose of obtaining the seeds which it contains. Grasping these, his paw, when closed, is too large for the hole, and either because he is too stubborn and willful to open his paw, or because he has not sufficient intelligence and presence of mind to do so, he holds on and pulls, and pulls and holds on, until one very much his inferior in climbing trees discovers and captures him. Though higher in the scale of life, and rounding out a larger and more showy link, man, in ways equally stubborn and stupid, often rushes upon and invites his own destruction. Let us therefore, pity these unfortunates, and not laugh at them.

A specimen of the Ficus Indica, or banyan tree of India, is erroneously supposed to exist near Nassau, and strangers often leave that city firmly convinced that they have added to their new and pleasant experiences a personal acquaintance with that famous tree of the Orient. An intelligent native merchant of Nassau, who is officially connected with our own Government, informed us that the (so-called) banyan tree near Nassau had been imported—that it bore no fruit, and that it is the only genuine India banyan tree upon the island of New Providence. He did not intentionally misrepresent, and would generally be considered good authority, but he was mistaken. Confident that we had seen little figs growing upon the tree in question, we visited it again, examined it more critically, and severed and carried away from it branches of wild figs in every stage of development. It is a species of the Ficus, has the same habit of growth with the Ficus Indica, but is identical in kind with the other wild fig trees upon the island of New Providence, and exhibits far more strikingly than any of the others those peculiarities which have made the banyan tree of India so famous.

An intelligent and pleasing correspondent of the *Troy Budget* (the Hon. C. L. McArthur) writes concerning the Nassau banyan tree, that "after its main limbs have grown out from its trunk some twenty or thirty feet, the *branches turn down to the earth,* taking root, and forming a column of support for its parent branch, as well as another tree of itself." "It is a very curious tree, furnishing friendly shade, ever extending by new **trunks,** ever widening its circle *by its top striking down and*

S

taking root, and every new growth and stem being still a part of the parent tree to which it is ligamented as were the Siamese twins." No doubt Mr. McArthur visited the tree he has undertaken to describe, and being a man of ability and literary culture, his testimony is that of a credible witness—and yet, he is contradicted by the facts. He was, as all are who see it, astonished and delighted to find a tree possessing such a peculiar habit of growth, and multiplying itself into a large grove or small forest. But he failed to make such a close and critical examination as was necessary in order to enable him to enlighten his readers in regard to the method by which the singular result is produced. Had he done so, he would have discovered that the branches do not "turn down to the earth and take root," nor does "its top strike down and take root," but from the outstretching branches, at various distances from the stem or trunk, *roots* descend a distance of from ten to fifteen feet *through the air,* fasten to the rocky bottom, enlarge from year to year, and thus by single and clustered living columns support the immense branches from which *as roots* they descended. These roots thicken and enlarge as they grow, and we saw some on their way to the surface rocks from one to three inches in diameter, *bearded* at the end with a long hairy fibrous covering, which, we presume, absorb nutriment from the surrounding air.

Milton makes a similar mistake, and if he did not originate the error he has given it a wide circulation. He refers to the *Ficus Indica,* but this tree also is extended by means of roots which the lateral branches send down to the ground from an elevation above it of a number of yards. In the following lines in Paradise Lost he has, in describing it, drawn in this respect upon his imagination:

"The fig tree, not that kind for fruit renowned,
But such, as at this day to Indians known
In Malabar or Decan, *spreads her arms,*
Branching so broad and long, that in the ground
The bended twigs take root, and daughters grow
About the mother tree, a pillar'd shade,
High o'er arched, and echoing walks between."

These roots grow and become important columns of support
to the wide and ever extending branches, many of them being
multiform or clustered, forming

"Huge trunks—and each particular trunk a growth
Of intertwisted fibres serpentine,
Up-coiling, and inveterately convolved —
＊　　＊　　＊　　＊　　＊　　＊　　a pillar'd shade."

Some of these root trunks are not only singularly entwined
and twisted, but they have looped upon and attached to them
small aerial rootlets which add a new feature unlike anything we
had observed. Evidently little roots, in dropping down from the
nearly horizontal branches, stopped on the way at different distances, varying from a few inches to a foot or more, to rest and
establish new bases of supply, and fastening, by a living growth,
to one of the root columns of support, they have pushed out
again into the air, and after making a further growth of a few
inches, they have again stopped for a similar purpose, fastened
to the same column in the same way, then pushed out again, re-
peating the process until either the rocks are reached or they are
absorbed and lost in the older and larger growth to which they
have in different places adhered.

This tree is situated upon a clearing a little to the east of Nassau, and a few rods from the highway which skirts the harbor.
It is near a dwelling house known as "Thompson's Folly"—a

tall wooden building, unsheltered, and so exposed to the wind
that the natives believed that it would fall an easy prey to the first
hurricane that should visit Nassau after its erection. They
therefore gave it the name which it still bears. But the evil
prophets of Nassau seem to have been uninspired, and, as if to
discredit and confound them, the fearful and most destructive
hurricane of 1866, while it turned many a solid and costly structure into a ruin, left this house intact and unharmed. Although
it survived the hurricane, it has been ruined by a bad name.
There it stands, gloomy and solitary—treeless, unprotected, and
unoccupied. Commanding a fine view, cooled by the trade winds,
fanned by every breeze that ruffles the surface of the neighboring
ocean, stately as an English official, seemingly in a good state of
repair, and having a very famous and curious tree for its nearest
neighbor, it has been rendered absolutely worthless, good for
nothing but for fire-wood in a place where fires are a nuisance,
because some meddlesome people have given it a bad name.
Thus has it often happened that Slander has given to Innocence
a name which has ever after remained like the brand of the divine
displeasure upon the forehead of Cain.*

A low terrace has at some time been made under this tree out
of small fragments of coral limestone, thereby securing a more
level surface for those who might repose or have picnics in its
cool and grateful shade. This is now thickly covered with a net-
work of roots, and the branches and roots have extended far beyond its limits. Springing out of the rocks under the tree there

---

* Since this was written, and during the time of our second visit to Nassau,
"The Folly" was temporarily occupied by a medical gentleman and his family, who, it was currently reported, for prudential reasons, left their more
central city residence, (located not far from our hotel,) which a malignant
disease had invaded. In a subsequent chapter this disease will be more particularly mentioned and considered.

is growing a species of cactus, wild coffee bushes, and vines and shrubs with which we were not familiar. The top of the tree towards the harbor, being more exposed to the wind, was evidently rudely trimmed and dismembered by the hurricane, and the growth and development appear to have been mostly on the opposite side.

It was under a wild fig or banyan tree that Black Beard, the noted pirate, in the early history of Nassau, "used to sit in council amongst his banditti, concerting or promulgating his plans and exercising the authority of a magistrate." The trunk of it existed and was seen by McKinnen nearly a hundred years afterwards, in 1804, as he states in his "Tour through the West Indies." The author of "Letters from the Bahama Islands, written in 1823–4," states that "the remains of an immense tree are to be seen on which it is said the renowned Black Beard hung his prisoners, and it is supposed by many that large treasures were buried near it by the pirates." A recent Nassau magazine writer states that "Black Beard's tree" used to stand at the north-west corner of the eastern parade ground.

Some of the highway fences in the outskirts of Nassau furnish strong evidences of the favorable influence of this climate upon vegetable life and growth. The posts in a green state, unhewn and unmorticed, having in some ingenious manner been made to assume an upright position, are pushing out and developing branches, apparently unconscious that from some tree in the forest they have been dismembered.

There are upon the island many species of air plants, and one of these being suspended upon the wall of our room, obtained nutriment enough from the surrounding air alone to make it an object of attraction to a vegetable parasite, and a beautiful and delicate little vine was soon discovered feeding upon its juices, which grew, budded, blossomed and flourished, until the poor

little air plant, tired of keeping boarders while only living upon
air, turned yellow and died.

A most remarkable specimen of the ceiba or silk cotton tree
may be seen in the rear of the central one of a collection of public buildings which form three sides of a quadrangle at the south-
west corner of Bay and Parliament streets. It has a spread of
one hundred and sixteen feet from east to west, and of ninety
feet in the opposite directions. Its trunk is immense. Around
and forming part of it are huge leaves or partitions of wood some
five or six inches thick, which are more or less twisted; these
start from a point from ten to fifteen feet from the ground and,
reaching the earth at an angle of something like forty-five degrees,
form around the tree half-a-dozen large openings or chambers
resembling somewhat horse-stalls. There are a number of silk
cotton trees upon the grounds of the Royal Victoria Hotel, and
being deciduous, and developing their leaves at different times,
we were much interested in observing the rapidity with which
they fully leaved out after their buds commenced to swell. One
of these is very large, many of its huge branches are almost horizontal, and a spacious platform, with seats for the accommoda-
tion of musicians and others, erected in the tree, is reached
by a wide wooden railed stairway. These trees have large seed
pods, which are packed with cotton of a soft silky texture. The
long large roots, like huge anacondas, traverse the surface of the
limestone rock, and fasten the trees down with innumerable living clamps and threads. As if aware of the fact that they have
been brought by man from a land of comparative meteorlogical
quiet and repose, to an island that lies in the favorite track of
the hurricane, it does not, like the cypress of Florida, the pines
of the North-west, or the elms of New England, proudly push its
branches high up in the air, but with more modesty and prudence
than elegance, abruptly stops the upward growth of its limbs,

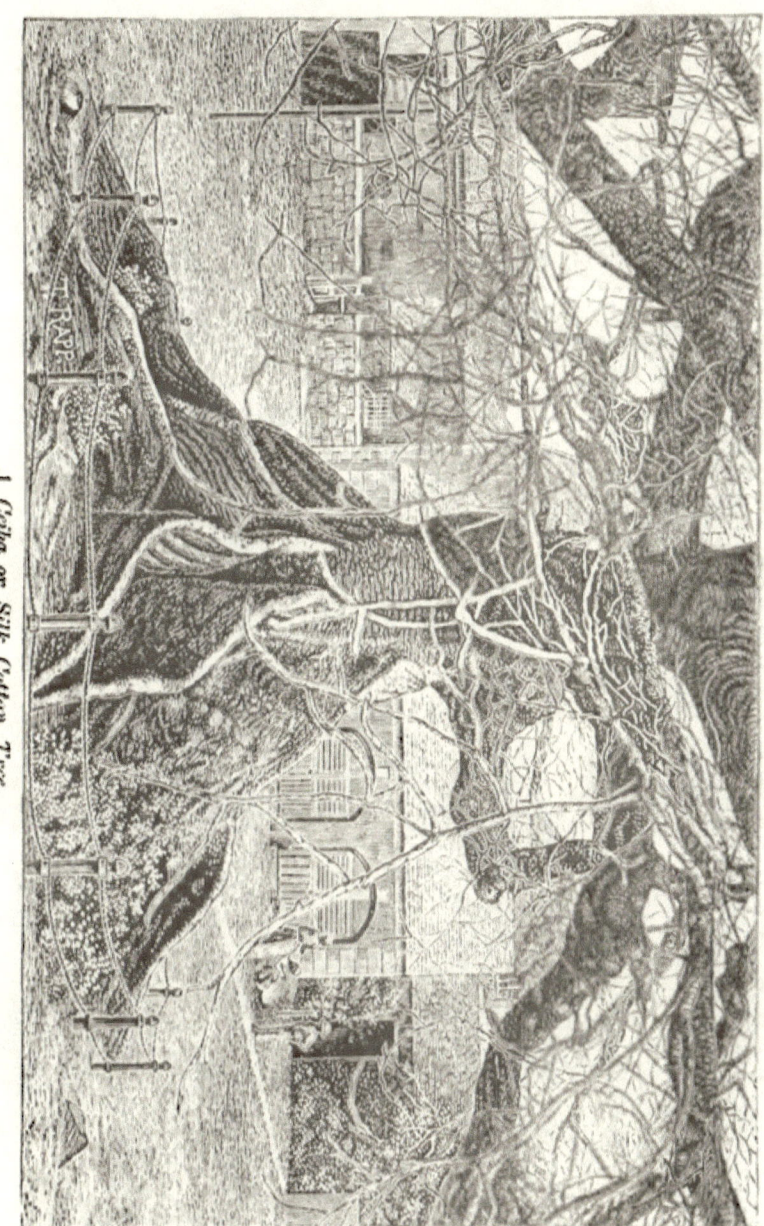

A Ceiba or Silk Cotton Tree.

and makes up in lateral spread what it lacks in elevation. The first mentioned silk cotton tree is believed by an apparently well informed Nassau writer, whom we have heretofore quoted, to have been brought from South Carolina, and, as he thinks, all the others upon the island have been derived from it. None of the latter that we saw, exhibit the wonderful formation of booths around and constituting a portion of the stem which characterizes and makes famous their "ancestral tree."

"The negroes," says Charles Kingsley, "are shy of felling the ceiba. It is a magic tree, haunted by spirits. There are '*too much jumbies in him*,' the negro says, and of those who dare cut him down, some one will die or come to harm within the year." The one we have described looks indeed as if it was "possessed," and it is easy for any one to imagine that viewless goblins sport among its roots and branches, and repose in the strange open chambers of its buttressed trunk. Mr. Gosse says that in Jamaica the negroes believe that " if a person throws a stone at the trunk [of a ceiba] he will be visited with sickness or other misfortune," and that " when they intend to cut one down they first pour rum at the roots as a propitiatory offering." We have no doubt but that the favor of many embodied spirits has likewise been secured by a liberal use of good Jamaica rum, a little differently administered.

An old writer states that the silk cotton tree sometimes grows so large that fourteen thousand persons can assemble under its branches.

There is a remarkable specimen of this singular tree at Trinidad, which is thus described by Mr. Higgins, an English gentleman, in his recently published " Notes by a Field Naturalist."

"We came almost suddenly upon a true monarch of the woods, a silk cotton tree, (*Bombax Ceiba*), said to be the largest tree but one on the island. When young, the trunk of the tree is round,

and beset with sturdy spines, capable, as we well know, of in-
flicting a severe wound. As it increases in age and size, the
thorns fall off, and five or six broad buttress-shaped supports are
developed, star-wise, from the trunk, propping the tree in various
directions against the enormous overhanging force which must
bear upon it during tropical storms. * * * A rough estimate
of the buttresses gave a circumference of eighty yards, or a
diameter of about eighty feet. The compartments between the
buttresses resembled small angular courts separated by high
walls." He estimates that in these compartments, outside of
the solid trunk, if the thin dividing buttress were removed,
"2,400 people could stand round this ceiba," allowing each two
square feet of standing room.

In tropical and semi-tropical countries there is no tree or bush
which so attracts the attention and interests the mind of the
stranger from the North as the palm. It is one of God's most
valuable gifts to man, and he has few physical wants that it cannot be made in whole or in part to supply, while it greatly ministers by its strange and varied beauty to his esthetic taste.
Botanists in classifying and arranging it divide it into five or
more families, seventy to a hundred genera, and a thousand or
more different species.   In South Carolina, Georgia, and Florida,
we made the acquaintance of two of these,—the scrub palmetto,
with its beautiful long, green, radiating leaves, from which palm
leaf fans are made, and the palmetto tree, from whose tall,
straight, branchless stem or body, a rich cluster of similar leaves
spread out in every direction at the top.

The cocoanut palm has the same habit of growth, and thrives
upon the island of New Providence. But its leaves are quite
unlike those of the palmetto, being long and graceful, crowning
the tall, straight, branchless stem, and drooping in beautiful
curves over the thickly compacted fruit that nestles under the
shadows of its evergreen wings.

There are in and near Nassau a few African palms which are much admired. They are tall, stately, branchless and truly royal trees, pre-eminently graceful and beautiful. The stem of this palm is very delicately moulded, of small diameter, enlarging at or near the center, and gradually tapering each way, presenting a novel and pleasing outline. Its long, feather-shaped, curved and drooping leaves stretch out from its top on all sides, a chaplet, light, airy and so exceedingly attractive that we never ceased to look at it but with regret. While strongly resembling the cocoanut palm, this tree appeared to expend less of its vital energies in the production of fruit, and more in the development of a higher type of beauty. The palms, esthetically considered, rank high among the trees of the forest, and in the perfection of grace and comeliness the African palm surpasses them all.

In this connection, the cabbage palm is entitled to a passing notice. In some more favorable localities it is said to attain a height of one hundred and twenty feet—nearly twice that of any we saw in the Bahamas. As if animated by a noble ambition, it wastes none of its energies upon "side issues," but, pushing its branchless stem up boldly towards the heavens, it towers above its less successful rivals, and in the bright, warm sunlight of the upper air matures those long, drooping, graceful and feathery leaves which reveal, even to the casual and distant observer, the noble family to which it belongs. Young, tender and succulent leaves, at the base of those which are fully developed, are formed and compacted into a light-colored head, which is eaten as a salad. It is also cooked and prepared for the table like the cabbage—hence its name.

Mr. Kingsley in his "At Last," gives the following description of some cabbage palm trees which he saw in the West Indies. "We stopped at a manager's, with a palmiste (*oreodoxa oleracea*) or cabbage palm on each side of the garden gate—a pair of columns which any prince would have longed for as ornaments for his lawn. It is the fashion here, and a good one it is, to leave the palmistes, a few at least, when the land is cleared, or to plant them near the house, merely on account of their wonderful beauty. One palmiste was pointed out to me in a field near the road, which had been measured by its shadow at noon, and found to be one hundred and fifty-three feet in height. For more than a hundred feet the stem rose straight, smooth and gray. Then three or four spathes of flowers, four or five feet long each, jutted out and upward like; while from below them, as usual, one dead leaf, twenty feet long or more, dangled head-downwards in the breeze. Above them rose, as always, the green portion of the stem for some twenty feet; and then the flat crown of feathers, as dark as yew, spread out against the blue sky, looking small enough up there though forty feet at least in breadth. No wonder if the man who possessed such a glorious object dared not destroy it."

In the low, wet, rocky hammocks the scrub or dwarf palmetto is abundant. With consummate art nature thus hides her blemishes with a countless number of palmetto fans, brightly and beautifully adorned with "living green," and supplemented with a luxuriant growth of flowering shrubs and climbing vines. Is it a cropping out and development of the divine in woman when she utilizes the fan to hide her beauties? The palmetto yields a fibre, from which, when reduced to a pulp, the strong paper is made upon which the bills of the National banks are printed. An ingenious gentleman in Washington has lately invented a machine by which the tedious process of crushing the fibre by hand is avoided.

Upon the premises of Mr. Charles Burnside we were shown an India rubber tree—one of a class which, thanks to American genius, has proved in modern times to be of incalculable value.

It has been utilized for man's benefit in so many ways that it has become almost a factor in the problem of civilized existence. As a representative tree, filled with juices of such great practical value to the whole civilized world, we approached it with a feeling of reverence and of gratitude. Like all true merit it was unostentatious and modest, and put on no airs. It flaunted no gaudy colors, while looking down from its giddy elevation upon its less gifted neighbors. It was perhaps as large as a medium sized maple, and its leaves were thick and leathery, resembling somewhat those of the magnolia grandi flora, but of a darker shade, and less glossy and waxy. When Mr. Burnside's boys desire rubber balls they, by tapping the tree, quickly secure an abundance of sap, which hardens into rubber upon being exposed to the air and sunlight. Upon the banks of the Amazon, where it abounds, man is satisfied to simply live and propagate his lazy and indolent race, but the stimulus of the crisp and frozen airs of northern climes, thousands of miles away from the source of supply, causes a demand that essentially aids in the development of commercial enterprise—as Creative Wisdom intended it should.

Several kinds of trees in Nassau mature their seeds like the bean, in pods. One of these has upon its branches in the winter season a large number of delicate light-colored, silvery, translucent pods, about eight inches long, which, being swayed and shaken by the wind, so fill the air with soft, soothing music, that the tree has been called the "singing tree." Some sour, cross, crusty and ungallant individual has had the temerity to name it "woman's tongue"—because it is never still!

This tree is of a large size, and loses its leaves some time after it has flowered. Its blossoms have been described as particularly beautiful but odorless, resembling the finest floss silk. Before the tree leaves out, the blossoms hang, crescent shaped, from the top of long stems. We arrived too late for its flowers, but in season for its soft murmuring music.

A northern person naturally looks for the tamarind upon tropical vines, but it grows in green pods, in great abundance, upon trees tall and widespread. Negroes frequently brought for sale to the court of the hotel a few of the green pods. They were purchased, not so much for use, but as objects of curiosity, although the tamarinds, when unpreserved, have a pleasant acid taste, and, with the aid of sugar, make a palatable drink. From the tamarinds of commerce the pods are removed, but the seeds are enveloped in a second covering, and are connected together with a fibrous string, as the reader has no doubt observed.

The trees of the Bahamas which grow valuable timber are principally pitch pine, Madeira mahogany, horse flesh mahogany, olive, cassava, mastic, fustic, cedar, button, white and black torch, satin and lignum vitæ.

Some Bahama trees, like the cinnamon, are valuable for their bark; others, like the logwood, for their dyes; while certain trees and many plants possess valuable medicinal qualities.

While at the Bahamas, we were more than ever before impressed with that Divine Wisdom which pervades, as with a living spirit, the most common phenomena of nature. If man should first observe them in the maturity of his intellectual powers, he would be lost and overwhelmed in wonder and astonishment. In the early dawn of his existence, before the reflecting and reasoning faculties are developed, he sees and accepts them as facts, and thus swallows unawares and without difficulty, whole caravans of camels. Having thrived upon such a diet, and experienced no injury from his childish credulity, it seems foolish, in the later stages of life, to wrench and strain himself over the little troublesome gnats that float, like moats in sunbeams, in an atmosphere mysterious and apparently supernatural.

Living upon the same meagre diet of rock, water, air and sunshine—and upon nothing else—it seems incredible that the small islands constituting the Bahama group should produce forms of vegetable life so widely dissimilar and infinitely varied. Nature has provided but one table, with a bill of fare exceedingly short and simple, for all the wondrous display of fruits and flowers and forests which these islands exhibit—a table which must, to the rampant growers, look very discouraging. In the valleys and deep rich soils of the river bottoms in the United States, the observer naturally concludes that the vegetable commissary department is in quantity, quality and variety, on a scale corresponding with the magnificent floral world which it supports. But with a soil nearly as scant as that which is found upon the Belgian pavements of northern city streets, the miracle of producing much out of nothing is performed under our eyes.

Roots creep over the rocks and penetrate their crevices and crannies, searching and collecting materials for the green, polished, waxen leaves—the pure, white, and exquisitely perfumed flowers—the golden balls and delicious pulp of the orange. Near them are other roots entwined among and persistently pushing into the little pockets of the same and similar rocks, and, by an inexplicable alchemy, obtaining from them nutriment for the growth of the tall stately stem, the large and graceful plume, the dry husks, the hard shells, the soft and palatable pulp, and the cool, sweet milk of the cocoanut palm. In like manner the sapodilla, with its russet apples of "sugared honey" —the long, large leaved, branchless banana, feather-crested like the palm, with its large, pendent, purple fruit bud at the end of a long drooping stem, around which its gloved ambrosial fruit is thickly clustered—the lime, the lemon, the pawpaw the pine apple, the guava, the star apple, the bread fruit, the shaddock, the mango, the date, the almond, the sweet sap, the sour sap, the fig, plums of different kinds, and many other fruit-bearing and other trees, each, from lowest root to topmost

9

branch, having its own marked and widely dissimilar characteristics and qualities, fasten to the same common rock and eliminate and perfect their juices out of the same scanty and most unpromising materials. So also with the flowering shrubs and vines,—a world of itself, teeming with blooms in unending variety, radiant with every shade of color, and redolent with unnumbered perfumes of marvelous sweetness,—upon the outer margins of which we stand appalled, and lay down our descriptive pen, conscious that we cannot do it justice.

How such wondrous growths are rendered possible upon islands so destitute of the rich fertilizing elements which are deemed necessary for the proper development of vegetable life at the North, it is difficult to understand or conceive, and we are compelled to fall back upon that Divine fiat, whose faint murmurs, recorded in Genesis, come to us through the dim shadows of a past that shroud the mysterious beginnings of time.

CHAPTER VI.

> " Pomona bore me to her citron groves,
> To where the lemon and the piercing lime,
> With the deep orange glowing through the green,
> Their varied glories blend."—THOMPSON.

> "Gorgeous flowrets in the sunlight shining,
> Blossoms flaunting in the eye of day,
> Tremulous leaves, with soft and silver lining,
> Buds that open only to decay."

WHETHER we adopt the theory that nature has stocked the earth with luscious fruits for man's benefit, or created man for the benefit of the fruit, and to secure its more perfect development from the sour, crabbed, wild, unseemly, primitive condition, in which, when uncultivated, it exists, we must admit that fruit is an important, if not an essential factor, in the problem of the health and happiness of the human race. At all stages, and in all conditions of life, man craves and requires the ripened fruits in their season. One of the pleasures incident to visiting foreign lands arises from the opportunity which is thus afforded to pluck and eat them in their freshness and maturity. In these days of rapid transit by sea and land, when the ends and distant corners of the earth are brought together, and space is almost annihilated, so that oranges in our cities are nearly as cheap and plenty as apples, it is less necessary to visit the lands where they are indigenous, or in which they have become naturalized, in order to enjoy their beauty of color, delicious fragrance, and exquisite flavor. But some fruits are too delicate and destitute of keeping qualities to admit of exportation to distant lands. Others are taken from the trees before they are fully ripe, and never acquire on shipboard or in northern markets the perfection which only the tropical sun and air can impart. Besides, a tropical orchard loaded with fruit, some in all stages of development from flower to fruit, is a most charming sight, and alone compensates for the discomforts and fatigues of a long journey. Each member of the whole citrus family must be seen at its home to be fully appreciated. Boxes, barrels and baskets are a very poor substitute for the waxen and varnished leaves in which the golden balls nestle by thousands in the closely compacted tree tops.

In Nassau, as well as in Florida, oranges and bananas and other tropical fruits have a prominent place, in their season, in the breakfast and dinner bills of fare. Every morning at the Victoria Hotel, with some few exceptions, as soon as we had taken our seats at the breakfast table, there was placed before us a large fruit dish filled with oranges and bananas, together with a bill of fare, a pencil and a slip of paper. After making out and giving to our neatly dressed, polite, and generally efficient table servant, our breakfast order, the fruit, regaled and consoled us while our breakfast was being prepared. With the fruit dish before us, there was no limit to our indulgence except that which appetite and a wise discretion imposed. We found the Bahama oranges of good size, and excellent flavor, a trifle sweeter than those of Florida, owing, we conclude, to the fact that they matured and ripened in a warmer climate. The bananas were of a superior quality. After the long fast of the night, the rich,

sub-acid juices of the former were particularly agreeable and grateful. They soothed and gratified the nerves of taste, took away
the rough edges of appetite, and prepared the stomach for the
heavier work it was soon to be called upon to perform. At dinner the same thing was repeated, except that the order was re-
versed, and the tempting dish of golden and yellow fruit came
to stimulate the appetite after it had been subjected to the tempting influences of a long and varied bill of fare. It does not take
a great while for these agreeable customs to become deeply and
firmly rooted. Oranges to daily break our fast in the morning,
and delightfully crown our afternoon meal, are felt to be a necessity. Without them the most elaborate feast fails to satisfy.

New Providence relies upon Abaco for a very material part of
the oranges which its market requires, and in the spring of 1879
our landlord imported some from Florida, and yet the island
abounds with wild, waste land and idle people.

The banana resembles the pear in this, that its quality is improved when it ripens dissevered. The long stem, thickly
covered with fruit in various stages of development, hangs pendent, with a large purple terminal bud, which constantly matures rings of fruit blossoms as it grows and gravitates towards
the earth, with its leaves—narrow, very long, green and gracefully drooping,—rising from a green sheath, is beautiful to
behold, and its novelty never wore off, so that almost daily we
had to stop and admire it. Our readers are all familiar with
this fruit, for it is in New York and in other northern cities
what it is in and near the tropics; its habit of growth, aside
from its large and beautiful terminal bud, is readily seen in the
bunches so extensively exhibited wherever at the north southern
fruits are offered for sale.

The opinion we heard frequently expressed that the banana is
unhealthy. Some assured us that it always distressed them when

they ate it.   Others indulged in its use freely and with apparent
impunity.   We were at first very incredulous when stories reached
us seriously reflecting upon it as a disguised enemy of the human
stomach and constitution.   We gave it our confidence, and also
room very near to our hearts.   We defended it to the best of
our ability, with zeal if not with knowledge.   We said it was an
impeachment of Divine Providence to allege that its golden links
of most delicious sweetness—so tempting to the four senses—
sight, touch, taste and smell—were indigestible, health-destroy-
ing, deceitful and bad.   But we began finally, to have doubts,
and at last thought we perceived after eating them, an unpleasant sensation right in the center of one of our seats of happiness.
We inquired concerning it of physicians, and found, as in other
cases where experts testify, that they widely and materially differed.   Very reluctantly and with some misgivings, we are compelled to admit, that, being plucked when quite green, for that
or some other reason, it does not agree with all, and in many
cases is injurious to health, yet the banana is said to be "extensively used for food, and in many of the Pacific islands it is the
staple on which the natives depend.   In its immature condition,
it contains much starch which on ripening changes into sugar.
* * * From the unripe fruit, dried in the sun, a useful and nutritious flour is prepared."—[British Encyclopedia.]   It would seem
from the published analysis of the fruit, and of the flour made
from it, that it must generally be a healthy article of diet for
healthy people, and our advice, if asked, would be that once given
to us by a skillful and experienced physician—"eat of it, if you
like, until you ascertain by your personal experience that to you
it is hurtful."

The banana is an herbaceous plant, and, after fruiting, its top
dies, but it annually sprouts again from its roots.   It attains a
height of from fifteen to twenty feet, and its curved and drooping leaves have a width of from one to two feet.

Among the tropical fruits that we were always pleased to give house room in the frozen north, was the pine apple, and now that we were upon one of its native rocks, or upon rocks where it had become thoroughly naturalized, we had a desire to see for ourselves the manner of its cultivation, and the processes and stages of its growth and development. Our curiosity was gratified in the following manner:

In going to the caves in the Blue Hills we took the shore road, or the extension of Bay street to the west, and skirted for several miles Delaport Bay—a body of water which Silver, Long, and North Keys, with their connecting submerged reefs, shelter from the ocean, and which as you approach Nassau, after crossing its bar, stretches away to the right. Passing the caves nearest to the highway, we ascended a little hill, turned abruptly to the left, followed for a few rods a carriage road through the dense low woods, and, leaving our carriages near some small negro cabins, and following our very dusky guides, started on a footpath for the more extensive caverns which hide in the hill from half to three-quarters of a mile further to the east. The trail led us through the center of a pine apple field which covered fifteen acres. It was termed an "orchard," but there was nothing in its appearance suggestive of such a name. We found it humble, lowly and modest. It put on no airs, and evidently had no ambition to occupy a conspicuous position and make a show in the world. This West India "apple" does not grow in clusters like the cocoanut, nor upon high, wide branching trees like its northern namesake—but singly upon plants which attain an average height of about one and a-half feet. The lowly plant has long narrow leaves or fronds, hard, thick, coarse, bayonet-shaped, and with sharp serrated edges. A single fruit stem pushes up from the center of the root, blossoms, and in about eighteen months from the time of planting matures a single apple. One plant, producing one apple at a time, will continue to yield an annual crop for three or four years. There are three varieties; the *Sugar Loaf*, which is juicy, of excellent flavor, and excels the others in keeping qualities; the *Cuba*, which is of larger size, firmer texture, and less sweet than the sugar loaf and commands a higher price; the *Bird's-eye*, the cultivation of which has been pretty much abandoned because of the destruction of the crop by rats and land-crabs. Gov. Rawson states that of a forty acre field of the sugar loaf variety, the rats destroyed 6000 dozen, or one-third of an annual crop. Land-crabs, he says, "like locusts elsewhere, march straight through a field and consume all the fruit in their course."

It is raised from slips—2000 dozen of the sugar loaf, and 1600 dozen of the Cuba to an acre. In the "orchard" we crossed, the cocoanut had been planted among the pines so as to insure a cocoanut grove when the pines ceased bearing. The rocky surface was covered and concealed by the pines, and in "clearing" the plantation, (they evidently could not if they would hoe it), it is said "the laborers are obliged to wear canvas leggings and gauntlets to protect them from the spines of the leaves." Gov. Rawson says, the fields are "or ought to be cleaned six times in the year." He states also that the average weight of the sugar loaf is three pounds, that it yields one-third of the quantity planted, and lasts five years; that the Cuba has an average weight of three and a-half pounds, yields one-half of the quantity planted, lasts only three years, and will thrive upon soil considered unsuited for the other varieties; also that the Cuba is preferred in the United States, and that the sugar loaf, by reason of its superior keeping qualities, is preferred for the English market; that it is uncertain whether the pine apple is a native of the Bahama Islands, or has been introduced from the Windward Islands or Cuba; that the value of 229,226 dozen exported in 1864 was £21,299—which makes them average about four cents a piece; that in shipping the pine to the United States it is stripped of every thing but its head, while the whole plant was formerly sent to England, the leaves and shoots being wrapped round the fruit to keep it fresh, but that since 1858 only the shoots are left on the stalks ; that the fruit is arranged in tiers, great attention being paid to ventilation; the hatches are left open during the voyage ; serious losses often occur on shipboard arising from exceptionally bad weather and long voyages, as well as from other causes. The shoots are used for new plantations, and as these are sent with the apples to England the price is for that reason increased. There are two annual cuttings: the Cuba is cut early in May and late in June, and the sugar loaf from the 1st to the 20th of June, and in July and August. As in 1879 and also in 1880 we left the Bahamas in April, much to our regret we were unable to test the quality of pine apples fully ripened in the field.

The sapodilla is very abundant and cheap in Nassau. The tree is large and is a good bearer. The fruit is of a uniform dull dark brown color, and almost unpromising in its outward appearance as a cocoanut. Its skin is very thin, its flesh yellow, soft and sweet, its shape oval, and its diameter from two to three inches. A taste for it has to be acquired, so that while it is discarded by the many, the few strangers who have learned to love it, esteem it very highly. It is conceded to be a very healthy fruit. We saw but two varieties. Some specimens of the fruit in size, flavor, and richness of the coloring of the flesh, were very much superior to those offered ordinarily for sale.

The cocoanut is cultivated in the Bahamas, and thrives in some parts of New Providence. Gov. Rawson includes it in a table containing the names of twenty-three varieties of fruit which were growing upon the Bahamas in 1864, and which he claimed were indigenous. Others, however, think that it is an exotic. Upon general principles we should, in the absence of positive testimony to the contrary, incline to the Governor's opinion.

It flourishes best in the vicinity of salt water, and is found upon most of the inhabited islands all over the ocean world within and near the tropics. It is, perhaps, God's most valuable gift to the people inhabiting not only almost innumerable islands, but large portions of the main land. Every part of it ministers very materially to man's wants. The milk and meat of its fruit constitute a considerable part of the food of the people who bask in its shade or live where it grows. In the island of Ceylon (it is credibly stated) the wealth of men is estimated by the number of cocoanut trees which they own.

This one fruit of itself furnishes full and ample evidence, to an observing and thoughtful mind, of the existence and goodness of God. Having made it, and in so many ways fitted it to supply the prime necessaries of human life in those parts of the world where frosts are unknown, He has provided in a most wonderful way for its preservation and propagation. Wrapped up in a shell so hard and impervious that it is carried a thousand miles and more for the purpose of holding the cool water brought to the earth's surface in " the old oaken bucket that hangs in the well," we find the life-germ from which it is developed. Around that shell are placed and compacted innumerable threads which require, when dry, the aid of an axe to detach them from the treasure they so persistently guard. Around these wrappings there is another hard vegetable shield, wisely designed and curiously made, and the whole is so wonderfully contrived and adjusted that it will float safely for months upon the ocean in calm or storm, secure from molestation by reason of its outward destitution of comeliness, flavor and fragrance, from any of the hungry and voracious monsters of the deep, until, at last, some huge, angry mountain wave hurls it, as if in anger, a seemingly useless thing, high upon the land, where, when the fingers of decay have sufficiently loosened the strings and hard envelopes which have so securely confined and guarded it, the enclosed life-germ sends down its little rootlets into the congenial soil, a vigorous stem pushes up into the air and the sunshine, as if, like a little Columbus, to learn what sort of a new world it has finally landed upon after its long sea voyage. From this little and un-promising beginning, on many an ocean isle, the invaluable and graceful cocoanut palm has multiplied and extended, and made it possible for man to live and flourish in comparative idleness, with few substantial wants that the cocoanut cannot abundantly supply.

Upon Mr. Charles Burnside's grounds we saw a " hog plumb " tree with a plentiful supply of small, green fruit in clusters upon the branches—but not a leaf in sight. The juices are not in this instance perfected in the leaves for the growth of the fruit.

The shaddock was there with its large glossy leaves, and per-fumed the air with its white blossoms. The mistletoe had estab-lished itself upon its branches, and, as if lineally descended from the old Nassau pirates, flourished upon the rich sap it had done nothing to eliminate. Both the shaddock and the grape fruit belong with the orange, lime and lemon, to the citrus family. The former is sometimes over two feet, and the grape fruit over one foot in circumference. Almond trees, large and beautiful, were just leafing out. Mr. Burnside showed us also, the " For-bidden Fruit " tree, and we would willingly have followed the example of Adam and Eve, and tested the quality of its sweet fruit, if we had had an opportunity to do so, even at the risk of being forever banished from the pleasant fruit garden where it was growing.

Gov. Rawson states in his report, that "The soil and climate of the Bahamas are admirably adapted for all tropical and semi-tropical fruits." His table of those which are indigenous embraces the following: the sapodilla, cashew, pine apple, sweet-sap, sour-sap, papaw, sour orange, lemon, star-apple, cocoa plum, cocoa nut, seaside grape, water melon, mamee, plantain, banana, love-in-a-mist, guava, spanish hog plum, hog plum, scarlet hog plum, tamarind, and wild grape.

"The luscious fruits, which of their own accord
The willing ground, and laden trees afford."

The following, he states, have been introduced at different times: the Jamaica (custard) apple, ground nut, bread fruit, ackee, citron, orange (*citrus aurantium*), mandarin orange (*citrus decumana*), two species of shaddock, lime, rose apple, fig, mangoe, avocado pear, pomegranate, date, balsam apple, mulberry, broad-leafed almond, grape and jujube.

In Nassau, as elsewhere, every month has its own special and peculiar floral display, although many flowers continue from month to month to unfold their blossoms. Some varieties of indigenous flowers are always to be found in the wild and tangled woods. The ladies, returning from their rides near the close of day, generally bring with them the curious growths of tree, and shrub, and vine, which nature has spontaneously produced and scattered with lavish profusion on every hand. The flowers are massed in trees and ambushed in thickets. Here a flowering vine festoons a wayside tree with garlands of beauty, and reaches out for a caress as the stranger rides by; while there, from their little many-hued censers, flowers of more rank and stately growth shed upon him their sweet tributary incense. One soon is compelled to adopt as his own, the enthusiastic sentiment of the charmed poet who sings:

"Were I, O God, in churchless lands remaining,
  Far from all voice of teachers or divines,
My soul would find in flowers of thy ordaining,
  Priests, sermons, shrines."

The following extracts from "Letters from the Bahama Islands," written by an American lady in 1823-4, give an account of some of the more prominent flowers to be seen in Nassau and its suburbs.

"The indigenous plants and flowers, and flowering shrubs are abundant and beautiful; and, it is said, there are five thousand varieties. I am very fond of the mignonette tree: it bears pale yellow and green flowers, and has the most powerful and delicious fragrance. The acacia is very different from that of the same name with us; the flower is a little, round, yellow ball, about the size of a chestnut, looks like a tuft of fringe, and is filled with a yellow powder and has a sweet perfume. The blossom of the mahogany tree is beautiful, and so is the yellow and crimson flower fence or Barbadoe's pride. The coral tree is very curious; the flower looks like a bunch of red, cut coral, and grows at the top of the branch distinct from any leaves: the stem, which is five or six inches long, stands perfectly erect, and, though beautiful, it is ungraceful. The coral vine bears a blossom of the same color and shape, and runs in wild profusion over all the stone walls and hedges, but has no odor. Myrtles, jessamines, tuberoses, and roses, the amaryllis of every species, the convolvulus, the sensitive plant, and Arabian jasmine, are seen in every direction, and grow wild among the rocks. Groves of the oleander are very common, and, prized as they are with you, are thought almost vulgar here, as well as the beautiful south-sea rose. The mutable rose is a native of this climate: the bignonia bears a yellow trumpet flower; the blue passion flower, which hides its head among clusters of dark green leaves, is one of my favorite flowers. * * * The yellow jessamine, and a variety of flowering myrtles, fill the air with their perpetual fragrance. * * * I have seen the sweet briar and the multiflora rose in blossom, growing very luxuriantly."

"The bayonet plant is properly named for its leaves are thick and sharp like those of the aloes, and point upwards like those of the pine apple : it grows about thirty feet high, and forms an impenetrable hedge. From the center of the leaves, directly on the top, bursts a stem about two feet long which is thickly covered with dazzling white flowers, the size and shape of a crown imperial; the inside of the calyx is of a pale yellow, and hundreds of these little bells hanging downwards, cover the stem, and the whole is two or three feet in circumference. It has the most powerful and oppressive fragrance. The flower of the cocoanut is very beautiful. There is no end to the variety of pretty flowering vines and shrubs which spread forth their rainbow colored flowers to charm the eye, and mingle their spicy odors with the soft winds to delight the senses. The coffee and cotton trees are not very numerous, but the air is eternally filled with the fragrance of the orange, lemon and mahogany blossoms. There is a wonderful variety of medicinal plants here, and almost every leaf affords a panacea for some disease."

Oleanders are very common and grow to a large size. They adorn many homesteads, but lose something of their value by reason of their great abundance. They continued in bloom during all the time we remained in Nassau; the blossoms of some were white, others pink, and others a dark red color. A prickly pear species of cactus of a vigorous, large, rank growth, is also found upon the island, and is in many localities very abundant. A large, exquisitely beautiful, plume-like and delicate blossom, called the shell plant, was frequently offered for sale in the court of the hotel, and was greatly admired. Colored girls daily frequented the court well supplied with beautiful boquets of flowers of various kinds, and particularly of roses, to give to their friends whose good will they wished to cultivate, or to exchange for the money of the strangers. There is also to be seen a beautiful running vine which blooms about Christmas time, and for that reason is called the Christmas flower. It is not a favorite with the agriculturists of Nassau because of its rank and persistent growth.

Occupying conspicuous places in the flower borders in front of the hotel were large clusters of rank growing lillies, whose bells, suspended upon long stems, with silent eloquence spoke to the mind and rang out peals of perfume upon the surrounding air. They also grow wild upon the island. We were surprised to learn that the healing balm of which squills are composed is obtained from the bulbous roots of this species of lilly. The little negroes are accustomed to steal these and other flowers belonging to the hotel before they have time to fully mature, and with as innocent a look as they can command, offer them at the court of the hotel for sale. But while fully appreciating the delicious perfumes that gave such a charm to the soothing air, and the endless variety in form, habit of growth and color of the flowers, we could not at times refrain from unfavorably contrasting the animal life of the Bahamas, with their flora, and to harbor the thought which one of Shenstone's stanzas, slightly altered, expresses:

"Boast, favored islands, boast thy flowery stores,
   Thy thousand hues by chemic suns refined,
'Tis n t the dress or mien the soul adores,
   But the rich beauties of the immortal mind."

The floral display upon the islands and in Florida was less

abundant and brilliant than usual in the early part of the year 1879, by reason of the fact that the season was exceptionally dry.

Shore View West of Nassau.

CHAPTER VII.

> "Not poppy, nor mandragora,
> Nor all the drowsy syrups of the world
> Shall ever medicine thee to such sweet sleep."—SHAKESPEARE.

The Bahama air is very soothing, and soon makes itself felt upon nerves that are sensitive, disordered or unstrung. It enervates like an opiate, and the newly arrived stranger soon succumbs to its influence. It is difficult to do anything in the warm and languid air, when not overcome by sleep, but muse and dream. It is very entertaining to observe the new comers from the states when a passenger steamer arrives. They step so quick, and talk so fast, and inquire so earnestly, and commence so soon to crowd an immense amount of walking, riding and sailing into a single day, economising time, and drawing upon their capital of latent strength and vitality as though in vigor and endurance they were millionaires. The amount of sight-seeing they accomplish in two or three days is astonishing. But in less than a week the warm air takes all the frost out of them, and wilted, languid and limpsy, they loll, and lounge and loaf

113

in the shade as though "to the manor born." It requires the stimulus of a steamer nearly ready to return to the States, to energize one sufficiently to write a letter home. It is a luxury to breathe and feel the soft air, but it inclines to repose; it puts us in a state or condition of rest. Bold enterprise and tireless energy are quickened into life by cold winds from the snow-fields.

"There's iron in our northern winds,
Our pines are trees of healing."

Not only is ambition not indigenous in the Bahamas, but, like many other exotics, it has but a sickly and short-lived existence when introduced from abroad. The primal curse that doomed man to a life of labor, does not seem to have extended to these isles of unending summer. In fact, it is only in such a climate as these islands possess that labor is a curse and not a blessing. Indolently reposing in the shade of a tropical orchard, fanned by the sea-god's invisible wings that seem ever in motion, the inhabitants of these favored islands have no occasion to work (as we of the north understand that word) in order to supply their simple wants. It is therefore apparent that the original Garden of Eden must have been less favorably situated for lazy people than this part of her majesty's possessions.

New Providence has been called by one of its enthusiastic admirers, in the pages of Scribner, "The Isle of June." It may with equal propriety be named The Isle of Indolence. At all times, in sunlight and starlight, it seemed as if unseen spirits

"Spread forth their downy pinions, scattering sleep
Upon the drooping eye-lids of the air."

Man there soon passes into a semi-torpid state, and while the wear and waste incident to an active life is avoided, the recuper-

ating powers are, as in sleep, quietly at work. Entering the
dining room of the Victoria Hotel for our breakfast soon after
eight o'clock one morning, and finding as usual at that early
hour nearly a hundred seats at the tables unoccupied, we said to
the head waiter, "There are a good many lazy persons in this
hotel." "Yes," he replied: "it's the place to be lazy—that's
what people are here for." It is only occasionally that the ama-
teur fishermen have life and vim enough even to fish, being, like
the author, satisfied to simply sail over the beautiful waters.
Some persons explained to us, upon their return from a fishing
excursion, that the fish they caught were not "gamy," and made
none of those heroic struggles for freedom which give spirit and
zest to piscatory sports in northern waters. The fish which they
caught were large, fat and beautifully colored. Sharks abound,
and come near enough to the surface to be soothed and quieted
by the Bahama air. As the tempting bait floats near the top of
the water about three rods from the boat, it is very interesting
to watch, in the clear water, the movements of the sharks as they
reconnoiter and cautiously approach the savory but deceitful
prize. The larger ones manifest the prudence so characteristic
of age, while those smaller and younger, as our sable yachtman
forcibly expressed it, "jess like de children what den no' no better," impetuously rush forward and are caught, towed to the
boat and shot for their temerity. One of the captured was, without any court-martial trial, shot in the head, and, with his jaws
extended to their utmost capacity, exhibited in the court of the
hotel. It was seven and one-half feet long, and had a capacious,
well-armed and ugly looking mouth—extremely repulsive to all
except those who have a romantic desire to take part in the old
drama of "Jonah and the Whale." It should be said to the
credit of the Nassau sharks, that while the black divers in the
clear and transparent waters of the Bahamas must look to them

exceedingly attractive, especially when hungry, we heard of only
a single instance in which any one of these usually voracious
monsters has dined upon a negro, and the report in that case is
not very well authenticated.

While in Florida, a gentleman having a plantation upon the
St. John's, mentioned to us that he could not give credit to all
the claims that had been made and published concerning the
Bahamas, and upon being pressed to state particularly what
claims he considered unfounded, he replied—"Well, take for
instance the Bahama sharks; it is affirmed that they never injure
people. Now I can't believe that story. Why, last summer, at
the mouth of the St. John's, Mr. —— and his family left their
cottage to bathe in the river. His wife entered the water first,
and while she was wading out, in the presence of her husband
and children, she uttered one loud scream of pain and terror and
disappeared. Her body was afterwards recovered, minus one
arm. A shark had seized her by the arm, drawn her under
water, and bitten her arm off. I do not believe that over in
Nassau where sharks are plenty, they are so different from ours."

It is proverbial that every story has more than one side—and
we found it so in this case. Upon inquiry, we ascertained from
some friends of ours who own a cottage at the mouth of the St.
John's, that the lady in question, in company with another lady,
went out upon a sand bar, and remained there about an hour;
that in the mean time the tide rose, increased the depth of the
water, and the force of its current between them and the shore;
that in attempting to return, one lady got into a hole beyond
her depth; that her companion, in endeavoring to rescue her,
also got into deep water; that one was in consequence drowned,
while the other floated away quite a long distance, upon the surface of the water, but was rescued at last unharmed, by a gentleman who went in a boat to her relief, passing on his way through

water infested with sharks, a dozen or more of them being in sight.

A gentleman who has spent considerable time in the West Indies, assured us that sharks are cautious if not cowardly, and that they will never bite a man if he splashes the water. Perhaps, before trusting too much even to the warm water sharks, it will be prudent to first make sure that their hunger has been satisfied. When looking for his breakfast or his dinner, in the absence of fish, now and then a shark may make a bold dash for human flesh. The very great clearness of the Bahama waters may operate in favor of safety, and the fish that they crave for food may be less abundant in the colder water of the Florida Gulf. If the Bahama sharks are very dangerous, it is singular that so few facts are reported which indicate it, and that the divers continue to be so numerous and so bold.

In our sleeping room at Nassau, it was sometimes found necessary to use the mosquito bars with which our bed was provided. We found this insect unlike the little nocturnal musicians so common at the north. When hunted upon the wall in the morning, a Nassau mosquito appears strangely indifferent. Often when first struck at and not hit, it does not seem at all disturbed and remains in the same place. Then when aroused sufficiently to fly from the threatened danger, it makes a very short journey to another resting place not far from the first, and looks around with a calm quiet expression of supreme indifference. A lady justly remarked—"you don't see them sitting 'round that way at home, but here they breathe a lazy atmosphere and live on lazy blood."

Little facts and circumstances evidence great truths. The influence of climate may be as well shown by a mouse as by a man or a mammoth. Therefore, it is, that we give another little incident that came under our observation.

With more curiosity than discretion, a mouse one day came out of its hole to look at some of the newly arrived guests of the Victoria Hotel. Upon being pursued, it took refuge under a mat at the foot of the grand stair-way. A little girl turned up the end of the mat, and we then expected to see a lively display of the quickness and agility of the pursuer and pursued. But, to our astonishment, the mouse, with quiet resignation, remained perfectly passive, and made no noise, while the little girl seized it by the tail with her fingers, and suspended it, head downwards, in the soft and soothing air. Such passive resignation in a cold climate would have been impossible.

In further evidence of astonishing climatic results, we copy the following seemingly incredible fish story from a well written article upon Nassau by Epes Sargent, the proprietor of the Sargent House in that city. Speaking of fish, he says :

"The jew-fish supplies the place of our Northern halibut. It is cut into steaks and fried in a similar manner. It is the largest edible fish we have, often weighing six hundred pounds. At certain seasons this fish lies dormant at the bottom, and refuses to take the hook. Under these circumstances *the fishermen dive down and place the hook in his mouth!* This may appear to you to be a very heavy fish story, but it is nevertheless true, as can be vouched for by many here."

Mr. Sargent, who thus affirms the truth of this story, is a highly respectable citizen of Nassau, but it will be noticed, he does not claim that his testimony is founded upon his personal observation. If the fish has regular hibernating periods, its torpidity at such times may not be chargeable to the climate. It seems that this singular mode of capturing large fish is not without its perils, for Mr. Sargent adds, that "at Long Cay a man had his hand taken off while performing this feat."

Our landlord kept his hotel well supplied with green sea turtle.

One turtle we particularly examined.   It had then recently been taken from the water, weighed fifty-seven pounds, was alive and fat, and was soon, in the form of soups and steaks, to grace the tables of the dining-room.   This huge reptile, (though quite an infant compared with some of the same species), while he must have had some vague suspicions of the cruel fate in store for him, and was turned over upon his back so that he could not crawl away, and rudely punched to wake him up and to see if he was fat, seemed perfectly contented and happy.

A large number of servants of both sexes were employed in and about the Victoria Hotel, yet there was no jarring, scolding, complaining or quarreling.   Some were grave, but none appeared sad or discontented.   Light hearted and good natured, polite and respectful, attentive and faithful, they performed the tasks assigned them in a very unexceptional manner.   Petulant and unreasonable complaints did not disturb their equanimity or elicit tart replies.   When a number were assembled to perform some labor in common, they lightened their tasks by finely singing with rich musical voices sacred songs.   They were never boisterous, and ever exhibited a respectful deference and a politeness which was the more agreeable because unstudied and natural.

We seldom heard in any of the suburbs of Nassau, teeming as they do with colored people, a harsh or profane word ; we never there witnessed a fight, nor do we remember to have heard a child cry.   When sailing on one occasion, we heard some loud unpleasant talk between two white men, near a public dock, each on board and apparently in command of a vessel.   Finally one said to the other—" Now look'er here ! If you get me mad I'm going to wrestle, or run, or *do something !*" This old salt had evidently breathed the air of the Bahamas for some time.

It seemed to us while in Nassau that if we had any enemies any where in the wide world that it was a good time to heartily

forgive them while we were not only too lazy to get mad, but too
languid to keep fast hold of any but the most pleasant and sensuous emotions, and before we returned to a climate where one's
nerves are all so "strung upon wires" that they vibrate painfully
when the atmosphere is in the least disturbed by untoward events.
Nor did we feel like the very sick Dutchman who promised if
he died to forgive his enemy, but to give him a good licking if
he recovered. We would also suggest to those restless spirits
that cannot wait for the coming of the millenium in the due
course of time, and who are anxious to have the lion and the
lamb, without any further delay, lie down together in peace, the
propriety of trying the efficacy of physical forces, independent
of or in conjunction with moral ones, and that they now in-
augurate a great migratory movement, by which the whole
human family shall be transported to the Bahamas, or to other
similar islands, where men lack the life and energy to commit
crime, or to accumulate fortunes, or to engage in great enter-
prises, and every passion (save one) is as torpid and seemingly
dead as though it never had a lodgment in the human heart.
We suspect that when the millenium is witnessed in the northern
states, great climatic changes will have first taken place.

As might be expected Nassau is a very quiet and orderly city.
Strangers are much impressed by the absence of scenes of violence, drunken brawls and profane, abusive and irritating language in the public streets and places of popular resort. We
were told that more persons are arrested for improperly wagging
their "unbridled tongues," than for more serious offenses. The
"keeping of the peace" is not, however, due to the climate alone.
The criminal code, the swift and sure administration of justice
by the courts, the police department with its efficient and fine
looking black patrolmen—all are material factors in accomplish-
ing so desirable a result. Convicts are made to labor upon the

streets, and the chain gangs, in their white prison uniforms, while at work in the hot sun, exert a moral influence which is widely and deeply felt. A future punishment by hard work and not by fire is what makes an impression on the indolent mind. Nor should the peaceful and conservative operation of a very efficient Church—represented by a goodly variety of different sectarian organizations, from the humble Methodists with their untiring zeal and spiritual sledge-hammers, up, through the more pretentious cathedral, to the loftiest kind of high church, with its choir of colored urchins in holy vestments within the walls of "Saint Agnes," in Grantstown, back of Nassau, be omitted. The extent of its salutary influence may be fairly inferred by the manner in which Sunday is here kept. The first day of the week is marked by solemn stillness, entire absence from all secular employments, a display of neat and tasty costumes, and by a general attendance upon the devotional services of the churches, as strongly as it is in any of the country towns of New England. In this respect the neighboring island of Cuba, with its Sunday theatres and bull fights in its chief city of Havana, furnishes a most striking contrast, and leads the seeker after the best practical ecclesiastical system to ask, whether English Protestantism or Spanish Catholicism furnishes the most desirable religious foundation for a prosperous and well ordered community.

It is apparent that the Royal Victoria Hotel is an active agent in demoralizing the colored boys who frequent its court. Novelty speedily degenerates into nuisance. To them the crowds of winter visitors are like the sugar hogsheads to northern summer flies. The "rich Northerners" constitute a great living tide, with deep, broad currents of unfailing wealth, and all are most eager to catch some of the drops of the golden spray. Not all of them who have a love of money are endowed with the gift of song, and as the choirs are not selected, and most of the black urchins believe that the louder they scream the better they sing, the extent of the disturbance and annoyance may be in some small degree comprehended. This, together with an inveterate habit of begging at all times and on all occasions for money—a vicious practice constantly encouraged and fostered by the well-meant liberality of the guests—occasionally causes some of the old habitues of the hotel, when the salutary influence of the lash is not brought into requisition, to hire them to go away.

Although you have only to tickle the Bahama rocks with a crowbar to make them smile with tropical and semi-tropical harvests, yet agriculture languishes and maintains but a sickly struggle for life, the wildness of untamed nature being only here and there to a very limited extent disturbed. In and near Nassau many places, once made beautiful by enforced slave labor, now look sadly neglected. A thick growth of bushes and small trees cover the rocky fields, and many dwellings, once the happy homes of men who owned their workmen, have a deserted, tumble-down look not at all in keeping with their natural attractions. Some sugar cane is raised, and several small sugar mills are in operation. The cane is crushed by horse power between three small cylinders, connected together at the top by projecting cogs, so that while one cylinder is turned by a horse traveling in a circle at the end of a long connecting arm, (as in the old-fashion cider mill), the other cylinders are made to revolve. They are so adjusted that the third cog gives the cane a tighter squeeze than the first two. One of the receiving cylinders has either vertical grooves or spaces which help to maintain and keep a hold upon the cane, constantly fed to the machine by a negro seated on the ground by its side. While in operation, a steady stream of saccharine cane-juice, having a strong corn-stalk taste, runs into a large tub, from which it is taken in pails to the sugar house, where it is boiled in large kettles; the cane from which the juice has been extracted is used for fuel in making the sugar, and is fed to stock. Some lime is put into the juice when it is boiled. Six men were employed in the mill we visited, who worked from 5 o'clock in the morning until sundown. Each horse grinds twice a day, two hours at a time—making four hours per day for each horse. The mill yields only one and a-half barrels of sugar per day. It was made in Cincinnati, Ohio. One of the other three mills on this island makes four barrels of sugar per day. It is only quite recently, we believe, that sugar has been made upon the island of New Providence. Commencing in December, sugar-making continues four months. The sugar seems of very fair quality.

A marine railway for the repair of vessels is maintained upon Hog Island, but we searched in vain for a single factory upon any of the Bahamas, bearing the faintest resemblance to the thousands that are found in every northern state. A very few little shops, like those often seen in small American villages, where some of the simplest of the mechanic arts are practiced, exist. But there is very little demand for skilled labor. We have a photograph of a Nassau joiner shop. It is very roomy, being located out-doors. It is well ventilated, having for its ceiling the blue vault of heaven. It is stable, being founded upon a rock. It is amply furnished and manned for the successful prosecution of a limited business, as it has a single joiner's bench and jack plane, which are in the sole possession and use of one of the Queen's colored subjects. A negro, mounted upon a rather unprepossessing looking mule, is the nearest approach which the Bahamas have yet made towards establishing either a steam or horse railroad. Telegraphs and telephones are of course unknown. Nassau has been described to be " a city without chimneys," though a few have been built for culinary purposes.

A lady of our party having broken either the main-spring or

chain of her watch, it was placed in the hands of a man who held himself out to the world in Nassau as competent to repair it. He kept it some four or five weeks, and until the owner was on the point of leaving the island, and charged her a good price for his worse than useless services. She found her watch in a worse condition than she believed it would have been if she had sent it to a northern blacksmith of average mechanical ingenuity and intelligence.

While Prof. Dana concedes that a coral island is a good temporary sanitarium when well supplied with foreign stores, "including a good stock of ice," and is especially attractive to those "who can draw inspiration from its mingled beauties," he well says, that "even in its best condition, it is but a miserable place for human development, physical, mental and moral," although "there is poetry in its every feature." "How much," he pertinently asks, "of the poetry and literature of Europe would be intelligible to persons whose ideas had expanded only to the limits of a coral island? What elevation in morals should be expected upon a contracted island, so readily overstocked that threatened annihilation drives to infanticide, and tends to the cultivation of the extremest selfishness. "Assuredly," he adds, "there is not a more unfavorable spot for moral or intellectual progress in the wide world than the coral island."

The situation of the city of Nassau, and its commercial relations with the outside world, save its people in a measure from the consequences which naturally result from a location upon a small island, of very limited resources, entirely destitute of mountains, and where neither rivers nor rivulets are seen wending their way to the sea, to the music of their everflowing waters. The generosity exhibited by many of the poorest of the negroes, was often the subject of favorable comment by people from the States.

CHAPTER VIII.

Absence of Wild Animals upon Coral Islands. Pleasures of the Chase Unknown. Diet of the Aborigines. How Alligators Taste. The Guanas as a Table Luxury. They are Intoxicated with Whistling Music. Vassar Girls Charming Turtles. Mountain Crabs. The Hermit Crab a Freebooter. The Lizards—Changing their Color and Hunting Game. Animals upon the West India Islands when Discovered. Snakes. Sea Turtles. Turtle Shell. How Sponges Grow and form Communistic Communities. The Sponge Fisheries. Value and Quantity of Bahama Sponges Exported.

"The world was made to be inhabited by beasts, but studied and contemplated by man."—THOMAS BROWN.

BUT upon the Bahamas man finds few animals to study and contemplate. At the time of their discovery by Columbus in 1492, they were destitute of all the higher forms of animal life. The Bahamas belong to a recent geological age, and are some of the ornamental appendages with which the earth was decorated, thousands, and perhaps millions of years after it was made, and while, with its little partner, the moon, it was, as now, waltzing around the sun. This, in connection with the fact of their small extent and isolated position, accounts for that absence of animal life to which we have referred. Some domesticated animals— the cow, the horse, the hog and the sheep—are now found upon the islands, but they are a part of the old world's gift to the new. That pet of many a household—man's friend, companion, guard and protector—the much abused dog—is not only frequently met with upon the islands, but it is reported that a native breed once existed that never barked. While we are unable to vouch for

125

the truthfulness of the tradition, we are ready to believe that
even ill-natured beasts would soon become amiable in the mild
and soothing air, and that a canine millennium might, by the
silent operation of natural laws, soon be established on those
emerald isles.   Perhaps we owe an apology to the dogs of the
Bahamas for having stated that they are too lazy and indolent
to bark—it may be that we should have said instead, that they
are too amiable.   The loud and persistent crowing of the roosters, during all the hours of the night, we have been recently
assured is the crow of hunger, and not the genuine John Bull
expression of a self-satisfied sentiment of conscious superiority.

Killing for sport, and "the pleasures of the chase," whether
brutal or refined, could not have been among the pastimes of
those who received and welcomed Columbus and his companions
when they first landed upon the shores of the New World.   And
they had yet to learn the game of cruel and merciless war from
the more educated and cultured savages of a higher civilization.
In that they had no accumulated capital they were poor indeed,
but free from the fevered dream of ambition, the unquenchable
thirst of avarice, and the tortures of unsupplied and constantly
increasing wants, they were vastly richer than any of the envied
millionaires of either ancient or modern times.   Simple, amiable
and guileless children of nature, unlearned and uncultivated,
happy and cheerful as the birds that flaunted their gay plumage
in the spicy and perfumed air, they lived and loved in their little
Gardens of Eden, with no ban upon the delicious and golden
fruits of their uncultivated tropical orchards.

These fruits, a limited supply of vegetables, and the fish which
the surrounding ocean supplied at all times in great abundance,
constituted their food.   A vegetable and piscatory diet infused
no frenzied fever in the blood or brain; and with no wild beasts
in the forests or jungles, there was no savagery to be transmuted.

Mr. McKinnen in his "Tour," when speaking of his visit to Acklin's Island in 1802–3, says: "Alligators were sometimes brought in for the table, but it required considerable address to destroy them. The negroes, however, never display so much ingenuity or patience as in pursuit of prey. The flesh of an alligator which I tasted was hard, white and very much resembled the sturgeon's." We heard of no alligators at New Providence, and, as the Bahama Islands are destitute of rivers, we think it probable the alligators referred to had strayed away from their accustomed haunts, and that this huge reptile contributed little to the support of the ancient Lucayans.

Lizards of small size are very common in New Providence. They are from six to twelve inches in length, and their ancestors could not here have very materially contributed to the maintenance of human life. But Mr. McKinnen, speaking of the condition of the island and their inhabitants in his own time, states, that "the guana [*iguana*] of the lizard tribe is found in the holes in the rocks in all the islands. In the cultivated parts the guana soon disappears, as they are easily taken, and their flesh is much esteemed by the negroes."

Mr. Bryan Edwards, of the island of Jamaica, in his history of the West Indies, published in Dublin in 1793, says, concerning the island, that

"The woods were peopled with two very extraordinary creatures; both of which anciently were, and still are, not only used for food, but accounted superior delicacies. These are the iguana and the mountain crab." The former "is a species of lizard— a class of animals about which naturalists are not agreed whether to rank them with quadrupeds, or to degrade them to serpents. * * * From the alligator, the most formidable of the family, measuring sometimes twenty feet in length, the gradation is regular in diminution of size to the small lizard of three inches;

the same figure and conformation nearly (though not wholly) prevailing in each. The iguana is one of the intermediate species, and is usually about three feet long, and proportionally bulky. It lives chiefly among fruit trees, and is perfectly gentle and innoxious." He says they had then "become generally scarce," except in places seldom visited by man. Also that "the English, even when they were more plentiful, did not often serve them at elegant tables, but their French and Spanish neighbors, less squeamish, still devour them with exquisite relish." Also that a lady "of great beauty and elegance," assured him, from her own experience, that they are "equal in flavor and wholesomeness to the finest green turtle." That "P. Labat likewise speaks of a fricasseed guana with high approbation. He compares it to a chicken for the whiteness of its flesh and the delicacy of its flavor."

He quotes from the work of this "good father," (Tom iii, p. 316,) his description of the novel mode then in vogue of capturing this species of game. "We were attended," he says, "by a negro, who carried a long rod, at one end of which was a piece of whip cord with a running knot. After beating the bushes for some time, the negro discovered our game basking in the sun on a dry limb of a tree. Hereupon he began whistling with all his might, to which the guana was wonderfully attentive, stretching out his neck and turning his head, as if to enjoy it more fully. The negro now approached, still whistling, and advancing his rod gently, began tickling with the end of it the sides and throat of the guana, who seemed mightily pleased with the operation, for he turned on his back, and stretched out like a cat before the fire, and at length fairly fell asleep, which the negro perceiving, dexterously slipt the noose over his head, and with a jerk brought him to the ground; and good sport it afforded to see the creature swell like a turkey-cock at finding himself entrapped. We caught others in the same way, and kept one of them alive seven or eight days, but it grieved me to the heart to find that he thereby lost much delicious fat."

That other members of the reptilian family are also keenly sensitive to whistling music, and greatly pleased and soothed by it, is evidenced by the following account which the author received from his daughter. She says: "Upon the college grounds at Vassar, there is a small artificial lake which is utilized for boating in mild weather, and for skating in winter. It is well stocked with turtles, varying in size from one to about nine inches in length. It was common for the lady students to keep small ones in their rooms as pets. Perceiving that the one I had thus utilized and "adopted" had evidently an ear for certain kinds of music, especially whistling, I was induced to try an experiment upon other and larger turtles in the lake. The result far exceeded my anticipations. Pushing out from the shore in my little row boat, I could always, when so disposed, secure at once at my whistling concerts for turtles, a numerous audience of all sizes, from three to nine or more inches in length. They would mount a log close to me, first one and then another taking its place, until the sittings were all occupied, and listen with wrapt and pleased attention. While the whistling continued, they turned their heads from side to side, and stretched them out from their shells to the farthest possible extent, as if anxious to see and hear to the uttermost. They would suffer me, at such times, to handle them, and the music, if such I may be permitted to call it, appeared to produce a very quieting effect upon them. They seemed intoxicated with what must have been to them a new and strange pleasure. They would remain so long as I would whistle, and jump off into the water when the whistling stopped. They liked the soft sweet airs, and were frightened by a lively tune, but I found that I could retain them as auditors of the more spirited tunes if I first quieted them and secured their confidence by whistling tunes which harmonized better with their sluggish natures. When the whistling stopped, the reptilian audience retired, and carried, perhaps, the news of the strange sounds they had heard to the more domestic turtles which had remained below in their watery abodes. They were not all alike gifted with a musical taste, for some evidently enjoyed it very much more than others. I found, after a time, that this novel sight caused often the attendance upon the shore of a large number of the lady students, who were much interested and amused at these whistling turtle concerts."

No doubt the New Providence guanas were long since exterminated. The small lizards of to-day are certainly in appearance not very attractive as table luxuries. Capt. Fox, a near neighbor of ours at the hotel, secured a few living specimens, and held them in captivity for a few days, that he might critically examine them and observe their movements. We were, by his courtesy, also enabled to learn by personal observation some of their peculiarities, although generally we are content to get our reptilian knowledge second hand.

The Bahama lizards possess the power of changing their colors, like the chameleon. How this result is accomplished we do not know. They may have little vessels containing fluids variously colored, and as one set is expanded or contracted upon the surface, the lizards blossom out in brown, red, green or satin as the case may be. Thus each, without changing its dress, has at pleasure all the benefits of an ample and varied wardrobe. This may result in frequent cases of mistaken identity, and cause much trouble and possibly no little innocent amusement. Their eyes have movable lids: some species have dew-laps, which look like pouches under their chins, and all are considered harmless, although possessing teeth, which are simple in their structure. They have an elongate round body, a snaky looking tongue, four

REPTILES.

1. *Chelonia imbricata.* "Hawkbill Turtle." About one-sixth natural size, from Holbrook's Herpetology. Tortoise shell, used for combs, jewelry, &c., is taken from this species.

2. *Sphæriodactylus notatus.* Natural size. 3. Head of same, enlarged. 4. Foot of same, enlarged, showing the suckers. From Report of Mexican Boundary Survey.

5. *Anolis principalis.* Natural size. From Holbrook's Herpetology. Color, bright green, changing to brown, acording to health and weather.

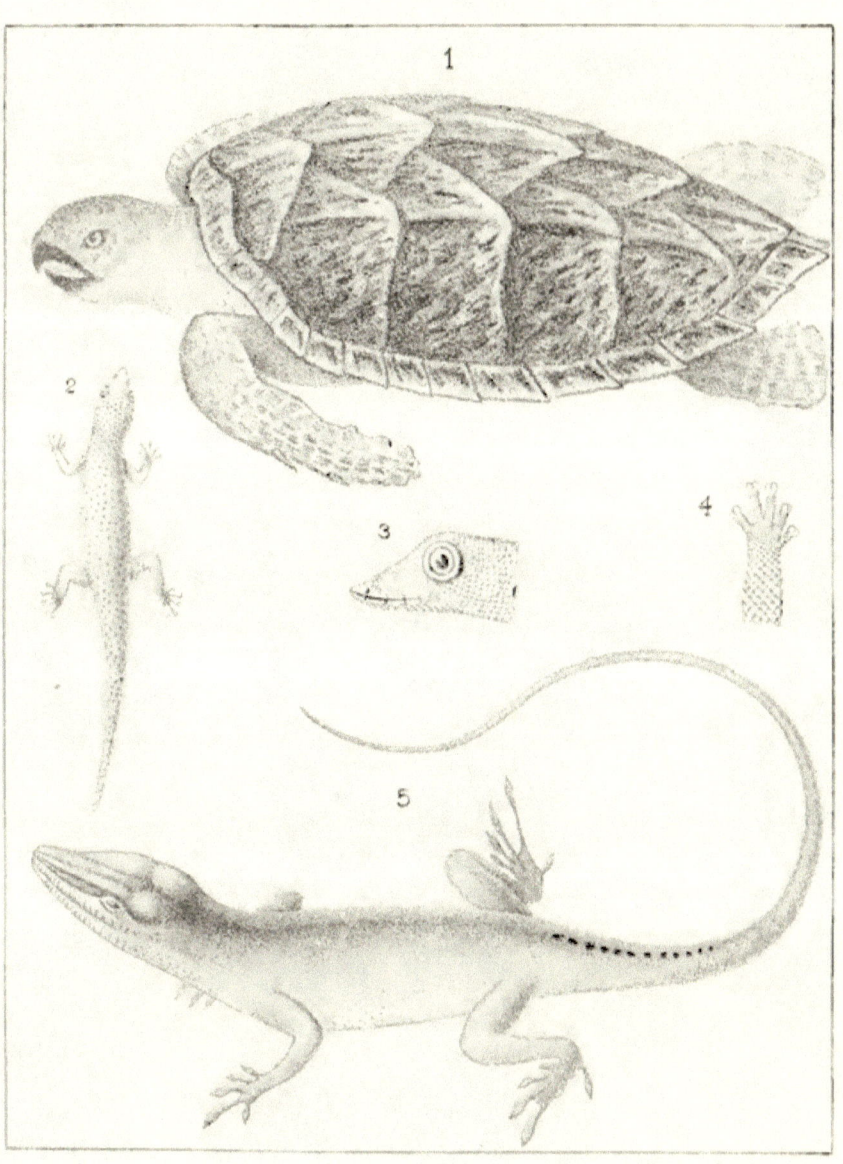

REPTILES.

short legs, each with five digits, and travel upon the rocks and over the bushes and trees with considerable dexterity and agility, being essentially aided by a wiggling motion of their bodies and long tails. They always excited in us such a decidedly repugnant feeling, that we did not consider ourselves at all slighted when we observed on their part an evident desire to avoid us as disagreeable intruders; and yet these reptiles are decidedly good looking and attractive when contrasted with another genus of the same family in Australia, whose ferocious appearance, armed as they are with horns on their heads and spines on their bodies, have secured for them the descriptive and suggestive name of "Horrid Molochs."

One of our passengers from Nassau to Fernandina in the Western Texas, was Mr. Albert H. Phelps, of West Pawlet, Vt.— a self-educated naturalist, only seventeen or eighteen years of age, having a most ardent love for natural history, who, while at Nassau, so taxed and exposed himself in the intensely hot sun, collecting and preserving as many specimens as possible of the singular forms of life in and out of the water, that he was attacked with a dangerous and malignant fever, and nearly lost his life. In regard to the New Providence lizards, he in substance said: "I have ten or more species; some of them, including their long slender tails, are ten inches long. One, of a dark brown color, is very showy. It has five golden spots, and its back is so raised as to form a ridge. It has also a dew lap. After I knocked it down with a cane, the bright colors and the dew lap disappeared, and the reptile was all of a pale ash color. I killed another before he had time to change color. It was of an umber brown, with clusters of lemon yellow spots, very minute, so that a little distance off each cluster seemed a little spot. The dew lap was a rich shade of dark umber brown, with a rich stripe of yellow 'round the small bone under its jaw, and 'round its forehead and head of its nose. I read in Appleton's American Encyclopedia that there are no four footed reptiles that are dangerous. I have allowed the lizards of all descriptions to bite me, and never suffered any inconvenience from it. Their bite is like that of turtles; they pinch hard, and have great strength in their jaws. The small lizards will stand and turn their heads and listen if you whistle. It is amusing to see them out hunting. They hunt insects that are large enough to attract their attention. At a place where I used to go to get sea-eggs to dry, flies collected, and I would sit and watch them. They would see a fly when two feet distant, and then lie down and creep towards it like a dog after a wood-chuck, or a cat after a mouse. I have seen them jump and catch flies, and catch them on the wing. Salamanders are not dangerous. I have tamed little red ones so that they would walk 'round on my finger. I never could get one of them to bite me. They are perfectly harmless."

In a communication received from our young friend, Mr. Phelps, of Vermont, while this chapter was in the printer's hands, he states: "Many of the people of Nassau consider the flesh of the iguana a great delicacy. I was unable to test it personally, because none were offered for sale in the Nassau market. I obtained one from Cuba for my collection. They grow to a length of from three to four feet, including the tail, which is two-thirds the entire length. The head is large, and its capacious mouth is armed with about fifty teeth upon each jaw. The dew-lap has a depth about equal to the diameter of the head; it is triangular, and has about a dozen separations on its anterior border. Along its neck and back is a comb-like crest of fifty-five scales, which, extending to the tail, becomes simply a serrated ridge. The color above is greenish, with blue and slate tints; below it is a greenish yellow; generally, upon the sides, there are brown, zigzag bands, with a yellowish border; on the front of the shoulder there is a yellowish band; some are dotted with brown, and have yellow spots on the limbs. The tail is ringed broadly with alternate brown and yellowish green colors."

Mr. Phelps adds: "There are a great many small iguanas every where about Nassau. The most numerous species are about five inches in length, and are generally of a light gray color, but like the chamelion, they can change to several different hues at will. It is constantly on the hunt for small insects, and may at any time be seen on trees, walls and houses, running about in quest of its prey.

"Another small species abounds in all gardens. It is about seven inches long, and of the brightest grass-green color. It is much more slender than the one just described, has a tail which is twice the length of its body, and a very prominent dew-lap of a rich umber-brown tint. The dew-lap is peculiar to this order of lizards. It is capable of expansion and contraction at will, and, through its changes, an interchange of ideas seem to be effected; sight taking the place of sound as a medium for transmitting thought.

"The blue-tailed lizard frequents hot, sandy places, and may be commonly seen about the battery. It is about ten inches long.

"The lizard is small but very useful. Its mission is to keep insect life in tropical countries within reasonable and proper bounds. They are exceedingly spry, and very amusing in their habits. They never molest any one, and their mission, so far as man is concerned, is decidedly friendly and beneficial."

Mr. Phelps states that he saw upon the island of New Providence, three species of the tree frog, one of which was very large.

Also that he had collected while at Nassau, from fifteen to twenty species of crabs, including three or four kinds of land crabs. Mr. Edwards, in his history of the West India Islands, speaking of the mountain crab, says:

12

"It is, without doubt, one of the choicest morsels in nature." It formerly was found in immense numbers, and the observation of Du Tertre that they were "a living and perpetual supply of manna in the wilderness, equalled only by the miraculous bounty of Providence to the children of Israel when wandering in the desert," is said to have been no exaggeration. The Indians relied upon them with confidence when all other provisions were scarce, and the supply was always equal to their wants.

When Edwards wrote it still existed in large numbers, but he thought the time of its extinction was then near at hand.

Du Tertre described them as living in a kind of orderly society in their retreats in the mountains, and as having annual night marches to the sea, by the shortest and straightest lines, like a well drilled and admirably organized army under able and experienced commanders. The waves relieve the crabs of their spawn; the eggs are soon hatched in the sand of the shore, and millions of young crabs, impelled by a power invisible, mysterious and divine, are soon seen slowly making their way to the mountains. Crowding each other upon the eastern coast of the Atlantic states, the human instinct has to be quickened by the loud clarion notes of command to induce the young men to "go West," but these little crabs seem to be endowed with more practical wisdom, and to push inland of their own accord.

The hermit crab, a singular and well known species, is common upon the shores of the Bahamas. It has very loose ideas upon the subject of the personal rights of its fellow creatures, and is to the full extent of its capabilities, a first-class freebooter. Having captured a little circular shell fish, it uses the shell of its prisoner to cover and protect the vulnerable portion of its own organism, makes itself perfectly at home in its new but stolen house, occupies it as tenant in common, pays no rent, compels its captive to make all the repairs, and to accompany it on its travels over the rocky shore.

Mr. Edwards states that there anciently existed upon the Windward or Caribbee Islands all the animals that were found upon the larger islands, and some others in addition. The latter were found at the time when he wrote in Guana, and few or none of them in North America, which helped to make him believe that the Windward Islands were anciently peopled from the south. He mentions only eight kinds of land animals as having been found in the West Indies, viz.:

1. The agouti—("the *mus aguti* of Linnaeus, and the *cavy* of Pennant and Buffon") "constitutes an intermediate species between the rabbit and the rat." He believed it extinct except in the larger islands.

2. The pecary—(" the *sus tajacu* of Linnaeus, and the *pecary* and *Mexican musk hog* of English naturalists.") It differed from the European hog in that it had a gland upon its back from which there was a musky discharge, while it sported gay colors, its bristles being pale blue tipped with white. It was also more courageous, and would attack the dogs that hunted them. In 1793 it had been exterminated in the West Indies, but it abounded in some portions of Mexico.

3. The armadilla was called "the *nine banded*. It was covered with a jointed shell or scaly armor, and rolled itself up like the hedge-hog. As an article of diet it was very delicate and wholesome." It was once found in all the West Indies, but was extinct when Edwards wrote.

4. The opossum (or *monitou*) grows its own bag in which under its belly, it shelters and carries its young. This animal like the pecary, Edwards thinks was unknown in the larger islands.

5. "The raccoon was common in Jamaica in the time of Sloane, who observes that it was eaten by all sorts of people." It was believed to have been exterminated when Edwards wrote.

6. The musk rat—(the *piloris* of naturalists)—abounded on some of the islands, and may have been the agouti.

7. The alco or native dog, that did not bark, was carefully fattened by the natives, and esteemed a great delicacy as an article of diet. Edwards quotes the following from Acosta: "In St. Domingo at first there were no dogs but a small mute creature resembling a dog, with a nose like that of a fox, which the natives called alco. The Indians were so fond of these little animals that they carried them on their shoulders wherever they went, or nourished them in their bosoms."

8. Monkeys. These were used for food, and are said to have very much the flavor of hare. Englishmen seem to have had a sort of Darwinian instinct, and to have deemed an invitation to dine upon monkeys substantially the same as to pick the dry bones of their dead ancestors.

The only snake we saw while at the Bahamas, was discovered and killed near the west gate of the hotel enclosure. We think they are neither numerous or dangerous.

Mr. Phelps writes that the chicken snake is the only representative upon the island of New Providence of the whole family of serpents; that it resembles the milk snake; and that it is reported to attain sometimes a length of fifteen feet, but that the largest one he saw and measured was six feet long, and two inches in diameter in the largest part. He adds: "They are perfectly harmless. The only venomous creatures on the island are the tarantulas, or ground spiders, as they are called by the natives. They are found but rarely, and only upon the plantations. In my many excursions I never came across either a tarantula or a scorpion. My specimens were obtained of the negroes, whose services were secured through the stimulating influence of pecuniary rewards. Centipedes are occasionally met with, but their sting, though very painful, is not fatal."

Several large and valuable kinds of sea turtles are found in the Bahama waters, as was evidenced by the bountiful supply of excellent turtle soups and turtle steaks often seen upon the dining room tables of the Royal Victoria Hotel. The Hawk's Bill turtle yields the beautiful tortoise shell that figures so prominently in ladies' toilets. The shells of the Green, and also of the Yellow or Mulatto turtles, are said to be in lamina too thin for practical use. The name "Green Turtle" we suppose was given them on account of the green color of the fat under their shells. Turtle steak is very light colored, and looks and tastes like the tender meat of a chicken. Stepping upon a platform adjoining a Nassau dock, we looked down through a trap door into a crawl which contained a large number of sea turtles, varying in weight we should think, from fifty to one hundred or more pounds. The shells of some of them at least, equalled in size the one the poet Wadsworth thus very unpoetically describes:

> "The shell of a green turtle, thin
> And hollow; you might sit therein
> It was so wide and deep."

We observed them with much interest. They appeared contented and happy although somewhat restless. Our first impression was that they were either holding a mass meeting or a sociable. Then we queried whether they had not come to Nassau on a marooning excursion. But they were so dignified and solemn, and seemed so loaded down with a heavy weight of cares, we finally concluded they were holding a session of the sub-marine reptilian "Parliament." That they were loyal and patriotic may be inferred from the fact that they were soon to lose their lives for the public good. Turtles and turtle shells are exported from the Bahamas of the annual value of from three thousand to four thousand dollars. It is said that the sea turtle

will live several weeks without food—consuming meantime we
suppose, its own fat. Upon unfrequented and desolate little
islands or keys, covered with sand, weeds and bushes, the sea
turtles lay their eggs in great numbers, which are incubated by
the sun—each newly hatched little reptile thereby, all unconsciously, acting the part of the infant Moses in the bulrushes.
The turtle as a pedestrian is not a great success, as his four legs
are very short and widely separated.   But it is apparent from the
size of the turtle steaks that he has great muscular power, and in
" paddling his own canoe " in the water, although weighted with
a complete coat of mail, he can make very good time.

The aborigines of the island of Cuba captured the sea turtle
by a process novel and ingenious.   Tying a long cord to the tail
of a sucker-fish, which the Spaniards called the *reves*, (of the
Echeneis genera,) they cast it into the water in the narrow and
winding channels frequented by the sea turtles, and the fish
first fastening its suckers, which surrounded a flat disc upon its
head, upon the turtle's coat of mail, retains its hold until the
piscatory captor and captive were safely drawn out of the water.
Columbus alleged that the reves would suffer itself to be dismembered rather than relax its hold upon its unfortunate victim.   It
may be presumed that this singular method of fishing for turtles
was followed by the natives of the Bahama Islands.   Humboldt,
in his " Island of Cuba," states that when this new mode of fishing was reported in Europe, the story was discredited and considered "only a traveler's tale."   He adds that on the eastern
coast of Africa, near Cape Natal, a similar artifice was used.

The most valuable product of the Bahama waters is the Spon-
gida, which yields the sponge of commerce—an article which
ministers in so many ways to the comfort and wants of man.   It
has been growing in popular favor for the past forty years, as its
capacity for varied and extensive usefulness has been gradually

developed. Fastened to the rocks by roots, maturing germs like buds, and looking like a fungus, an ordinary observer can hardly believe the learned men of science when informed by them that it is an animal. The spongidæ are found in water from twelve to thirty feet deep, and are detached from the rocks by divers or by fishermen with the aid of long poles having hooks with two prongs. Water glasses, like those hereafter described in our chapter upon corals, are also used when the water is rough. A large number of boats and men are employed in the business.

When we went to Nassau we supposed we knew sponges, but we were greatly mistaken. When taken from the water they are dark colored, and in appearance resemble liver. The sponge of commerce consists of the flexible fibrous skeletons of a large colony of sponges. The very small and clustered animals are so closely united, and so arranged, as to form a mass of tubes, through which the sea water containing their food is made to circulate by means of very small hairs or cilia which line the cavities, and vibrate at the will of the animal, so that each can take its appropriate nourishment as the water passes through. It seems to be a communistic community, where each works for the common benefit of all. The principle works well, and would produce equally good results in human societies if man had only a little more of the nature and disposition of a sponge conferred upon him. The water is discharged through the larger orifices. It has been well said that "the sponge represents a kind of subaqueous city, where the people are arrayed about the streets and roads, in such a manner that each can appropriate his food from the water as it passes along." The supply of water is stopped when the orifices or gates of these marine cities are closed, but how such multitudes of animals, that are inseparably united and permanently attached to one spot, can be so regulated and managed as to secure harmony and the common good of all, we cannot fully understand.

Aside from its many curious forms, some of which are beautiful, the sponge when first taken from the water has a very unpromising appearance, and its odor is offensive. The sponge of commerce is merely its skeleton or framework. This is surrounded by a glairy, gelatinous substance, which formerly was removed by burying the sponges in the sand for a few days, and afterwards whipping them with sticks. But now they are kept upon deck for two or three days, when they lose their vitality; afterwards they are placed in a crawl and kept there from eight to ten days; then they are cleansed and bleached in the sun and air upon the beach. Afterwards, upon their arrival in Nassau, the roots are cut off, and they are trimmed and packed for exportation. Some of those offered for sale in the hotel court were doubtless bleached with chemicals. The result in such cases is that the strength of the fibre is impaired. The sponges grow sometimes in forms so singular and unique that they command from strangers a good price as curiosities.

We were shown at Judge VanVolkenberg's house in Florida, what seemed to be a package two or three feet in length, of beautiful small glass threads, and were very greatly surprised to learn that it was a species of Japanese sponge. It was obtained in Japan when the Judge filled the office of United States minister to Japan.

We also saw in the little embryo museum which is connected with the Nassau public library, a delicate foreign sponge, packed in cotton wool, which closely resembled handsome thread lace.

In a recent official report of the Governor of the Bahamas, he states that it has been discovered in Germany that the sponge may be propagated by cuttings from living specimens, which, when fastened to pieces of board, are placed in the sea. Skilful cultivation may hereafter result in the production of the more valuable sponges in many parts of the ocean world where they are not at present found.

SPONGES.

1. *Tuba plicifera.* "Bouquet Sponge."
2. *Pachychalina rubens.* "Silk Sponge." Color, when living, red.
3. *Hircinia purpurea.* "Wire Sponge."
4. *Spongia tubulifera.* "Finger Sponge." A peculiar variety of the "Glove Sponge."

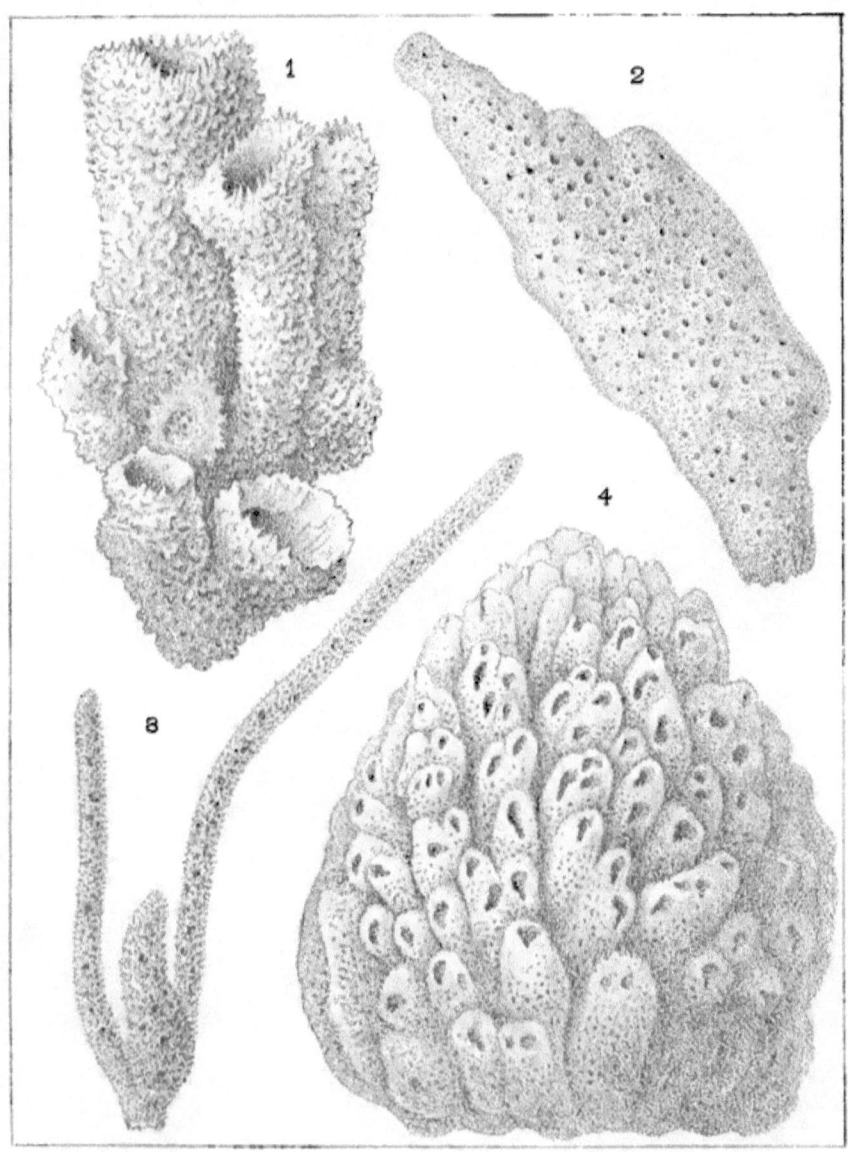

SPONGES

Our Bahama experience has secured for the sponge a conspicuous and pleasant place in our memory. It is no longer what it has been. It has become glorified and hallowed. We look at it with new eyes, and handle it with a feeling of respect akin to reverence, for it reflects something of that divine and creative wisdom that caused it to grow, in part at least for man's benefit, upon the white limestone floor over which the clear, warm waters of the ocean surrounding the coral islands ceaselessly roll. Perhaps a more thorough and extensive exploration of the beds of the ocean world may bring to light new and valuable additions to the sponge-producing waters. In the sea dredging off the coast of Massachusetts some specimens of Spongidæ have been obtained.

The Bahama sponges differ very much in quality, and consequently in value. Some are quite small and fine—others large and coarse. Some have a texture so firm that the hardest wringing and pulling does not tear them. Others, having the same general appearance, are easily picked to pieces with the thumb and finger. The difference in softness is also very marked. The novice needs to be on his guard, and to exercise much caution in making purchases, for he is not only in great danger of buying a poor and perhaps worthless article, but of imposition in the matter of price. It is never pleasant to feel that we have been imposed upon, but it is mortifying for one boasting of Caucassian blood to be cheated by an ignorant and unlettered negro.

Sponges are daily offered for sale in the court of the Royal Victoria Hotel. They are strung together, a dozen or more upon a string, and most visitors purchase a supply for home use. They are much cheaper than those sold at retail in the States, and when dried and pressed occupy but little room. In the waters surrounding the islands of Abaco, Exuma and Andros the sponges are found in the greatest abundance, and the Abaco sponges were represented to be the best by those who sold sponges at the hotel.

For the purposes of sale the Bahama sponges are divided into eight classes, and though they find a ready market, they are considered inferior to those which are found in the Mediterranean—and this is equally true of corals. I was informed by an extensive dealer in sponges, that the Florida waters produce sponges of a quality superior to those of the Bahamas, though not equal to those of the Mediterranean.

The quantity and value of sponges annually exported from the Bahamas has not been uniform. In 1855, sponges were exported of the value of nearly $50,000; in 1861, of over $150,000; in 1877, over $90,000; in 1878, nearly $125,000; and the average for ten years prior to 1864 was nearly $87,000. The increase in quality and value in 1878 was caused by the re-opening of the Cuban sponge fisheries which were closed during the Cuban insurrection. The Bahama sponge fleet entered last year the Cuban waters, and by over production soon broke down the market. Some of the finer qualities were exported to France, but the largest portion of the Bahama sponges are sent to the United States and to England.

CHAPTER IX.

THE people of Nassau, owing to their isolated condition, are compelled to rely upon their own resources for amusement. A Bahama nimrod has no horn or hoof or hide among his trophies. His game is in the sea. In the variety and abundance of its fauna, the ocean to some extent, makes up for the absence of animal life in the impenetrable jungles. The birds have mostly been compelled to build their nests and rear their young upon secluded and uninhabited islands. Nassau's "back country" is small in extent, and the continuity of the shade and the profound depth of the solitude which ever rests upon the island beyond the city's borders, can hardly be said to be broken by the two or three little hamlets where a few negroes have their humble homes. Hence the almost entire absence of the thousand and one entertainments that compete for a portion of the time and money of the people in all the cities of the Union. These, with us, are largely due to our facilities for inter-communication. They multiply as our steam commercial marine increases, and with every enlargement of our railroad system. Theatrical exhibitions, menageries, concerts by companies of eminent musicians, lectures

113

from famous and gifted men, and great gatherings of representative men in science, religion and politics, and for moral reforms, must inevitably be as rare in the Bahamas as skating rinks. During the wild excitement that prevailed in Nassau when, during the late rebellion, it was practically a confederate port, under the protection of the flag of Great Britain, a stone building was erected for theatrical exhibitions. The astonished winds immediately blew its roof off and otherwise damaged it, so that its bare monumental walls alone remain to commemorate the important part which Nassau played in the great war of the Southern rebellion. But no inference can properly be drawn from the fact of its destruction by the angry elements, that the theatre was especially objectionable to the spirit that rides upon the whirlwind and directs the storm, because churches as well as other public and many private buildings were blown down at the same time. We have no doubt that the Bahama government, in these calm sober days, would prefer as a paying investment, warming pans to theatres.

Nassau and its surroundings have much to interest a stranger, especially if he has spent his life in more northern latitudes; but to her own citizens, it must be a very dull place notwithstanding an occasional hurricane and frequent wrecks. In the winter of 1878, '79, a traveling circus company chartered a steamboat and visited some of the West India Islands. Their arrival in Nassau produced a deep and profound sensation. The landing of Columbus and his followers upon a neighboring island nearly four centuries before, with gilded cross and emblazoned banner, was not a greater surprise or productive of half the pleasure. No alloy of fear marred the happiness which the arrival of the acrobats occasioned. Heralded from afar, and accompanied in their grand march through the streets of Nassau by musicians who made the soft and languid air vibrate with a melody it never had before experienced, richly clad in costumes, striped, bespangled and radiant with burnished silver and shining gold, they seemed to many an unlettered and untraveled looker-on, fourfold more the children of the sun than did the Spanish discoverers of 1492. The new Jerusalem, as seen in the fervid dreams of Nassau's dusky, religious devotees, surely cannot boast so gorgeous a chariot, nor do horses of equal grace and beauty tread the golden and jewelled streets of their celestial city. A wild and bewildering excitement took possession of Grant's Town, and, like an electric atmosphere, pervaded the thoroughfares and by-ways of Nassau itself. While the show lasted, the contributions levied upon the guests of the Royal Victoria Hotel, to enable the little negroes to see it and be forever happy, were quite formidable in number if not in amount. Indeed, some of the juveniles were smart and enterprising enough to make it an excuse for obtaining a good supply of shillings for future use. We suspect that the circus as a motive power and moral force in the world has been underestimated. We esteemed it more highly after we witnessed its effects in that island of unending summer. Indolence retired, and ambition came out of its tomb of death at its approach. Long live the circus!

As we have elsewhere shown, the forms, ceremonies, symbols, trappings and paraphranalia of a royal government, furnish an integral and very important part of Nassau's amusements. In this point of view, colonial institutions on a monarchial model are a real godsend. For people living outside of the limits of the great world of human activity and life, without railroads, telegraphs, steamboats, telephones, capital, enterprise, or business, it seems to be a pleasant but expensive diversion.

A whist club exists at Nassau. It is composed of the governor, and a few high officials and prominent citizens, numbering, as we were informed, some fifteen in all. They meet twice a week, in the evening from eight to eleven o'clock; Friday at the "Government House," (the Governor's residence,) and Tuesdays at the houses of the other members. They play nothing but whist, and loyally follow the English custom of putting up sixpenny stakes, "just to increase a little the interest, and keep things lively," as my informant expressed it. We were also told that on these occasions "they never drink to excess, and no excess of any kind is indulged in." Excess, as applied to drinking, is a very flexible uncertain word. Such of the high officials as we saw drink could not be called "hard" drinkers, for we never saw men drink more easy than they did, or appear to take to it more naturally, or enjoy it more. In carrying capacity, also, they are at least the peers of their American cousins. The belief is wide spread, that spirituous liquors moderately used as a beverage in warm climates, are conducive to health. Where malarial poisons are exhaled, quinine and alcoholic drinks are considered by many absolute necessaries. We have no doubt about the value of quinine as a tonic and malarial antidote, but have no sufficient basis of fact in regard to the use of alcohol, in such cases, upon which to form an opinion satisfactory to ourselves, or of value to others. It is a question which has two sides. If that which we saw drank was used for sanitary reasons, the quantity imbibed indicated a country most alarmingly unhealthy. The treatment we thought partook of the "heroic."

Nassau formerly had a yachting club, and in all probability its organization remains, but nothing occurred while we were there to indicate that it still lives. It certainly was torpid if not dead —chloroformed by climate. No regattas, as of yore, pleasantly disturbed the ocean tides, or the dreamy quiet of the city's every day life. Something of the sadness which follows in the wake of pleasure, and of the melancholy which hovers over departed joys, surrounds and envelopes the yacht club's silent boat-house.

The ambition of the young men is not excited or increased by bat and ball, or boat and oar. Archery, an out-door diversion, which connects the high-toned men and maidens in England to-day, with the people of pre-historic times, and which, with feathered shafts and twanging bow, projects the distant stone age into the age of gold, has not as yet, been re-established upon these islands, where it flourished in the time of Columbus. Requiring little physical exertion, arousing no fierce passions, stirring the bosom with only pleasurable excitement, its highest enjoyment secured when both sexes participate in its sport, a semi-tropical climate would seem to be peculiarly favorable to its practice and cultivation. But the more violent games of foot-ball and polo flourish instead, and call out many spectators on the afternoons of Tuesday and Friday of each week, including the élite of the town in carriages. Polo results occasionally in a broken bone, and foot-ball excites to spirited struggles for the mastery. The negroes in the military department when off duty, are perhaps more to be commended, for, when not idle, or occupied with their lady friends, they are satisfied, (according to one of the official medical reports,) with flying paper kites, and the lowly and quiet game of marbles. No doubt many of the Queen's ebony subjects would rather be the humble turtle, that idly basks and meditates upon a rock in the sun, than the most beautiful antelope that ever scaled the craggy heights of a mountain. With the thermometer in the eighties in the shade, I could the better understand the wisdom and good sense of such a preference. But, then, upon us high-toned English precedents produced but little effect.

One result of the absence at Nassau of the innumerable and varied private sports and public amusements which exist in all cities and large towns in the States is, to give greater prominence and importance to the church. Religion has its social side, and, in the States, it is apparently often deemed advisable if not necessary, to unite all who worship or statedly attend devotional exercises in the same place, in what is practically a social club. It is difficult for the church to secure the attendance of people generally to its meetings of a purely religious and devotional character, where the cities are constantly placarded, and the columns of the newspapers teem with notices and advertisements of an endless variety of shows and public entertainments. Hence the number of church fairs, church festivals, church feasts, church concerts, and church picnics. It has been deemed necessary, not so much to aid the church as an aggressive force in the world, but in self-defense, to surround religion with some of the rational enjoyments and healthy diversions which otherwise will be practically used by the devil to undermine its influence and destroy its power. At Nassau, religion dominates without these adjuncts, as it did in New England in the days of the pilgrims—and for the same reason.

Public attention is called to some of the holy days and fasts of the church by placards, printed in large type and posted upon the street corners and in other public places. Good Friday was thus announced, and the following we copied from one of the hand-bills.

"GOOD FRIDAY.

"Is it nothing to you, all ye that pass by?

"Good Friday is the most solemn, the most awful day in the whole year to the Christian.

"On Good Friday, the Lord Jesus Christ, God in the nature of man, suffered on the cross of shame, dying that He might save you.

"It is everything to you that He died, for He suffered for your sin—yes, your's!

" How then will you spend Good Friday? If your father, mother, wife, or husband, son or daughter, died—if they died to save your life, would you choose the anniversary of their death to make merry and take a holiday? No, you would not."

We omit the three concluding paragraphs.

Another street hand-bill read as follows:

ASH WEDNESDAY.

" The first day of Lent;

" The church's special call to repentance.

" Blow the trumpet in Zion; sanctify a fast; call a solemn assembly;—

" Gather the people; sanctify the congregation; assemble the elders; gather the children and those that suck the breasts; let the bridegroom go forth out of his chamber, and the bride out of her closet.

" Let the priests, the ministers of the Lord, weep between the porch and the altar, and let them say, spare thy people, O Lord, and give not thy heritage to reproach, that the heathen should rule over them; wherefore should they say among the people, where is their God?"—Joel ii, Chap. 15—17 verses.

That these solemn occasions are to many quite attractive is doubtless true. They diversify the every day life of the people, although they are not, in the strict sense of the term, amusements. But they are a real recreation no doubt, for some, and not a cross. The old lady exhibited something akin to this feeling when she complained of the solitary situation of her dwelling house; she did not like it, she said there was " nothing going on there—no funerals, nor'nothing."

Could Black Beard and the other pirates who rendezvoused and dominated in Nassau in the early historic times, walk its streets to-day, they could not but be greatly impressed with the moral and religious changes which have taken place. While the little capital has doubtless its full share of the vices which mar the civilization of modern times, and is by some declared to be a very wicked place, yet, compared with what it was in Black Beard's day, it is the very garden of the Lord.

Judging from outward appearances, religion at Nassau is built upon a very democratic basis. In their public assemblies all are "one in Christ." There is no "color line."

No seats are set apart in the churches, where the white element preponderates, for colored people. The blood of the two races is greatly and curiously mixed, mingled, and combined. The line that marks the division between day and night is not more uncertain and difficult to determine than the color line in Nassau. A prominent white citizen informed us, and it seemed both to amuse and astonish him, that the whites upon Abaco island persist in exclusively occupying one side of the church. These people, who place such a high value upon their blood, descended, he said, from the pirates! Much to their chagrin the Governor appointed a negro to fill the office of resident magistrate upon that island, because he excelled them in a competitive examination. The black squire occupied a seat in the isle which separated the "children of darkness" from the "children of light."

Many of the visitors at Nassau find in fishing pleasant and useful occupation for some of their leisure hours. Arrangements for boats and bait are consummated, the party made up, and the time and place agreed upon a day or two in advance. The expenses, divided per capita among the gentlemen forming the party, are trifling. Good sailing and good fishing can be calculated upon with confidence, as it is very rare indeed that there is any failure of a favorable wind, or of an abundance of piscatory game. The boatmen are accustomed to bring "the catch" to the court of the hotel, where their captors, with a laudable pride exhibit the substantial evidences of their skill. Sometimes a huge shark is thus exhibited. The great variety of the fish, (often a dozen or more different kinds,) the large size of most, and the brilliant colors and wonderful beauty of many when first taken from the water, attract the attention of the guests of the hotel, and secure many exclamations of astonishment and pleasure. Some usually are then given to the hotel steward, and the balance to the boatmen. But the dead sharks often yield up their large and well armed jaws, and sometimes their spinal columns, as trophies to their captors, who esteem them as souvenirs.

It is often amusing, and always interesting, to watch and listen to the boatmen while they canvass for customers. In this business Sampson is an adept, and always eminently conspicuous. His good sense, experience, volubility and zealous and persistent attention to his business, place him naturally in advance of his competitors. His dress is always neat and showy, but his wardrobe is evidently pretty well stocked, for he frequently blossoms out in costumes of varied styles and colors. Neither does his ever active tongue vibrate always alike, or his thoughts and illustrations run in the same well oiled groove. We add a little pen picture as a sample of what is daily seen and heard on such occasions.

To a group of gentlemen and ladies sitting cosily in large arm chairs in the cool shade of the court of the Royal Victoria, Sampson is telling his story, and answering questions. He is about six feet high, muscular, well-formed, bright, active, ingenious, good-natured, and cunning. He on this occasion sports a clean, white jacket, with a wide turn-over collar, lined with blue cloth, and having a white line running round it. Its pockets are adorned with blue binding. In one of the pockets is a white handkerchief, ornamented with red lines and red corners. His shirt has no collar, but it is well laundried, and its bosom sports a gold stud. A substantial palm leaf hat of good quality rests jauntily a little on one side of his head, the body of which is encircled and almost covered with a wide, black ribbon, upon which is stamped in golden capitals, the word "TRIDENT," the name of his yacht. He has on a pair of neat, dark colored, woolen pantaloons, turned up a trifle at the bottom, which, by their length, are suggestive of the probable fact that they once belonged to a man who boasted a longer and probably whiter pair of legs.

He addresses his remarks more particularly to several gentlemen who arrived in the last steamer, with a dignity and gravity calculated to inspire respect and confidence. He insists that

"If de gentlemen choose ter go, dare aint no difficulty 'bout der fish—I ken promise yer dat. We'll just anchor der boat at soundings, with her tail to der ocean, when we get where der fish ar. The moment I gets over whar dey ar, you haint got to feel for 'em, but jess pull 'em in. If der sharks don't bother yer, there's no mistake about it. We ken wait till Thursday, 'cause der wind is sou-east now; it will be south to-morrow, and Thursday she'll fetch 'round all right. I want to wait till Thursday, 'cause I know for sure Thursday."

"Is there no danger of accident, Sampson?"

"Deres no trouble if der boatman don't lose his head. Samson has got along so far and never lost his head, thank God. I never had any accident; God has spar'd me thus far; hope I shall alers get along and not lose my head."

"Sampson, now tell us truly, have you ever studied circumnavigation?"

"I karnt say honest, I knows dat. I don't claim I ever larned circumnavigation; but I do know for sure that I ken sail der Trident any whar in dese yer waters when any one can, and I don't kar who he is."

"But how about the sharks, Sampson?"

"Der sharks bother us sometimes. Dey comes in wid der tide. T'other day one jest swallowed der bait, hook and all, and towed der boat where he liked. We wouldn't let him go, and der shark couldn't get away. After that my boat hit him with an oar and confused him. We brought him ashore, and had him in a hand-cart, a great big fellow. It was a bonnet-cub shark. We'll kill some when we go fishing, but they'll not let us bring 'em ashore now 'cause of der smell."

"You call 'em *bonnet*-cub sharks—why is that?"

"Kause there's something 'bout dar heads that looks like an old fashion ladies' bonnet."

"Aren't the sharks dangerous, Sampson? Don't they sometimes attack men?"

"I never see 'em hurt any one. One year arter der war I was a diving for conchs, the water was deep, and I took der first shell I could find. Then I has a way of putting my foot on der bottom and giving a shove to come up. I was finning up, and when I got near my boat, what did I see but a great big bonnet-cub lying there looking at me. He was seventeen feet long. Wasn't I skar'd! He was as long as my boat. He looked at me kinder anxious like. When I got to my boat I rolled in all in a heap, quicker—you may bet on that. He just missed me. He 'peared disappointed like, wiggled his tail and went off. I've been skar'd ever since. I don't forget his eye and der look he gin me. I never knew dey had eyes in der outer edge of der heads that way afore."

"You don't mean to say, Sampson, that you was afraid of a shark?"

"I mean to say he confused me. I had a heap rather look at 'em from der Trident, den to see 'em star at Sampson in der water so wicked, der way he did."

"But do you think if they are not disturbed they will attack people? Some say if you splash the water it will frighten them away; that they are timid, or at least cautious and scary."

"Every one of 'em will eat men. I wouldn't trust any of em. Der last shark we caught had a dozen fish in him, and leads, and lines, and hooks, all to pieces in him. We got one t'other day seven feet long. Some are twelve feet and more. A man went fishing some time ago to Andros island, in his boat. His name was Carter. He didn't come back. They 'spected something had happened, and sarched for him next day. When they got near der reef whar he war, they saw his boat—der man, he warnt there. The boat either swamped or tipped over. It had some turtle and fish in it he had caught. Der man was gone. Afterwards, two large cubs were seen cruising 'bout dar. One was caught, and in him they found some turtles and two-quarters of a man—so I 'spose der sharks divided even."

Sampson's persistent zeal and unfailing eloquence made him always a success in securing his full share of business, and his experience and skill as a boatman were always conceded by his customers.

CHAPTER X.

> "The winds, full of sound—they go whispering by,
>   As if some immortal had stooped from the sky,
>   And breathed out a blessing—and flown!"—JOHN NEAL.

FOR safe and attractive boating facilities, Nassau is pre-eminently distinguished. Its navigable waters combine more elements of varied beauty than we often see crowded into the same number of square miles. In ordinary weather, when the bosom of the ocean gently rises and falls in graceful undulations, the eye searches in vain for some trace of the grand, the thrilling and the sublime. The waters ripple with a silvery and soothing melody.

> "The airs we feel,
>   Which 'round us steal,
>   Seem murmuring to the murmuring keel."

Clouds of satin and silver float in the soft air, the fitting drapery of slowly moving but invisible gods of idleness and repose; while upon the sea and its fairy isles, in unending variety, are seen in great profusion, the evidences of a hand divine, **that**

155

adorns with exquisite loveliness, all forms and every variety of matter which it touches.

There being no mountains upon any of the Bahamas, and no high surrounding hills, those who seek for health and pleasure upon the water at Nassau, have very little to apprehend from sudden and dangerous gusts of wind during the visiting season. These, sometimes occur, but the Bahama winds blow with remarkable uniformity and steadiness. There is, at times, too much wind, but it is rarely unsafe to sail in Nassau harbor, on account of its strength, and we were only twice becalmed, and then only for a short time. On one of these occasions, we soon came in with the tide.

The Nassau yachts, as a rule, have a good breadth of beam, are strong and staunch, and with competent boatmen at the helm, they are much safer than ocean steamers. They have no complicated machinery to get out of order, no large and infernal looking furnaces to threaten purgatorial fires in advance of the appointed time, and no high pressure steam boilers or drunken officials to blow one up. It is true, however, that the master of a Nassau pleasure boat is just as liable to be overcome with liquor as the officers of steamships, but they do not have bar rooms on board their yachts, and if sober when they take their passengers on board, it may be safely assumed that they will remain so until the return of the boat to her dock.

It is reported that Captain Sampson, a few years ago, sometimes when on shore, failed to put a sufficient quantity of water in his rum, or, to speak perhaps more charitably, occasionally, by mistake, put more rum in his water than was necessary to neutralize the effects of the unhealthy salts it contained when taken from Nassau wells, and that, like his great namesake, when on a certain occasion his hair was cut too short, he was **temporarily weakened and unmanned.**

But Sampson's good sense proved to be stronger than his appetite, and the native force of his character secured a very creditable victory for his higher moral nature, and vindicated the goodness and strength of his judgment. When sailing with him on one occasion, after we had delicately alluded to this subject, he said,—"I ha'nt drinked no sperits since '76. I know'd it wouldn't do. Why, when I used to drink, I was 'fered to talk to the missuses—'cause I 'fered they'd smell my breth. But now I isn't 'fered at all. I goes 'round 'em, and 'mong 'em, and *to windward of 'em*, or any how—and none of 'em kan't smell no liker when Sampson talks to 'em, 'bout goen sailen in his boat."

We have been informed that in Boston harbor several lives are lost every summer from the capsizing of pleasure boats; that Boston yachts are long and narrow, and that in their construction, as well as in sailing them, safety is subordinated to speed. But here, surrounded by intricate channels, and the waters abounding with submerged rocks and reefs, where the vessels of commerce, in formidable numbers, are stranded, and the business of "wrecking" is pursued by many of the islanders under licenses purchased of the government, we have yet to learn of an instance where a serious accident has ever happened to a pleasure boat. The "Triton" carries eight thousand pounds of iron ballast and draws five feet of water. It grounded once when we were on board of her, upon a bank of coral, and a ton of ballast was thrown overboard to get her off, but Sampson declared such a thing never happened to the "Triton" before, and he would not have the affair known for fifty dollars. He was overboard in the water so long trying to get her off, and was so excited and nervous about it, that, alas for the fast color of his ebony complexion, he fairly turned white. Aided by the friendly crew of a passing boat, the "Triton" was extricated from her difficulty at last, and the diplomatic Sampson made all his pas-

14

sengers happy by a perfect shower of encomiums upon the noble
and unexampled manner in which they " laughed at their calamity," declaring that never in his life had he before seen ladies
and gentlemen behave so well.

An old U. S. naval commander, (Capt. Fox), addressing our
favorite yachtman one day, said:

" When you go out with sailing parties and have ladies on
board, why don't you take along your small boat, for, ballasted
with 8,000 lbs. of iron, if the 'Triton' should upset she would
go right straight to the bottom like a shot.   In the United States
navy they will not allow a boat to be ballasted with anything
but water, so that it cannot sink.   Now, with four tons of ballast
on board, what would you do should your boat with its load of
passengers upset?"

With emphatic and graceful gestures and a flashing eye, Sampson answered:

" But de 'Triton' karn't upset—'tis impossible.   Why I sails
all round dese yere waters in all kinds 'er weather for mor'n ten
years, and I knows what she ken do, and I tells yer der 'Triton'
karn't upset—kause I wont let 'er."

" Well, Sampson, you think she'll not upset, and a great many
men as experienced and capable of managing boats as you are,
and equally confident, have been drowned at last.   Now why
don't you take your small boat along so that if an accident happens, and you have ladies on board, they may be saved?"

" I say," replied Sampson, speaking with an energy and earn-
estness with which a native deference, respect and politeness were
singularly and pleasantly combined, " I know'd what der Triton
ken do; for many a time, when I ha'nt got no passengers, I goes
all alone by myself and tries her in every place 'bout yese here
waters, and I studies her, and tries her, and larns what she ken
do, and I tells yer—not to say as how I do'snt 'spect your opinion

—I knows de Triton, and I knows she karn't upset—'taint possable—'cause Sampson wont let her. Why, Sampson karn't 'ford ter have 'er upset—'twould ruin him. I couldn't live. No; I keeps watch all der time; I keeps my eye on 'er; I doesn't 'pend on luffin' 'er up alone, but yer see—with one hand on her tiller, I hold the main-sheet in t'other hand on a bite, so I ken instantly shake der wind all out of 'er main-sail if I seed it coming nor furrer den dat house. And if I 'spects der wind any, I makes one man hold 'er jib sheet on a flying turn—'cause e'en if I empties 'er main-sheet, der wind in der jib mite upset her—no sah! I tells yer der Triton can't upset—'cause Sampson wont let 'er. But I 'spects yer opinion, an' 'twont do no harm to take der small boat along—but no sah! she karnt upset."

And Capt. Charley Mitchell, (now, we regret to say, deceased,) between whom and Sampson a friendly rivalry formerly existed, upon another occasion expressed equal confidence in the Frolic, (a center-board yacht which he sailed,) and in his ability to avoid serious accidents while prosecuting his vocation in water around the island of New Providence. "Why," said he, "now s'pose Mr. I., ye're way off heah, ever so far from yer home, with only a hundred dollars in yer pocket—wouldn't you be karful of dem hundred dollars? Wouldn't yer mind and study how yer spend 'em? Well, now, der Frolic is for Mitchell dem hundred dollars. No, sah! Mitchell isn't gwine to lose his boat, 'cause he'd starve."

It is pleasant at times, notwithstanding some increase of danger, to sail outside the natural breakwaters of the harbor of Nassau, and cultivate a more intimate acquaintance with an ocean which has and requires great continents to restrain and confine it when tossed and maddened by the tempests, or when stirred to its profoundest depths by the hurricane. A little peril adds an agreeable condiment to prosaic life, and breaks a monotony which finally becomes oppressive even in an atmosphere that

seems ever freighted with sensuous pleasures, and never stimulates
to heroic deeds, or to labors and duties which in colder latitudes
characterize all forms of life outside of the vegetable kingdom.
We were therefore predisposed to respond favorably to the proposition of Sampson, when, upon the morning of the 20th of March,
1879, the day the equinoctial storm arrives at the north, if it is
on time, he proposed that, as the wind was more lively than
usual, a few gentlemen should put the Triton to the test as an
ocean boat by going outside the bar.   He is always a ready and
fluent speaker, but on this occasion he seemed to have more and
better wind than usual to fill the capacious sails of his eloquence.
Like his great namesake, of biblical fame and memory, he accomplishes great results with a " jaw-bone."

"I don't want no ladies dis time," said he, " there's a leetle
too much wind to take der ladies along.   I jess want to shake all
der reefs out of der Triton's sails and let her go.   I'd like for
once to show der gemmen what der Triton ken do."

Half an hour afterwards two gentlemen and the author were
seated in Sampson's boat, and flying down the harbor of Nassau
under full sail.   Amos, from Harbour Island, a colored man of
much nautical experience in Bahama waters, and of more than
average ability, was greatly complimented by the captain, because,
without waiting to be told, he went quietly to work and prepared
the yacht before crossing the bar for the washings he evidently
anticipated she was destined to get.   He lashed to the boat the
anchor and the oars, put carpets and cushions away in the little
forecastle, made fast every coil of rope, got ready for immediate
use the large sponges which are here employed to keep boats dry,
and brought out for the use of the passengers oil-cloth suits, more
useful than ornamental, and sufficiently capacious to keep the
salt water on the outside of a man in case the ill-mannered waves,
presuming too much on our very limited acquaintance, should

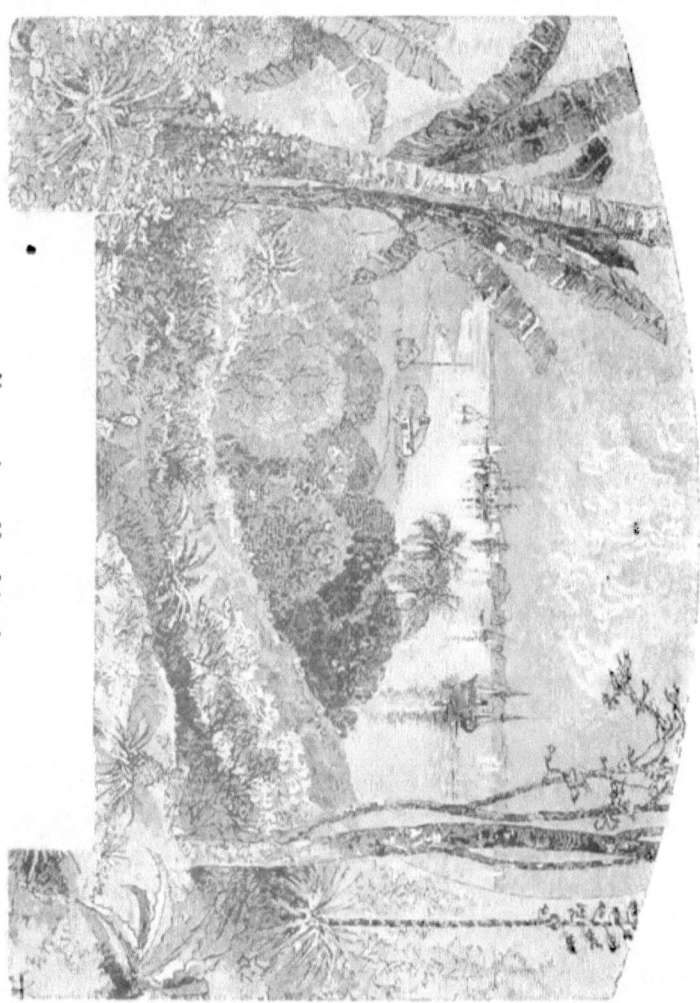

Nassau from Hog Island.

persistently attempt to take possession of our temporary "house and home." William, also from one of the outer islands, obeyed orders, and made himself generally useful.

We were soon out upon the broad Atlantic, and Sampson, like the rider of a winning horse at a race, experienced a gratification he could not entirely conceal, as, with the gracefulness and seeming speed of a sea gull, his yacht pluckily met and mounted the high rolling billows, which we could not but remember had, in their angry moods, strewn with wrecks the neighboring shores. A portion of one of those wrecks was in sight, being all that remains of a blockade runner, whose captain took his steamer to the left instead of the right of Nassau lighthouse. Some claim the officers were all drunk; others say, "it was a put up job;" but all the boatmen united in affirming, that, as a consequence, "boots and shoes were plenty on Hog Island"—those articles having constituted a part of her cargo. Certain it is, that having sailed out of Nassau harbor one afternoon, the vessel returned in the evening of the same day, and was beached. Sampson said, with an exultant chuckle, after alluding to the cargo scattered along the shore, that "der Cap'n mistake Nassau light for der 'Hole in der Wall,'" (a well known light upon Abaco, nearly sixteen miles distant.)

The larger waves moved towards us in stately grandeur, in a regular order of succession, as if marshaled and marching over the bosom of the ocean under the guidance and direction of some invisible god of the seas. After every nine smaller waves had passed by, and under us, the long liquid platoon was marked and bounded by a billow whose approach was watched with much interest, and with an exhilarating but peculiar pleasure, as it would often not only wash our forecastle and submerge our gunnels, but drench us from head to foot, and make lively work for William and his sponges. The pure ocean air, pleasantly cool

and more than usually lively: the soft white clouds moving so
majestically across the clear blue sky: the exquisite beauty of
the islands and keys, and of the city of Nassau, which quietly
rested upon the rocky hillside, spiced with an excitement produced by a sail designed to demonstrate " what der Triton could
do " in a free wind outside of the shelter which the natural breakwaters of Nassau afford—all combined to give us a very high
degree of exquisite and unalloyed pleasure.

After we had sailed in a northerly direction out into the ocean
to vindicate the truth of Sampson's claims in reference to the
good qualities of the Triton in rough water, we sailed in an
easterly or northeasterly direction along the windward side of
Hog Island, crossed Silver Key bar, entered water that seemed as
warm as any confined and heated by a July sun upon a northern
shore—skirted the southern line of Silver Key—passed through
"the Marine Garden," a region of submarine coral bowers of
marvelous and wondrous beauty, situated between the east end
of Hog Island and the west end of Athol Island,—then, turning
to the west, we traversed the easterly portion of the harbor of
Nassau, and were landed safely at the stone steps of the wharf
which we had left some three hours before. The latter portion
of our sail having been in waters somewhat sheltered, Sampson
was better able to amuse us with a chapter or two taken from the
volume of his personal experience.

The account he gave of his visit in the summer of 1878 to the
city of New York was particularly interesting. The impression
made upon his wondering and astonished mind, graphically and
faithfully described, furnished an entertainment of the most droll
and comical character. Quick to see, sensitive to feel, and gifted
to describe with a genius and eloquence all his own, this unlettered
and untraveled negro, mounted upon any northern platform,
could not have failed to convulse and bring down the house.

Never before had he left the peaceful quiet of this little island world. Passing over nearly a thousand miles of a solitude such as only the immense, pathless, treeless wastes of the ocean can produce, he landed at last in that immense, seething, boiling, noisy whirlpool of intensified human life—the great city of New York. Afraid of being cheated—afraid of being robbed—afraid of being run over—afraid of being, in a hundred ways new to him, killed—not merely a stranger in a new land, but an ignorant, semi-tropical, Bahama African in a babel and pandemonium far surpassing anything his imagination had ever conceived, he seemed for a time to have every particle of life taken out of him. The ferryboats, constantly passing and repassing loaded with passengers—the immense labyrinth of streets and avenues, stretching away in every direction farther than he could see—the great, elaborate and expensive buildings of every description—the street railroads, and particularly the vast crowds that made it necessary to carry people on elevated railroads over the heads of those rushing in a ceaseless tide below—and the loud, harsh, deafening and infernal mingling of noises that ever ascended day and night—all wonderfully impressed him, and revealed a much more new and strange world to him than his own Bahamas did to Columbus nearly four hundred years ago. He got lost in New York seven times the first day after his arrival; paid ten cents to go to Central Park, and, after a long ride, he was astonished (and almost scared at the seeming witchcraft) to find himself at the precise place he started from. "Why," said he, "der ting had turned round and I know'd nothing 'bout it, and I had to pay my ten cents over agin." He still retains a vivid impression of the delicious flavor of northern strawberries, but ate so many he declared that at night "dey confused" his stomach. His sea voyage seasoned to his taste everything he ate. "Why," said he, "I'd give more for jess wun mutton chop like as dat I had in New

York, den for all der mutton in Nassau." Though much interested in, he was glad to escape from New York, and affirmed
that he did not get the deafening din of its horrible noises out
of his head for more than two weeks after he left that city.

For two or three hours after we landed, we were busy at times
wiping the crystals of salt out of our eyes, which were occasioned
by the waves outside of Nassau light endeavoring to take possession of our boat. As we recall this rather foolhardy sail, it brings
to mind the anecdote of the newly-converted negro who was per-
suaded to be baptized by immersion in the ocean, and having
accidently slipped from the grasp of the officiating clergyman
while his woolly head was under water, declared, so soon as he
could get the sea out of his eyes and mouth—"Some gemman
kum nare losing a good nigger by dis yere cussed foolishness."

Man is a gregarious animal, and when circumstances bring together a large number of persons who are mostly strangers to
each other, they soon feel the influence of some subtle social law,
and form into groups. The foolish walk in company over the
paths of folly in search of pleasure. Here music binds together
with her tuneful strings and harmonious cords, those whose
hearts are attuned to melody. There, sparkling wit, and amusing story, and clever anecdote, flash and scintillate from the
crystalizing centers of another happy group. The staid, sedate,
practical, matter-of-fact people, in their little corner, meditate
and moralize upon the solid and substantial things of life, and
mourn over the fast and foolish ways and the constantly increasing extravagance of the present degenerate age. Some are solitary, and get all the light and heat they seem to need by burning
oil in their own little lamps.

We cannot explain how it happened, but at Nassau we generally found ourselves surrounded by congenial people. We frequently speculated upon what we had lost by not having known

them before, and wondered, when we finally separated, if we should ever meet in this world again.

The yachting circles to which we were attached, form clusters of unfading flowers in the garden of memory. They were composed of persons as enthusiastic as we were in their expressions of delight when viewing the exquisite beauties of the Bahama isles and waters. Some were successful merchants from the cities of the great west, who had run away from business, and left all their heavy cares behind them. They seemed as gay and sportive as children at play. Light-hearted and joyous, they winged with a peculiar pleasure the flying hours. A log was kept, and it was the source of much amusement. Its keeper, being the head of the log, was voted to be, without any intentional disrespect to the turtles, a loggerhead. Many wandering ideas and gay fancies were shot on the wing, captured, and embalmed in its pages. It contained much entirely new matter, which never had been before and never will be again added to the wide domain of letters.

Several portable mills ground out upon the water detached stanzas of machine poetry. It was soon suspected that some of our party, when preparing to enter upon the voyage of life, had made mistakes, and gotten on board the wrong boats. Teas and not tragedies, sugars and not songs, pork instead of poetry, had occupied their time and engrossed their thoughts, to the great loss of themselves and the world.

A dignified, courtly gentleman, who, several years before, had crossed the dividing line which runs mid-way between youth and old age, and in whose bright and pleasant eyes humor was lurking in ambush, on one of our sailing excursions perpetrated the following:

> We venture in the gay Gazelle,
> Because with Amos all is well,
> But what may happen none can tell.

Instantly, upon his giving utterance to the last word of the last line, a lady added as a refrain or snapper,—"my mudder!" borrowing it from a tenderly filial poem which little Sankey sometimes gave us, standing in a chair in the court of the hotel. It would have brought down the house had there been one.

This caused the crank of another mill to revolve, and the following stanza was thereupon ground out:

> Who learned us all this much to tell,
> While sailing in the gay Gazelle,
> And o'er us came this magic spell?
>   My mudder.

After the laughter and applause had sufficiently subsided, a third stanza was added by still another of our happy group, as our yacht glided before the wind.

> To landsmen all we say, farewell!
> Your troubled hearts you now may quell,
> With Capt. Amos all is well;
>   My mudder.

A lady contributed in pencil the following, which was read by the keeper of the Log:

A POEM.   CANTO I.

> It was in breezy, blustering March
>   That we, a jolly crew,
> Went sailing in the gay Gazelle
>   Upon the waters blue.

>   To be continued.

This literary gem was deemed all that could be expected in such a climate as the result of mill work for one forenoon.

The loggerhead, meanwhile, had not been idle, and occasionally added a stanza to complete the literary bill of fare. We give them connectedly:

Like mountain lake—as smooth and calm—
  The waves are hushed in dreamy sleep,
While perfumes float from isles of balm,
  And murmuring voices from the deep.

We float like sea-birds on the tide,
  We tread the deep with muffled keel,
Like spirits of the air we glide,
  And something of their rest we feel.

Like sunset isles in western skies,
  Where viewless spirits joyous flit,
Before us lie the coral isles,
  And happy angels, wingless, sit.

When weary toilers picture heaven,
  Unending rest is their ideal;
That boon to coral isles is given,
  Here soon we learn that heaven is real.

On some of these excursions we took along Thompson's " Castle of Indolence," and when the wind was not too strong, it was read aloud and very greatly appreciated. It seemed as if its author must have visited the Bahamas before composing the poem, his pictures so perfectly mirror what one there ever sees and feels. Take, for example, the following:

" A pleasing land of drowsy head it was,
  Of dreams that wave before the half-shut eye,
And of gay castles in the clouds that pass,
  Forever flushing 'round a summer sky;
There ekes the soft delights that witchingly
  Instil a wanton softness through the breast."

While sailing in the Bahama waters, the famous sargasso or gulf weed, cannot fail to attract attention. It is constantly in sight, and in that portion of the ocean world, is

> "Ever drifting, drifting, drifting
>   On the shifting
> Currents of the restless main."

Columbus encountered it upon his first voyage to the new world, a few days after he left the Canary islands. The frequent mention which he makes of it in his journal is evidence that it abounded then as now. He also noticed the crabs that it contained—for little crustacea, it seems, have long been accustomed to have their domicils in these fragile and floating abodes, which, no doubt, withstand the violence of an angry ocean better than the strongest ships of oak and iron that man can make. This weed is sometimes encountered in such quantities as to constitute what has not been inappropriately termed "sea gardens."

The following very interesting and suggestive description, we copy from Kingsley's "At Last:"

"One glance at a bit of the weed as it floats past, shows that it is like no fucus of our shores, or anything we ever saw before. The difference in looks is indefinable in words, but clear enough. One sees in a moment that the sargassos, of which there are several species on tropical shores, are a genus of themselves and by themselves; and a certain awe may, if the beholder be at once scientific and poetical, come over him at the first sight of this famous and unique variety thereof, which has lost ages since the habit of growing on rock or sea bottom, but propagates itself forever floating; and feeds among its branches a whole family of fish, crabs, cuttlefish, zoophytes and mollusks, which, like the plant that shelters them, are found no where else in the world. And that awe, springing from the "scientific use of the imagination," would be increased if he recollected the theory—not altogether impossible, that this sargasso (and possibly some of the animals which cling to it), marks the sight of an Atlantic continent sunk long ages since; and that, transformed by the necessities of life from a rooting to a floating plant,

"Still it remembers its august abodes,"

and wanders 'round and 'round as if in search of the rocks where it once grew."

"When fresh out of the water it resembles not a sea weed so much as a sprig of a willow leaved shrub, burdened with yellow berries, large and small; for every broken bit of it seems growing and throwing out ever new berries and leaves—or what for want of a better word, must be called leaves in a sea weed. For it must be remembered that the frond of a seaweed is not merely leaf, but root also; that it not only breathes air, but feeds on water; and that even the so-called root by which a seaweed holds to the rock is really only an anchor, holding mechanically to the stone, but not deriving, as the root of a land plant would, any nourishment from it, therefore it is that to grow while uprooted and floating, though impossible to most land plants, is easy enough to many seaweeds, and especially to the sargasso."

The expense of yachting at Nassau is generally apportioned per capita, and the charges of the boatmen are quite moderate, so that a great deal of enjoyment is thereby secured for a very little money. Although there is a good circulation of air on shore, the change to that of the harbor is, when the hot sun is well up, a decided improvement, and outside of the barrier keys the wind over the ocean seemed more strongly medicated and tonic. For sanitary reasons, therefore, we would strongly recommend Nassau visitors to spend a portion of each pleasant day

15

upon the water. There is no part of our Nassau experiences which, when far away, gives us more happiness in the retrospect; and often

> The white-winged boats with sable crew,
>   The fleecy clouds that draped the skies,
> The gales of health that constant blew,
>   The waters striped with brilliant dies,
> The cradle-waves that ever rocked
>   'Gainst far off cloud-embroidered wall,
> The skies whose blue the deep sea mocked,
>   The sunny hearts that gilded all—
> Return with e'en an added power
> To brighten many an idle hour.

CHAPTER XI.

> " The breath of a celestial clime,
> As if from heaven's wide open gates did flow
> Health and refreshment on the world below."—BRYANT.

IF Nassau has any great value to the American people, it is as a health resort. It is claimed to be the " Great Sanitarium of the Western World." Much that is written and published upon this subject is inspired by personal interest, and in such cases a one-sided and warped presentation of the facts of the case is a natural consequence. Many confidently express crude opinions, hastily formed, and bottomed upon a few ill-digested surface facts, and thus act the part of blind leaders of the blind. We have strongly felt the great responsibility which rests upon those who volunteer their advice or opinion in matters so important.

It is not without a good deal of hesitation that we publish the result of our diagnosis of the Bahamas. We made the best of our limited opportunities, and we have endeavored to collect and decide upon the facts with judicial fairness. We do not ask the reader to adopt our views, but only to take our testimony for what it may seem to be worth, and to consider it in connection with that of others whose opinions may be entitled to more weight.

The climate of the Bahamas, in its normal condition, seemed to us fairly described in the lines we have quoted at the commencement of this chapter, although they were written of the mountain air of Western Massachusetts. But when the poet declares—(we substitute the word "ocean" for "mountain")—that

> "Suns cannot make
> In this pure air the plague that walks unseen;
> The ocean wind, that faints not in thy ray,
> Sweeps the blue stream of pestilence away,"

he states what cannot be truthfully said of Nassau or its suburbs, and what is not probably true of any of the thickly inhabited portions of the globe.

Nothing is easier than to poison the purest air. Without constant care and vigilance, the waste matter—the sewage incident to permanent abodes—will become any and everywhere, (the regions of unending frost alone excepted,) the prolific source of disease and death. Through window and door, through crack and crevice the pestilence will enter. Nature affixes penalties to her sanitary laws which execute themselves. The code of health which she has established is learned at a fearful cost in sick rooms, in cemeteries, and in mortuary records. In pushing our inquiries into the sanitary conditions of Nassau, it will not do to look only at her ocean winds, "the breath of a celestial clime." We must examine "the earth, and the waters under the earth." It is proverbial that there may be "death in the pot;" but we should never forget that it is equally true that there is often death in the pitcher and the pail; and good physicians in our day, when a malignant disease is developed, immediately examine the character and condition of the water supply.

The reader must, in regard to this question of health, keep ever in mind those peculiarities of the Bahama islands which we have endeavored to describe. Perfectly shielded from the cold by the Gulf stream, which throws its warm, wide, watery arm around them on the west and north—a shield which the frost king finds absolutely impenetrable—it is ensured an atmosphere of unending summer. Winter, in our sense of the word, is literally unknown; while, at the same time, the islands are exempt from the dry, scorching heat, which banishes the white race from tropical regions in many parts of the world. The polar currents, aqueous and aerial, are completely transformed when they encounter the Gulf Stream, and all the discomfort is quickly taken out of them, so that the Bahamas, languidly reclining in the lap of summer, are slightly but agreeably refreshed by the coldest winds that ever reach them from the north and west.

It is in this that their superiority as a winter resort for the American people over the states of the Gulf consists. Upon the main land, the north winds make a clear sweep to the Gulf of Mexico. There is nothing to obstruct their course. The valley of the Mississippi seems to have been scooped out to facilitate their progress. With the Appellachian chain of mountains on one side, and the Gulf Stream on the other, a great highway is formed for Boreas over both the land and water sides of our Atlantic coast. And he travels over it in his icy chariot altogether too frequently for the health and comfort of those who leave their northern homes to search for summer in either of the states of the south.

The remarkable uniformity of the temperature of Nassau will appear from an examination of the following meteorological table copied from the official report of Gov. Rawson for 1864, page 14, compiled from the records kept at Nassau's Military Observatory. It gives the "Mean of Daily Observations on Week Days for Ten Years, from 1855 to 1864."

Months.	Thermometer at 9 A. M.			Wind at 9 A. M.				Rainfall on Ground in Month. Inches.
	Max.	Med.	Min.	Four Chief Points in Order of Prevalence.				
Jan.	75	70	66	N. E.	E.	S. E.	N.	2.4
Feb.	76	71	66	N. E.	E.	S. E.	S.	2.4
Mar.	78	72	66	E.	S. E.	N. E.	N.	4.5
April	81	75	68	N. E.	E.	S.	S. E.	2.4
May	84	78	71	N. E.	S. E.	E.	S.	6.9
June	83	81	74	S. E.	E.	N. E.	S.	6.4
July	88	82	75	E.	S. E.	S.	N. E.	6.5
Aug.	88	81	75	E.	S. E.	S.	N. E.	6.7
Sept.	86	81	75	E.	N. E.	S. E.	N.	5.2
Oct.	82	77	73	N. E.	E.	S. E.	N.	7.4
Nov.	79	74	70	N. E.	E.	E.	S. E.	2.8
Dec.	77	73	69	N. E.	E.	S. E.	N.	2.4
Average	82	76	71					4.6

From the foregoing and from an examination of other special tables contained in his report, Gov. Rawson draws the following conclusions:

1. *Barometer.* That the mean height of the barometer at Nassau is exactly thirty inches.

2. That it attains its greatest height in the three months from December to February, and is lowest in October and November.

3. That there is a constant difference in the observations taken in the morning and afternoon, averaging for the whole period a decrease of 0.05 height in the afternoon.

4. That the difference between the average of maximum and minimum observations in the ten years has fluctuated between 0.25 and 0.46.

Thermometer. 1. That the four months, June to September, are the hottest, and of nearly equal temperature, viz.: 88°.

2. That January, February and March are the three coldest months, and of nearly equal temperature, viz.: 66°.

3. That the greatest maximum heat exceeds the average heat by not more than 12°, and that the greatest minimum falls short of it 10°. The extreme variation, therefore, is 22°.

Rainfall. 1. That the chief yearly rainfall is from May to October, and is heaviest in October. During these six months it amounted to forty-four inches, and during the remaining six months to nineteen inches; and that the greatest rainfall does not correspond with the greatest pressure of wind.

Wind. 1. That the highest winds prevail in November and January, and the average from October 1st, March inclusive, greatly exceeds the average of the remaining six months, and that there is little difference between morning and afternoon.

2. That north-easterly and easterly winds are the most prevalent from September to February, during which months they blow during one-half or two-thirds of the whole time. Northerly winds seldom blow except during those months, and then only for three days in a month. From June to August, the average is less than a day. Easterly and south-easterly winds prevail chiefly from March to August. South-western are most prevalent in February and March, to the extent of two to three days in a month; westerly winds from February to April to the extent only of one to one and a-half days in a month, and dur-

ing the rest of the year of less than a day monthly; northwesters from November to March, about two days in a month. Their relative frequency throughout the year is shown in the following statement of the percentage proportion of days in a year, during which they prevailed at 9 A. M.

North,	7.2 per cent.	South,	11.0 per cent.
North-east,	26.2 "	South-west,	5.0 "
East,	24.4 "	West,	2.3 "
South-east,	18.6 "	North-west,	5.3 "

The following tables are copied from official reports:

METEOROLOGICAL TABLE FOR 1878.

Months.	THERMOMETER.				RAINFALL.		
	Max. in shade at 9 A. M.	Min. in shade at 9 A. M.	Max. in sun in 24 hours.	Mean at 3 P. M	Rainfall, Inches.	Number of rainy days	Max. fall in 24 hours
January,	76.5	61.0	140.0	73.3	5.15	16	1.10
February,	78.0	62.5	146.0	73.9	7.05	11	2.00
March,	82.5	65.2	149.5	76.7	2.36	7	1.05
April,	82.2	70.0	150.2	80.4	3.19	8	1.00
May,	86.5	75.5	156.5	81.8	7.28	7	2.40
June,	89.8	71.0	154.0	84.0	6.56	19	1.60
July,	89.5	74.5	159.0	85.8	6.05	20	1.88
August,	88.8	78.8	157.9	85.8	9.25	18	2.13
September,	87.2	78.0	153.0	84.2	7.15	24	1.60
October,	83.5	75.5	153.0	81.1	7.37	12	4.50
November,	79.0	71.0	157.5	76.1	2.84	10	1.21
December,	77.5	65.8	155.0	73.8	1.38	7	0.55
Sums,	1001.0	848.8	1830.7	956.9	65.64	159	21.02
Means,	83.5	70.7	152.6	79.7	5.47	13	1.75

METEOROLOGICAL TABLE FOR 1879.

Months	THERMOMETER.				RAINFALL.			
	Max. in shade at 9 A. M.	Min. in shade at 9 A. M	Max. in sun in 24 hours.	Min. in sun at 3 P. M.	Rainfall, Inches.	Number of rainy days.	Max. fall in 24 hours.	Date.
January, ...	77.0	61 0	145.0	73.6	0 92	6	0 41	23
February, ...	76.5	64.2	148.0	74.4	1.29	8	0 95	11
March, ...	78 5	69.5	153.5	75.6	2.84	6	2 45	14
April, ...	82.8	73.5	154.0	78.8	0.42	5	0 20	3
May, ...	83 8	70.5	155.5	80 5	3.85	13	0 90	9
June, ...	85.5	74.0	155 0	82 4	12.77	14	5.37	26
July, ...	88.0	71 2	157.0	85 3	7.43	18	1.80	30
August, ...	88.5	77 0	157.0	86.4	9.85	13	3 11	16
September, ...	87.5	70 0	153.5	84.6	8.02	20	2 27	13
October, ...	85 0	74 5	153 0	81.9	6.50	18½	1.60	25
November, ...	81.5	66 5	148.0	77.2	7.98	6	7.41	7
December, ...	78.2	67.0	150.5	76.6	1.60	11	0.95	1
Sums, ...	992.8	839.1	183.0	957.3	63.47	138½	27.42	
Means, ...	82.7	69.9	152.5	79.8	5.29	11	2.28	

Gov. Robinson vouches for the correctness of these tables by inserting them in his reports for the colonial Blue Books.

The weather was so charming when we were at Nassau in 1879, the thermometer at 7 A. M., week after week, marking substantially the same temperature, with no storms, and only an occasional shower, that Capt. Fox believed that we were favored with weather exceptionally good, and through the kindness of the librarian of the Nassau public library, he obtained from the Nassau military observatory the following table, showing the highest and lowest temperature and the rainfall at the end of every week, for six months, from November to April, both inclusive, for the years 1878 and 1879.

	1877.				1878.		
		Thermometer.				Thermometer.	
Week Ending	Rainfall.	Deg.	Deg.	Week Ending	Rainfall.	Deg.	Deg.
Nov. 3	.12	90	72	Nov. 2	.54	87	71
10	3.98	99	71	9	.19	81	67
17	.49	84	65	16	2.44	82	64
24	.24	82	66	23	.11	82	65
Dec. 1	.80	85	61	30	.10	85	66
8	.19	85	67	Dec. 7	.68	82	62
15	.00	78	65	14	.55	81	65
22	.20	78	67	21	.13	82	65
29	1.26	83	61	28	.02	82	63
	1878.				1879.		
Jan. 5	.00	80	56	Jan. 4	.00	83	62
12	1.50	82	61	11	.03	81	62
19	2.12	84	59	18	.05	85	62
26	.32	82	59	25	.84	83	58
Feb. 2	1.13	81	59	Feb. 1	.00	74	71
9	1.00	81	59	8	.03	74	64
16	2.19	85	62	15	1.09	74	68
23	1.44	83	60	22	.02	76	66
Mar. 2	2.42	84	61	29	.15	75	66
9	.40	83	63	Mar. 8	.10	72	69
16	.04	89	66	15	2.50	75	73
23	1.87	84	64	22	.24	76	73
30	.05	89	63	29	.00	78	76
April 6	.56	89	62	April 5	.20	80	74
13	1.20	83	61	12	.00	79	74
20	.31	86	65	19	.15	83	74
27	.22	85	67	26	.02	78	73

There are serious discrepancies between the tabulated reports which we are unable to reconcile or explain, and we give them to our readers as we find them. It appears that the temperature at Nassau from November, 1877, to May, 1878, was not very dif-

ferent from that of the same months in 1878 and '79; but the
rainfall during the same months in 1878 and '79, aggregated only
10.18 inches, while during the corresponding period in 1877 and
'78, it amounted to 24.05 inches. Indeed, during our visit in
1879, there was so little rain that a consequent failure of the
fruit crop was apprehended. The average rainfall for the ten
years covered by Gov. Rawson's summarized meteorological table,
during corresponding months, is 16.9 inches. It thus appears
that the Nassau weather from November, 1877, to May, 1878,
was very exceptionally wet, while during the next following corresponding period the weather was exceptionally dry.

While at Nassau in 1879, we were accustomed to daily observe
the thermometer and barometer, and a pencil meteorological
record upon the white wall of the hotel court was made by a very
intelligent and reliable gentleman from Canada, every morning
at 7 o'clock. The unvarying steadiness of the temperature and
atmospheric pressure, seemed so incredible to some of the guests,
that, half in earnest and half in jest, they declared that the thermometer and barometer had been "fixed up and doctored." I
give the state of the thermometer at 7 A. M., for each day, from
February 1st, to March 12th, inclusive:

1879—68, 67, 63, 64, 66, 68, 72, 77, 70, 70, 71, 70, 71, 70, 69,
68, 69, 71, 70, 69, 65, 65, 68, 70, 69, 70, 72, 72, 70, 69, 68, 69,
70, 69, 70, 70, 70, 70, 70, 71 degrees. For the four last days, at
two P. M., the thermometer stood at 75, 74, 74, 75 degrees, and
generally the difference between seven A. M. and two P. M. was
very small in the shade. The barometer varied but a trifle from
thirty inches.

But in the noon-day sun, especially in the narrow streets lead-
up from the water, over the hard, white limestone, and between
the high white-washed stone walls, the heat is very excessive,
and, but for the breeze that constantly blows from off the water,

it would be too much for any but salamanders and Congo negroes.
This side of the picture is seldom given to the public. The
tables I have copied from Gov. Robinson's reports are a marked
exception in this particular, to which the reader is referred. It
is easy, however, to avoid exposure at mid-day, and to take one's
rides or walks in the morning or in the latter part of the afternoon. While yachting, little inconvenience is experienced from
this cause, as it is customary to take along a supply of umbrellas
to assist the sails in throwing shadows upon the passengers. The
water is, without exception, of a most agreeable temperature,
and the tireless wind, that with remarkable constancy, ruffles its
surface, while leaving a tawny and enduring impress of its most
welcome caresses, is freighted with the grateful benisons, uttered
or unexpressed, of all who feel its cooling and rejuvenating influences. The simile, "as fickle as the wind," seemed there to
have little applicability.

Writing from beneath the shade of one of her noble moss draped
live oaks, at Mandarin, upon the right bank of the St. John's
river, in Florida, the gifted author of Uncle Tom's Cabin, speaking of Florida, says in her " Palm Leaves:"

"Sudden changes from heat to cold are the besetting sin of
this fallen world. It is probably one of the consequences of
Adam's fall, which we are not to get rid of till we get to the land
of pure delights. It may, however, comfort the heart of visitors
to Florida to know that if the climate here is not in this respect
just what they would have, it is about the best there is going."

If the word "about," in the last sentence quoted, is used in
the sense of "*near to*," then it is strictly correct, for the climate
of Florida is "near to," (being only two days sail from) that of
the Bahamas. Whatever may be said to the discredit of these
islands, they are certainly not chargeable with that " besetting
sin of this fallen world" to which Mrs. Stowe refers.

While no one can be any more sure in Nassau than he is at home, or anywhere else, of escaping an exceptionally wet, and to that extent disagreeable, winter, he can rely with great confidence upon having there, night and day, an atmosphere of a pleasant and uniform summer temperature.

It is difficult for a native and untraveled Bahamian to appreciate what is written at the north about "the domestic hearth," and "cheerful fire-side." As poets do not confine themselves exclusively to the truth, but use their "poetic license," the Bahamians naturally deem Longfellow's lines the out-cropping of a wild fancy when he sings:

> "Each man's chimney is his golden milestone;
> Is the central point from which he measures every distance,
> Through the gateways of the world around him."

Certain it is, there are few such "milestones" in Nassau.

Persons who, for any reason, find it necessary to avoid the cold, damp winds and storms of the North, will find at Nassau a climate that fully fills the measure of their wants from the middle of November to the middle of April. But temperature and clear skies are not the only points to be considered in determining the question of the importance of Nassau as "a great sanitarium," and we have therefore extended our observations and pushed our inquiries in other directions.

The drinking water, the drainage, the existence and observance of sanitary regulations, the topography and condition of the adjacent back country, as well as the quality and direction of the winds that pass over it, are all important factors in the problem of health, and should be carefully examined and critically considered.

It is just here that Nassau's most vulnerable points are discovered, and, but for the superior sanitary arrangements of the Royal

Victoria Hotel, they would be much more damaging to the place as a health resort. Wells and cisterns, in the absence of sand, are sunk in the soft, porous, limestone rock, in the vicinity of cesspools and privy vaults, so that the water they contain can hardly fail to become more or less unwholesome. In many wells the water is said to rise and fall with the tide, but whether its quality is impaired by sea water we are not informed. There being no general sewerage system, the surface rock is likely to become saturated with the waste and effete matter that is suffered to accumulate around human habitations where the climate disinclines to exertion, and exhalations may be expected to arise therefrom, which will jeopardise health and life.

The colored people who are crowded together in the suburbs of Nassau, pay little, if any regard to nature's sanitary laws, and apparently conform to few of the conditions of healthy human existence. While they live in the open air during the day, they at night are crowded together in the one or two rooms of their little cabins, from which the outside air is religiously excluded by closed doors and wooden shutters. Perhaps they have learned by experience the necessity of thus excluding the damp and poisoned air that rests upon the low, wet lands of the interior of this island. Their poverty denies to them the advantages of a generous diet of varied food which is everywhere within the reach of honest labor in the States.

That the seeds of disease, at least during the night, float in the air above the swamps and lagoons of the central portions of the island of New Providence, is apparent to any thoughtful observer who either crosses it or sees it from any of the neighboring hills. The germs of sickness existing there are never destroyed or rendered torpid by frost. In the mild, soft, damp air, disease is present, and often dispenses his fevers with a liberal hand, as the official records and statistics clearly demonstrate. Consumption also, upon a galloping steed, rides in the suburbs of Nassau with an unchecked rein to his goal—the portal of death. It is possible for leprosy to lurk in the dense chaparral of low lands, and under the thick mangro groves that, with living arches and festoons, beautify and adorn the miniature islands that rise out of the shallow waters of the brackish and stagnant lakes.

The city of Nassau, as we have shown, is, in a sanitary point of view, very favorably situated. Bottomed upon a rock of a porous nature, which dips towards the harbor, and speedily absorbs or carries off the heaviest rain-falls, facing the north and skirting the sea, having within its limits no low and wet lands, the prevailing winds come to it directly from the ocean laden with refreshment and health. We examined the annual medical reports of the surgeon connected with the military department at Nassau for eleven years, from 1867 to 1878. Only that of 1873 gave statistics of the wind. From that report it appeared that during the year 1873 the wind blew from the south at nine o'clock A. M. only three times—once in June and twice in November—and at three o'clock P. M. only once during the entire year, and that was in November. The report states that in 1873 the wind blew from the north-east on 175 days, at nine A. M., and from the south-east 111 days, and that at three P. M. it was north-east 185 days, and south-east 121 days; while it blew from the west only two days. During the ten years covered by Gov. Rawson's table, which we have quoted, the wind from the south is stated to have averaged eleven days in a hundred. The wind was from the south very rarely while we were at Nassau in 1879, but it atoned for its long intervals of absence by being very sultry, debilitating, and exceedingly disagreeable. As it sweeps over the low, wet surface of the center of the island, we believe it unfavorable to health, although the distance is measured by a very few miles. While we were at Nassau in 1880, the wind was more frequently from the south and the weather was, as in the States, exceptionally hot, and for that reason Nassau was much less attractive.

The Royal Victoria Hotel is provided with tanks for the storing of rain-water, which are said to have a capacity of 300,000 gallons. The water is exclusively used for drinking and culinary purposes, and it always appeared to be of most excellent quality. Ice, from the state of Maine, is procured under a contract which the government made for the supply of the city, of which there was always an abundance at the hotel. The water of the hotel is therefore most excellent and unexceptional provided proper care and vigilance are exercised in cleaning the tanks, and guarding and keeping them from impurities. During the latter part of the hotel season of 1878–9, after a long protracted drouth, dysenteric complaints were alarmingly prevalent at the Victoria Hotel, and, although physicians were numbered among its guests, no one seemed able to discover their cause. There was nothing disclosed in the taste, color or smell of the drinking water which indicated that it had anything to do with the trouble. The more we pondered upon the cause, the more we were puzzled. Before leaving Nassau we read the "Brief Auto-biography" of the former rector of one of the churches in Nassau, the late Rev. Wm. Strachan, D. D., who, in 1822, established a church and was for sometime its rector upon one of the Turks Islands. The latter part of the following extract from the little book (p. 58) excited in us some incredulity:

"I found no wells in the island, and learned that the only water to be had, either for drinking or cooking purposes, was the rain which drops from the clouds, and is received into capacious tanks attached to the several houses. A stranger must be cautious how, and in what quantities, he imbibes the rain-water at first, as it is liable to produce a severe dysenteric attack."

In calling the attention of one of the military officials at Nassau to this subject, and to the paragraph we have quoted, he said :

"Soon after my first arrival in Nassau, I was, in common with some other officers of the garrison, troubled with severe griping pains in the bowels, which I suspected was caused by impure water, and I caused the water in the cisterns to be drawn off. At the bottom I found a dark colored, dirty deposit, two to three inches thick. I had the cisterns thoroughly cleaned, and the result was the griping pains disappeared."

When in April, 1879, we returned to Jacksonville, Fla., we learned that dysenteric complaints had made their appearance among the guests of the St. James Hotel, that the water in the cisterns of the hotel was discovered to be very impure, and offensive to the taste and smell. In Jacksonville as well as at Nassau there had been a long season of dry weather, so that the cisterns were drawn down low, and the dirt at the bottom no doubt in both places poisoned the water—hence the sickness that followed its use.

Upon our return to the north we sent the substance of the foregoing facts to the proprietor of the Royal Victoria Hotel, and he promised to have the cisterns of his hotel emptied and cleaned.

Thus disease and death sometimes lurk, and wait, and watch for victims, where they are looked for least. While at Nassau, in 1880, we had no evidence of the existence of any of the dysenteric troubles that existed in 1879. Spring water is utilized at the hotel for some purposes, and a bountiful supply is carried to tanks elevated over the water-closets by means of a steam pump, and a suspicion existed when the bowel complaints made their appearance, that some of it had been used for cooking purposes. The hotel officials, however, denied that it had been so used.

The dews at Nassau are often very heavy, and it is prudent to follow the poet's advice, and

> "The dews of the evening most carefully shun,
>   Those tears of the sky for the loss of the sun."

Some old residents of Nassau informed us that they considered the evening air in Nassau prejudicial to health. One of them—a lady—said that she was obliged to exclude herself from it to avoid lung disease. But when night after night so many bright stars call to us from a cloudless sky to come out and look up—and especially when the moon rides in great splendor across the bluest of heavens on purpose to be seen, it seems hardly courteous or creditable to ignobly ensconce ourselves under mosquito bars, and be content with indolent repose or oblivious sleep. When we occasionally accepted of the invitation, it was only to be overwhelmed with the magnificence of the display, as was Moses on Sinai.

The official Bahama mortuary statistics which we examined, failed to discriminate between the races, and to so localize the results that a comparison can be made between Nassau and its suburbs. The medical reports of the military department describe the colored troops as being very licentious, and a large portion of them suffer from venereal diseases. These complaints are said to have been introduced into Grant's Town by French troops, when, upon the breaking up of Maxamillian's Government in Mexico, the vessels which were transporting them to France stopped on their way at Nassau.

As a matter more of curiosity than of practical utility, we subjoin an abstract of the reported causes of death in all the Bahama islands in 1864. It is taken from Gov. Rawson's report for that year.

CAUSES.	Average Quarterly Number.				Percentage Proportion.			
	January to March.	April to June.	July to September.	October to December.	1st Quarter.	2d Quarter.	3d Quarter.	4th Quarter.
Fevers:								
Ordinary, ...	32	38	63	58	16.6	19.7	23.0	25.4
Yellow, ...	1	5	35	14	.4	2.4	12.7	6.1
Scarlet Eruptive, &c., ...	14	6	12	9	7.3	2.9	4.4	3.7
Diseases of Lungs and Heart,....	34	38	55	26	17.8	19.8	20.1	11.5
" " Bowels and Liver,.	14	22	26	19	7.3	11.4	9.4	8.5
Dropsies, ...	7	5	6	7	3.6	2.6	2.1	3.1
Diseases of Brain and Nerves:								
Apoplexy and Palsy.......	6	4	3	6	3.1	2.1	1.1	2.6
Convulsions and Spasms,	24	14	21	27	12.6	7.4	7.5	12.0
Sudden and Violent,..............	10	10	7	9	5.0	5.0	2.7	4.1
Stillborn, ...	2	1	2	1	1.2	.7	.6	.6
Childbirth,........................	2	3	3	5	1.0	1.3	1.2	2.4
Other causes,......................	45	47	42	46	24.1	24.7	15.2	20.0
Total, ...	192	192	274	230	100.0	100.0	100.0	100.0

Gov. Rawson says, "The inferences to be drawn from this table are that the latter half of the year is much more fatal to the population, to the extent of nearly one-third, and that this is owing chiefly to the prevalence of fevers, including yellow fever, which contributed one-third to the excess."

"These islands are, without exception, remarkably healthy. They are free from, and are seldom visited by epidemic diseases. Intermittent fevers, which prevail to so great an extent on the neighboring continent, are comparatively infrequent here, and usually assume a mild form. During the last thirty-five years, Nassau has been visited by the cholera but once, viz.: in 1852; by small-pox in 1845 and 1860, when it was introduced in both

instances from St. Domingo, and by the yellow fever at distant
intervals, and attended with very slight mortality, viz.: in 1829,
1843 and 1853, until 1861–2, when from transient circumstances
it assumed a more malignant form, and carried off a greater number of victims, including the first bishop of the diocese. It repeated its visits in 1863–4.

"The inhabitants are, for the most part, a hardy, robust race.
They consume little animal food, and live chiefly on Indian and
Guinea corn, vegetables, fish and shell-fish. Many of the petty
cultivators on the Windward Islands, who cling to their small
plots, and refuse to seek employments as hired laborers in their
own or other islands, are often reduced to much distress when
their meagre crops of corn fail them through drought or other
causes; and these are in the course of deterioration, both physical and mental, enervated, indifferent to improvement, and bringing up their families in ignorance and sloth.

"Nassau is usually very healthy and free from disease. In
1862–64, during the height of the blockade-running trade, when
the town was filled with strangers, the lodging houses were over-
crowded, and the elements of disease were festering in the heart
of the city, it is not surprising that the yellow fever, whether
introduced by vessels coming from infected ports, or engendered
by the unusual condition of the city, should have broken out.
But *it was confined to strangers and to unacclimated persons*,
and was not by any means fatal as compared with other places.

"The Board of Health, a body constituted under a local Act,
with large powers for the protection of the health of the colony,
reported that in 1861–62, about 400 persons were attacked, and
ninety-five died, in a population numbering in 1861, 11,503; and
that in 1864, out of a population estimated at 15,000, the number of cases was 700, and of deaths 137. Of these, 153 cases
resulting in forty-five deaths, were admitted into the Quarantine
Hospital from the shipping and lodging houses."

It should be considered that in the settlements upon some of the islands, the population is very much crowded, and that the health of the people suffers in consequence. Gov. Rawson, in his report for 1864, estimated that the population of Dunmore Town, upon the island of Eleuthera, was 2,500, and that the density was "about forty persons to the acre, or 124 square yards to each individual, which is nearly six times the average of the 781 principal towns in England" in 1861. He adds, "the consequence is that for the last two or three years the place has been very sickly, and typhoid fever has committed considerable ravages among the inhabitants.

Upon a little key at the extreme north-west point of Eleuthera, and about five miles from Harbour Island, the settlement of Spanish Wells is situated. Gov. Rawson states in his report of 1864, that the inhabitants of Spanish Wells "have continued to divide and sub-divide their lots among their children, so that the houses almost touch each other, and in some places the (so-called) street is not over three or four feet in width. The area of the settlement does not exceed three acres; so that the population is upwards of 150 to the acre." He adds, "they are uncleanly in their habits, and all attempts to introduce sanitary rules among them have hitherto failed. Consequently, typhoid fever has lingered here, too, for the last three years."

Gov. Rawson also speaks of another settlement upon Eleuthera, called Governor's Harbor, where, he says, "the density of the population equals, if it does not exceed that of Spanish Wells." He says it is situated upon a rock, about 300 yards long, by 100 yards wide, which is connected with the main land by a narrow neck of land, and that this rock is "in miniature, very like the Rock of Gibraltar."

He also states that "the people at Devil's Point, upon St. Salvador, have the worst reputation of any upon that island,"

and of "being not only lazy, but addicted to the most vicious and immoral habits," Also, that upon Acklin's Island, "the commonest comforts and the ordinary necessaries of life are evidently wanting," which he attributes in part to the indolent habits of the people. He says that upon Fortune Island, the people (numbering 470) "are all poor and unable even to repair their own dwellings, and that but for the fish, conchs and crabs, they would absolutely suffer and perish from want of the commonest necessaries of life, for they are too indolent and inactive to go where their labor would be useful to themselves and others."

We give these facts, not as fairly indicating the average character and condition of the people living upon the Bahama islands, but as illustrating, 1st, that no air, however pure and delightfully tempered and medicated it may be in its normal condition, will save a people from diseases of a malignant type when laws of health are disregarded; and 2d, that very elaborate health tables are of little value if they fail to discriminate between places where the sanitary conditions and habits of life of the people are very unlike—although they have some degree of geographical and political unity.

We did not learn of any cases of yellow fever, cholera or smallpox, from 1864 to 1879. In Gov. Robinson's report for 1878, he states that "an epidemic of whooping cough prevailed for several months, causing much distress and some mortality amongst the children of the laboring classes." One would suppose that in such a climate, if whooping cough made its appearance at all, it would have been of a very mild type. It seems to have been otherwise in 1878.

During the winter and spring of 1880, a malignant fever resulted in quite a number of deaths at Nassau, and it is our belief that it was yellow fever, and we will state the evidence upon which our opinion is predicated.

Upon the morning of the day the steamer left New York, on which we had engaged our passage out, a gentleman startled us a little by announcing that "Nassau had got a black eye." He said it had been reported in the States that the yellow fever had broken out in Nassau, but that the Governor of the Bahamas and the foreign consuls at Nassau had published cards denying the truth of the report. Our steamer stopped at Fernandina, and a gentleman there told us that a physician, recently from Nassau, and then at the Egremont Hotel, in Fernandina, stated that before he left there had been in Nassau two deaths from that disease. The steamer City of Austin had then just arrived at Fernandina from Nassau, and one of its passengers assured us that there was not any yellow fever in Nassau when he left. None of our passengers were alarmed sufficiently to alter their plans, and when upon the day of our arrival in Nassau we entered the dining room of the Victoria Hotel, and saw how merry and healthy and hungry everybody seemed to be, the last vestige of the yellow fever scare disappeared. For some days no allusion was made to "Yellow Jack," but after a while pretty well authenticated reports reached us of quite a number of cases of sickness and death within the city limits, but outside of the hotel. It appears that the disease attacked at first the children of the natives, some twenty or more of whom died. It was said that it could not be yellow fever, first, because it was confined to the children, and second, because none but children belonging in Nassau had been attacked; whereas unacclimated adults were the first to be stricken down when yellow fever prevails.

After which we learned of a few cases of alarming sickness among the visitors from the States and elsewhere, several of which resulted in death. One of the latter was the wife of Dr. Aiken. She was previously a healthy woman, but the doctor was an invalid. They had been boarding with a Nassau gentleman who held the office of Assistant United States Consul. This case occurred in a house situated upon high ground very near to the hotel, which the owner and his family thereupon, for prudential reasons, vacated. Dr. Aiken then came to the Victoria Hotel to board, and he was afterwards our fellow passenger when we left Nassau for Florida. He told us that the disease was yellow fever, and that the sanitary conditions of the Vice-Consul's premises outside of and close to his dwelling house were very offensive and bad.

Our young friend from Vermont, Mr. Phelps, arrived at Nassau in November with his invalid mother. He had the fever, but his mother escaped, although she took care of him night and day, with the exception of two nights, when, by advice of a local physician, she entrusted her son, while convalescent, to the care of a nurse whom the doctor recommended. This nurse got drunk, neglected the sick man, who took cold in consequence, and had a relapse. His life was then despaired of by the physicians, but he was saved at last by an experiment which the mother had the sagacity and courage to make upon her own responsibility, and without the knowledge of the medical attendants. She administered, in connection with the prescribed medicines, some kind of salts, (we have forgotten what kind,) first in small but frequent doses, watching him closely all the while, and had the great satisfaction of seeing the fever gradually give way, and finally disappear. The doses were increased as the salutary operation of the medicine was developed. When she afterwards told the doctors what she had been doing, they were (as she represented to us) offended, although she had apparently saved the life of her son after they had announced that he could not recover. With the exception of keeping a little piece of camphor gum in her mouth, she did nothing to escape the contagion of the disease. One of the attending physicians, who was accustomed to sit upon the bed of the sick man, she believed carried the disease to his own home, for two of his daughters thereafter had the fever and died. He then abandoned his house upon East Hill street, within a block or block and a-half of our hotel, and moved with the remainder of his family to "Thompson's Folly," where he was sure of the best kind of Bahama air, and a plenty of it, although he took the chance of being blown some day half across the Atlantic ocean by a hurricane. The disease was not pestilential but sporadic, and although it was near to, it did not enter the hotel. It was evidently a very undesirable fever to have, whether entitled to be called yellow or not. Two out of three of the resident physicians persistently denied that it was yellow fever, while the third one, who was in Nassau when the yellow fever prevailed at the time of our late American war, differed with them on this point. A gentleman on familiar terms with the prominent men of Nassau, informed us before we left, that it was not at first believed to be yellow fever, simply because it was confined to children, and especially to the children of natives, "but now," said he, "that it has attacked adult strangers, they admit it to be yellow fever." These admissions were not publicly made or generally known.

Our attention was occasionally attracted by consultations, private and mysterious, of persons who traveled in company. A growing and constantly increasing desire to speedily return to the land of the starry flag was discernable, and we learned, after a while, that the state-rooms in the Nassau steamers for their return trips had been secured for sometime in advance by certain wise and thoughtful ones—among whom we, alas, were not numbered. There was no panic, but only a quiet and commendable exhibition of prudence. So far as we could learn, no cases of fever had occurred at our hotel, and nothing was observed in its immediate vicinity calculated to generate or invite disease.

17

Unfavorable rumors floated more or less loosely in the soft and silky air, but, notwithstanding, the wings of fear were kept wonderfully well clipped. Nor did we permit ourselves to be made unhappy by unfavorable possibilities. We knew that borrowed troubles are worse than real ones; but still the fact was too patent to be overlooked or ignored, that only a single floating bridge, of limited capacity, connected us with Florida's wet and flowery land, and that if it, for any cause should give way, as several of its predecessor's had done, it might be some weeks before its owners in New York would learn of the disaster, and span the Florida gulf with a substitute. Nor did we feel any strong desire, personally, to "lie down to pleasant dreams" in the white coraline rock of "the greatest sanitarium of the western world," even though a colonial capital should in consequence thereof be beautified and made forever famous by our monument.

After a while our turn to depart came, and a feeling of great satisfaction—not to say relief—came over us when we bade adieu to the great sanitarium, and the charming picture of jewelled isles in a turquoise sea disappeared from view. Proudly our steamer skimmed the smooth, untroubled and tranquil world of waters, slowly and grandly the day god

> "Steeped
> His fiery face in billows of the west,"

while the night was made glorious with its canopy of brilliant stars. It spoke well for our ship, and for the hotel in which we had spent so many happy hours, that in neither of them had there been a single case of serious sickness of any kind.

Mr. Phelps and his mother, and Dr. Aiken, were our fellow-passengers, so that it seemed—especially while they detailed to us their sad experiences—that we were brought almost into the very presence of the much to be dreaded fever itself. But a kind and merciful Providence so ordered it, that we escaped entirely unharmed the perils of sickness and of the sea, and as our steamer had a clear bill of health, we were saved from numbering among our experiences, a practical acquaintance with the indescribable attractions of the quarantine system in southern ports in very warm weather.

About four weeks afterwards we took passage in the screw steamer City of Austin, at Fernandina, for New York. She had just arrived from Nassau with a large number of passengers, including Mr. Morton, the proprietor of the Royal Victoria Hotel, together with his principal assistants. The children of the American Consul were also on board, and we learned that the Consul and his wife designed to follow them so soon as his official duties would admit of his leaving. We had also the Episcopal Bishop and his children. The Bishop's wife was one of the victims of the fever, and we had no doubt he had left Nassau because he was not willing to incur the hazards incident to a residence there during the warm and wet season of the year. We could not but deeply sympathise with him in his great affliction, and half regret that we had allowed ourselves to be amused at the high sounding titles which, upon his arrival the year previous, helped so much to inspire the Bahamians with reverence, if not with awe. Upon ship-board there were certain peculiarities in his every day costume, as striking as a Chinaman's pig-tail, which were well calculated to attract attention. They were strongly suggestive of the fact that the man whom they adorned was not an ordinary individual. But in the shadow of his great bereavement, surrounded, as he was, with his pretty but motherless little ones, we were not disposed to unfavorably criticise or inwardly smile at the peculiarities of his costume. We did not make the Bishop's acquaintance, but he was dignified without seeming vain and conceited, and his intelligent, amiable and good natured countenance quite prepossessed us in his favor.

Our ship was very much crowded, and some passengers slept upon the floor of the main saloon, but being favored by pleasant weather, and no pestilential or other diseases having made their appearance, little inconvenience was experienced. We ought not, perhaps, to omit one instance of sickness which occurred on board, and was said to have occasioned at first some uneasiness. The sick man was employed upon the steamer, and a physician, after looking him over, and making a thorough diagnosis of his case, reported that his patient had only an attack of "whiskey fever," and that he would be all right in the morning.

As we made our way up the beautiful harbor of New York in the early morning of a charming day, and felt the thrilling and exquisite pleasure incident to a safe return to our native shores, we almost forgot that a malignant disease had recently thrown unpleasant occasional shadows over us upon one of the isles of summer, and had almost brushed against us with the hem of its garment as it passed by.

Mr. Phelps has written us that he has, since his return, received letters from Nassau, and his mother has entertained several persons who reside in Nassau, at her house in Vermont; that his Nassau corespondents stated that at the time of their writing, the yellow fever prevailed extensively in Nassau, and that it had occasioned many deaths; that the wife and two children of the Wesleyan minister at Nassau, Major Simpson and two of his children, and a lady visitor from Ontario, Canada, were numbered among its victims. Also, that the local physicians there now admit that Mr. Phelps had "the genuine yellow fever."

Another gentleman, whose sources of information through correspondents in Nassau are at least equally good, though less disinterested, writes us as follows: "The fever has shown itself spasmodically at Nassau this summer, but to very little extent.

The town has been very thoroughly cleansed, and if the recent hurricane has visited Nassau, as it probably has, the germs of the disease will be destroyed." It is, therefore, now altogether probable, that the sickness which occurred in Nassau in the winter and spring of 1880, was of the yellow fever type. That it did not more generally prevail, is no doubt due to the fact that Nassau is so well ventilated with ocean winds. In certain localities there existed conditions favorable to its spread, and in these the fever germs took root, so that the disease was sporadic and not pestilential, and the result of local causes.

The fact should in this connection be stated, as a matter of justice to Nassau, that all the cities of the Southern States and of the West India Islands, have been occasionally subject to the same disease.

An apparently intelligent and well-informed correspondent of "The Semi-Tropical,"—a monthly magazine formerly published in Jacksonville, Florida—in the December number of that periodical for 1877, gives some instances of the prevalence of this disease which are worthy of consideration. He says: " In 1857, Jacksonville was visited by a fatal epidemic, generated by the opening of the railroad through a swamp hole in the heart of a little hamlet during the warm season, when the exhalations were fœtid with miasma. It was confined at first to those residing in the immediate vicinity of this swamp, and radiated from that center, but did not cross the river. It was as destructive as yellow fever, though in many respects, it lacked some of the essential features of that disease. It proved fatal to an alarming degree, but more from the impossibility of securing nurses and proper assistance, than from any necessity of the disease." He adds that before that, yellow fever cases from the West Indies had not spread.

He also refers to "a few fatal cases of what is termed in the

West Indies, butcher's fever, which occurred two years since, [1875,] in Jacksonville, Fla., about the market."

Under date of November 20, 1877, while his article was partly in type, he adds—" Yellow fever has been proclaimed in Jacksonville, and in such a manner as to cause the most false ideas and groundless apprehensions abroad." He adds that " not more than five cases have occurred, and in regard to these, some of our most experienced physicians express the greatest doubt." But it seems to be consistent with the code of medical ethics, to doubt and deny if thereby the spread of disease may be prevented or checked. The materia medica includes moral as well as physical poisons, experience having shown that they are the antidotes of fear. A medical man from Boston, told us in Nassau that Dr. —— of Nassau, could not be much of a physician, for if he was, he would not say that yellow fever existed there, even if it did in fact.

The magazine writer refers to the exemption of St. Augustine from yellow fever for fifty years during its occupancy by the Spanish and British authorities, and to its prevalence in 1821. We were assured that cases of this disease occurred in St. Augustine a few winters since, and some cases are occasionally to be expected perhaps in all cities not favored with frost.

He says that " in 1822, the yellow fever was introduced into Pensacola, by a cargo of spoilt fish being cast upon the wharf."

That, " when the yellow fever prevailed in the town of St. Mary's, Ga., about 1808—a place of great general health—such, he was informed, was the state of the atmosphere, that beef, twenty-four hours killed, fell from the hook by putrifaction, and water drawn from the well in the evening, was in a state of mucilage next morning."

In 1878, the yellow fever prevailed at Port Royal, and we were there told, that fifty persons died of the disease. And yet, the place is quite small. The fever is supposed to have been caused by digging up the ground to make certain improvements which the railroad's freighting business demanded.

The city of Fernandina in Florida, is pleasantly situated on a rise of ground upon Amelia Island. Its vicinity to the ocean, whose winds and the tides that flow through the spacious water-ways that lead to it, would seem to secure for it immunity from malignant diseases, although there are low and wet savannahs in its immediate neighborhood. It is something of a health resort in winter. We learned while there, from some of its residents, that the yellow fever scourged the city in the summer of 1877. The magazine writer whom we have quoted, refers to it in his article, and says that in a population of 3000 there were 1000 cases of yellow fever, which resulted in 100 deaths. He states that it was caused by opening ditches through wet lands in hot weather, and by the discharging of a large amount of ballast from a vessel with yellow fever on board, "into the heart of the town, and in the midst of this reclaimed swamp;" and that, "according to a well established law, the introduction of a quick, virulent disease will drive out or characterize all local diseases, and become epidemic."

Notwithstanding the grave and serious importance of the subject, one can hardly refrain from smiling when he sees the inhabitants of a fever-stricken city looking to a hurricane for their deliverance, as travelers and pioneers upon the great western prairies sometimes fight fire with fire. Destructive cyclones have commissions of mercy and beneficence to execute, and God not only makes "the wrath of man," but the angry winds "to praise him." The blessed angel of health, when driven out of its strong-holds in the cities of the South, and upon the beautiful coral isles, harnesses itself to a hurricane and returns, driving out, scattering and destroying its enemy. Incidentally huge trees are torn up by the roots, houses blown down, and some lives destroyed, but health and happiness pitch their tents upon the ruins. Since the great hurricane of 1866, and until the year 1880, the yellow fever, so far as we have been able to learn, though domiciled in Havana, has been a stranger in the Bahamas. We trust Nassau will for many years to come be free from its visitations.

Although Nassau's sanitary character has not always been unsullied, and it has occasionally suffered a "fall from grace," its reputation as a sanitarium has generally been not only good but well deserved. It never has been and never will be safe, especially in countries where frosts are unknown, to violate the laws of health which nature has imposed. The operation of these laws, and the enforcement of their penalties, is as sure and silent as the revolutions of the stars. Disease and death sleeplessly watch from their coverts at the gates of every stronghold of health. Eternal vigilance is the price of safety. "A little slumber, a little folding of the hands to sleep" in the drowsy air, by the boards of health, has caused many happy homes to be made desolate in the past, as it will in the future, when hard but salutary lessons are forgotten.

If Nassau, for six consecutive months out of every twelve, is not one of the healthiest places in the world, it is the fault of its people. From November to April, the seeds of malignant diseases will not germinate in its healing and healthful air, if wise sanitary regulations are made and enforced. She owes it to herself, and to valetudinarians in the British American Provinces, and in the States of the Union, who desire to seek for health within her limits, to see to it that the pure air which nature wafts to her constantly from the ocean, and the pure distilled water from the clouds, artificially or naturally stored in its coralline rocks, shall not be polluted and made inimical to health by a criminal neglect of the first and plainest hygienic principles.

"It is an ill-wind that blows no one any good," and the people of Nassau live largely upon the misfortunes of others.   Disabled hulks from the stormy ocean, and from the troubled sea of human life, fly to it as a harbor of refuge, and the amount paid for salvage in each class of cases, aggregates every year a large sum.   By a liberal expenditure of money in mapping and lighting the channels of commerce, the British government has curtailed one source of income, which will be in a measure made up by the adoption and rigid enforcement of wise sanitary laws.

For the benefit of our readers, we give the views of a number of intelligent gentlemen in regard to the merits of Nassau as a health resort.   They were written from different stand points, and cover periods of time widely separated.

Peter Henry Bruce, an English engineer, was commissioned in 1741, to build and make good the defenses of Nassau.   After speaking in his Memoirs of its climate, and characterizing it "as the most serene and most temperate in all America," he says, "it is, therefore, no wonder that the sick and afflicted inhabitants of this [English] climate fly here for relief, being sure to find cure here."   Thus it appears that its fame as a health resort in winter was well established nearly a century and a-half ago.

Dr. W. T. Hutchinson, of Providence, R. I., highly recommends Nassau for those who suffer from diseases of the nervous system, and who require rest for body and mind, for brain and muscle.

Dr. W. Kirkwood, of Florence, Italy, affirms his belief "that the climate of Nassau, during the winter months, is superior to any winter resorts for pulmonary invalids" which he has visited, and he had spent four years in Italy and the South of France. But we conclude it was a hasty opinion based upon a short experience of Nassau's mild and uniform climate.

Gen. James Watson Webb, said in 1870, that "from the first of November to the first of June, there is not, in all probability, any spot on the face of the earth so desirable for persons suffering from pulmonary complaints." From the facts and opinions we have given, the reader will judge whether this unqualified recommendation is not too broad and sweeping.

Dr. F. A. Castle, editor of "New Remedies," with more discrimination, and we think truth, said in 1877, that "in those forms of lung trouble where there is profuse expectoration and perspiration, we should hardly think of recommending patients to visit the Bahamas. But in the early stages of chronic pneumonia and catarrhal pneumonia, in tubercules, convalescence from acute diseases, and in exhaustion from over-work and worry, the advantage of being able to live, if necessary, out of doors, without the fatigue of heavy clothing, the comparative freedom from risk of catching cold, and the purety of the atmosphere, render this one of the most healthful as well as available resorts of which we have any knowledge."

The Rev. Dr. Nelson Millard, writing from Nassau in March, 1876, said, "Such a climate, if resorted to in time, often works with wondrous curative power upon affections of the throat, bronchia and lungs—as in the case of bronchitis, I can testify from personal experience."

Epes Sargent, Esq., a gentleman of considerable literary culture, but whose opinion may be unconsciously biased from the fact that he keeps a boarding house at Nassau, says, "that for all [?] diseases of the lungs, throat, liver, kidneys, or spine, there is no climate on the face of the earth superior, and I doubt if any equal, to the climate of Nassau." And again, "some most wonderful cures of pulmonary diseases, asthma, rheumatism, neuralgia and bronchitis have been performed almost entirely by the climate. In the first stage of the disease, recovery is almost certain." Mr. Sargeant has had unquestionably superior opportunities of learning the facts, and his opinion, notwithstanding his personal interest, is entitled to considerable weight.

We were interested in 1879, to hear two of our Nassau friends who had been at the Bermudas, compare them with Nassau. One declared that the Bahamas weakened and debilitated, while his system in the Bermudas was refreshed and invigorated. Both winter resorts have the ocean air, but one is cool and tonic—the other so warm it wilted and unstrung him. He did not want to see the Bahamas any more. The other declared the Bermudas no place at all for a sick man: that it rained there all the time, and was therefore damp and wet, while its temperature was subject to great fluctuations, and was very trying to invalids. But Nassau, he affirmed, was just the place for a sick man to enjoy himself and get well. A large, healthy looking and intelligent man who was returning home with us after a six months' residence at Nassau, spoke very strongly against it. He did not like boating, and preferred to take his exercise on foot. When the sun was up he could not walk out because it was so very hot, while the damp and unhealthy night air made out-door exercise at that time unsafe. He had no desire to go there again. Other passengers on the Savannah steamer in 1879, including the author, felt that to them Nassau had been a great sanitarium, while its bland air, beautiful waters, coral bowers and bright skies, will ever secure for it a most prominent place in the mind's store-house of pleasant memories.

The wife of the author of this book was relieved of bronchial and asthmatic troubles at Nassau, in 1879, which did not return while she was at our sea-side residence upon the north shore of Long Island Sound during the following summer. In the succeeding fall and early winter the old troubles again made their appearance in a modified form, but the air of Nassau in March,

1880, supplemented by that of Florida in April, affected an apparent cure.

We knew of an instance where a person suffering from catarrh of the bladder found great relief at Nassau.

A judge from the city of New York was stopping at the Victoria Hotel when we arrived in 1879, who was suffering from what was thought to be a softening of the brain. In such cases, perhaps, a more tonic atmosphere is desirable. He attempted to resume his judicial labors soon after his return, but found himself incapacitated.

We made the acquaintance at Nassau, in 1879, of a lady who was then apparently cured of a bronchial disease, but she had some return of it the following summer in the mountains of North Carolina.

It is impossible in a great many cases to know beforehand with certainty what effect the air of the Bahamas will produce—whether favorable or unfavorable. It is not adapted to meet the necessities of all. Nassau is unlike the pool of Siloam, that cured all comers. Some are prostrated in its warm enervating air. A medical gentleman informed us that in confirmed consumption it relaxes the tissues, and that severe hemorrhages follow. If good in that complaint at all, it is only in its early stages. This we learned both from observation and from the testimony of physicians on the spot. One of these said to us, "Don't recommend these islands for consumption and rheumatism." A resident physician of good repute declared the climate bad for rheumatism. A young clergyman, prostrated by a pulmonary complaint in the dawn of what promised to be a most useful life, went over in the same steamer with us, in 1879, and for sometime it seemed doubtful if he would ever be able to leave the island alive. We were told in Nassau, in 1880, that his health was improved.

As Nassau's position is isolated, and so far removed from the cities of the north, with only one weekly line of steamers, and no telegraph, as yet, to connect it with the States, it is not the place one would ordinarily select in which to be very sick, and many better places nearer home can be found in which to die. A physician whom we met in Nassau, in 1879, said to us: "It costs a thousand dollars to die here. In one instance, last year, (1878,) $300 dollars was paid for the use of a small building as a dead house, and other charges were in proportion." If one is dangerously sick, there is no place for him like home, with its comforts and unbought sympathies.

To those who are weak, debilitated, over-worked and run down, whose feeble hold on life is constantly endangered by sudden fluctuations of temperature, and the severe storms and cold winds of the north, the warm and beautiful Islands of Indolence and Sensuous Repose, attract with flattering promises of permanent benefit. New leases of life are doubtless accessible to many such in Nassau. But we do not believe that either shore of the Mediterranean Sea, the banks of the Nile, Madeira, Florida, or any Isle of Unending Summer, can furnish desirable homes for white people in health. We have only to compare the natives of the States north of the old Mason's and Dixon's line (including cold and bleak New England), and their works, with "the children of the sun" and their neglected opportunities, to be satisfied on this point. The cold north wind stimulates, braces and builds up. Every blast, fearlessly and boldly breasted, invigorates the healthy body, enriches the blood, and gives vitalizing and enduring strength and power to the mental and moral forces. In the temperate zone the mental, moral and physical powers of man reach their highest development. Frost is an essential factor in the problem of civilization. All human progress is bottomed upon ice. The great and profound truths, the

18

hidden laws of the world of matter and mind are born of the north wind sweeping over the snow fields.

Wandering through the wilderness of streets in the noisy Babel of the Empire State, only seventy-four miles from home, a little unassimilated globule in a great eddying, boiling sea of human life, separated and isolated from familiar scenes and faces, and from warm and sympathetic hearts, a murky and crushing feeling of loneliness that we cannot dispel pervades the soul, and life for the time loses its value by reason of its comparative insignificance. But the frequent mails, the long lines of railroad, the locomotive with its ribs of steel and mouth of fire, the bridges of steamboats over all the deep separating water-ways, the perfect net-work of telegraph and telephone wires, like great life-roots, still closely unite and bind to the familiar places and faces that we have left behind us; while the morning press, that miracle of modern enterprise and invention—seems to so closely connect us, that we realize that we are indeed a component part of the great world of human life, and we feel every pulsation of its great heart. But upon the little island of New Providence—a rock fast anchored in the great ocean—communication with the outside world is so infrequent and contingent, that we seem when anxiously waiting, watching, and vainly longing for the arrival from Jacksonville of the only steamer that connects these islands with the mainland, like a little colony of Robinson Crusoes.

On stepping from the deck of a steamer, upon one of the docks at Nassau, we have a consciousness that we are mere waifs on the ocean of life, dissevered and far away drifted from everything that makes a residence upon the sun's little satelite desirable.

The tired worker, needing absolute quiet and rest, can find it there. But he must make up his mind not to be anxious or fussy about friends and business in his distant home. If, day

after day, the expected steamer fails to arrive, and he looks a
hundred times in vain for the signal of her approach upon the
flag-staff at Fort Fincastle, he must not allow himself to think
even of the possibility that she has foundered at sea, or has been
wrecked on some of the dangerous rocks or reefs or shores that
have made the Bahamas so noted in the past.   He must not indulge in speculations upon the probable results of such a misfortune, nor strive to find out how long it will be before the outside
world will hear of the disaster and make provision for his return
to the living busy world from which he is separated.   If he has
a sick relative in charge, he must not undertake to solve the con-
undrum what he ought to do in case the sickness assumes a very
dangerous form, and how he will manage in case of death.   But,
on the other hand, by all means let him feast and fill his soul
with the sensuous, ambrosial delights that surround him, thank
God for the clear, blue skies, the mild uniform temperature,
the soft and balmy airs, the tranquil and beautiful seas, the
strange, wonderful fauna of the emerald water, the picturesque
islets and keys, and the new and most charming vegetable world
that is ever spread out in unfading beauty before him; let him
enjoy the present, trust in the future, and in a Divine Providence
that wisely directs, rules and overrules with unerring wisdom
and unflagging benevolence, and leave to fools and madmen the
bad business of distilling, like wasps and hornets in flower gardens, poisons from present joys.

While considering Nassau's advantages as a health resort in
winter, we ought not to omit to mention the facilities which it
offers for sea bathing.   In this particular nature has done for it
all that could be reasonably asked or desired.   She has furnished
both air and water of a most agreeable temperature at all seasons
of the year, and during all the hours of both day and night.
No cold currents of either air or water are encountered.   The

islands are situated within the limits of the isothermal belt, that in the neighborhood of the equator, nearly encircles, with a warm watery girdle, the earth. The Gulf Stream protects it upon the west and north, while the strong winds, that sometimes prevail, seem unable to bring to the surface the colder water that fills the bed of the vast oceanic basins. Besides private bath houses along the city's harbor front, bathing facilities are furnished near Fort Montague. Crossing the harbor in a row-boat, the north shore of Hog Island is soon reached, where the surf rolls in from the ocean, and bathing of a lively and exciting description can be enjoyed by those who experience an exhilarating pleasure in breasting the strong and foaming billows. Some gentlemen who occasionally tried surf bathing there before breakfast, spoke very highly in its praise, but regretted that no one had life, energy and enterprise enough to smooth the surface of the rocks—a work requiring but a few hours of labor with a hammer.

Some indulged every morning in a sea-water sponge bath in their rooms.

CHAPTER XII.

> "There with a light and easy motion
> The fan-coral sweeps through the clear deep sea,
> And life, in rare and beautiful forms,
> Is sporting amid the bowers of stone,
> While the waters murmur tranquilly
> Through the bending twigs of the coral groves."—PERCIVAL.

WHILE at Nassau it was our happy destiny to make the partial acquaintance of some of the members of a family of the most ceaseless, and indefatigable builders that have ever existed since the world first commenced to keep step to the "music of the spheres," and sweep in grand cycles around the sun. Called into existence by the fiat of Jehovah, in that vague and mysterious "beginning" when "the earth was without form," and "darkness was upon the face of the deep," the little corals, with the first peep of creation's early dawn, commenced, in the warm clear waters of the great primeval sea, their silent, unobtrusive and apparently insignificant work—evidences of which, clear and indisputable, the researches of modern scientists have discovered far inland, hundreds and thousands of miles from where the Western Atlantic billows "beat the sounding shore." In an unbroken line of descent, from the depths of a past so vast and

245

profound that the minds of the wisest men reel, totter and give way when they attempt to grasp and follow it, the little, tireless, plodding, stone-secreting corals of our own times have descended. The monuments of their Past are the islands and continents, whose foundations they laid, that have arisen out of the sea—while the Future patiently, in solemn majesty, awaits the completion, in tropical and semi-tropical latitudes, of those new foundations, now being so quietly and noiselessly laid by these diligent builders, upon which the "new earth" of prophecy is to rest.

Looking at them in the perfectly clear waters of the Bahamas, how insignificant they appear! Studying them more carefully in the light of the vast results which they have already accomplished, they seem foremost among the great builders, made and set apart by God for the erection of homes, in a vast and wild waste of waters, for all the varied forms of vegetable and animal life. Individually they are seemingly as insignificant as the motes in a sun-beam. Collectively, as seen through the dim mists which shroud in gloom the vast unknown periods lying back of the small cycles of recorded time, they glow and are hallowed with a radiance reflected from a divinity whose decrees they execute. "The mill of the gods grinds slow;" to Him who had no beginning and is ever existing, "a thousand years are as one day,"—and as we, from time to time, gazed at and reflected upon these little but most important creatures in their ocean homes, they revealed to us more of the divine than did ever the lofty cloud-capped mountain in its sublimity, or the vast ocean when vexed and tossed by the wildest and most angry storms. Upon our arrival in Nassau they were the first to attract our attention, and, before leaving, they were among the last to engage our thoughts and employ our pen. When we would propose the task of attempting some description of them, we felt an indescribable reluctance to commence, and were awed into silence, knowing that we could make but a faint picture of the corals as they appear to the eye, or give satisfactory expression to the moody speculations which they naturally suggest to an inquiring mind.

The coral was formerly believed to belong to the vegetable kingdom, but naturalists have for some time agreed that it is one of the lowest forms of animal life. To those whom "proud science never taught to stray," it appears, upon casual inspection, to be in some of its forms nothing but a curious and beautiful kind of limestone, and in others a marine vegetable having such a stony habit of growth as closely to ally it to the inanimate rock upon which it builds, and to which it is securely attached and apparently rooted. It belongs to the large family of *coralligerous zoöphytes*, and is found not only in the Bahama waters, but off the coast of Florida, around the Bermuda and West India islands, Madagascar and Mauritius, off the coast of Zanzibar, in the Persian Gulf, in the Red and the Mediterranean Seas, and in the Indian and Pacific oceans; but, as it cannot live and work except in water of the temperature of not less than 68° of Fahrenheit, it is only found within a belt of ocean thirty-six hundred miles wide, through which the line of the equator runs. In colder latitudes, and off the western coast of South America and Africa, it is not found. Some of its reefs are over a thousand miles long.

The most important of the coral-making animals are the Polyps, which in external form and delicacy of coloring Prof. Dana compares to the garden aster. Both have a central disc, fringed with petal-like organs called tenacles. Below the disk the coral polyp has a stout cylindrical pedicel or body which contains the stomach and internal cavity of the polyp. The mouth is in the center of the disk. The coral animal is very domestic, from necessity, being as it were, "tied to its own door-post." Like a tree

or shrub, through its little round of life it remains fastened to
the same spot, and the process of increasing and multiplying
never stops. Closely compacted in compound groups, a single
zoöphyte is formed by a budding process differing little from the
budding process in vegetable growth. The coral animals while
thus closely associated, living together and constantly multiplying, secrete the beautiful corallum or coral of commerce and cab-
inets, which is merely the skeleton on which the soft and perishable
portion of the animal rests, and to which it adheres. Coral reefs
are, in their outer surfaces, mainly composed of great communities of these flowering zoöphytes, below which the dead skeletons
are compacted and solidified.

The coral reefs were divided by Charles Darwin in his Voyage
of a Naturalist, published many years ago, into three classes.
The first, which are found in the immediate neighborhood of the
land, in shallow water, he called fringing reef corals; and the
second, barrier reef corals. These two surround islands or skirt
continents, but they are separated from the neighboring shores
by navigable channels, while their outer margins often border
ocean depths as vast as those seen from lofty mountain tops. A
barrier coral reef is formed off the coast of Australia, of sufficient
length to more than reach from Nassau to New York. It is from
twenty to thirty miles from the shore, and is a breakwater to a
great natural highway, having a depth of water of from sixty to
six hundred feet. The remaining class of coral reefs are circular
in form and are called atolls. They encircle great lagoons, or
large areas of ocean water, to which access is generally obtained
through breaches or openings upon their leeward sides—where
we would naturally anticipate the little corals would be most actively at work, as they would be there less exposed to the force
and fury of the ocean when its billows are storm-tossed. But
Creative Wisdom has secured their services for the windward side

by making it a law of their existence not merely that they shall be constantly under water which is clear and of a temperature of not less than 68° Fahr., but that the water shall be aerated; the ceaseless dashing of the waves against the rocks and reefs on the windward side saturates them with air, as the foaming breakers and sparkling spray clearly indicate; and hence it is that here, in the ever seething, boiling, foaming waters, these silent, unobtrusive and seemingly unimportant creatures, with a lineage reaching back to "chaos and old night," are found in the greatest numbers, reach their highest development, and accomplish the best results. Thus do the ocean depths below us, where by an alchemy far surpassing the skill and genius of man, the little corals secrete from the ocean waves the limestone foundations for islands and continents that are yet to be, equally with the depths above where suns and systems of worlds revolve, forever reveal to the observing eye and inquiring mind the perfect and profound wisdom of their common Creator.

We have spoken of the corals as builders, and in practical results, such they pre-eminently are, but, as Prof. Dana has shown, they do not labor like the bird in constructing its nest or the beaver in making its dam, but, by a law of their nature, they secrete the corallum or coral as man makes his own bones or the oyster its shell, and the vast coral formations found upon the land and in the ocean are composed of the skeletons which they have left behind them.

No costly sarcophagus of deceased royalty—no mausoleum which human skill and ingenuity has ever erected—no Egyptian pyramid rising grandly out of the shadows of four thousand departed years, can even in a remote degree rival in beauty and sublimity the vast and varied tumuli of these little dwellers in tropical and semi-tropical seas.

The corals and corallum in extensive beds abound in the Bahama waters, and afford one of the principal attractions for those who visit this part of Queen Victoria's possessions. We have seen and studied them at various times and under different circumstances, and yet we feel, not only that our knowledge of them is imperfect and superficial, but that we can convey to others only a crude and unsatisfactory reflection of the impression they made upon our own mind. The effect is heightened by all the surrounding circumstances. There is nothing to annoy or produce any but pleasurable sensations. New but congenial friends meet together by a subtle law of attraction, recline on the cushions, occupy the comfortable chairs, or sit on the circular seats of the "Trident," the "Gazelle" or the "Frolic." It is, to be sure, mid-winter, but no northern summer air ever seemed half so soft, soothing and voluptuous. We have not known each other long, and yet there is such an absence of reserve, such an interchange of thought, such an expression of pleasurable emotions, and such a telling of rich and racy anecdotes, that a looker-on would have supposed we were life-long acquaintances and friends. Feasting and surfeiting upon types and forms of beauty never seen or even imagined in our colder climes, it was a relief to be aided in the audible expression of delightful emotions by the combined vocabularies of our little group of explorers.

Visits to the coral beds and reefs are made exceedingly attractive by reason of the peculiar clearness and beauty of the water over which we sail to reach them and in which they are found. No snow fed mountain torrent was ever more clear and transparent, and, as the water-bed is white limestone, objects at the bottom can be seen with great distinctness. On one occasion of relatively smooth water, a mile or so outside of the bar of Nassau harbor, we clearly saw the bottom at a depth of about seventy feet. The sounding line showed seventy-six feet, but some discount must be made, because, as our yacht was in motion, the line could not have been perpendicular.

The water of the harbor is most exquisitely colored. It is a soft, delicate, brilliant green, wholly unlike any of the countless shades of green seen in the vegetable world. When the waves are gently rolling in a brilliant sunlight, they gleam and sparkle in a manner but faintly represented by the most beautifully tinted silks when their graceful folds are in motion under a strong light. It cannot be properly described upon paper, and if faithfully imitated upon canvass by the most gifted artist he would be charged by art critics and connoisseurs with painting the ideal, and with being color mad. One never tires of looking at it, but soon gets out of descriptive and eulogistic adjectives, and rests with a final declaration that it is a brilliant, moving, liquid, sparkling, lovely torquoise. At times, when the winds and sunlight are particularly favorable, such color effects are produced that practical, prosaic men seem to vie with the more susceptible and appreciative ladies in their exclamations of astonishment and pleasure. A lady in our party on one occasion when we visited the corals, exclaimed while gazing, feasting and almost getting intoxicated upon this wonderful exhibition of color, "What would our friends at home say if they could only see this! They think that they know water, but they don't."

Occasional rifts in the limestone bed of the harbor vary the prevailing color with ribbons of the deepest and darkest blue, while the ocean outside is seen to darkly mirror the softer blue of the sky. Often also there is at midday a warm glow above the horizon like that which heralds the ushering in of a new day.

As we near the homes of the corals the foaming and dashing of the breakers over coral reefs and submerged rocks reminds one of our party of the icy spray of an Alpine avalanche, and adds a new and pleasing variety to the view, while the neighboring

islands with honeycombed shores, and short patches of white
sandy beaches, also contribute other elements of beauty. The
purple haze resting upon the island of New Providence also re-
calls the aerial investiture of the shores of the Mediterranean Sea.

We are soothed and lulled by a soft silvery melody, the water
rising and singing sweetly to us as we glide along; the music
perfectly harmonizes with the calm and voluptuous beauty which
nature has lavishly bestowed upon this favored locality.

Snatches of poetry long concealed in some of the nooks and
corners of the mind, and forgotten—the gathered gems of earlier
years—emerge from their hiding places amid scenes and surroundings so congenial, (just as the beautiful and perfumed blossoms of the arbutus awaken from their winter's sleep in the warm
breath of the opening spring,) and we again exclaim with Fay :

"Blow scented gale, the snowy canvass swell,
And flow, thou gleaming eddying current, on ;
Grieve me to bid each lovely point farewell,
That, ere its graces half are seen, is gone.

"Nor clouds in heaven, nor billows on the deep,
More graceful shapes did ever have or roll,
Nor came such pictures to a poet's sleep,
Nor beamed such visions on a poet's soul."

The "Marine Garden," through which the reader may remember we passed when returning from our yachting excursion to
test the capabilities of Sampson's Triton in a strong wind outside
the bar, is nearer to Nassau and more accessible than any of the
other localities where the corals abound in this vicinity. Hence
it is the most visited and the best known. Situated between
two islands, it is more sheltered from the wind, and the consequent comparative smoothness of the water enables the visitors
at all times to examine it. Being a flower garden under water,

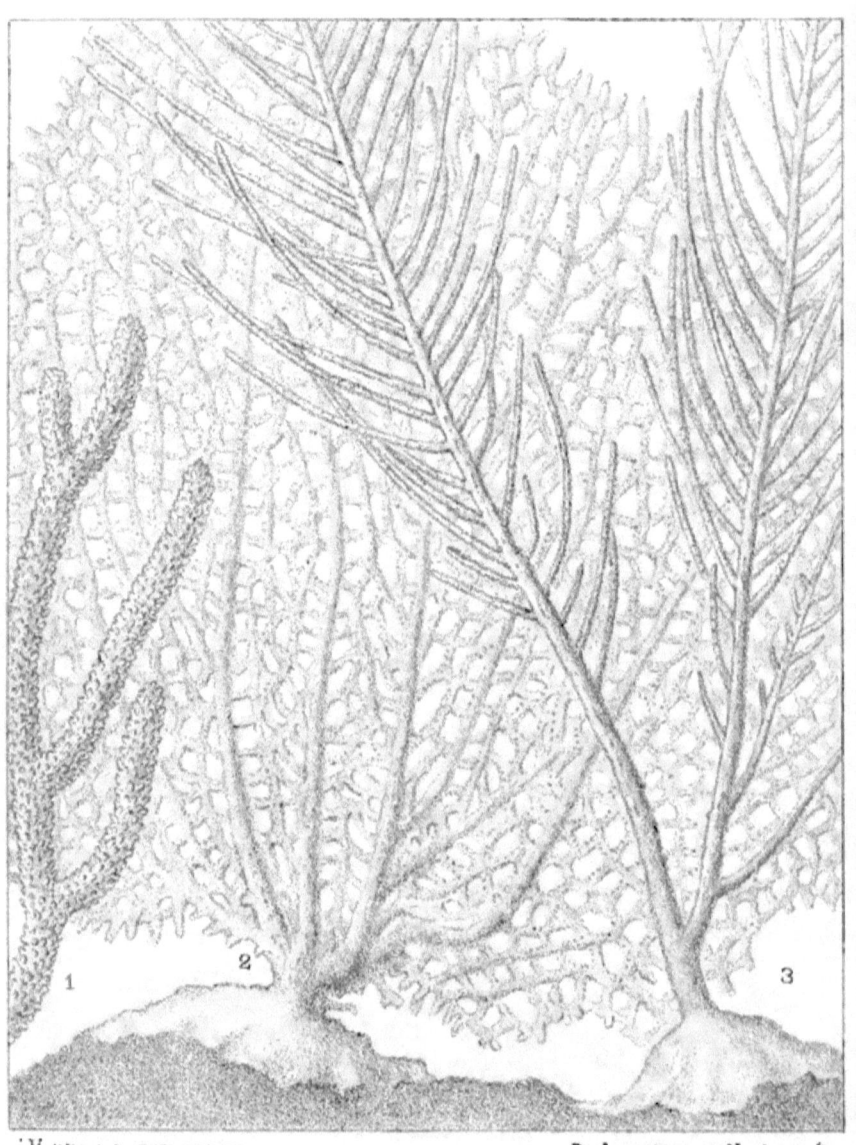

CORALS

WHITE STONY CORALS.

1. *Agaricia agaricites.* A piece from the edge of a large mass. Natural size. In life each hole was occupied by an animal with separate mouth and tentacles, but connected at the base with all the others around it.

2. *Porites clavaria.* End of a branch. Natural size.

3. *Eusmilia fastigiata.* "Rose Coral." A branch. Natural size. Formed of four distinct animals, two of which are nearly divided across the middle.

4. *Millepora alcicornis.* "Sea Ginger." When fresh it has a biting taste. A branch from a large piece. Natural size. This belongs to the *Hydroids,* a different class from most corals. In life the soft parts of the animals are extended through minute holes on the surface, marked by dark spots in the figure.

5. *Madrepora prolifera.* "Finger Coral." Branch from a large piece. Natural size. Each animal forms a cup-shaped projection. The terminal one, from which those below have branched, is larger than the others.

6. *Manicina areolata.* A young specimen. Natural size. Attached to the rock. From Agassiz's Report on Florida Reefs.

FLEXIBLE CORALS (GORGONIAS.)

Corals with a hard, flexible core, covered with a softer outer layer, which is usually brightly colored.

1. *Muricea muricata.* A branch. Natural size. Light orange-color in life.

2. *Gorgonia flabellum.* "Fan Coral." Light purple or bright yellow in color. A small specimen. Natural size. The black spots along the edges of some of the branches mark the holes from which the mouths and tentacles extended when the coral was alive.

3. *Gorgonia setosa.* "Sea Feather." One-fourth natural size. Color, light pink or purple.

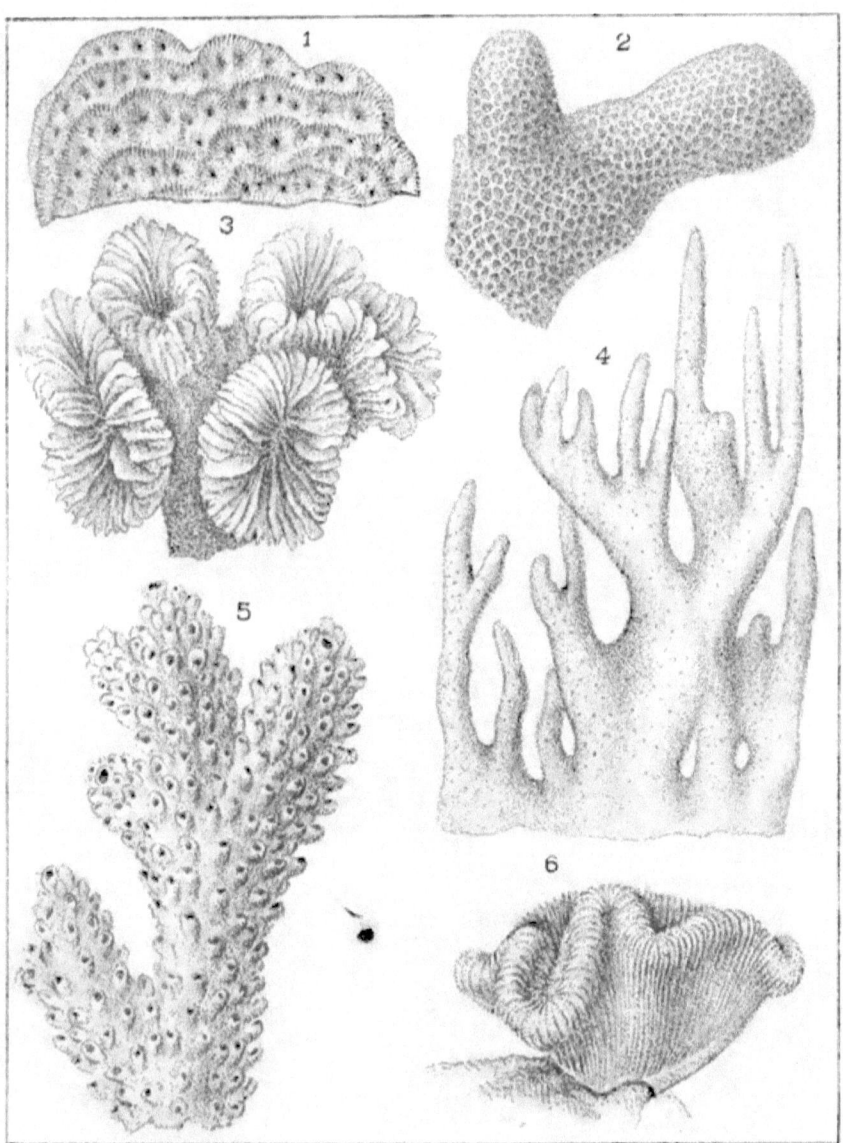

CORALS

the eye cannot explore it when the surface is rough. Each boat is therefore provided with "water glasses," wooden boxes about eight or ten inches square, open at the top, with window glass bottoms; to the boxes are attached wooden handles from eighteen inches to three feet long. Holding this little instrument over the side of a boat at anchor, in such a manner that the glass bottom is immersed, the observer who looks through the open end of the water glass can see all the "wonders of the deep" in the line of his vision as plainly as he could if no water intervened.

This marine garden is made up of the most exquisite submerged coral bowers and grottoes, which rival the choicest productions of the floral world in form and color. We can hardly believe our eyes when such charming and unexpected beauties are first revealed by the water glass. The madrepora or branching coral is very abundant, and is here and there seen of a large size. The astræa or brain coral also abounds, and masses of it are seen many feet in diameter. Alcyonoid polyps, (delicate coral shrubs,) vie with the gay, varied and luxuriant algæ in decorating the garden with their curious growths. They are peculiarly delicate in form, graceful in motion, and attractive in color. The gorgonias or sea-fans, also diversified in size and color, unite with the large clusters of tall, purple sea-feathers in challenging the admiration of all beholders, as they gracefully wave in the clear water like tall flowering shrubs in the wind.

Sponges are here also seen, clustered and combined in their little miniature cities, and immovably fastened to the rocky shelf upon which the warm, clear, beautiful waters rest. New and exquisite forms of coral beauty startle and charm us as our yacht slowly circles round her anchor in different portions of this curious nautical exhibition. Into deep alcoves and recesses, and far under shelving masses of corals, we inquiringly gaze, but an im-

18

penetrable mystery hides in the shadows where no sunlight enters, and, by a most striking contrast, helps to glorify and adorn the beautiful and unique forms that the light reveals.

New and wonderful combinations of these (to us) strange forms of marine animal and vegetable life, when first observed and closely studied, is the occasion of new expressions of delight. If sea-nymphs and ocean fairies exist anywhere in the world of waters, their chosen home should surely be in these coral bowers and grottoes; and if they are ever embodied, their outward adornments cannot in color surpass that of the fish we saw sporting in the sunlight, and darting into the dark recesses of this beautiful submerged coral world. Exquisite in form, the perfection of gracefulness in motion, the peers of birds of gayest plumage in color, they seemed specially adapted to harmonize with, and grace and adorn this lovely spot. As with water, so "our friends at home think they know fish—but they don't." Some are brilliant yellow, others a rich scarlet, and others a glossy indigo blue. Here are seen fish in suits of emerald green, and others in clerical black. Costumes of satin and silver may also be observed. Besides all these there is in the piscatory dwellers among the corals a most gorgeous color display, resulting from the ringing and striping and fringing and tipping and spotting of the fish. Indeed, it seems as if all the tints of the floral world and of the rainbow had been used in the most perfect and lavish manner to beautify and adorn these small specimens of the native dwellers of the ocean world. One of these, most gorgeously colored, was brought to us in a pail of sea water at our hotel, and we had an opportunity to more critically examine it. It was six inches long. Capt. Sampson called it the humming bird fish. We bottled it in alcohol, but its beautiful colors soon faded away. A description of some of these remarkable fauna of the sea the reader will find in the next chapter of this book. The real in the coral bowers is more gorgeous than the ideal.

Besides the coral beds there are two "aquariums," as they are very appropriately termed, in the harbor of Nassau, easily accessible, which few, if any, of Nassau's visitors fail to see. One consists of the keel and small portions of the attached ribs of a wrecked vessel lying upon the bottom of the harbor. The other is what is left of another vessel wrecked not far from the first, with its load of lime in barrels: these barrels are distinctly seen in the clear water. Great quantities of fish like those we have partially described, are at all times to be seen swimming in and around these old wrecks; as the coral bowers are so much more beautiful, we conclude they are here not from choice but from compulsion, and that they have been driven out of the Marine Gardens of Eden to these forbidding-looking places on account of their piscatory "indiscretions." Possibly they colonized for want of sufficient room. Perhaps, like ourselves, they are "on an excursion." It may be that they have some religious system and are here doing penance for real or imagined sins, or hope to secure divine favor by thus renouncing the gay world in which the voluptuous marine Epicureans are indulging. For surely no one can doubt that living, as such fish for the most part do, in a little world of more than oriental magnificence of fact and fable, they have a delicate and refined taste and an esthetic nature which peculiarly fits them for the enjoyment of nature's most lavish gifts to them of the beautiful in form and color.

Another marine garden very much visited is called "the coral reef." Being much farther off, and lying to the windward, in a position more exposed to the ocean, it is only occasionally that there is such a combination of force and direction of wind as to favor a visit to the reef. It must be sufficiently fair to enable the yacht to go and return in a certain limited time, and not so strong as to make rough sea. The water at this reef being more aerated, the corals thrive better, and their works are on a more extensive scale. Here the branching coral of a large size is very abundant—a variety familiar to all our readers. When taken from the water, it is of a light drab or yellow color, and for a while has a disagreeable odor, both of which it loses when exposed for a time to the air and the sunlight. We took the liberty to give this "reef" a better descriptive name, and, with the permission of Her Majesty Queen Victoria, and of her official representatives in the Bahamas, to call it, "*Coral Bowers and Grottoes*"—for such it literally is. It is the "Marine Garden" enlarged and magnified. It abounded with "wood paths wild," in miniature forests of coral,—dark recesses in groves that gleamed in brightness and beauty—alcoves carved in forms grotesque but beautiful, and profusely ornamented—vaulted isles of an architectural design and finish that dwarfed and belittled the products of human skill and genius—cave openings, elaborately wrought and strangely configured and adorned, yawning beneath coral banks and bowers wild and endlessly varied—all constituting a vast natural aquarium, the home of large numbers of fish like those seen in the Marine Garden, brilliantly and most gorgeously colored, which bore the same relation to the little aquariums that man makes that the vast and magnificent tropical forests, clothed in perennial green, adorned with graceful vines, teeming with flowers of every hue, and vocal with countless birds of the most varied and of the richest plumage, bear to a lady's little but luxurious boudoir, with its evergreen branches, climbing vines and captive birds in their small but gilded cages. Turning our eyes upward, surfeited as they were with the truly wonderful display below the surface of the water, it was restful to look again at the soft but resplendent beauty of the blue heavens, here and there draped with light curtains of satin and silver, and at the gem-like setting in the green and blue waters of the islands, keys and rocks, with their varied outlines and colors visible in every direction, while we inhaled, meanwhile an atmosphere delightfully cooled and medicated by the ocean, and yet sufficiently warm to saturate us with an indolence we could not shake off, and with a feeling of languid and voluptuous ease, satisfaction and content. We seemed tenants of a new world where ambition is unknown and the passions are either dead or lost in a sleep profound and dreamless. Let not the reader for a moment indulge in any suspicions that this picture is overdrawn, for it is not within the power of any man to so color his descriptions of the coral bowers as to convey any proper idea of their marvelous beauty, or to do justice to the original. The most gifted pen can only caricature nature's perfect works. He who is not greatly exhilarated, excited and charmed while viewing the coral beds of the Bahamas, under the favoring circumstances which we have attempted to describe, is certainly color blind, and, as H. W. Beecher would say, "dead in the eye." In the language of Shakespeare, when speaking of music, "let no such man be trusted."

On a charming forenoon in March, 1879, when sailing in the "Gazelle" in a very light wind, we were for the first time becalmed just as we came to anchor over a large bed of coral to which we were piloted by Capt. Johnson, of the existence of which we were until then ignorant. For half an hour the wind failed to make itself felt, and the water was perfectly smooth and glassy. To our great joy we found that we could stand upon the deck of our yacht and see, without water glasses or any artificial aid, an extensive tract of corals with their swarms of beautiful fish, and even the shadows of some of them on the white bottom of the harbor, at a distance, we judged, of about twenty-five feet from the surface. Among the corals we observed here, as elsewhere, many algae, gorgonias and sponges growing upon the limestone floor to which they were attached. One

sponge was of the size and shape of a half bushel basket.   It was
secured for us, but proved to be old and rotten.

Here also, as in the "Marine Garden," and in the "coral
bowers and grottoes," way down in the edges of the lowest and
darkest shadows, we occasionally observed fishes repulsive in form
and diabolical in expression, whose movements were most decidedly stealthy and suspicious.   What business had they to grope
in the caverns and peer into the sunlight?   What was their mission in the garden of the sea gods?   Were they piscatory bull
dogs to guard and protect, or piscatory demons bent on marring
a happiness which their lower nature was unfitted to enjoy?

Our crew consisted in part of expert divers, who, as soon as we
anchored over or near to a coral bed, entered the little forecastle,
and soon re-appeared in costumes, not of Parisian, but of the
Garden of Eden cut—and truly "Solomon in all his glory was
not arrayed like one of these."   When a growth of coral was discovered by any one of the passengers, peculiarly beautiful and
coveted, the diver immediately plunged overboard and soon detached and brought it to the surface, unless it proved to be too
large and heavy, or too securely fastened for his strength.   It
is a novel and very amusing spectacle, and we could not refrain
from speculating upon the probable impression these black intruders made upon the gay and sportive dwellers in coral bowers.
If to us they seemed like imps of destruction, marring a beauty
they could not make, and disturbing a felicity they could not
appreciate or enjoy, no doubt the little gorgeous finny philosophers were not only shocked and appalled by the desecration and
destruction which they witnessed, but sorely puzzled to reconcile
it with their ideas of what infinite justice and goodness should
either do or permit.

Slowly moving out into view from under cover at the base of
the corals there is seen at times the sea-urchin, a shell fish from

two to four inches in diameter, which bristles with long, black,
needle-like spines. When these spines are removed it is seen to
be a shell-fish, round but flat like a large biscuit, very prettily
shaped and marked. The negroes daily bring these shells to the
court of the hotel and sell them to visitors under the name of
" sea eggs."

These curiously armed shell-fish appear to perform police duty,
and their sharp spines often cause the colored intruder discom-
fited to retire. One of our divers was made quite lame by one
of these creatures, the broken spine in his foot irritating and in-
flaming the flesh, and requiring for its proper removal the instruments and skill of the surgeon.

The barbs with which the spines are covered, are like so many
minute fish hooks; they readily admit the entrance of the spines
into the flesh of man or fish, but prevent their removal; so that
as an enemy, although small, they are somewhat formidable.

In consulting the works that have been occasionally published
concerning the Bahamas, we have been astonished at finding in
them so little in regard to the great clearness and brilliant hues
of the water, and the strange and exquisitely beautiful sub-aque-
ous world which the water glass reveals. Catesby appears to
have seen and described more than most, if not all, the authors
who have succeeded him.

There was occasionally brought to us by the divers specimens
of corals and gorgonias with some of the soft coraline rock to
which they adhered, and to which they seemed rooted, and we
were surprised to see that these fragments of the rocky floor of
the sea gardens abounded with worms and other forms of life.
Mr. Phelps states that he broke a large piece of this rock into
small fragments, and found in it a number of small crabs, two
or three small star fishes, three or more shrimps, three worms
organized like a centiped, and some monopod worms. He be-

lieved it contained not less than fifty living creatures. Channels had also been cut in the stone six inches deep, by stone-boring mollusks. When Capt. Basil Hall wrote a description of the corals in his "Voyage to the Islands of Loo Choo," which the author of "The Pelican Island" used as a text for his poem, he evidently supposed that corallum is the work of the "worms of different lengths and colors" with which the bottom rock is "full,"—hence the great mistake which both authors made.

We deem it not improbable that it will ultimately be discovered that corals, as well as sponges, can be artificially propagated; if so, we see no reason why the more valuable red varieties may not be successfully cultivated in the Bahama waters. The colonial government, at a small expense, can by wise legislation cause experiments looking to such a result to be made. The old world has colonized the new with men, choice live stock, delicious fruits and destructive insects—why should it not give us its superior sponges and corals?

Referring the reader to the excellent work of Prof. Dana, upon "Corals and Coral Islands," for full and complete information from a scientific standpoint upon the subject of this chapter, we take leave of the corals for the present, fully aware that we have hardly crossed the threshold where we would have been only too happy, had we been able, to fully enter and thoroughly explore.

ECHINODERMS.

1. *Echinanthus rosaceus.* Upper side. One-third natural size, covered with short purple or olive spines when alive.

2. *Oreaster gigas.* It is sometimes more than a foot in diameter. Covered with hard knobs connected by low ridges. Bright red or orange, when alive.

3, 4. *Cidaris tribuloides.* 4. A small specimen in its natural state. 3. The same after the spines have been removed, showing the knobs to which they are attached. One-half natural size.

5. *Diadema setosum.* A "Sea Egg" with very long spines. Black, or banded with black and yellow. When the spines are removed it resembles fig. 3, but the knobs are smaller and more numerous. One-half natural size.

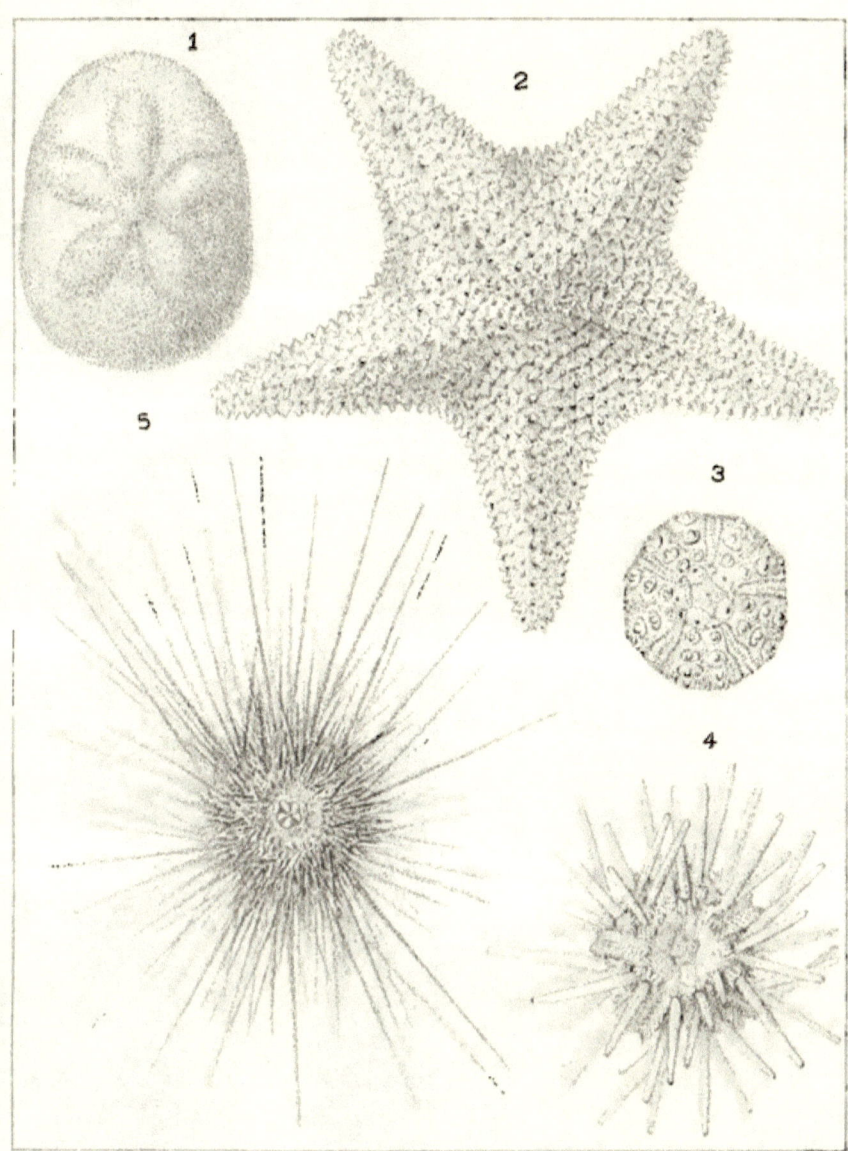

ECHINODERMS

CHAPTER XIII.

The Extent of the World of Waters and its Wonderful Fauna. Bahama Fishes. Some Eminently Distinguished for their Brilliant Colors, and Others for their Singularity, described. Fish that are Poisonous. Table Fish. The Bahamas Rich in Beautiful Mollusks. They Harmonize with the other Exquisite Forms of Life, and with the Brilliant Waters. The Shores Paved with Shells Wonderful in Form and Color. The Conch.

> "In the free element beneath us swarm
> Fishes of every color, form, and kind,—
> Strange forms, resplendent colors, kinds unnumbered—
> Which language cannot paint, and mariner
> Hath never elsewhere seen."—MONTGOMERY.

WHEN we consider that the sea occupies more than two-thirds of the earth's surface; that its normal temperature is, from the equator to the arctic circle, nearly uniform every where, below a few hundred perpendicular feet of its surface; that its depths are most profound, being measured by miles; that although it is for man's convenience geographically divided, and called by different names, yet that all the so-called oceans are in fact one, and that it abounds throughout the whole of its vast extent with animals that are created and fitted to live in the water as others are upon the land, we cannot fail to see that in all probability its fauna is far more extensive and varied than that of the land, and that man's knowledge concerning it is very meagre, superficial and imperfect. It is quite recently that the gigantic cuttle fish has been taken out of the realm of fable and

225

placed in the wide domain of fact. While Victor Hugo's "devil fish," closely resembles, in many particulars, the gigantic cuttle fish, yet, to some extent, it is a creature which the imagination has constructed upon a substantial basis of fact. A scientific gentleman, learned in all the piscatory learning of the present day, stated in our presence before the Connecticut Academy of Arts and Sciences, that he had no doubt of the existence of the sea serpent, and that before many years it will be captured and critically examined by scientific experts. There is something truly grand in the movements of the monsters of the deep through the vast depths and immense spaces of the great world of waters. But it is apparent that while some fish are able to wander at will in various directions around the world, others are localized by their necessities, and complete their little circle of life very near their family spawning ground. Hence the water that surrounds the Isles of Summer, and that covers the Banks out of which they rise, has its own peculiar and wonderful fauna, some glimpses of which were revealed to us while we were looking through the water glasses at the corals, and the curious and wonderful forms of life which surround and adorn them.

Many of these fish Mr. Phelps secured and preserved, and having carefully and critically examined them at his home in Vermont, and closely studied them both in and out of the water during his five months stay in Nassau, he has furnished us detailed descriptions of some of them, which we have utilized. We have edited his notes, and shaped them somewhat to fill the limited space that we have been able to spare for them in a volume which treats of so many other subjects. We did not ourselves make the fish a special object of study. We have retained, as far as possible, the language of Mr. Phelps, and to him and Mr. Catesby should be given credit for whatever of merit there may be in nearly all our piscatory pen pictures.

The *Rainbow fish* is from six to twelve inches long. Its color is a dark green. Its scales are large, and their tinted margins reflect the light in all the colors of the rain-bow—hence its name. Its teeth are like those of the bluefish, with two plates upon each jaw, which protrude from its lips.

The *Parrot fish* is most brilliantly colored. It is principally of a bluish green, with purple marks on the back and near the mouth, and yellow and red marks near the tail. The scales are edged with a dark wine color.

Catesby's description of it is more full; he says the body of the Parrot fish is covered with large green scales; the eye is red and yellow; the upper part of the head brown, the lower part and gills blue, bordered with dusky red; a streak of red extends from the tail to behind the gills, at the upper end of which there is a bright yellow spot. It has five fins; one extends almost the length of the back, and is of a bay or cinnamon color; there are two behind the gills blended with black, green and purplish colors, with their edge verged with blue. Under the abdomen is another red fin, verged with blue; under the anus extends another long, narrow green fin, with a list of red through the middle of it. At the basis of the tail, on each side, is a large yellow spot. The tail is large, forked, and green, with a curved line running through the middle, parallel to the curve of the tail, and ending in white points. It is more remarkable for its beauty than esteemed for delicacy.

The *Spanish Hog fish* is about ten inches in length, and weighs about one pound. The color of its upper portion—being all above a line drawn from the extremity of the dorsal fin to the pectoral fin—is a dark purple wine color, with dark brown bands on the edges of the tail; below this line the color is yellow, deepening in some places into orange. It is beautiful but poisonous.

The *Yellow Angel fish* is unsurpassed for the admiration which

its beauty elicits.   Colored plates are necessary to give any ade-
quate idea of the wealth of coloring with which it is endowed,
The body is short and high.   The dorsal and anal fins are very
large, protruding at the anterior parts, and thick at the base and
corners with scales, so that they seem to be a continuation of the
body.   The scales are large and delicate, of a brown color, with
a shade of olive green, and each of them is edged with a lighter
tint.   The chin, nape, upper eyelid, base of the pectoral and
neutral fins, and the margin of the dorsal and anal fins are a
bright cobalt blue, with lines of the same color extending over
the operculum.   The caudal fin, and the continuation or appendage of the longest spines of the dorsal and anal fins are bright
yellow.   The motions of this, as of all the other angel fish, are
slow, and it is usually to be seen about the docks, reefs, and old
wrecks.   Its flesh is not much prized.

The *Black Angel fish* is of a much larger size than the preceding, and is of an uniform black color.   The inner surfaces of the
pectoral fins and the margin of the tail are of a bright yellow.

The *Spanish Angel fish* is one of the most beautiful of fishes.
The anterior part of the body is a jet black, while the posterior
and tail are a light yellow.   The edges of the gills, and margin
of the tail are a salmon red color.   It is seldom over five inches
in length, and is caught in nets and traps, its mouth being too
small and delicate for the hook.

Catesby truthfully says, that this fish is "gorgeous, and may
be called the butterfly of the sea, it is so beautiful."

The *Moon or Crescent Angel fish* has a body much compressed
and elevated.   It has six dark vertical bands.   The third dorsal
spine is elongated, and the anterior portion of the dorsal and anal
fins are protruding.   The four crescent-shaped marks on the body
are of a bright yellow, the margin of the tail is edged with the
same tint.   It sometimes is found eighteen inches long.

The *Four-Eyed Angel fish* has a black spot on each side of its tail. The fishermen believe these spots to be an extra pair of eyes—hence its name. The color of the body is a pearly gray; the vertical fins are a bright yellow, and a black band runs across the eye. It has a nearly circular outline, with a projecting and protruding snout. It is a delicate, graceful fish. It is seen among the sea-feathers, and around the coral reefs. It seldom exceeds four inches in length, and must be caught with net or trap, as its mouth is too small for the hook.

The *Bahama Turbot* is of a bright bluish green above, and of an orange and orange blue beneath. The dorsal and anal fins are very large, and these, with the tail, have long continuations, all of which are of a dark green color. There is a light green band between the tail and body. Extending round from the mouth are two curved, slate-tinted marks running back to the gills. The pectoral fins are small. From the eyes radiate slender umber-brown lines, some of which pass around in front of the head from eye to eye. The scales are very rough and strong, and are often used for scouring and polishing wood and metals. The first dorsal fin is very prominent: the first spine, being very stout, is often used as a weapon. The body is very much depressed, and resembles that of the angel fish.

The *Trumpet* or *Unicorn fish*, much resembles the turbot in structure, but its body is more elongated and compressed, being about twenty-four inches in length, and nearly half an inch in thickness. Unlike the turbot, the dorsal and anal fins are very transparent, with a slight yellow tinge. The tail is long and very small; the mouth is situated on the upper edge of the snout; the teeth are large and compact; the color is a light ash tint, with many peculiar lines and marks of a light slate blue; a long slender spine rises from the head—hence its name. The scales are minute and resemble those of the shark.

Catesby says that this fish is sometimes three feet long; that it is shaped like a rolling-pin, and tapers towards the head and tail; that it can raise, and point backwards and forwards at its pleasure, the tapering sharp pointed bone that is found a little behind the eyes, but that this bone is brittle and easily broken. He also states that this fish feeds on shells and coralline substances, and is considered poisonous, and is found where corals are plentiful.

The *Cow fish* is from five to twenty inches in length. The appearance of this fish is exceedingly queer and comical. This is especially true of its face, which is that of its great namesake in small miniature. Whether this shell fish has infringed upon the cow's facial copyright, or the cow upon that of this odd fish, we are unable to decide. Its body is shaped like a beech nut, being triangular. The shell in which it is entirely enclosed (except the lips, base of fins, hind part of tail and eyes), is composed of hexagonal osseous scales; the parts excepted are covered with a soft skin; over each eye there is a prominent conical spine, which points straight forward, and helps much to give the face of the fish its cow-like appearance. On each neutral ridge there is a flat spine directed backward. The carapace is of a rich, bright blue color, with brown lines, and is very beautiful when seen in a good light, but it changes a good deal and the colors soon vanish after death. Its motions are slow and cautious, and it sometimes ejects water from its mouth to a distance of four feet.

The *Triangular fish* or *Cuckold Shell-fish*, (as it is called by the natives), is about twelve inches in length, and sometimes weighs two pounds. The integuments of the body are modified into a three ridged carapace, composed of hexagonal osseous scales. The snout-like mouth, the basis of the fins, and the hind part of the tail are covered by soft skin. On each neutral ridge is a flat prominent spine, directed backwards. The color is quite changeable; it is usually of a bluish cast, with brown spots and marks. It is a slow swimmer, and is often seen resting on the bottom. It will live several hours out of water without undergoing any apparent change, but when returned to the water, it is at first unable to sink to the bottom on account of the air it has absorbed. Its pectoral fins are constantly in motion, apparently for the purpose of fanning a current of water through the gills. Its flesh is of a light color, and its appearance and taste is like the breast of a chicken. It is best baked, but is said to be at times poisonous.

The *Squirrel fish* is very beautiful. Its color is scarlet, and in brightness exceeds that of the gold fish. Its body is elongated and slightly compressed. Its head is well proportioned, and has prominent spines. It swims quickly and vivaciously. The local name refers to a noise uttered by it which resembles the bark of a squirrel. It is very common in the Bahamas, and is usually the angler's first prize. It is little valued as a table fish on account of its small size.

The *Hind* is a very common and very handsome fish, and sometimes attains a length of eighteen inches. It is of a brownish or rosy-white color, and is marked with numerous deep rose-red spots. Being very voracious, it is easily caught. Its flesh is finely flavored, and is seldom, if ever, poisonous.

The *Blue fish* is from ten to eighteen inches long, and weighs about two pounds. Its color is ultramarine, with a few pink marks about the head and eyes. Catesby says the iris of its eyes is red. Its scales are relatively large, and are used in the manufacture of fancy work.

The *Bone fish* has scales which are used in making the most exquisite fancy work. The scales, after being washed in several waters, are cut into the desired shape, and pierced in two places for the very small silver wires with which they are fastened. Several weeks time is required to make a single scale basket.

The *Alewife* is of a greenish color, and is closely allied to *Slippery Dick.*

The *Great Hog Fish* is named from its swine-like profile and dentition. Its body is compressed and elevated; its snout pointed; its dorsal fin protruding, and its skin resembles brown and red marble, being light beneath. When it swims, the dorsal fins and their long streamer-like appendages give it a singular and graceful appearance. It is quite common, attains a length of thirty inches, and a weight of thirty pounds. Its flesh is hard, white and exquisitely flavored, and it is numbered among the choicest table fish.

The *School Master* is fifteen inches in length, weighs three to four pounds, and its color is an attractive bronze. It is not a safe table fish.

The *Porcupine Fish,* or *Sea Hedge Hog,* is a truly wonderful creature on account of its peculiar armor, and of its capacity to swallow either air or water, and thereby become ball-shaped. Its body is covered with triangular plates, from each of which rises a sharp spine, and some of the spines are an inch in length. When alarmed, it fills its body with air or water, thereby assuming a globular form, erects all its spines, and presents a formidable appearance. In this position it resembles an immense chestnut burr. Its color is brown above and light beneath, with spots of darker brown near the operculum. One of the smaller ones which Mr. Phelps secured, he says, was five inches long, and four inches in diameter.

The *Swell Fish,* or *Puffer,* is of an olive green color, and its surface is roughened with prickles. Its body is oblong and cylindrical. It derives its name from the swollen ball-like shape which it assumes when taken from the water, and irritated. It is from

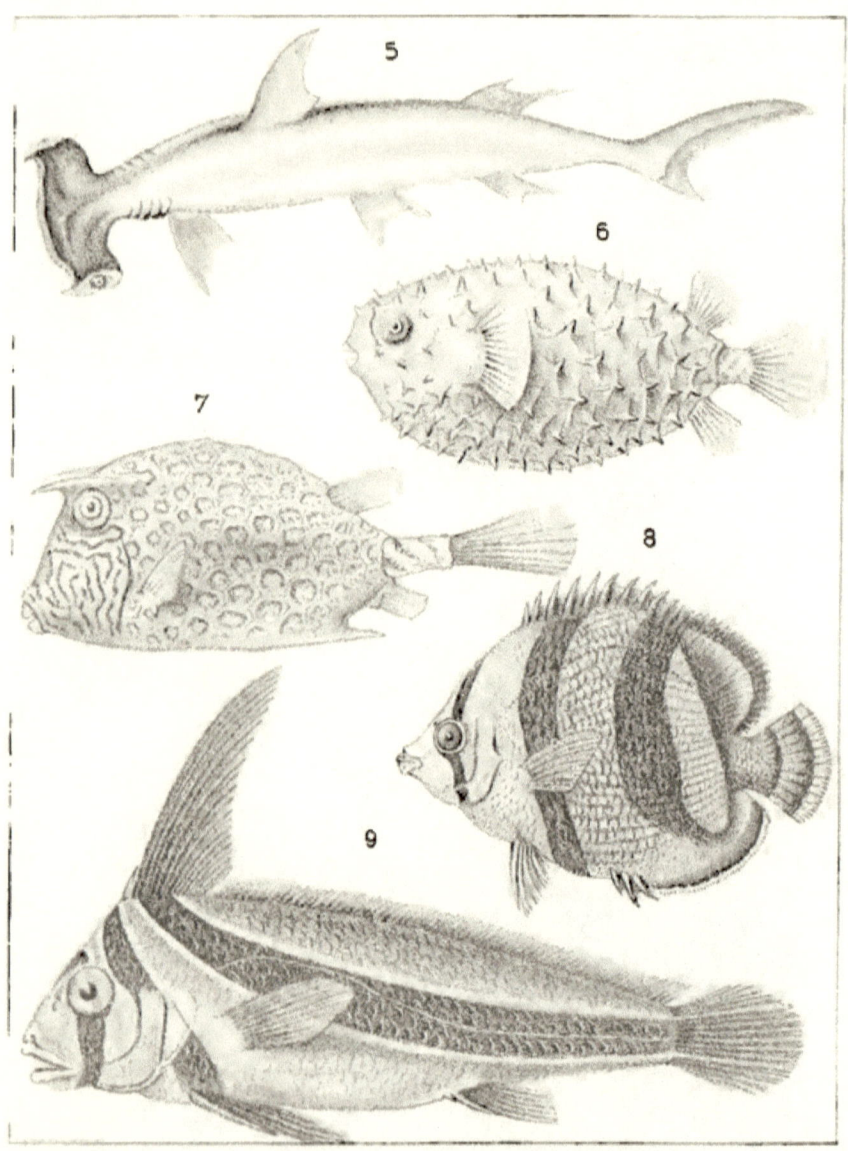

5

6

7

8

9

FISHES.

FISHES.

1.   *Echeneis albicauda*, "Sucker," from "Storer's Fishes of Mass." One-fourth natural size. Attaches itself to other fishes by the sucker on its head.

2.   *Fistularia tabaccaria*, "Trumpet Fish." One-fourth natural size.

3.   *Malthea vespertilio*, "Bat Fish." One-half natural size.

4.   *Coryphaena hippurus*, "Dolphin." Colors, metallic green and yellow with black spots. Remarkable for its changes of color when taken from the water.

5.   *Zygaena tudes*. "Hammer-head Shark."

6.   *Chilomycterus reticulatus*, "Porcupine Fish." One-fourth natural size.

7.   *Ostracion quadricornis*, "Trunk Fish," "Cow Fish." One-fourth natural size. This and the last are drawn from stuffed specimens.

8.   *Chaetodon striatus*, "Angel Fish." One-half natural size.

9.   *Eques lanceolatus*. One-half natural size.

   Figures 2, 3, 4, 5, 8 and 9 are reduced from Cuvier.

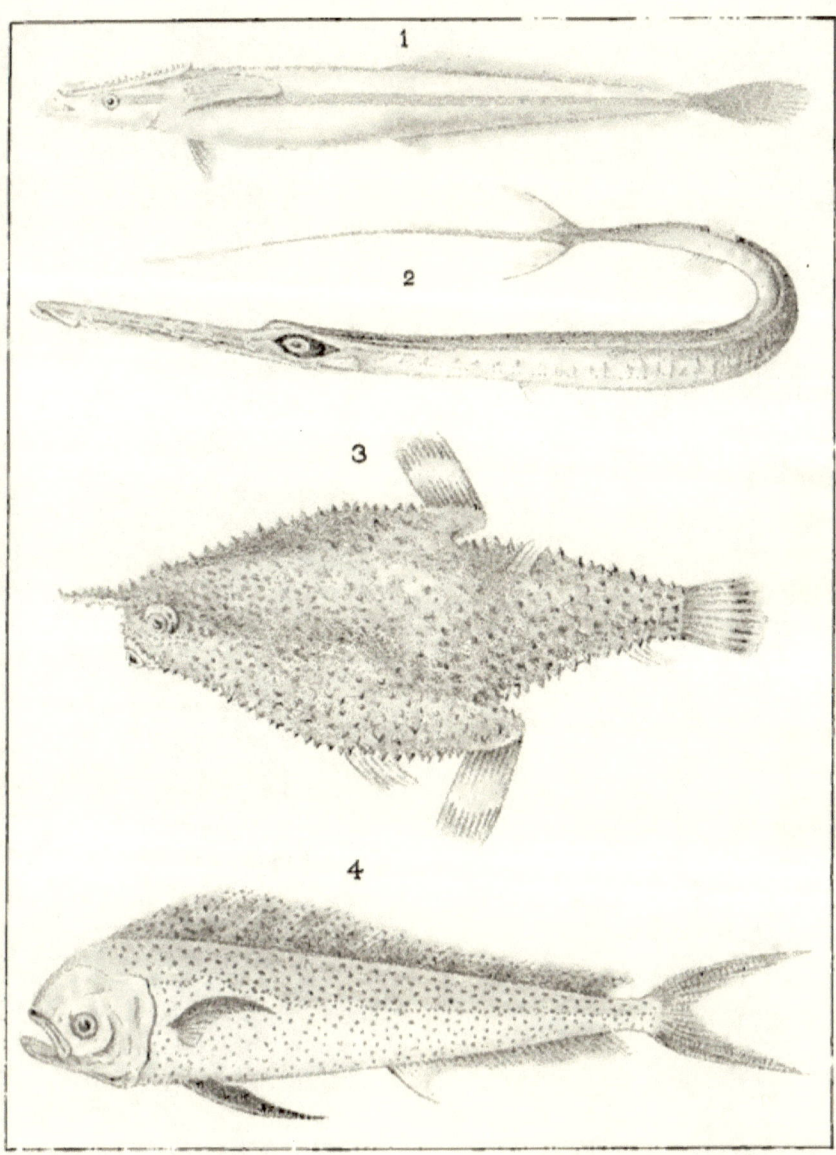

FISHES.

six to twelve inches long, but has no value as a table fish. It is abundant near Nassau, and is sometimes called the *Globe* fish.

The *Sucking fish* has a flattened disk on the upper part of its head, into which the first dorsal fin is transformed. This disk is composed of numerous transverse, cartilaginous, movable plates. By means of the suction or adhesive power of this disk, its owner fastens to a shark or other free and far-roving swimmer, "dead-heads" itself about the ocean without any labor or expense to itself, visits distant seas, and forages its supplies from the marine monsters that provide it, *nolens volens*, with a free, unlimited traveling ticket for life. This is the fisher fish to which we have heretofore referred.

Catesby says it is a foot in length, and that its head is equal in size to its body; that "the crown of its head is flat, and of an oval form, with a ridge of rising, running longitudinal and cross-ways to its sixteen ridges, with hollow intervals between, by which structure it can fasten itself to any animal or other substance;" that he has taken "five of them off the body of a shark, which were fixed so fast to different parts of its body, that it required great strength to separate them;" that he has "seen them disengaged and swimming very deliberately near the sharks without the latter attempting to swallow them."

Some of the Bahama fish are very poisonous. We were told by a Nassau gentleman that in some cases the question of the safety of eating certain fish depends upon the place where they are caught—the same kind of fish being in one place wholesome, and poisonous in another. Some are said to be safe for the table only when young. It is probable from these facts that the fish are poisoned by their food, but whether that food is of a mineral nature, (which we are inclined to doubt,) or vegetable or animal, we are not informed. Very likely some localities produce marine vegetable growths which are poisonous to the fish that feed upon them. As some kinds of Bahama fish are always poisonous, these may infect other fish when they happen occasionally to dine upon them. The toad fish is so poisonous that in one case the exhalation from it severely affected a gentleman who was mounting it.

Flying Fish are very plentiful in the Bahama waters. While yachting outside of Nassau harbor, and during our steamship voyages between Florida and the islands, it was an agreeable pastime to observe them. They looked like small birds, and skimmed along above the water like flocks of ducks, maintaining themselves in the air for so long a period of time that those not familiar with them would naturally suppose them to be a species of water fowl. Catesby says that this singular fish has a somewhat long and round body, and a small mouth, without teeth; that the two fins behind the gills are extraordinarily large, and spread very wide; that upon the hind part of its back there is another small fin; that under it there is a fourth one, thin, large and forked; that its scales are like those of the herring, but of a darker color; that, as they are a prey to both fish and fowls, nature has given them large fins which serve them not only for swimming, but for flight, and that it is a good table fish.

The *Rudder Fish* is described by the same author as being quite small, but able, notwithstanding, to keep pace with ships of the largest class. The upper part of its body is brown, with large specks of dusky yellow. The under part of its body is alternately streaked with white and yellow. He adds that in crossing the ocean, ships are seldom free from them.

The *Murray*, says Mr. Catesby, in its structure resembles the common eel; the iris of the eye is white; two fleshy barbels hang from the nostrils; a fin with an even white ridge begins behind the head, and extends the whole length of the back. The whole body is covered with a light gray skin, sprinkled with innumer-

CEPHALOPODS.

1. *Loligo Plcii*, "Cuttle Fish." One of the "Squids." One-half natural size. Color light yellow with dark spots, changeable. Reduced from D'Orbigny's figure.

2. *Octopus vulgaris*, "Devil Fish." One-fourth natural size. A specimen with arms five feet long is said to have been found at Nassau. Color, dark purple and reddish brown, changeable. Reduced and altered from D'Orbigny's figure.

1

2

SQUID — OCTOPUS

able black spots. One kind of this fish is green and spotted in the same manner with the black; perhaps it is of a different sex only. He adds—"the inhabitants of the Bahamas will eat only the green sort; they reject the black as poisonous. It is customary for this fish, as they lie lurking among the hollow rocks and corals, to bite peoples' legs that are exposed to them, though the bite is of no other ill consequence than fetching blood."

The *Mutton fish*, he also states, for the excellence of its taste, is in greater demand than any other at the Bahama islands. It has five fins; a long spiny one on its back, like that of the perch, of an amber color. The upper part of its head is a dusky black; the irides of the eye are a bright red; the upper part of the back is a dark reddish brown, the red brightening gradually to the portion below, which is white, faintly traced with red. The gills are shaded partly with purple and red.

The common *Cuttle fish*, (*Loligo special*,) is found in the vicinity of Nassau. It has two large prominent eyes of a greenish hue—one upon each side of its head; eight arms project out from its head and surround its mouth. These arms have on their inner sides rows of suckers in the form of muscular cup-like discs with serrated edges, with which the animal can strongly fasten itself to any living or inanimate object within its reach. It is also armed with two long tentacles which push out from the head and resemble the arms, but exceed them in length. At the end of each tentacle or long arm there is a sort of fingerless hand, armed also with suckers. This curious creature has a sack in which it secretes a brown or black fluid, which contains a large amount of a carbonaceous pigment, ("*sepia*,") and various mineral salts. When pursued by an enemy, this colored fluid is discharged in jets, and by means of its color, and perhaps by reason of its offensive character, it aids the cuttle fish in escaping from or contending with enemies who are not prepared for this kind of sub-marine warfare. The coloring matter of its "ink" is very indestructible, and has been handed down with fossils from a far distant geologic age. In making sepia paint it was formerly utilized. The cuttle fish is a kind of sea acrobat, and frequently walks by the aid of its arms upon the bottom of the sea, not exactly upon its head, but head downwards. When troubled, its arms enable it also, while in a perpendicular position, to swim through the water.

The integument of the cuttle fish consists of several layers, one of which (corresponding to the lowest layer of the epidermis) contains numerous large cells which are filled with pigment granules; and the expansion and contraction of these cells causes the marvelous play of changing colors, which the cuttle fish exhibits when excited.

A gentleman who was recently gathering algae in the harbor of Nassau, unintentionally shook hands with a cuttle fish which was clinging to a rock in the water. He mistook it for a rare marine plant, and experienced considerable difficulty in inducing his new piscatory acquaintance to let go. The latter was finally disabled and captured. We are informed that another species of the cuttle fish is found near Nassau.

The star fish and other members of the family of radiates are found in the waters of the Bahamas.

Mr. Sargeant, in giving some account of the Bahama fish, says:

" The hound fish are shaped very much like an eel, for which it is a good substitute. It is semi-transparent, with bones resembling light blue glass thread. Its snout or bill is often eight or ten inches long, slim and sharp, with a row of teeth running the entire length on either side. The maray and stingray are a species of the eel. The whipray has a body shaped like a flounder, with a tail often ten feet long, tapering from about one inch in diameter at the butt, to one-eighth of an inch at the small end.

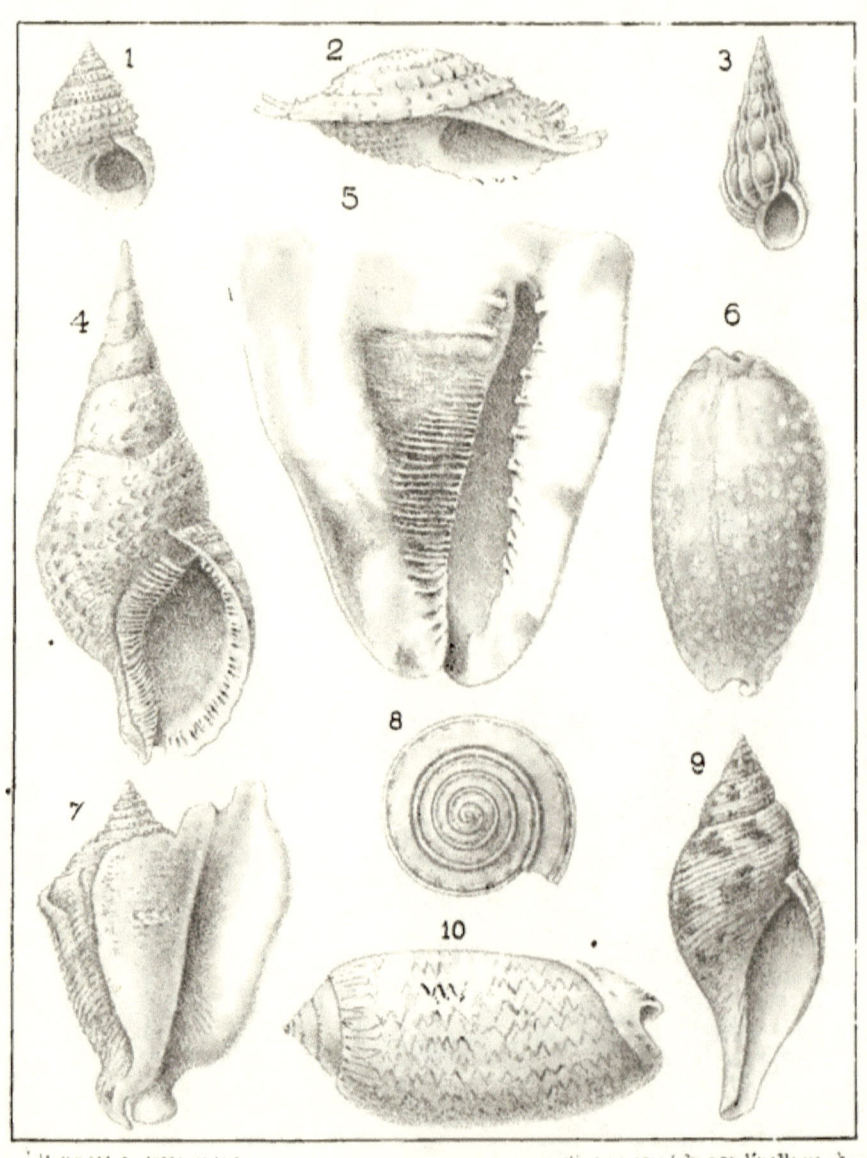

SNAIL SHELLS.

SHELLS OF MOLLUSKS.

1. *Tectarius muricatus.* Natural size. Color gray and purple.

2. *Uvanilla.* Natural size. Color yellow and pearly white.

3. *Scalaria.* Natural size. Color light brown, with a silky lustre. Ribs white.

4. *Triton variegatus.* "Trumpet Shell." One-third natural size. Brown, with dark spots.

5. *Cassis cameo.* "King Conch." One-quarter natural size. The smooth lip is light brown, with dark brown markings. From this species of shell cameos are cut.

6. *Cyprœa exanthema.* "Cowrie." One-half natural size. Brown, with white spots.

7. *Strombus bituberculatus.* "Small Conch." One-half natural size. Inside of the lip white and pink.

8. *Solarium granulatum.* Top view. Natural size. Color gray, with brown and white stripes.

9. *Fasciolaria tulipa.* One-third natural size. White, with brown spots and spiral lines.

10. *Oliva litterata.* Natural size. Polished white, with brown zig-zag lines.

11. *Janira ziczac.* One of the "Scollops." One-half natural size. Color, brown.

12. The same seen from the side. Lower valve nearly flat.

13. *Tellina radiata.* "Rising Sun." Natural size. White or pale yellow, with pink radiating stripes.

14. *Callista maculata.* Natural size. Light brown with darker spots.

15. *Pecten nodosus.* A "Scollop." One-half natural size. Dark red.

16. *Byssoarca Noæ.* "Noah's Ark." One-half natural size. Brown and white, partly covered with a rough epidermis.

17. *Avicula Atlantica.* One-half natural size. Color, brown and green. Rough on the outside and pearly within.

18. *Ostrœa folium.* "Racoon Oyster." Attached to root of a mangrove tree growing in the water. Small specimen. Natural size.

19. *Chione paphia.* A small one. Natural size. Polished white, with brown markings.

When dried it resembles whalebone, and makes a very nice coach whip.   Our bone fish are very similar in flavor and appearance to the northern shad."

Mr. Sargeant states, that the dolphin, king fish, Spanish mackerel, bonita and rock fish weigh from fifty to one hundred pounds, and that the jew fish often weighs six hundred pounds.   Among the remaining Bahama fish, he mentions the margate, cat, king, Hamlet, Miss Nix, grunt, runner, yellow tail, snapper, stripped snapper, gray snapper, pork, soldier, jack, goggle-eyed, cockeye, pilot, mullet, plate, grouper, shad, goat, trumpeter, sunset, porgy, sailor's choice, sand porpoise, balahoo, and crawfish or lobster.

The shell-fish found in the Bahama waters harmonize perfectly with the element in which they live, and with all the varied forms of vegetable and animal life with which they are surrounded. Exquisitely beautiful are they all.   There is no shock to the most delicate and refined taste in passing from corals and corallines to the fish that live and sport in the stony submarine bowers and grottoes,—and from gorgonias and algae to mollusks—all are wonderfully beautiful in form and color, and live in water that pleases by its warmth, and charms by the sparkling brilliancy of its hues.   These combined, constitute exquisitely pictured leaves of a most captivating chapter in the book of nature which God himself has illustrated.   The perfection of the work will not surprise us if we reflect that the Artist is divine.   It has been estimated that there are not less than four thousand different species of shell-fish in the waters of the Bahamas, and Mr. Phelps claims to have collected of the shells nearly one thousand.   The shores abound with them, and they seem in many places almost as numerous as pebbles.   We were astonished to find how large a number of handsome specimens we were able to collect within a small circle almost anywhere upon the shore without changing

our position. They constitute an important item in the daily
stock in trade of the negroes who frequent the court of the Royal
Victoria Hotel. Excepting the conchs, they are generally of
small size and very delicate. No lady, and very few gentlemen,
leave Nassau without securing a large supply for home use
and distribution, and they constitute when away, happy re-
minders of amusing scenes in the hotel court, and of occasional
rambles upon the honey-combed and shell strewn shores of the
islands and keys, when healthful pleasures filled the flying hours.
Large, richly but darkly colored and finely polished turtle shells
are secured by many at a cost of from two to fifteen or twenty
dollars each.

The common *Conch*, (*strombus gigas*) the "winged-shell," is
by far the most valuable shell-fish of the Bahamas. It is from
six to twelve inches in length, and weighs from one to five
pounds. It weighs from four to sixteen ounces after it is dressed.
It constitutes an important article of diet, and its shell is utilized
in various ways. The conch often secretes a pearl of a light pink
tint, mottled with water marks and having much the appearance
of the eggs of dragon flies. Many persons obtain a livelihood by
diving for conchs, in which they become quite expert; some divers, it is said, being able to thus secure them in water ten fathoms (sixty feet) deep. The local market for them is at Nassau,
where they are carried when alive. After breaking off the apex
of the shell, the animal is taken from its shell and first examined
for pearls, and then sold for food. They are considered, by some,
a very good substitute for clams. Some are eaten raw, and
others made into fritters. They are generally considered palatable, and are said to be nutritious. The shells are used in the
States for ornamenting gardens, and in Europe in the manufacture of cameos. Lime is made of them in the Bahamas.

The *King Conch* is less useful than the *strombus gigas*, being

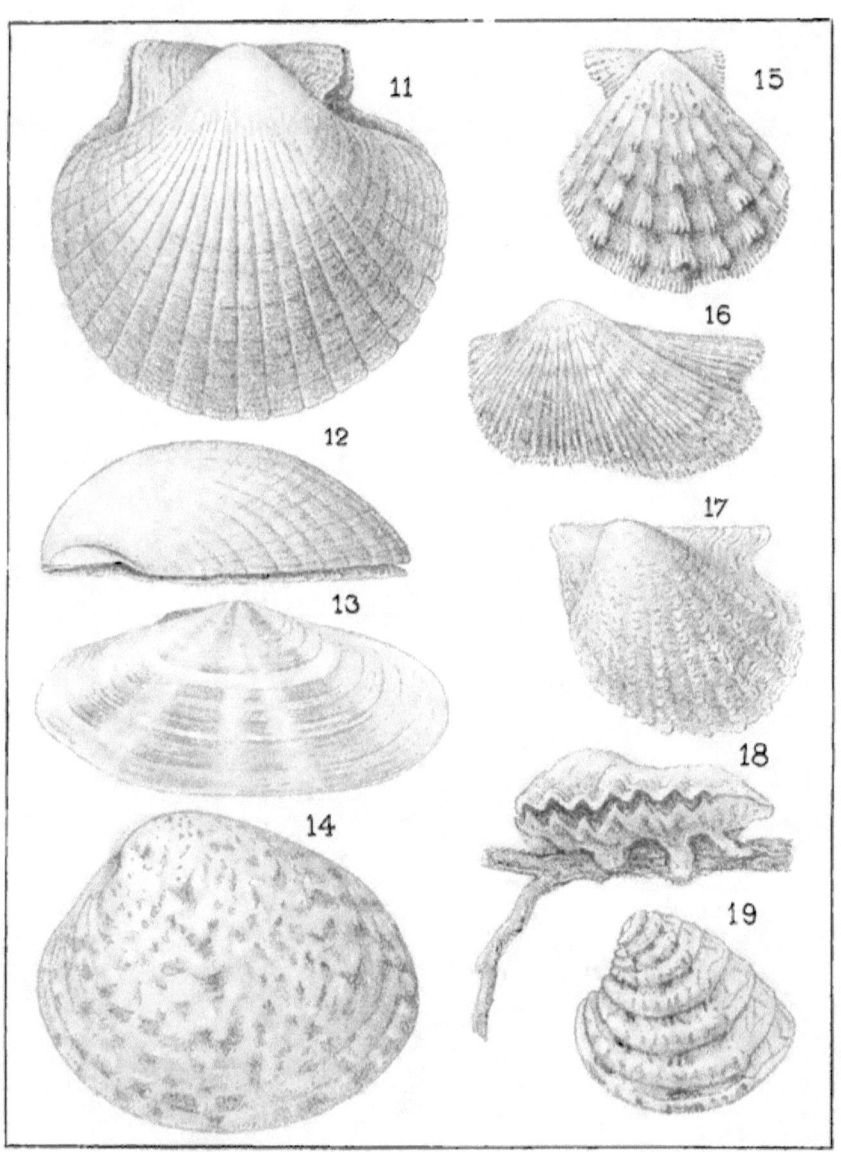

11

15

12

16

13

17

14

18

19

BIVALVE SHELLS

chiefly prized for its beautiful shell, the color of which is a light cream profusely mottled with brown umber and black. Its rarity and beauty secures for it a relatively very high price.

The *Queen Conch* is far more common than the King Conch, and its shell is larger in size and somewhat smoother in outline. The back of the shell is pure white, and the tip a yellow tint, while the interior is a dark brown. It is extensively used in the manufacture of cameos.

The *Twist Conch,* (*triton tritonis*), is very rare and always commands from visitors a high price. It is regular in form and beautifully mottled with brown and wine colors. Mr. Phelps deems it unquestionably the most exquisitely beautiful shell of its size found in the Bahamas.

A separate volume with illustrations, would be required to do anything like justice to the small mollusks whose shells pave and adorn the shores of the Bahamas.

Mr. Bruce in the work from which we have already quoted, published nearly a century and a-half ago, expresses the opinion that, "a beneficial whale fishery might be established here, [in the Bahamas,] as that fish comes in great numbers to wean their young among the islands, and several have been thrown ashore full of spermaceti." While we were at Port Royal, S. C., recently, we learned that several vessels from that vicinity are now prosecuting a successful business in capturing whales off that coast. Between Nassau and Florida, we also occasionally observed specimens of that great mammal of the ocean, which has done so much to dispel the darkness of the civilized portion of the world.

In taking leave of the Bahama fishes, so far as unsatisfactory printed descriptions are concerned, it is a consolation to know that they and their gorgeous surroundings will continue with us through life—for memory has embalmed them. The poet sings of flowers "blushing unseen," and "wasting their fragrance on the desert air," merely because they are not enjoyed by man. This is an exceedingly contracted view to take of the matter, and is bottomed upon man's egotism. There is no insect however small, no reptile however repulsive, no fish in any brook or sea, no animal that roams in pathless woods, and no bird that disturbs with its wings or songs the deepest solitude of the sea or land, that does not find much which its nature is fitted to enjoy in the great world of which they as well as man, form an integral part. The same great Father made all and provides for all, and when we looked into the coral grottoes, caves and bowers, and saw the lavish display of exquisitely beautiful forms and colors which the water glass reveals, we felt that it was no more made for man than is the magnificence of the celestial world made for the few spirits outside, who, perchance, may occasionally be permitted, with or without eye glasses, to look at the inner glories through the key-hole of heaven's great front door.

A book has been recently published in England by Mr. Higgins, entitled "Notes by a Field Naturalist." The author spent a few days in Nassau, visited the "sea garden," and after giving some account of what he saw there and in its vicinity, he adds—

"At last! There it all was, even as the great naturalist of H. M. S. "Beagle" had said more than thirty years before, 'how be it, I believed not the words until I came, and my eye had seen it—and, behold, the half was not told.' Description is not the proper vehicle for conveying the impressions made by such a spectacle. If the description be full, it is labored; if concise, it is nothing. I longed for the power of putting it into music."

"There is no doubt that the 'garden' is a thing of beauty, and that of a very high order."

" The stars—they are the poetry of heaven,
And in their bright leaves we may read the fate
Of men and empires."—CHILD HAROLD.

"The eye
Breathed on by fancy, with enlarged sense
Through the protracted and deep hush of night,
May note the fairies, coursing the lazy hours
In various changes, and without fatigue ;
A fickle race, who tell their time by flowers,
And live on zephyrs, and have stars for lamps,
And night dews for ambrosia."—SIMMS.

WE found in the Bahamas not only a new earth, but the canopy of stars at night was in some respects unlike that to which we had been accustomed. Our astronomical knowledge was too limited to enable us to indulge in a roll call of the heavenly hosts; but, from the extreme north, old stars had disappeared, while others, new to us, with seeming modesty, shone with a subdued light from lowly positions in the southern sky. Planets and great central suns appeared to have wandered from their spheres, and, with renewed fires, brilliantly gleamed from new positions in night's blue dome. The constellations of Orion and the Great Bear were, with a few others, too marked in their individuality

not to be readily identified, notwithstanding their changed positions and the increased brilliancy of their quenchless fires.   The
moon, when at and near its full, mounted almost to the zenith,
glorified Nassau as she lay embowered amid trees of fadeless verdure, imparted to the long, narrow, encircling islands a sort of
weird and unearthly aspect, and illumined with dancing light the
waters of the harbor and of the more distant ocean.

Among the stars of those "new heavens," which are unknown
to the northern skies, and which we especially desired to see,
were those composing the *Southern Cross*.   Many of the Moham-
medans—the followers of the *Crescent*—discover in every new
moon which hallows and adorns the unfathomable and awe-in-
spiring depths of ether, a divine recognition of the supernatural
origin of their religion, and are more confirmed in their belief
in the truthfulness of its doctrines, the wisdom of its precepts,
and the sacredness of its rights and ceremonials.   A Christian
may be pardoned for earnestly desiring to see with his own eyes
the universally recognized symbol of the religion he professes
emblazoned among the stars.   In various articles of personal
adornment—on sword and shield and scepter—in the form and
ridge lines, and in the internal and external embellishments of
the largest and most costly churches—upon altars, sepulchres and
decorative slabs—in knightly adornments, kingly crowns, and
imperial diadems—and upon national banners proudly floating
over the land and sea, *The Cross* has symbolized and proclaimed
a widely dominant system of religious belief and faith.   Christian
voyagers in southern seas discovered in their lonely vigils this
characteristic, significant and hallowed emblem, gleaming with
all the brilliancy of quenchless fires, in those distant heavens, and
naturally hailed it as a divine token that from the world's "beginning," when "the morning stars sang together," the Great
Creator had placed upon the sky this prophecy and endorsement
of the dominant religion of their time and country.

The Southern Cross consists of four stars, and their relative positions, when seen upon the meridian, is indicated by the following:

                     *

         *   *

               *

Were the upper and lower stars connected by a straight line, and the remaining two also connected by a straight line, the form of the cross would be apparent. When, in looking at the stars, this symbolic form is suggested to the observer, then (as in the case of seeing the face of a man in the moon) the resemblance is ever afterwards so vividly impressed on his mind, that the stars never fail to remind him of the cross whenever he sees them occupying a similar position. When they are not upon the meridian the form of the cross is not revealed.

Nassau being some distance north of the equator, the star gazer from that point can only see the cross when the stars which compose it occupy a position near the southern horizon, and he is consequently obliged to look at it through a large extent of the earth's atmosphere, resting so near to the land and sea as to be charged with their vapors. He who desires to see at Nassau the Southern Cross, will be more likely to have his wishes gratified if he makes his observations from some elevated position, where the air is particularly clear and the wind is blowing with some force from the north.

It was upon a favorable evening in March, 1879, that on going

to bed, we imposed upon our mind the task of waking our body
up a little before midnight, in order that we might make an
effort to see this beautiful symbol from the cupola of the Royal
Victoria Hotel.   We awoke on time, and, only so far dressing as
to meet the supposed demands of the invisible spirits of the
night, we made our way through long corridors, up several
flights of stairs, and into the profound darkness of the attic of
the hotel, where, like many another seeker after "the light of
the cross," we groped our dubious way.   Finally a faint glimmer
from above gave us hope, and after ascending another flight of
stairs we emerged into a spacious glass enclosed observatory, from
the inside of which and from its surrounding gallery, in the starlight and moonlight, we watched and waited for the cross.   Here
and there above the southern horizon, a few scattered stars appeared for a few moments through the rifts of slowly passing
clouds, while a thin veil of mist curtained a low belt of sky from
view.   But having concluded to find the cross, we were not dis-
couraged but determined to persevere, knowing full well that
though for the time unseen, it was surely there.   The sea air
was delightfully cool, and we seemed more than ever before to
realize how

> " Sweet are the gentle winds at night
>   That breathe when all is peaceful 'round,
> As if some spirits downy flight
>   Swept silent through the blue profound."

Below us the city of Nassau, with its low diamond-shaped roofs
and tropical and semi-tropical trees, was clearly and beautifully
revealed; the harbor with its shipping and beacon light, was
slightly ruffled, and reflected a soft and silvery radiance; the
barrier islands disclosed their picturesque shores, and beyond
their low but verdant summits, the Atlantic seemed soothed and

lulled to sleep by the sweet murmur of its own gentle billows. Above us were the new heavens to which we have referred, and in the resplendent light of its eternal stars, we seemed but an atom of thought in the boundless and magnificent universe of God. Nor could we banish the pleasant thought that there may be a deep and broad basis of fact in the mystic dreams and visions of the poets and prophets of the buried ages, whose mental vision discovered not only in all the surrounding air, but also in the profound depths of illimitable space, a vast universe of spirits viewless as the wind and swift as the sun-beams. Amid the chaotic desolation of the bleak summit of Mount Washington, with a piercing cold wind blowing at the rate of seventy miles an hour, we instinctively look earth-ward for fairies and fairy land, spirits and spirit land, but in the warm, clear, aromatic air of the summer isles, sporting in the moonlight and starlight, or lurking in the soft shadows, it is easy for superstition and credulity to believe in the existence of invisible spirits whose actual presence the quickened senses seem to actually perceive and recognize.

While gazing upward at the magnificent stellar display, the crushing feeling of one's utter insignificance was somewhat relieved by the comforting thought that the human soul was created by the same divine power that filled the vast dome above us with its brilliant display of revolving suns and systems of worlds; that great and small are relative terms invented and used only by mortals; and that an indestructable thread, real but invisible, connects and binds all to each other and to God.

If this is so, we can give an affirmative answer to Whittier's momentous question—

> "This conscious life, is it the same
> That thrills the universal frame?"

And the tiny insects hum, the song of the feathered minstrels, man's hymn of praise and adoration, and the music of the heavenly spheres, are not separate and discordant sounds, but one harmonious anthem, or, as Longfellow expresses it:

> "And the poet, faithful and far-seeing,
>   Sees, alike in stars and flowers, a part
> Of the self-same universal being
>   Which is throbbing in his brain and heart."

And still musing, wondering, watchful and appalled, we hopefully waited until we should see a blue banner unfurled above the southern horizon glorified and emblazoned with the gleaming and quenchless light of its cross of stars. Nor did we long wait in vain, for one star after another emerged from behind its curtain of vapor, occasionally again disappearing, until at last we had the great gratification of seeing, clear and indisputable, gleaming at that still midnight hour, above the earth's great central encircling line, from the unfathomable depths of space, that heavenly sign and symbol of the religion of the most advanced civilization of modern times—"THE SOUTHERN CROSS." Reaching at last the meridian, it was fully and completely revealed in all its fair proportions, a beautiful CROSS OF STARS!

Soon afterwards we retraced our steps, entered the darkness and gloom of the attic of the Royal Victoria Hotel, descending long staircases, and traversed seemingly interminable corridors, but the mind was luminous and buoyant, for it still glowed with the light of that starry cross in the sky. Thus, amid the doubt, darkness and gloom of the world, may the Christian Cross "towering above the mists of time," as a true and faithful type of a higher life in this world, and a happier life in the world "over the river," ever cheer, elevate and inspire with a faith that never wavers and a hope that is ever steadfast and enduring.

CHAPTER XV.

—— "The birds, great nature's happy commoners,
    That haunt in woods, in meads and flowery gardens,
    Rifle the sweets, and taste the choicest fruits,
    Yet scorn to ask the lordly owner's leave."—ROWE.

THE islands and keys of the Bahamas furnish every year, for a longer or shorter period of time, a pleasant and appropriate home for a great variety of birds, some quite rare, and many very beautiful. And yet, at Nassau, the absence of bird life is very noticeable. Surrounded by perpetual verdure, and inhaling in midwinter the softest airs of a northern June, we naturally expected to be awakened at day break, or to have our morning dreams shaped and colored by the rich and rare music of feathered songsters. But we were doomed to disappointment, and had to be satisfied with the unmusical vocalism of hungry roosters.

The cities of Florida in this respect are eminently superior, and upon landing, both at Fernandina and at Jacksonville, nothing impressed us more than the bird melody with which the air resounded. The turkey buzzard, that important member of the Sanitary Boards of our Southern cities, performs no scavenger duties at Nassau. Dr. Bryant states that it is abundant upon the islands of Andros, Abaco, and Grand Bahama, and he attributes its absence from Nassau to the fact that it cannot find there its appropriate food, as the blacks literally devour all the offal and waste of slaughtered animals, while death from disease or old age yields very meager and inadequate supplies. The buzzards are too wise and sagacious to remain in a place so poor and healthy as not to furnish them with a decent support, and the "living" which "the world owes" them they seek elsewhere.

Many birds frequent the pathless solitudes of the interior of the island of New Providence, and some parts of its shores and Lake Killarney abound with water fowl.

We have no doubt the absence of birds from Nassau and its immediate vicinity, is the result of a persistent and long continued war upon them by the people. For sport, for food, and for sale, they have been killed or captured, and children have no doubt thoughtlessly and wantonly rifled and destroyed their nests. To the court of the hotel we have seen young fledglings brought, and money paid by sympathetic ladies to secure their release.

Had suitable laws been made and enforced for the protection of the birds upon the island of New Providence, Nassau and its suburbs would present a new and very attractive source of enjoyment for visitors from abroad, hardly second to any for which it is now distinguished. Nature was almost as bountiful in giving to the air of the coral isles gay and beautiful forms of life, as she has been to the waters which encircle them. But this part of the colonial capital's inheritance of beauty and melody has been thoughtlessly squandered. Wise legislation may do much to retrieve the loss, and to cause the soft, warm air to vibrate as in the olden times, with the rich and varied melody of tropical birds. The orchards with waxen leaves and golden fruit, the fadeless foliage of shade trees and forest, and the thickets with their flowering shrubs and climbing vines, belong rightfully to the beautiful birds. For their benefit they were in part created, and their possessory title is older than that of man's.

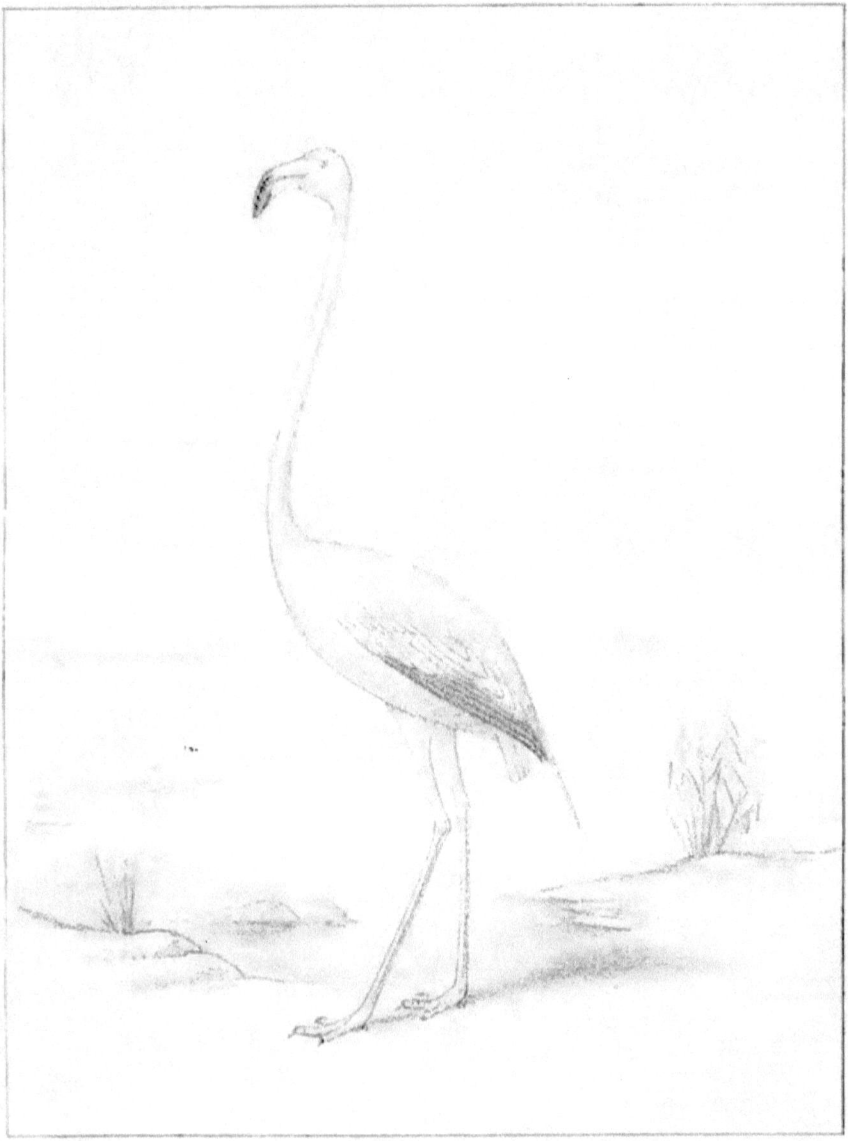

J. H. Emerton. Lith. Punderson & Crisand New Haven, Ct.

FLAMINGO.

A large and finely illustrated volume entitled "Birds of the Bahama Islands," has, during the present year [1880], been published in Boston by its author, Mr. Charles B. Corey. It contains the fruits of his own personal observations, and valuable information derived from other authors. We glean from it most of our information concerning the ornithology of the islands.

The *Flamingo*, for the size and brilliancy of its plumage, is most remarkable. To be appreciated it must be seen. With a small delicate neck longer than its body, and with lean and lank legs longer than its neck, it stands more than five feet high, dressed entirely in scarlet, and with lake-red legs. Most of its primaries are black, as is also the terminal half of its bill; the basil half of the lower mandible is orange. The only bird of this kind which we saw in Nassau was tame, and was kept as an unique and beautiful curiosity. Mounted upon stilts, it was quite amusing to watch it stalk around among feathered creatures less curiously made and less flashily dressed, and still more amusing to see it drink—which feat it accomplishes only by turning its head upside down so as to use the beak as a cup—a feat which is rendered quite easy of accomplishment by reason of its long flexible neck.

Mr. Corey says:—"This beautiful species was at one time very abundant throughout the Bahama Islands, but of late years they have been so persecuted by the inhabitants that at the present time they are to be found in any numbers only upon the inland ponds and marshes of Inagua and Abaco; they are gradually dying off, or seeking some more inaccessible locality as yet undisturbed by the presence of mankind, and in all probability, with the next century the flamingo will be unknown in the Bahamas. The inhabitants find their breeding places, and gather hundreds of their eggs. They kill great numbers of the young birds before they are able to fly, and carry away nearly as many alive to

sell to passing vessels, most of which die for want of care. They
are killed by hundreds for their feathers, and thus gradually
their ranks are being thinned, until at last the Flamingo, like
the Dodo and Soltaire, will be a thing of the past. * * * *
While on the nest, this bird sits with its legs hanging down on
either side, and it presents a most ludicrous appearance."

They were formerly seen in immense flocks, and Mr. Sargeant
states that one flock which he saw numbered five thousand—but
he omitted to add that he counted them.

Whether seen upon the beautiful water of the shallow lakes
and mangrove swamps, or among the green leaves of a tropical
forest, a large flock of flamingoes, with their bright scarlet uniforms, must present a most gorgeous appearance.

Mr. Corey's book contains a " General Catalogue of the Birds
of the Bahamas," in which he gives the names of one hundred
and forty-nine species. Of these, all but twenty-five it seems,
are also found in the United States. Some are limited in their
range, being confined to certain islands.

THRUSHES.

Plumbeous Thrush, (called by the natives Blue Thrasher).
This bird is found upon New Providence and Abaco, but remains
generally concealed in thickets.

Paw-paw Thrush.   It inhabits Inagua.

Little *Mocking Bird.*   It is a common resident at Inagua.

Bahama Mocking Bird.   It is very abundant throughout the
year in the Bahamas.   Dr. Bryant says: "On those keys which
are barely large enough for any land birds to inhabit them, this
bird is sure to be the first settler; and on some of them, as Ship
Channel Keys for instance, which are only a few acres in extent,
there would be two or three pairs, each occupying its own domain,
which they did not allow to be invaded by the others without

giving battle at once. It was singular as well as pleasing, to hear on one of these lonely and almost desert keys, this graceful bird, mounted on the topmost spray of some dwarf shrub, singing with as much fervor and satisfaction as if surrounded by listeners, instead of having for sole auditor his faithful mate."

Cat Bird. It is only a winter visitor.

Blue-gray Gnat-catcher. It is a resident of the Bahamas, and Dr. Bryant found it abundant at Inagua.

WARBLERS.

The *Black and White Creeper* is not uncommon during the winter upon some of the larger islands. It searches the stems of trees for insects, like the Woodpecker.

The *Blue Yellow-backed Warbler* is not uncommon during the winter, and Mr. Corey found it among the small trees bordering the road at Nassau.

The *Worm Eating Warbler* was seen by Mr. N. B. Moore while at Nassau in November, December and January.

The *Dedrœca Petechia.* This warbler was not uncommon at Inagua and Long Island in May and June.

Gundlach's Warbler. This was abundant in summer, but not seen north of Long Island.

The *Yellow-rumpled Warblers* were numerous near Nassau in December and January. It is tame and pretty, frequents the heavy growth, and is recognized by the yellow on the rump.

Black-poll Warbler. Dr. Bryant found it abundant in the Bahamas from the 1st to the 10th of May. It searches the trunks of trees for insects.

Chestnut-sided Warbler. Dr. Bryant saw a few early in May.

Black and Yellow Warbler. Dr. Bryant thinks it as abundant as it is in the United States.

Cape May Warbler. It is found in the Bahamas in winter,

but is not abundant.   On the 26th of January, Mr. Corey saw several in the trees in front of the hotel.

Prairie Warbler.   Pretty and abundant.

Yellow-throated Warbler.   Common in winter.   It frequents tall trees—generally the pines.

Kirtland's Warbler.   It is rare and prefers the thick brush.

Yellow Red-poll Warbler.   Pretty, and in winter abundant. It runs along the roads and in low brush.

Pine-creeping Warbler.   A winter visitant, abundant in the pine woods.

Golden Crowned Thrush.   It prefers the thick undergrowth. Dr. Bryant found it common in Nassau in 1866.

Water Thrush, (local name, Night Walker).   It prefers damp ground, and to be surrounded with impenetrable undergrowth, hence rarely seen, although a regular winter visitant.

Maryland Yellow-throated Warbler.   A beautiful ground warbler, and common in the larger islands.   Dr. Bryant saw a flock which was two hours constantly flying past his vessel, though not in a compact body.   He states that on May 10th, "they were still abundant in the neighborhood of Nassau."

Greater Yellow-throated Warbler.   Local and rare.   All the known specimens have been taken upon New Providence.

Redstart.   Abundant in winter upon the larger islands.

CREEPERS.

Bahama Honey Creeper.   Pretty, small and abundant upon all the islands visited by Mr. Corey.   It is fond of the honey in the blossom of the leaf of life (*Verea Crenata*), which it obtains by thrusting its bill through the petals—according to Mr. N. B. Moore.   When this supply fails, it devours the juice and pulp of the sour orange, and the small insects attracted to the sour orange trees, according to Dr. Bryant.

SWALLOWS.

Bahama Swallow. Small and beautiful, confined to these islands; it was found by Mr. Corey abundant in the neighborhood
of Nassau in June. Dr. Bryant "saw them during the whole
of his stay at Nassau, but only on the first mile of the road leading to the west of the island. They were so abundant there that
thirty or forty could be seen there at almost all times," skimming
along the road near the ground.

White-bellied Swallow. Seen occasionally during stormy
weather at Nassau.

VIREOS.

Black-whiskered Vireo. Very abundant after May 1st.

Common Vireo. Small and abundant throughout the islands.
It is a resident, and Mr. Corey found it especially common in the
neighborhood of Nassau.

FINCHES.

Purple Grosbeak; (local name, *Spanish Paroquet.*) It is abundant throughout the Bahamas, is very retiring in its habits, and
in the thick undergrowth its peculiar notes are heard. Gosse
says that at the extremity of an immense horizontal limb of the
silk cotton, or some other gigantic and hoary tree in the forests
of Jamaica, "it builds a nest of rude materials, as large as a half
bushel measure, the opening being near the bottom." Dr. Robinson, (speaking of this bird as we suppose,) says: "the black
bull-finch builds a nest as big as a blackbird's cage, and, by the
artful contrivance of this little volatile, the whole has the appearance of a heap of trash, flung on the bow of some tree as if
by accident, so that nobody could suppose it to be anything else."
Those which Mr. Corey saw showed no signs of a purple color.

Black Grosbeak; (local name, *Black Charles.*) Mr. Corey found it common on Inagua during May and June.

English Sparrow. It is said to have been introduced into the Bahamas within the last few years.

Nonpareil. It sports blue, green, red, black and brownish red colors, and is believed to be only an occasional visitor.

Indigo Bird. Mr. Moore saw it in Nassau in November.

Black-faced Finch. It is small, domestic, likes human society, and is abundant everywhere.

Bahama Finch. A beautiful bird with an olive green jacket; is abundant upon the island of New Providence, and "is one of the first birds that attracts the visitor's attention, on account of its brilliant coloration."

STARLINGS.

Bobolink. Dr. Bryant saw flocks of them in May. They were called Rice Birds.

Red-winged Blackbird. A common winter visitor, and perhaps a resident. Mr. Corey found it to abound about the ponds on Andros Island.

FLY-CATCHERS.

Gray Fly-catcher. An abundant summer visitant, and perhaps a resident. It is common south of New Providence.

Rufous-tailed Fly-catcher. A resident, but less abundant than others of the same family.

Least Bahama Fly-catcher. Small and abundant in some localities.

Bahama Kingbird; (local name, *Fighter.*) A constant resident and abundant.

Goat Sucker; (local name, *Death Bird.*) Not common, and rarely seen on account of its nocturnal habits. It has a peculiar .

cry, resembling the syllables "chuck-wills-widow," and remains concealed during the day. The negroes believe that whenever it is seen a person in the vicinity will die in a short time.

Little Nighthawk; (local name, *Pirami-dink.*) It is abundant, and flies swiftly about sun-set in search of insects. It does not remain during the winter.

HUMMING BIRDS.

Bahama Woodstar; (local name, *Hummer.*) It is very abundant in the neighborhood of Nassau.

Lyre-tailed Humming bird. Like many others of its family, it is restricted to a single island. It is found only upon Inagua.

Ricord's Humming bird. Interesting in plumage and habits, it prefers the vicinity of the shore, and is common on Andros Island. Some writers suppose it confined to Cuba.

Brace's Humming bird. It has been seen near Nassau.

KINGFISHERS.

Belted Kingfisher. It is common in the winter, generally frequents small lakes and ponds, and Mr. Corey always, when visiting Lake Cunningham, near Nassau, saw it there.

CUCKOOS.

Bahama Cuckoo. Mr. Corey saw one near Nassau.

Yellow-billed Cuckoo. Mr. Brace has taken it in the vicinity of Nassau.

Mangrove Cuckoo. Abundant on the larger islands, and common near Nassau. It remains through the year, and keeps concealed in the thick undergrowth.

Ani; (local names, *Rain Crow, Blackbird*) A very abundant resident, and is generally in flocks. Abundant around Nassau.

WOODPECKERS.

Hairy Woodpecker.　Common at Nassau.
Yellow-bellied Woodpecker.　Abundant near Nassau in winter.

PARROTS.

Parrot.　Formerly abundant upon the islands; now common only at Inagua.　It frequents the cornfields in large numbers in July.

OWLS.

Barn Owl.　It is found near Nassau, and has many names.
Florida Burrowing Owl.　Mr. Brace secured one at Nassau.

FALCONS.

Marsh Hawk.　An occasional visitor.
Sharp-shinned Hawk.　Seen near Nassau sometimes.
Peregrine Falcon.　Not common.
Sparrow Falcon.　Has been seen at Nassau, and at Great Stirrup Key.
Red-tailed Hawk.　One was taken at Nassau, and one at Inagua.
Fish Hawk.　An abundant resident in the Bahamas.

VULTURES.

Turkey Buzzard; (local name, *Crow.*)　Abundant at Andros, Abaco and Grand Bahama.

PIGEONS.

White-headed Pigeon.　Is found on the islands, and in summer repairs in immense flocks to the outer keys to breed.
Zenaida Dove; (local name, *Wood Dove.*)　A beautiful species; is found throughout the Bahamas, but is not very abundant, and does not collect in flocks.

Ground Dove; (local name, *Tobacco Dove.*) Very tame, graceful and abundant.

Key West Dove. Beautiful and abundant.

PARTRIDGE.

Partridge; (local name, *Quail.*) Numerous near Nassau.

THE PLOVERS.

Black-bellied Plover. A regular winter visitant, but not common. It frequents the salt marshes and beaches.

Golden Plover. An occasional visitor, and frequents the marshes.

Kildeer Plover. An abundant winter visitor, frequenting the fields and marshes.

Wilson's Plover. A resident and abundant. It frequents the long open beaches, and the shores of salt ponds.

Ring-necked Plover. An occasional visitor.

Piping Plover. Abundant in winter.

OYSTER CATCHERS, ETC.

Oyster Catcher; (local name, *Sea Pie.*) Rather a common resident. Frequents beaches and sand bars.

Turnstone. Abundant in winter, and frequents the beaches. It loses in winter "the varied colors of its nuptial dress."

STILTS.

Stilt. Abundant as summer advances. Its trailing legs give it, when flying, a singular appearance. It utters, while flying, loud, sharp notes.

SNIPES.

Wilson's Snipe. Abundant in some localities in winter.

Red-breasted Snipe. Mr. Corey found three specimens upon Inagua in May.

Semi-palmated Sandpiper. An abundant winter resident.

Least Sandpiper. One of the most abundant winter visitants. Very social, and found in flocks on open beaches.

White-rumped Sandpiper. A regular winter visitor, but not common.

Sanderling. A rather scarce winter visitant. It frequents beaches and soft marshes.

Willet. Abundant on many of the islands.

Greater Yellow-leg. Not uncommon in winter.

SPOONBILLS.

Spoonbills. Curious, gaily colored, beautiful and abundant at Inagua.

HERONS.

Great Blue Heron, (local name, *Arsnicker*). Frequently met with on the beaches, or in the small inland ponds.

Inagua Heron. Very abundant in Inagua in Summer. They breed in large communities.

Reddish Egret. A resident, and much more abundant than any other species of its family.

Little Blue Heron. Abundant in winter.

Green Heron. An abundant resident, frequenting marshes.

Yellow-crowned Night Heron. Very abundant throughout the Bahamas.

Least Bittern. A rare visitant. It has been taken at Lake Cunningham.

RAILS, ETC.

Clapper Rail. Claimed for the Bahamas by Dr. Bryant.

Carolina Rail. A regular winter visitant; not abundant.

Florida Gallinule. Resident and abundant when Dr. Bryant wrote. Mr. Corey could not find it.

Purple Gallinule. Dr. Bryant saw but one specimen.

Coot. Some remain all summer; large numbers arrive in the winter from the United States. They annoy the sportsmen, because they frighten away more desirable game by their incessant clamor.

DUCKS.

Tree Duck. A not uncommon resident on some of the larger islands. It frequents the mangrove ponds.

Bahama Duck. A small, pretty species, which Mr. Corey found frequenting the large salt ponds of Inagua.

Blue winged Teal. A winter visitant, beautifully adorned with finely colored plumage. It is abundant upon several of the larger islands, and frequents the ponds in flocks.

Green-winged Teal. It is common during the winter, and is sometimes seen upon Lake Cunningham.

Lesser Black-headed Duck. It visits the lakes in winter.

Ring-necked Duck. It is abundant in winter, and is sometimes seen in flocks with other species.

Red-headed Duck. A winter visitant, and is abundant upon the New Providence lakes.

Ruddy Duck. A winter visitant. It is abundant in the lakes near Nassau. It is an expert diver, and will swim under water to a hiding place in time of danger.

GANNETS.

Booby Gannet. About the 1st of February birds of this species repair to desolate, uninhabited, unfrequented places to breed. Small keys of a few acres in extent, some lying so low that they are washed by the waves during severe storms, are, during the breeding season, literally covered with them, of all ages, but mostly young. At such times the old birds manifest little disposition to get out of the way of intruders, but will make savage attacks with their powerful bills if too closely approached. They are very quarrelsome, and make frequent malicious attacks upon each other. Dr. Bryant says it is the most expert diver of any birds with which he is acquainted.

There is also another species, lighter colored.

PELICANS.

Brown Pelican. A resident, and breeds in great numbers on some of the islands. A tame one at Nassau exhibited more intelligence than Mr. Corey supposed this bird possessed. It went to the fish market every morning, and helped itself to fish whenever it could elude the owner's vigilance. On one occasion it made known its wants, and secured the services of Mr. Corey when it wished to enter the closed gate of its owner, by "tugging at his trousers with its bill," while Mr. Corey was passing.

CORMORANTS.

Florida Cormorant. An abundant species. "Nothing could tempt" one which Mr. Corey had "to eat a fish which had been dead over night."

FAM. TACHYPETID.

Man-of-War Bird, sometimes called *Frigate.* It frequents all the Bahama islands, and remains during the year. Dr. Bryant visited some of their breeding places, the largest of which was upon one of the Ragged Island Keys, and was five or six acres in extent. He says: "The nests, thickly crowded together, were placed on the tops of prickly pears, which covered the ground with an almost impenetrable thicket. * * * I have visited the breeding places of many sea birds before, and some well worth the trouble, but none so interesting to me as this. It was a most singular spectacle; thousands and thousands of these great, and ordinarily wild birds, covered the whole surface of the prickly pears as they sat on their nests, or darkened the air as they hovered over them, so tame that they would hardly move on being touched. * * * Incubation is carried on by both male and females. * * * Its food is principally derived from the Booby, whom they rob as the Bald Eagle does the Fish Hawk. Why the Booby should submit to this, being much more powerful, and armed with a most formidable bill, is strange." He watched them for hours, but never saw them catch a fish. While quite tame during the breeding season, it is shy and suspicious at other times.

TROPIC BIRDS.

Tropic Bird. It is called by the inhabitants *Egg Bird.* An "elegant and graceful species, and in summer abundant. Its flight is hurried and rapid, resembling that of the duck more than that of the gull. They closely resemble the Terns in their habits and appearance." Mr. Bryant says that they breed in holes in the horizontal and perpendicular surfaces of the rock, which are often so winding that, though their harsh notes can be heard, they can only be procured by demolishing the rock.

GULLS, TERNS.

Laughing Gull. It is abundant throughout the Bahamas after April. About the time the winter visitors leave Nassau, it may be daily seen in Nassau harbor.

Bonaparte's Gull. Probably an occasional visitor.

Gill-billed Tern. Common in summer upon the southern islands.

Royal Tern. Abundant throughout the Bahamas, and distinguished for its large size.

Sandwich Tern. An interesting species, occasionally found in summer. Mr. Corey found them quite abundant during the latter part of May, at Bird Rock, Acklin Island. He adds that their flight is strong and very graceful, and that they dive and fish with great dexterity.

Common Tern. Probably rather uncommon in the Bahamas.

Roseate Tern. A beautiful, regular summer visitant, but not abundant. The adult male has a showy rose-colored breast.

Least Tern. Common in the southern islands in summer. It breeds in large flocks.

Sooty Tern. They frequent in large numbers the reefs and small islands.

Bridled Tern. Mr. Corey found it abundant at Long Island during June.

Noddy Tern. During the summer months immense numbers repair to the reefs and small islands to breed.

PETRELS.

Wilson's Petrel. Abundant a short distant off the coast.

Dusky Shearwater. An abundant resident, and very shy. It remains far out at sea during the day, often in large flocks, and does not return to the land until the darkness prevents it from being distinguished. Mr. Corey says: "that all night long their mournful cries can be heard, but that long before dawn they are off again." They breed in holes or under projecting portions of the rock, seldom more than a foot from the surface. Dr. Bryant says, " Why these birds and the stormy petrels never enter or leave their holes in the daytime, is one of the mysteries of nature, both of them feeding and flying all day, are yet never seen in the vicinity of their breeding places before dark. When anchored in the night-time near one of the keys on which they breed, their mournful note can be heard at all hours of the night. During the day they may be seen feeding in large flocks, generally out of sight of land. They do not fly round much, but remain most of the time quiet upon the surface of the water. I did not see one on the banks, and never saw them dive or apparently catching any fish, though they are often in company with Boobies and different species of Terns, all of which are actively employed in fishing. About half way from Andros to the Bank, I saw on the 26th of April a flock of Boobies, Sooty Terns, Noddies, Cabot's Terns, and the Dusky Petrel, that covered the surface of the water, or hovered over it for an extent of at least a square mile. Their number must be enormous." The inhabitants call it *Pemblico*.

GREBES.

St. Domingo Grebe. A pretty little resident, which prefers the dark recesses of the mangrove swamps, and is not uncommon upon Andros and some other islands.

Mr. Corey states that "the small keys which, during the winter present a desolate appearance, in the summer season teem with bird life; thousands of Terns of different species repair to these deserted spots to breed, and their eggs might be gathered by the barrelful, as the rocks and sand are, in places, almost covered with them."

For the benefit of any of our readers whose love for the birds may incline them to visit the Bahamas in the summer season, we ought perhaps to add that Mr. Corey says: that "the south-

ern islands are almost uninhabitable by reason of the myriad of
insects by which they are infested." Even the horses, according
to the testimony of the inhabitants, are sometimes killed by
them. Several of the islands, Mr. Corey thinks, have never as
yet been by any naturalist fully explored.

We are happy to recommend Mr. Corey's " Birds of the Bahama
Islands " to all desiring extended and particular information concerning the subject matter of this chapter.

We cannot close this chapter without again respectfully suggesting to the people of Nassau the very great importance of
securing the enactment and enforcement of such wise laws as
will secure the return of the birds of the Bahamas to their woods
and waters, and to their gardens and orchards.

The *Mallard* was omitted by mistake from the account of the
ducks of the Bahamas on page 259. It is of a large size, and
has a glossy green head. A white ring encircles the lower part
of its neck; its breast is of a purple chestnut color, and its wings
are tipped with white and black. It is a regular winter visitant,
and frequents the lakes and ponds. Audibon says: "its progress
through the air I thought might be estimated at a mile a minute,
and I feel confident that when at full speed, and on a long journey, they can fly at the rate of a hundred and twenty miles an
hour."

CHAPTER XVI.

The Influence of the British Court and Aristocracy upon the People of Nassau. The Landing of Prince Alfred upon the Island of New Providence. Nassau and the British Government During the Late War of the Rebellion. Blockade Running. Nassau Practically a Confederate Port. International Laws Construed and Enforced so as to Greatly Damage the United States. Fortunes Rapidly Made, Squandered and Lost. Wild Excitement and Great Dissipation. Great Increase of Disease and Crime in Nassau.

"No voice of friendly salutation cheered us,
  None wish'd our arms might thrive, or bade God speed us."—ROWE.

As the child apes the man, so the practices and sentiments of the court and aristocratic circles of Great Britain give tone and character to society in the dependencies of the British crown in all the ends and corners of the earth. In Nassau, English influences dominate, although from the geographical position of the Bahamas, and the natural course of trade, they are commercially more closely allied to the United States. As the home government retains and exercises the power of filling the high executive and judicial offices, and has the ultimate and deciding voice in all important legislative and judicial matters, a great check exists against the growth of a natural sentiment in favor of political independence, and free institutions. Much is done in the Bahamas to foster, keep alive and deepen the feeling of reverence for and true allegiance to the Queen, her family and her government. The landing of Prince Alfred upon the island of New Providence, upon the 3d day of December, A. D. 1861,

caused the 3d day of December in all future years, to be declared
a public holiday.   The flight of stone steps which lead, from the
harbor to Rawson's Square, upon which on that occasion he first
stepped, were called by his name on account of that auspicious
event, and thus keep him in perpetual remembrance.   Not that
Alfred had developed great genius, or purchased fame by his
attainments and exploits; not that the soft balmy air of those
coral isles had vibrated with a single great thought from his royal
lips that would be heard in future times: not that from his pen

> "A small drop of ink, falling like dew upon a thought,
> Had made thousands, much less millions, think;"

not that he had lightened the heavy burden of a single tax, or suggested administrative or governmental reforms, or caused any of
the wild and now waste crown lands of the islands to be conveyed
to their landless poor—but, being a prince, it was a crowning
glory, an event never to be forgotten in the coming years and
distant ages, that he had actually gone ashore at Nassau.   By
reason of his royal blood, his mere foot-fall has left a permanent
impress upon Bahama history, like the fossil tracks of great animals upon sandy shores in pre-historic times.   We trust that
we entertain a proper respect for Prince Alfred, both on his own
account and on account of his parents, whose virtues are sufficient
to make them illustrious, but to make the day of his landing a
great historic event because of his blood, looks very much like
an effort on the part of somebody to purchase favor at the court
of the Queen.   There is a day in the history of the Bahamas
which the outside world will keep in perpetual remembrance—
the day upon which the Old World first had an introduction to
the New.   No column, obelisk or temple, is seen upon Watlin's
island, where, as we believe, Columbus first landed, knelt, and
gave thanks to God.   No public recognition of that event has

been made by the Bahama government, and we doubt if many of the islanders know where it occurred—but they will not be permitted to forget the day the Prince of Wales was born, nor the time his sailor-boy brother first trod the white limestone streets of their little colonial capital. This is the result, no doubt, of governmental policy. Distance—the mists of space —impress the African mind, and Victoria's golden crown, on the other side of the broad Atlantic, reflects a mystic light, like that of "the great white throne" beyond the limits of time. The nearness of the Bahamas to the United States—the intervening waters of the Gulf of Florida being to some extent spanned by a bridge of ocean steamers—tends more and more to strongly bind them to the States by the strong ties of commercial intercourse. At least a hundred Americans visit those islands for a longer or shorter time, to one Englishman, and republican influences, if not studiously counteracted, would soon predominate.

The British ministry and aristocracy during the late civil war in the United States, from political and commercial considerations, openly and heartily sympathized with the South, and greatly prolonged the war by the aid and comfort they rendered the would-be founders of a great slave-holding oligarchy. Nassau practically became a most important naval station and depot of supplies for the Southern Confederacy.

Under the friendly flag of Great Britain, secessionists and blockade runners held high carnival upon the "Isle of June." Commanding, as New Providence to a limited extent does, our South Atlantic coast, the approaches to the West India Islands, and the entrance to the Gulf of Mexico, Nassau is very favorably situated to do great damage to our commercial marine in time of war; and the Confederates, with the British government and aristocracy on their side, were not tardy in availing themselves of its advantages. The wildest excitement prevailed. Steamers

and sailing vessels, built for speed, were constantly arriving and
departing. King Cotton was enthroned at Nassau and upon
Hog Island. The cotton famine districts of England, and the
destitute armies of the South, alike looked to Nassau for material assistance. Brave, daring and dashing men in gray were the
lions of the day, and were courted and feted by the high digni-
taries of Church and State in this miniature seat of royal and
sacerdotal pomp and power. Fortunes were rapidly made, and
the Bahama treasury overflowed with gold, which came in rich
streams from its custom house. All the Bahama negroes who
had anything to sell were made happy. The crumbs from the
Confederate tables that dropped upon Capt. Sampson and his
fellow boatmen, are vividly remembered to this day, and it is
very amusing to hear Sampson, in his graphic way, while his
yacht is bounding over the billows, describe the golden but now
departed days of Nassau during the war. The Bahama government was soon enabled to wipe out its debt of £47,786 (over
$238,000). The Royal Victoria Hotel, for the erection of which
the Bahama legislature made an appropriation in the year 1859
of only £6,000, that valetudinarians might be suitably accommo-
dated in Nassau, was elaborately and expensively finished in
the early part of our late war, at a total cost of over $100,000,
and the Nassau people were in consequence enabled to sumptu-
ously entertain their Southern friends—the daring and dashing
wearers of the gray. Gov. Rawson states in his official report
accompanying the Blue Book of the Colony for the year 1864,
that the hotel cost "up to the close of 1864, £19,804." As the
appropriation for the hotel in 1859, was only £6,000 it is probable that the tide of wealth which in consequence of our war,
filled to overflowing the coffers of the colonial treasury, led to
the erection of a more elaborate and expensive building, that the
Confederates and blockade runners might be suitably entertained.

Indeed, Gov. Rawson says, that "without such an establishment it would have been almost impossible to have provided for the influx of persons connected with the blockade trade." But alas! how unstable are human hopes! How speedily the shadows succeed to the sunlight! Changes great and unexpected thwart "the best laid schemes of mice and men."

A few short and fleeting years since then have passed, and the bold, rich and dashing Confederates are there nowhere to be seen, but in their places come the once hated Northerners, including not a few Yankees from troublesome New England, to repose in the pleasant chambers, and feast in the banquet hall of the Royal Victoria Hotel, so lately honored by the advocates and champions of "the lost cause." The Great Republic meanwhile rises with new strength and vigor from its baptism of blood, far more formidable than it ever was before as a rival in peace and an enemy in war.

Blockade running culminated in 1864 and the early part of 1865. The imports of Nassau in 1860 were in value only £234,029 and its exports £157,350, but the imports in 1864 were of the value of £5,346,112 and the exports £4,672,398. In January and February 1865, twenty steamers ran the blockade, and landed at Nassau 14,182 bales of cotton, which were of the total value of two and three-quarters million of dollars. Every one was wild with excitement. Fortunes were made in a few weeks or months. Gold eagles, and twenty dollar gold pieces were pitched instead of pennies, by fickle fortune's new favorites, in the Court of the Royal Victoria Hotel. Money was spent and scattered in the most extravagant and lavish manner; and, as a natural consequence, immorality and crime affected the moral atmosphere, and disease nestled and watched for its victims in the soft and balmy air of this great natural sanitarium.

In these calm and peaceful days a vivid imagination will find

itself impotent to conceive the extent of the dissipation, the prof-
ligate waste, the mad revel and riot, and the wild frenzy and
delirium which everywhere prevailed. What a contrast they
afforded to the mild, soft and lambent air,—the clear, placid and
beautiful waters,—the calm and quiet majesty of heaven's blue
dome,—and the fairy bowers with their flowers and unfading
verdure, which characterize this favored part of the New World !
But like the occasional great tidal waves of the ocean, which after
they subside leave little but wreck and ruin upon the shores which
they visit—when, soon after, the Confederacy collapsed, and only
the Stars and Stripes fluttered in a free air over all the recently
dissevered States, silence resumed its reign in the streets of Nassau, and much that existed, in the shape of fixed capital, was
turned into a ruin by the great hurricane of 1866. A lasting
monument was erected to commemorate and keep alive the memory of those days, which every inhabitant of these islands sees and
feels, in the form of a colonial debt of over a quarter of a million
of dollars.

If the American eagle and the British lion hereafter quarrel,
we recommend the former, (in settlement of accounts), to make
a breakfast of the Bahamas some pleasant morning,—saving their
insignia of royalty for our Peabody Museums.

Two rules were adopted by the English government during
the war, which operated (as it was well known at the time that
they would, and as it was designed that they should,) very much
to the benefit of the Confederates, and to the prejudice of the
United States government. One provided that if there was a
Confederate vessel and also a Union vessel in a British port, and
one sailed out first, the other should not leave until twenty-four
hours had elapsed. Now, as our vessels of war were always the
pursuing party, the rule greatly and exclusively aided the South.
To put it mildly, this was unfriendly conduct, and had for its
object the permanent dissolution of the American Union.

And when an armed Confederate vessel entered an English port, she was permitted to take in coal sufficient to enable her to reach a southern port. This was according to the rules of international law. But the English authorities gave it, (in the interest of the Confederates), a practical construction which conformed to its letter but violated its spirit. They held that a Confederate steamer having coaled once in an English port and departed, might return as often as its officers pleased, for fresh supplies of coal, without any troublesome questions being asked. So that, under this rule, a Confederate privateer, without making a home port, was able to continue its cruise along the great ocean highways frequented by our commercial marine, run into Nassau when it pleased for coal, capture our merchant ships, and levy forced contributions upon or destroy them. They held that no violence was thereby done to the principles of national neutrality, because the British government did not know and was not obligated to inform itself whether or not the privateer had since its previous coaling, returned to a home port, nor what had become of its previous supplies.

The unfriendliness of the British government to the American Union at that time, furnished a solid foundation upon which the rebellion rested its hopes. It greatly protracted the war, and largely increased the harvests of suffering and death, and, as a necessary consequence, impoverished the South, wasted the substance of the North, and stirred up bitter feelings of hostility between the two nations after the memories of old and bloody family quarrels had nearly faded away. And what did England and her colonies thereby gain? The cotton she received from blockade runners during the war, formed but a very small fractional part of the entire crop. The value of her vessels and cargoes captured by our cruisers while endeavoring to run the blockade, aggregated many millions of dollars. Nassau was rendered wild and delirious by becoming for a time a great commercial center, and awoke to find herself only weakened by the dissipations which the great carnival had caused; while England was humiliated by an award which compelled her to pay heavy damages for injuries we suffered from the rebel cruisers which she permitted to be fitted out in her ports. The two countries are bound together by the strongest of ties—blood, language, mutual dependence, religion, literature and law—but the love and respect of children for their mother can be greatly impaired and even turned into hate. It should never be forgotten, however, that the British Queen stood faithfully by the Union in the days of its sorest peril, and that the great body of the British people were also with us.

The yellow fever prevailed at Nassau in the years 1861, 1862, 1863 and 1864, and resulted in the loss of many lives.

The statistics of crime, disease and death, during this period in Nassau, clearly prove this bad business to have been equally unfavorable to sound health and good morals. There were committed to prison in the Police Court in Nassau in

1861,	Males, 375,	Females,	189.
1862,	" 523,	"	223.
1863,	" 639,	"	189.
1864,	" 891,	"	221.

There were tried for the more heinous offences in the General Court in

1861,	17.—Convicted, 13,	Acquitted,	4.
1862,	34.— " 22,	"	12.
1863,	82.— " 59,	"	23.
1864,	99.— " 75,	"	24.

The following table from Gov. Rawson's report exhibits the number of vessels which arrived from and departed for the southern states at Nassau, from 1862 to 1865:

Years	Arrived from Southern States.		Departed for Southern States.	
	Steamers.	Small Sailing Vessels.	Steamers.	Small Sailing Vessels.
1861	2	2	3	1
1862	32	74	46	109
1863	113	27	173	48
1864	105	6	165	2
1865	35	—	41	—
Total,	287	109	428	160
			287	109
Excess of Departures,			141	51

Of these, forty-two steamers are known to have been captured, and twenty-two to have been wrecked, chiefly off the ports of Charleston and Wilmington. Thirty-two were confederate vessels. Of the twenty-three steamers which remained in the harbor of Nassau, or arrived in it after the Southern ports were taken, twelve cleared for England, four for Halifax, two for Bermuda, three for Havana, one for St. Thomas, and one for Matamoras.

During the whole period, 1861–1865, 164 steamers, connected with the trade of the Southern States, entered the port of Nassau. Of these, 108 brought cargoes from the coast. Fifty-six are recorded as having left the port of Nassau, but do not figure among the arrivals from the coast. Fifty-one steamers made but one voyage each, and twenty-three two voyages each. Two steamers made ten trips, and the Syren eighteen. On her nineteenth voyage she was captured.

In 1863 the expenses of a vessel which could carry 800 bales (including wages, coal, provisions, labor, repairs and agent's commissions,) were about £3000 for a round trip, to and fro. In the following year the expenses were increased to £5000. The salary of the captain rose from £600 to £1000 for the trip, with the privilege of carrying ten bales of cotton on his own account. The purser and first officer received each £300, with the privilege of carrying two bales each, and the pilot received £1000, with the privilege of carrying five bales.

A first class steamer would run from Charleston or Wilmington to Nassau, in about forty-eight hours. She could be discharged in twenty-four hours, the laborers working day and night. But three days for loading and unloading was considered good dispatch. The excitement, extravagance and waste which prevailed under such circumstances may be easily imagined.

During the war, had the colored people who compose about three-fourths of the population of the Bahamas, known that the question of the enfranchisement of five millions of their race was involved in the struggle, we should at least have had their warm sympathies on our side. But nearly everything relating to the war that was published in Nassau, so far as we have been able to learn, was favorable to the rebel side. This may also be fairly inferred from the fact that the ONLY BATTLE of that war that the publisher of the "Nassau Guardian" has noticed in the columns of important events inserted in his Nassau Almanac for 1879, is that of BULL RUN, July 21, 1861.

It is charitable to conclude that the editor and compiler has never heard of the great Union victories that culminated in a restored Union, and we trust, a permanent peace between the two sections of our common country.

CHAPTER XVII.

*The Bahama Constitution. Opening of the Colonial Legislature. Impos-
ing Ceremonies. The Negroes Made Happy. The Governor and his Military
Guard of Honor. "Parliament" Prorogued. Martial Music and Booming
Cannon. Engrossed Bills Approved and Signed. Small Annual Crops of
New Laws. No Color Line in the House of Assembly. Wrecks and Wrecking
in the Bahamas. Salvors and Salvage. Bahama Hurricanes.*

> " Why, man, he doth bestride the narrow world
> Like a colossus; and we, petty men,
> Walk under his huge legs, and peep about
> To find ourselves dishonorable graves."—SHAKESPEARE.

IN 1879, the day after our arrival at Nassau was distinguished
by the opening of a new session of the Bahama Legislature. Our
landlord kindly secured for us tickets of admission, for only those
thus favored were allowed to witness the ceremonies. They bore
the official signature of the President of the Council. The chief
executive officer of the Bahamas was Governor William Robinson,
a man with black hair and eyes, a heavy moustache and long
beard. He was apparently not over forty years of age, five feet
eight or nine inches high, rather good looking, and had a practical business air about him. He appeared in most excellent physical condition. With the thermometer, even in the winter
ranging in the shade among the seventies, he bore up under the
following heavy weight of titles and descriptive appellations.

"His Excellency William Robinson, Esq., Companion of the
most distinguished order of St. Michael and St. George, Governor

and Commander-in-Chief in and over the Bahama Islands, Vice Admiral and Ordinary of the same."

These titles are not only harmless, but, under British rule, they very likely serve a useful purpose, and help to make the people respect and reverence those whom it is the pleasure of the home government to appoint and send out to rule over them. A Bahama negro especially, may be expected to be very greatly impressed when a new góvernor comes upon the island to represent the Queen with such an imposing array of titles.

In this case, we felt less disposed to be amused when we observed that the governor's public utterances indicated practical administrative talents, and a desire to promote the general welfare.

There is an Executive Council, composed of nine members; four who hold other high offices, are members *ex officio*.

"Parliament" (as in common speech here the General Assembly is termed) is composed of eight Councilmen, who are appointed for life by the Queen upon the nomination of the Governor, and a "House of Assembly" composed of forty-one delegates from this and neighboring islands, who are elected for seven years. To be eligible, they must own real estate of the value of $2,500. They receive no pecuniary compensation for their services.

It is common for citizens of Nassau to represent in the Assembly the people of some of the other islands. They desire the honor, and can better afford to hold the office, as the Legislature meets near their houses and places of business. This gives Nassau a controlling influence in all legislative matters.

Thus it will be seen that the Colonial government follows closely the English model. It is eminently fitted to secure stability, and we think, wise legislation.

The constitution is not based upon any charter, but originated in successive Royal Commissions to the governors empowering them to convoke a General Assembly. The number who voted in 1861, was 4,351.

The common law is the foundation of the jurisprudence of the colony, but the amendments introduced from time to time in England have been generally adopted without delay. In 1848, the Attorney General was made public prosecutor, and it was provided that in all civil cases, and in all but capital criminal cases, the verdict of two-thirds of the petty jury might be taken, and that in capital cases two-thirds might acquit but not convict.

We confess that we had a curiosity to witness the ceremonies attending the opening of a "parliament" possessing certain limited legislative powers over such a large number of islands, inhabited and otherwise.

To secure favorable seats, we went early to the Council Chamber. One o'clock, P. M., was the hour appointed for the services to commence. Our little piece of pasteboard was duly respected and honored by the colored officials who guarded the approaches to the Council Hall.

This hall is unpretentious, and can seat comfortably about 150 persons. It has windows on three sides. At one end of it was a platform slightly raised above the main uncarpeted floor, with its own backing all draped with red bunting, and surmounted by the red cross of St. George. Upon this platform stood the chair of the presiding officer.

The sound of martial music in the street as the hour of one approached, was quickly followed by the entrance into the hall of the members of the upper house. They were mostly not far from seventy years of age, intelligent looking, and had every appearance of being the right men in the right place. To see them was to have confidence in them. No Connecticut Senate ever impressed us more favorably. They occupied arm chairs with high backs, upholstered with leather, near to and in front of the president's chair.

24

A police force was in charge of the hall and its approaches, and gave seats to the citizens and visitors from abroad, who soon occupied all the seats back of the table of the Legislative Council. These policemen were all young and black, yet very bright looking. They wore blue jackets, white pantaloons, and fatigue caps. Belts encircled their waists, to which were secured clubs like those carried by policemen in northern cities. They seemed to be picked men, and were polite and gentlemanly in every respect, having nothing of that offensiveness of manner so common when ignorance and brutality are invested with a little brief authority.

The people there assembled to witness the ceremonies were evidently highly cultivated and intelligent, and all seemed to appreciate and enjoy the honor of this novel entertainment.

The Governor, having left the Government House, was received at the Legislative building by a colored military guard of honor in gay uniforms and white turbans. They formed a detachment from the First West India regiment, and presented arms while the national anthem was played by the band. The Zouave uniform has special attractions for the negro.

Soon the Governor, accompanied by high officers of state, and followed by the officers and members of the lower house, entered the Council Chamber, took a position upon the raised platform, gave a dignified bow to the venerable members of the upper house, who all rose to receive him, surveyed deliberately and with seeming satisfaction, his brilliant audience, and then, while still standing, read from manuscript his speech. The members of the Assembly and others who came with him remained also standing on his right. He was dressed in blue, while a moderate quantity of gold lace, and a sheathed sword by his side, indicated that while Governor he also filled the position of a military commander. His army then in commission at Nassau, consisted of two companies of colored troops. In the division of Legislative honors the negroes had a portion allotted to them, several of them being members of the lower house.

The Governor's speech was ably written, and effectively delivered. It covered matters of practical importance, and would compare well with the speeches and messages of our State executives.

The address concluded by a suggestion that sounded very home-like, that the present session of the Assembly might be even shorter than the last, which in brevity surpassed its predecessors.

After delivering his speech, His Excellency and his suite withdrew, and the members of the lower house retired to their chamber. Both houses afterwards voted replies. As the Governor left the building a salute was fired from three field pieces, the troops concluded their escort duty, and all the colored population of Nassau which had assembled to see the show, followed His Excellency's example, satisfied and gratified with the short episode which had broken the monotony of their every day life.

Before we left Nassau in 1879, the Bahama Parliament was prorogued by the Governor with imposing formalities. At the appointed hour, His Excellency, accompanied by his Secretary and other high officials, was escorted from the Government House, (as his residence is called,) to the building in which the Senate holds its sessions, by the colored troops, while martial music imparted life and spirit to the indolent air. The semi-royal pageant was a god-send to the negroes, as it broke in pleasantly upon the dull monotony of their every day life, and, in Bay street where the procession passed, they constituted, to the eyes of northern strangers, the most interesting part of the show.

The legislative "dissolving views" were witnessed by those only who had been favored with tickets which secured them a free pass to the Senate Chamber, and, being numbered among the fortunate ones, we repaired in good season to the appointed place, inspired by a natural curiosity to witness the "giving up of the ghost" by an integral and important part of the law making power of this out-lying portion of the Queen's possessions.

The Senators, (or colonial lords,) grave, dignified and prepossessing in their appearance, took possession of their high-backed arm chairs, and in low tones conversed with each other, until the sound of approaching footsteps indicated the arrival of their more youthful and less experienced superior in official rank and honors.

In the presiding officer's chair, (which was decorated with banners and bunting,) the Governor was soon comfortably seated and enthroned. His military dress and sheathed sword were mildly suggestive of the power which upholds government, and gives effect and potency to law. He received, as before, the speaker and members of the lower house, the former accompanied by his large and conspicuous mace of office, brought to Nassau from South Carolina by the royalists after the revolution of 1776, while a clerk or secretary carried the parchment rolls upon which were engrossed the unsigned bills of public acts which had successfully run the gauntlet of the two houses. Each roll was successively handed to the speaker, who, in an audible voice, indicated its character by reading its title, and handed it to the Governor, who signed it in the presence of both houses of the colonial parliament, and thus, by his approval and signature, united with the legislative branch of the government in making it a law of the colony. There were in 1879 but five rolls, so that only five laws were enacted at one entire session of the Bahama Legislature. We had no means of determining to what extent this extremely short law crop was chargeable to the climate. In the crisp, cool air of the north, crime is tirelessly active, and constantly assumes new and unexpected forms, rendering additional enactments necessary, while the rapid growth of new industries, the great accumulations of wealth in ever changing forms, and the constantly increasing complications of human affairs, public and private, give rise to countless and unending changes in the laws. But rest, repose, quiet, torpor, sleep—lie down and nestle in the soothing, languid air of the isle of unending summer. Industry and enterprise wilt and wither in an atmosphere that seems made for disordered nerves, and worn and weary minds, and for the development and growth of vegetable life and beauty. Only five new laws in one entire legislative session! But for the wrecking business, the ten commandments, with suitable penalties, appended like snappers to whips, would almost meet the requirements of these happy islanders so far as law is concerned.

There were sixteen engrossed bills in 1880 that received the Governor's signature upon a similar occasion when we were present.

The Governor, after giving his sanction, and adding his signature to the enactments, addressed the two houses separately and collectively, after the manner of the British Queen in Parliament, and said:

" Mr. President and Gentlemen of the Honorable, the Legislative Council;

" Mr. Speaker and Gentlemen of the Honorable House of Assembly;

" I am glad to be able to relieve you from your parliamentary duties, and thank you for your coöperation in all matters that have been submitted for your consideration;

" Mr. Speaker and Gentlemen of the Honorable House of Assembly;

" I am much indebted to you for the very liberal supplies which have been voted."

The Governor alluded to the government as " my government,"

which together with his reference to the supplies which had been voted, made the idea prominent that his excellency was the government itself, and not merely an executive officer authorized to see that a government of written laws is duly enforced.

After complimenting the Assembly by telling its members that "they had kept pace with the legislation of the mother country," he said:

"By virtue of the power invested in me by her majesty, I now prorogue this parliament until the 11th day of May next." The Governor then retired, accompanied by the officials who had graced and honored the occasion with their presence. They were followed by the members of the two houses, and by the amused and gratified spectators. The latter, for awhile, mingled with the crowd outside, whose loyalty may be fairly presumed to have been intensified by the inspiring notes of martial music, the thunder of deep-mouthed cannon, and the showy uniforms and soldierly bearing and evolutions of the colored troops who acted as a guard of honor to his excellency.

As the legislature was only adjourned for three or four weeks, the affair would have been a waste of time and powder, if time had there any money value, or public shows had been more common.

On those occasions when we attended the meetings of the House of Assembly, its sessions were in the evening, and only routine business that did not consume more than half an hour, was transacted. Members rose languidly from their easy seats and addressed a few words to the speaker in a low tone of voice. The speaker had reduced parliamentary brevity to a fine point. In putting a question, he very quietly said—"negatives rise—it is carried." This mode insured an unanimous vote in the affirmative, as something extraordinary would be required to induce a member to rise out of his comfortable and roomy chair. The

colored members looked intelligent, appeared well, and seemed
to command the respect of their white associates.

WRECKS AND WRECKING.

Much may be truthfully said in commendation of the delicate
silken web of the spider, as its gossamer threads, gemmed with
dew-drops, glisten in the morning sunlight,—but to many gay,
sportive insects it is a trap of death.   Little do they think of the
lurking peril as they fan the warm air with their tiny wings, and
voice their happiness in gentle murmurs.   Thus in the clear
warm waters of a summer sea, the Bahamas attract by their
beauty, and lull and disarm suspicion by their soft and languid
air.   But a more dangerous place is nowhere to be found in all
the paths of commerce. Numerous islands, keys, rocks and
reefs, deceitful currents and cross currents, and extensive shoals
and banks, constitute only a part of the perils which ever lurk
in these much frequented waters, for wreckers have succeeded
the pirates, and the salvage of the salvors, and the legal and other
expenses, not unfrequently absorb all that the destroying elements
and engulfing waters have left.   Deprived of the means of support which the varied industries of colder climates so lavishly
furnish, hundreds of the Bahamians wait and watch for wrecks,
as our northern cats wait and watch for summer birds.

The government officials and the courts of admiralty, under
the broad aegis of colonial revenue acts and maritime law, are
handsomely provided for in the division of the spoils of the sea,
so that in many cases the owners in distant States have to thank
Nassau for little more than a convenient and sufficiently roomy
burial place for their property and their hopes.

The number of wrecks reported in seven years, from 1858 to
1864, was 313, of which 259 were claimed to be total losses—
which means, we suppose, total so far as their owners were con-

cerned; the wreckers and government and court officials took all
that was saved as a compensation for their services. The hurricane months are August, September and October, yet of these
313 cases, 199 occurred during the six months ending May 1st
of each of these seven years, being nearly two-thirds of the whole
number.

The amount of salvage awarded from 1855 to 1864, in fifty-
nine derelict cases, was £11,318 10s. 5d., and in thirty-seven
salvage cases, £59,955 14s. 8d., making a total salvage for those
ten years, of over $350,000, being about six times more than
was paid to the proprietors by the English crown for the whole
group of islands. In 1865 the owners of the American steamer
Herman Livingston, which was stranded and got off, paid,
under an agreement with the master and salvors, $30,000. The
salvors, after discounting the bill, received £5,480 3s. This was
divided among thirty-two vessels and boats.

Governor Rawson says: "It is stated on good authority, that
the average salvage allowed, chiefly by arbitration, which twenty
years ago amounted to sixty per cent., has not during the last
five years, (1859 to 1864,) exceeded forty per cent., and that the
charges for commissions amount to ten per cent. on the mer-
chandise saved, and for labor, storage, &c., to four per cent.
more. From the above, the extent may be inferred, to which the
population of the colony, maritime and commercial, has been and
continues to be interested in this source of employment and income."

The total value of wrecked property, including hulks and
materials, paying *ad valorem* duties of twenty per cent., auction
duties of five per cent., and specific duties and of property re-
exported, aggregated £638,864.

Gov. Rawson also states that wrecking has had the necessary
and usual effect of demoralizing the persons engaged in such

occupations, of diverting their attention from agriculture or any other industrial pursuit, exposing them to the trials and temptations of alternate abundance and want, and accustoming them to rejoice in the misfortunes which bring calamity and ruin to others.

The local legislature has endeavored to bring the wrecking system under control by a law which requires licenses to be taken out for men and vessels, provides for the appointment of wreck masters, apportions the share of salvage which each vessel and its crew may claim, and imposes penalties for certain acts of misconduct. In 1858 there were licensed 302 vessels and 2,679 men; in 1865 only 176 vessels and 712 men. The late civil war in the States occasioned this difference.

HURRICANES.

As the hurricane has a great sanitary mission to perform in purifying the air and destroying the germs of malignant diseases in the West India islands, it is seldom that more than three or four years pass by without some manifestations of its presence and power. At such times the wreckers reap a rich reward.

The following list of hurricanes that are known to have passed over the Bahamas is taken from Gov. Rawson's report:

1780,	October,	3 to 4.	1838,	September,	5 to 8.
"	"	4 to 16.	1842,	August	2 to 4.
1796,	"	3 to 5.	1844,	October,	5 to 6.
1801,	September,	5 to 6	1846,	"	10 to 11.
1804,	"	7 to 9.	1848,	August,	22 to 23.
1813,	July,	23 to 24.	1853,	"	18 to 20.
"	August,	22 to 24	1856,	"	25 to 27.
1821,	September,	1 to 2.	1857,	November,	10 to 12.
1827,	August,	20 to 22.	1858,	October,	16 to 19.
1830,	"	13 to 14.	1861,	August,	13 to 15.
1835,	"	14 to 15.	1862,	"	27 to 28.
1837,	"	2 to 3.	1865,	October,	23 to 25.

This list includes those hurricanes only concerning which Gov. Rawson had reliable information. Probably there were others during the period covered by his table. We suppose also that many of the hurricanes mentioned visited only a portion of the Bahamas. The terrible hurricane which inflicted such serious damage upon Nassau in August, 1866, desolated many other islands, and damaged and destroyed a very large number of vessels. The recent hurricane that caused such a destruction of property in Jamaica, and wrecked the steamer Vera Cruz in the Gulf of Florida, with great loss of life, must have been felt to some extent on the island of New Providence. Very favorable official reports have since been received from Nassau in regard to the health of that city.

CHAPTER XVIII.

> "Fill the bright goblet; spread the festive board;
> Summon the gay, the noble and the fair;
> Let mirth and music sound the dirge of care,
> But ask thou not if happiness be there—
> Lift not the festal mask!"—W. Scott.

THE social life of a people cannot but be a matter of absorbing interest to the stranger, even if he does not acquiesce in the sentiment of the poet, who affirms that

> " The proper study of mankind is man."

In its main roots and cardinal elements human nature is the same everywhere; but traditions, education, customs, climate and other influences and surrounding circumstances, wonderfully varied and widely dissimilar, produce new and unlooked-for results which arrest the attention, awaken inquiry, furnish food for reflection and materials for a criticism which is only in appearance sometimes unfriendly. In Nassau, we were in such a hap-

287

py frame of mind, being relieved from all the harrassing cares and severe labors of professional life, and having all our nerves soothed and quieted by a most delightful climate, that while we were ready to heartily assent to one line of the poet that "every prospect pleases," we were by no means willing to unite in the severe charge partially concealed and ambushed in the expression that "only man is vile." But our eyes were neither blind nor bandaged, and no one tried to pull Bahama wool over them.

Small communities are inclined to overestimate their importance, magnify their merits, and to be unconscious of defects and foibles which immediately attract a stranger's attention. They often feel disturbed when unfavorably criticised, and the pen of the traveler sometimes leaves upon a thin and morbidly sensitive epidermis, an enduring mark. In our country, (which we are pleased to call "The Great Republic,") the inflated bladder of conceit has often been remorselessly punctured by English tourists. Across the wide and stormy Atlantic the derisive laugh has been distinctly heard. It has penetrated the depths of primeval forests, and embittered the perfumed air of the boundless prairies of the Great West. The people of the old world are amused and astonished to find their Yankee cousins so thin skinned. The latter are more vexed because they cannot successfully retaliate. Hoary with age, and rich with the vast accumulations of many centuries, the great countries of Europe know little and care less what may be published concerning them in the New World.

We found so much to enjoy and commend in the Bahamas, we trust its people will not consider us unfriendly if we allude to some few things which are less complimentary.

Completely isolated—an oasis in a wide waste of waters—Nassau is necessarily a little microscopic world, but slightly connected with the great old and new worlds which the vast ocean, which

George Street and the Government House.

surrounds the island upon which it is situated, divides and separates. This isolation has very naturally tended to foster some degree of self-exaltation, which could not have existed had its people been brought in closer contact with the great tides of human life and activity thousands of miles away.

It is proper, however, to suggest that our observations of the social life of Nassau were taken from an outside stand-point, so that the reader may very properly allow a wide margin for mistakes and imperfections. We did not plant our feet upon a single round of Nassau's social ladder, but, like Jacob of old, we occasionally saw as we supposed, the angels ascending and descending upon it. Had we been permitted by a kind Providence to climb, as some were to crawl, up the dizzy heights of official and social life in that little colonial capital, and been sufficiently calm and self-possessed to have observed with an undazed eye, and to take notes with a steady hand, we should be better qualified to reflect back upon our readers a little of that intoxicating pleasure, which, like a philter, is supposed to pervade that upper and truly aristocratic air. But, landing upon one of the wharfs of Nassau utter strangers to her people, we had no letters of introduction that opened for us the door of a single private dwelling. The Royal Victoria Hotel, with its numerous guests, varied and constantly changing, was a little miniature world in which we were satisfied to live and revolve, making but few outside acquaintances, and those slight and casual. We had no desire to commence a fresh set of books for new and short-lived friendships, nor to gratify an idle curiosity by crossing the thresholds of hospitality; but as one can learn much, and all he desires to know, about a gale of wind without being exposed to its fury, so a close and careful observer upon the outer margin of society sees many things—feathers in the air—that disclose to him much of the "true inwardness" of a high life of fashion and folly.

The eye of such an observer is not blinded, nor his judgment warped, by the subtle influences that envelope, like aromatic odors, the festive board, and infect the air where invited guests assemble to add new and stronger ties to friendships that are not always sincere, disinterested and genuine.

Small cities exhibit in miniature the different phases of human life which exist in large ones. Their inhabitants are never entirely homogeneous. The integral parts are radically unlike, and persistently refuse to assimilate. Great natural formative and organizing laws, subtle but powerful, are ever in operation, crystalizing and stratifying the elements of which society is composed. Brains and blood, rank and fortune, that never would be felt or known in a great metropolis, ruffle and disturb with their little eddies the insipid and otherwise stagnant waters of a small town.

However much we may admire the happy and contented spirit of the grim, hard-headed, stoic Greek philosopher of the tub, who wanted nothing of the dispenser of royal patronage but such a change of position as would secure the full benefit of the light and heat of an unclouded sun, it cannot with truth be denied that the love of rank, social position, office and high sounding titles is with most persons inborn and inbred. It is in the warp and woof of their souls. Nor can that be said to be an " infirmity of noble minds," which an all-wise Creator has made a part of their nature. Looking a little below the surface, we see and learn that these seemingly light and trivial objects of desire are great impelling forces, constantly stimulating and urging their possessors upward and onward. Gewgaws and trinkets are not to be ignored, belittled or despised, if, as objects of human desire, constantly coveted and labored for, they furnish healthful stimulus to indolence, and cause valuable additions to be made to man's stores of material and intellectual wealth.

In a little town upon a small island, from our position on the outside, perhaps we were inclined to be cynical and uncharitable, when we allowed ourselves to be amused at the apparent official and social exaltation of some of its more favored people. If the Governor at times seemed to us a little airy; if the young, newly-appointed and freshly imported Chief Justice, who blossomed out in a scarlet robe of office and a wig, (judicial toggery before unknown upon the judicial bench of Nassau,) seemed to us much more elated than any Chief Justice we had seen in the States; if the Bishop sported titles but little in harmony with the humble and modest spirit of the Apostles of the olden times; and if to our superficial view "the upper classes" appeared somewhat proud, supercilious and exclusive, it may have been because at the time we failed to remember that they were only exhibiting traits of character common to our race in all parts of the world; that they were playing the game of life, as it is everywhere played, only the stage upon which the chief actors performed their several parts was relatively small and insignificant.

But as we looked from our quiet nook upon the different phases of life in Nassau, what astonished us most was the great desire which certain ladies from the States manifested to mingle on terms of social equality with the aristocracy of Nassau, and to receive attentions from officials with high sounding titles. The poet is not correct when he affirms that

" Women, like moths, are ever caught by glare,"

though it is true that they frequently are, and a very large title occasionally surrounds with an attractive and dazzling effulgence small, bad, and repulsive men. As woman's sphere is domestic and social, it was natural that the lady guests at Nassau, finding themselves isolated and cut off from the outside world, should desire to cultivate the acquaintance, and stand or kneel on the same social platform with her majesty's Bahama representative, with his then reputed wealthy and very popular official secretary, with the brand new "lord" bishop, with his excellency's counsellors, with the venerable and very dignified members of the Bahama house of lords, with the honorable speaker of the lower house of the Bahama parliament, and with the few untitled gentry composing the *élite* of the town. It was perfectly natural that some of the more enterprising and ambitious should use all their arts, and every attractive and alluring blandishment, together with full and free libations of expensive wines, and other stronger, and, to some, more attractive beverages, in order to accomplish a result so much desired and coveted. It is true that the blood of a portion of the "gentry" is said not to be perfectly pure, but it is difficult in some cases of mixture to accurately draw the color line, and it is wise to ignore it, and ask no questions of one's partner in the voluptuous waltz, which might result in banishing the inquisitor from high-toned society. It is at times injudicious to scrutinize closely hair that appears straight or nearly so. One lady was quoted as saying that she preferred Nassau to London, because it is not so difficult in the former to gain admittance into good society, and move in its best circles.

To the few and favored strangers who have the *entrée* of the homes of the leaders of Nassau society, we have no doubt the social sky glows with a fervid and impassioned warmth unknown to colder climates, and sparkles with a fascinating brilliancy like the neighboring phosphorescent waters in the moonlight. Passions are more fervid in the warm latitudes; love is more ardent, friendship more demonstrative, and hospitality more liberal, open-hearted, kind, and assiduous to please. The islanders have established an enviable reputation for the agreeable and polite attentions which they bestowed in the past upon strangers so-

journing among them.   Formerly, from their isolated position,
intercourse with the outside world was infrequent, but now, with
a steamboat load of fresh arrivals in a small town once a week
during the winter season, what can the poor islanders do?   Hospitality withdraws appalled, if not disgusted, while Avarice and
Cupidity stalk boldly to the front, and with an enterprise and
industry remarkable in such a warm and enervating climate,
scramble for the greenbacks and gold of the new-comers.   Like
a few choice plants in a green-house, a little of the old time hospitality is preserved.

In the "Letters from the Bahama Islands," written by a lady
more than fifty years ago, much space is occupied with descriptions of the social gayeties of Nassau.   Then, as now, picnic
parties upon some of the islands, or "at some rural spot" in the
suburbs of Nassau, were of frequent occurrence.   "Most families"
were accustomed to devote each Saturday "to festivity," and
marooning parties upon that day were common.   All but the
invited guests contributed to the entertainment.   The particular
things which each furnished were previously determined by a
ticket drawn by lot from those which the managers prepared.
The authoress adds:

"The evening is generally passed at the town house of one of
the party, at cards and conversation, and ends with a *petit souper*,
and I am afraid the opening of the Holy Day finds many of these
Saturday revelers too dull and drowsy for morning prayers."

The same writer speaks of frequent and most charming dinner
parties which she attended, and of other festive occasions, when
the ladies "were pledged in full bumpers;" of supper upon the
deck of a brig after a marooning excursion upon Rose Island, when
"champagne and the choicest wines flowed like the waters below
them in sparkling abundance, and the hours flew swiftly and
gaily on;" of the storm that kept them out "in a pelting rain

till two o'clock Sunday morning;" of "state dinners" at half past six o'clock given by G——, a bachelor; of supper at twelve; also of supper on another occasion at one o'clock at night, followed by music and dancing for she did not know how many hours; of a ball in the Assembly Room, when the Governor and suite were saluted by the band with the "King's March;" of retiring at four A. M.; of a ball in honor of the King's birth-day, when flags ornamented the shipping in the harbor, guns were fired, fire-works displayed, and the "dear five hundred" were permitted to unite with their superiors in doing honor to their sovereign.

The pictures were drawn by a friendly hand, and though made more than half a century ago, we are inclined to believe that, with slight modifications, they will answer very well for the present day. From the little which we saw, and from information derived from others, we are of the opinion that the picnics, the balls, the nightly revels, the feasting and drinking, the whist parties and early morning hours for retiring, characterize to a considerable extent the fashionable and high life of this miniature colonial capital to-day, as in 1823–4. To the ball which the Governor gave at the Government House while his wife and children were in England, some few of our hotel guests we know went late and returned in the small hours of the morning. His Excellency manifested in our presence at the ball which some of the ladies of our hotel gave in its dining hall, a great fondness for the waltz, and was reported to have taken part in each of the eighteen dances at the ball given by himself. One gentleman who attended the latter observed that the Governor was so occupied, while the heavy load of official cares was laid aside, in honoring his lady guests by kindly consenting to embrace and spin them around in the rhythmic circles of the voluptuous dance of the German, as to seemingly forget what genuine politeness and ordinary courtesy demanded of him for the proper entertainment of his other guests. But as he has not then occupied his exalted and honorable position for many years, having been so recently as in 1873 simply "William Robinson, Esq.," and fervid passions lurk in the warm air, while the ladies who received his assiduous attentions were greatly pleased and flattered thereby, we must not criticise him too closely or judge him with severity. It is something to be a Governor of a British colony, even though it is poor and sparsely populated, especially where one, in addition to the free use of a palatial residence with ample grounds, has a salary of $10,000 a year. When we saw in the public library of Nassau a little volume made up of his official report of the exhibits of the British colonies in the Vienna Exposition, and observed upon the first blank leaf, in his own hand-writing, this entry: "Presented to the Nassau Library by H. E. Gov. Robinson, the author," we were at first disposed to smile, for we knew that certain of the able and very modest men of Connecticut, whom it had been our privilege and good fortune to personally know, while occupying the executive chair of a State that has brains and wealth, and industry and enterprise, and population sufficient to make a great many Bahamas, could never have been induced to write "His Excellency the Governor" before their honored names. But when we reflected that the Governor of the Bahamas had been educated and trained under institutions and a political system less democratic and radically different from our own, and where rank and honors and high-sounding titles are held in very high esteem, and when we further considered that Her Majesty's most loyal subjects upon these little islands had been trained and educated to treat with the most profound and deferential respect the men whom the Queen from time to time sends to them to represent her sovereign authority and power, we thought perhaps His Excellency knew what his subjects (mostly colored) required better than we did, and that possibly profound political wisdom existed, though concealed in acts that to plain democratic eyes appeared ludicrously egotistical and vain.

An old author states that "the general character of the West Indians is extremely pleasing to strangers. They are frank, lively and generous, and hospitality is carried to an extreme which is unknown in England; and there are few persons, we believe, who have ever visited these islands who have not separated from many of the inhabitants with regret." Speaking of the people of Kingston in Jamaica he says: "It is their pride to send away their guests so mellow as to be scarcely able to find their way. On this account much extraordinary attention is paid to the roads in Barbadoes." "The streets of Jamaica may almost be said to be paved with glass bottles." How many of these bottles had done service in "entertaining angels unawares," is among the matters mysterious and unknown. The miles of stone walls which enclose the private grounds of the people of Nassau, are to a large extent surmounted by the broken fragments of glass bottles, laid in mortar; the broken glass is strongly suggestive of the convivial habits of Nassau in the earlier times. One would suppose it extremely unwise to engraft the habits of the English aristocracy, who are accustomed to raise the damp and chilly fogs which envelope them with the contents of the bottle, upon the customs of a people who live in an atmosphere of almost tropical heat. But the leaders of fashion in Nassau are not only extremely loyal to their most excellent queen, but seem to aspire in every way to mould their habits and conform their lives to English models, without any regard to the wide differences which exist in all the circumstances which surround them. We should anticipate that, as a natural and necessary consequence, a rapid wasting of all the vital energies of mind and body, and a material shortening of the term of human life.

A Private Residence in Nassau.

The pleasant and agreeable attentions which are shown by the local clergy of Nassau and some prominent church members to ecclesiastics from abroad, who, by letter or otherwise, make themselves known, may be inferred from the following extract from a short descriptive and highly eulogistic account of Nassau, communicated to a New York religious paper by a clergyman. He writes under the date of March 25, 1876: "The hospitality of the inhabitants is as warm and genial as their clime. The polite cordiality extended to non-residents makes them forget they are strangers in a strange land." A burrowing animal from its little hole in the ground is about as well qualified to describe a universe which it has not seen, as is a Doctor of Divinity to accurately portray the hospitality of a place, because the doors of certain good, pious and appreciative persons have always been flung wide open at the approach of one of God's favored ambassadors. We doubt if the learned doctor was invited to the high-toned entertainments, where cards and wine and the waltz shortened the hours of midnight and of the early morning, and helped to place in full accord the best blood of the Bahamas with the aristocratic and royal blood of the mother country. And we know from observation and experience, what any one may know is true from the nature of the case, that forty-nine out of fifty strangers sojourning in Nassau will never know, except from report, that there is such a thing as a generous hospitality anywhere upon the island. This is not exceptional, for the same thing is and must be true in all places where strangers arrive regularly at short intervals and in large numbers. In a small, poor city, they constitute rich golden placers to be sedulously worked, and not disguised angels to be entertained.

We all know by report, and not a few by personal experience, the warmth and glow of a hospitality, noble and unselfish, that was indigenous to the soil, and flourished with tropical luxuriance

in many of the Southern States in former times.   When certain
loyalists fled with their slaves to the Bahamas after the breaking
out of the American revolution of 1776 from the States of the
Carolinas and Georgia, they carried their hospitality with them,
and found that it flourished better than cotton upon those rocky
isles.   And no doubt it still survives, but circumstances have
greatly changed.   While retaining an allegiance to the mother
country that, if mistaken, challenges admiration, they did it
largely at the expense of their fortunes, and at Nassau the exercise of hospitality on a large scale, sufficient to meet the requirements of weekly boat-loads of strangers, who are willing to be
received with open arms and to be entertained with princely
liberality, would soon result in their financial annihilation.   But
any gentleman of respectability and of fair social position, who
is able and willing to take with him to Nassau a large supply of
the choicest wines and other liquors, will only need to let his
position be known in order to be surrounded with troops of high-
toned friends, officially and otherwise well up among the gentry
of the island.   Liquors will open doors better than letters, and,
as a social currency that will circulate everywhere, even check
must give way to champagne.

But, as in the floral world, the shrubs that from leaf and flower
load the air with sweetest perfumes, seldom, if ever, spring spontaneously from the soil where trade has established her thronged
and busy marts, so it is in countries sparsely populated, and seldom marked with the impress of stranger foot-steps, that the resi-
nous, spicy and aromatic perfumes of a free, genuine and grateful hospitality rise like incense from censers sacred and golden.

CHAPTER XIX.

The First Great Voyage of Columbus. He Solves the Dark Problem of the Ages. His Land Fall. The Whole Group Made Forever Memorable. The Spirits of Columbus and Black Beard Indelibly Impressed Upon the Islands. Eminently Good and Bad Men Not Dead When They Die. The Natives As Columbus Found and Described Them. The West India Islands Occupied by Substantially One People. The Caribs. The Search Among the Bahamas for the Fountain of Youth.

> "There are great deeds that will not pass away,
>   And names that must not wither, though the earth
>   Forgets her empires with a just decay."—Byron.

THE Bahamas are objects of great historic interest to the whole civilized world, but to the inhabitants of the Western Hemisphere they have a peculiar charm. The life and voyages of Christopher Columbus, the son of a Genoese wool-comber, when faithfully recorded, give to literature a treasure of inestimable value, and to the department of fact, the absorbing attraction and dazzling brilliancy of fiction. For several weeks after our first arrival in Nassau, the great navigator and discoverer was almost constantly in mind. While yachting in the perfectly clear and transparent waters, so exquisitely colored, borrowing their rich hues not only from the skies but from the white sand beds and coral shelves and reefs over which they flow, we thought how, after his long and anxious voyage, he must have been impressed; and every ride we took over the hard limestone roads, upon the island of New Providence, now looking out upon the

299

neighboring keys, set like jewels in liquid colors so peculiarly rich in shades of green and blue that written language is too poor to furnish terms with which to describe them—and then, turning to a new world of trees, shrubs, vines and flowers, we seemed to commune with that great spirit of the past, and to participate in the wonder and astonishment with which his mind was absorbed and filled, when, nearly four hundred years ago, he preceded us in making the acquaintance of those fairy isles in that dreamy and seemingly unreal part of the world. Indeed, at times, it seemed as if we could almost feel the gaze of his gray, thoughtful and prophetic eyes.

The foot-fall of the great Genoese discoverer upon one of the long, low, Bahama islands, has ennobled the whole group. The subtle influence of that grand historic event pervades the surrounding air, and imparts a brilliant and prismatic radiance to objects in other respects insignificant. The woods and waters, the flowering shrubs, the climbing vines, the trees with their rich glossy foliage and luscious and golden fruits, and even the sable forms and faces of the happy negroes, glow with an added lustre in the light of that ever memorable event. Were those coral isles to-morrow "in the deep bosom of the ocean buried," their memory would remain, for the Genius of History will ever keep and guard it in her imperishable archives. Ocean has no abyss deep and dark enough to hide it from the view of the men of the future.

A diabolical presence also—the ghosts of bad men who have passed away—seems at times, even in our day, to lurk in the shadows, and to infect with distrust the light, upon the island of New Providence. Strong natures cannot be wholly shut up in hades. It is more than a hundred and fifty years since Black Beard rendezvoued at Nassau, and held his court under one of its trees. No robber of the sea, ancient or modern, surpassed him in courage, in cruelty or in crime. Columbus, by simply skirting the shores and landing upon one of the summer isles, secured for the whole group an immortality of fame. Black Beard infected them with an infamy as enduring as the memory of his crimes. The foot-fall of one hallowed the coralline rocks, the presence of the other so polluted the air as to permanently give to it the shadowy gloom of a lurking fear. The most charming flower bed loses much of its fragrance and beauty as soon as it is known that a serpent has nestled there.

Death cannot wholly destroy men who are good and great. They are not dead when they die. They enter upon that journey where the travel is all one way, and yet do not wholly leave us. Their suns descend behind the hills, but a zodiacal light still lingers in the heavens. So when earth's moral monsters pass away, shadows dark and chilly are for centuries projected into the sunlight. Hence we observed, that over the bright and beautiful waters, and along the shining shores of the emerald isles, the soft air is even now impregnated with a moral poison derived from pirates who have been dead more than a hundred years.

In the Old World the traveler is often so occupied with the relics, monuments, history, traditions and legends of a past hoary and venerable with age, that he is inclined to overlook the present. In the new world the dark and impenetrable shadows extend to modern times, and leave but a few centuries for the historic period. But even contemporaneous history is not wholly reliable, because of the bad habit of covering with the gay robes and bright ribbons of fiction, the simplicity and nakedness of truth.

It was upon Friday, (a day which superstition has branded as unlucky) August 3d, 1492, at eight o'clock A. M., that Columbus with his three caravals, two of which were only decked fore and aft, sailed from Palos upon what the world generally believed

26

to be a "fool's errand." Reaching the Canaries in safety, he
left Gomora on the 6th of September. At 10 o'clock P. M., October 11th, A. D. 1492, Columbus saw or supposed he saw a moving light gleaming fitfully in the darkness. For three weeks,
Herons, Pelicans and several other species of birds, had appeared
in sight almost daily, as if to cheer and welcome him on his
lonely way. Some even alighted on his vessels, and were hailed
as the bearers of good tidings. Other mute, but most reliable
witnesses, in constantly increasing numbers, had been encountered
by his caravals, floating in the calm, warm waters, and had conveyed to him the joyful intelligence that the great object of his
search was near at hand. Four hours later, a gun fired from the
Pinta, the vessel that led the little fleet, conveyed the thrilling
intelligence that terra firma itself was actually in sight. In
that supreme moment of his triumph a wild intoxication would
have possessed a less lofty and heroic mind. The inspired proph-
et of the fifteenth century, casting his eyes upwards, humbly
returned his thanks to that Divine Being that had enlightened,
sustained, guided and protected him in the great work to which
he had devoted himself for so many years, and for the brilliant
success with which at last his labors were crowned.

The author of the "Land Fall of Columbus" has, with great
boldness and apparent success, attacked the opinion heretofore
so generally conceded to be true, that Columbus first landed upon
the present island of St. Salvador, (sometimes called Cat Island.)
The old belief received the endorsement of Washington Irving,
(who did not deem it best "to disturb the ancient landmarks,")
and also of Baron Humboldt, but the author of the "Land Fall"
has reproduced the original text of the journal which Columbus
kept of his first voyage of discovery, as embodied in the letters
which he wrote at the time, closely and critically examined its
statements, and, with the assistance of modern official charts,

carefully followed the great navigator's every movement, as min-
utely described by himself, from his first landing upon the island
which the natives called Guanahani, until he anchored off the
island of Cuba. He arrives at the conclusion that Columbus
first landed upon Watling's Island and named it San Salvador,
and that he did not visit at all the island now known by that
name. After carefully considering the facts which lead to this
result, we are clearly of the opinion the author of the "Land
Fall" is entitled to the credit of exposing a great historical error
after it had received the sanction of eminent writers, and been
hallowed by time.

Watling's Island is one of the Bahamas, and nearly or quite two
hundred miles distant in a north-easterly direction from Nassau.
The great importance of this discovery as seen in the light of the
four centuries which will soon be completed—so apparent to us—
far exceeds all that Columbus had imagined in his wildest dreams.
No wonder that Europe was thrown into a ferment of intense
excitement when the intelligence of his wonderful success was
made known. Many a long cycle of a thousand years had been
completed, during all which time no human being, standing upon
the eastern shores of the Atlantic, could discern anything in or beyond the illimitable waste of waters but a GREAT UNKNOWN. A
deep and profound mystery, like the pall of the darkest night,
ever brooded over the billows that received the setting sun.
Philosophers gazed but to speculate, men of fervid imaginations
to dream, and poets, in measured numbers, to sing their weird
and wildest songs.

Upon the banks of the Tigris and Euphrates,—in Abyssinia
and Upper Egypt,—down the fertile valley of the Nile,—and
upon both shores of the Mediterranean Sea, civilization, empire
and imperial power had for thousands of years made their slow
but grand and solemn march, only to be at last barred and baffled
by a vast and unknown waste of waters.

Columbus, with his little fleet of three vessels, solved the problem of the ages, dispelled the deep and profound mystery, and bridged the dark and unfathomable abyss. Landing upon the Bahamas, he impregnated the newly found Western world with the seminal principles of the old Eastern civilization. This cluster of keys and islands constitute the cradle in which Young America, with all his inventions and revolutionary ideas in embryo, was first rocked. How murky were the shadows that four centuries ago shrouded equally the Christian church and the most famous institutions of learning! Out of them the tall and commanding form of Columbus rises, radiant with an effulgence that seems divine, ennobled and glorified by great truths in advance of his age. For eighteen long years he bore with marvelous fortitude and equanimity the unsupplied and pressing wants which his poverty engendered, the delusive and broken promises of kings, the mistaken fears and bigotry of the good, the narrow-mindedness of the learned, and the ridicule and contempt, the scoffs and jeers of the ignorant and doubting world.

The lesson of Columbus should never be forgotten by the eminent theologians and divines who minister at the altars of religion, and guard its profound mysteries in their small but sacred arks; nor by the votaries of science, who seem, while they explore the wonderful phenomena of nature, as disclosed upon our earth, or travel among the stars, to literally "walk with God." Let them ever remember that outside of cloistered cells and institutions richly endowed and furnished, in the future as in the past, the most valuable germs of progress will probably be found; that no proposition should be ignored because it is bold and startling; no truth ostracised because it is new. At the same time it may be well for some of the long haired, unshaved, and unkempt seers of our day, who have, as they think, some great revolutionary and reformatory mission to fulfill, to consider that it may not be less than two or three thousands of years before another Columbus will be born, and that like rank and noxious weeds in a good garden, superstition and error had root and flourished by the side of truth in the mind of the great discoverer of the New World.

Mr. Moseley, in his Nassau Almanac, states that Columbus visited New Providence and called the island Fernandina, in honor of the king of Spain. This is very clearly a mistake. The author of the Land Fall agrees with Washington Irving that Exuma is the island which Columbus thus discovered and named. If we remember rightly, Bruce makes the same mistake in his Memoirs.

The visitor at Nassau has ample time to muse and meditate. He is not wholly satisfied with the present. Looking at the dark murky shadows lying back of a few hundred years that envelope human history upon these islands, he asks the tangled woods, the coralline hills, the rude water-worn caverns, and the shell-strewn and honey-combed shores—WHAT OF THE PAST? There is no response. Neither records nor ruins furnish even historic riddles for its solution. Let us, therefore, stand where Columbus and his companions stood in October, 1492, and listen while he gives to his sovereign a description of what he then saw. We copy from his epistolary journal under date of the 13th of October, the day after his "Land Fall:"

"All were young persons, as I said before, and of good stature, and withal handsome, who came to the shore. The hair of these islanders is not crisp or wooly, but long and straight like that of Asiatics. The forehead is wide, more so, indeed, than any people I have yet seen. They have large handsome eyes, and are not black, but of the color of Canaries, as might be expected, since they are due west from the island of Hierro, one of that group. They are all well made, even to their hands; not pot-bellied, but exceedingly well formed.

"They came to the ship in canoes, formed from the trunk of a tree, as long as a boat, and all from one log, curiously worked after their own fashion, and large enough to carry forty or fifty persons. Others they have, also, sufficient to contain one person. They are propelled by a paddle shaped like a baker's shovel, and glide about rapidly. They overturn and right them again when on the water, emptying them with calibashes which they have always with them. They bring balls of cotton thread, and other things too numerous to mention, and would exchange them for anything in return. I watched them very narrowly, to see if they had any gold, but could only see that they had a little piece hanging from the nose."

In a subsequent letter he writes: "They swam out to our boats, bringing parrots and balls of cotton thread, with spears and several other things, all of which they exchanged for what we chose to give them—glass beads and hawk's bills. In fact we traded together most amicably, but they appeared to be a very poor race of people, deficient in many things. They go about naked as they were born, the women also, although I did not see but one [old] young one. Indeed every one that I saw was young; every one appeared to be under thirty years of age.

"The hair of some was thick and long, like the tail of a horse. The hair of some was short, brought forward over the eye-brows; some wearing it long and never cutting it. Some again are painted, and the hue of their skin is similar in color to the Canaries—not black nor white. Some are painted white, and some red, or any other color. Some paint only their faces, and others their whole person, and some only their eyes and noses.

"They have no weapons and appear to know of none, for I showed them swords, and they took them by the blade and cut themselves from sheer ignorance. They have no iron. Their spears are long, and instead of iron are pointed with the teeth of

DESCRIPTIONS BY COLUMBUS.

a fish, and such hard substances." He says that some had scars, caused by wounds received when repelling invaders, (Caribs undoubtedly.)

"This is a tolerably large island, very level, with pine trees and plenty of water, and a large lake in the middle of it, without mountains, all covered with verdure which is pleasant to the eye.

"These people are very amiable, and desirous of having our things, for when they have nothing to give us for them, they take what they can and jump into the water and swim off with it. But anything they have they give us readily for whatever we will exchange for it. They will even barter for broken crockery and glass."

Upon going to another part of the island, when the people saw the Spaniards were not going to land, some of them, he says, "rushed into the sea and swam out to us, and we understood them to ask if we had come from the skies. One old man even got on to the boat, and others, men and women, called out at the top of their voices—'come and see the men who have come from the skies; bring them something to eat and drink.'

"They are a simple-minded and handsomely formed race.

"I went after a canoe which shot away faster than any boat could; for speed they have great advantage over us."

Again he writes: "The islands are very fertile, and have a fine air.

"I saw even cotton cloth, made like mantles, and the people appeared more orderly, and the women wore a piece of cloth, which, however, scarcely concealed their sex.

"There appears to be no kind of religion among them."

He also speaks of the fishes as "of the most beautiful colors as if painted of a thousand different hues, and so brilliant that they astonish every one, who, on this account, is anxious to see them. There are whales, also parrots and lizzards, but of beasts I have seen none."

Again he says: "The people, one with another, are all of the same race, naked alike, and of the same stature.

" * * * Our men, who had gone for water, told me they went into their houses, which they found swept very clean, and that their beds and furniture were of cotton net. Their houses are like tents, and of a good height, with chimneys. But I have not seen among the many settlements I have met with, any one with more than twelve to fifteen houses."

Again: "The married women wear cotton aprons, but the girls none, excepting some above eighteen years of age." One man "had a piece of gold in his nose about the size of a half dollar.

"Your highness may depend that this country is the most fertile, temperate, and even there is in the world."

"My eye can never tire admiring so much beautiful verdure, and so different from ours too.

"And the singing of the birds, and the flocks of parrots which are so numerous as to obscure the sky, are so delightful that no one could desire to leave it. The birds are so numerous, and so different from ours that it is quite wonderful. And there are a thousand different kind of trees, and all with fruit and delicious perfume."

Under date of October 22d, 1492, he writes: "And many natives came to see us, similar to those of the other islands, all naked and painted, some white, some red, some black, after their fashion. They brought spears and some cotton balls for trade. * * * Some of them wore bits of gold in their noses."

The West Indian islands include the Bahamas, and, when discovered by the Spaniards, they were occupied by substantially one people. There existed minor differences, the results of their separation, but the early writers give them a common description. The Caribbean Islands were inhabited by a very different people. The two races were no doubt off-shoots from different portions of the neighboring continent.   While the Caribs were bold, rugged, aggressive and warlike, the former were amiable, docile, kind-hearted, generous and affectionate, and only fought when driven to it by the instinct of self-preservation.   The contrast was that of the wolf and the lamb.   The blood of the Caribs had not been exposed to the soothing influences of the atmosphere of their island homes long enough to have eliminated the cruel and savage taint it acquired in the cold, bleak, barren region where it no doubt received its race-mark.   The inhabitants of the West Indies were confiding, frank, gentle and good-natured.   The sexual passion was strong.   " Love with this happy people was not a transient and fitful ardor only, but the source of all their pleasures, and the chief business of life.   *   *   *   They gave full indulgence to the instincts of nature, while the influence of the climate heightened the sensibility of the passions."

" They had less strength and endurance than the Spaniards. Their limbs were pliant and active, and in their motions they displayed both gracefulness and ease.   They were expert divers, and their agility was eminently conspicuous in their dances, wherein they delighted and excelled, devoting the cool hours of night to this employment.   It was their custom to dance from evening to dawn."   Herrera says that their public dances, (for they had others highly licentious,) were appropriated to particular solemnities, and being accompanied with historical songs, were called Arretoes.

They had an elastic ball game like that of cricket, which was called Bato.   The ball was not caught in the hand, or returned with an instrument, but received on the head, the elbow or foot, " and the dexterity and force with which it was repelled was astonishing and inimitable."

" They had remarkable sweetness of temper, and native goodness of disposition."   " All writers agree they were unquestionably the most gentle and benevolent of the human race."

To their superiors they were submissive and respectful; to
their enemies forgiving; while for their ancestors in spirit land
they entertained an undying affection.

Superstition, that old inhabitant of earth, indigenous in all
climes, and existing in all ages, was domiciled upon the coral
islands at the time of the Spanish discovery, and was as active
as the indolent character of the climate permitted in forging
fetters for the human mind, and holding men in bondage to fear.
Priests performed ridiculous rites and ceremonies, interpreted
the decrees and communicated the messages of deities whose evil
designs they sought to placate with prayer.   They were also the
medical attendants of the sick.   The union of the clerical and
medical professions is to be expected wherever disease is believed
to be the result of diabolical agencies, and not the executed pen-
alty for violated physical laws.

The islanders believed that the heaven which awaited the good
after death, was a pleasant valley of luxurious repose and indolent tranquility—of cool shades and murmuring brooks, abounding in guavas and other delicious fruits, never scorched by drought
or desolated by the hurricane.   Its chief happiness consisted in
a re-union, forever indissoluble, with the loved friends and re-
vered ancestors from whom they had been separated by death.

They believed in one Supreme Being, and in many lesser
divinities, but sought to win the favor of the demons who were
permitted to rule and desolate their island world, by worshiping
hideous idols which symbolized their unseen presence, and clearly
manifested diabolical power.

The authority of their caziques was hereditary, and it has been
claimed that, in determining the succession, the children of a

cazique's sisters were preferred on account of the greater certainty of royal blood. The sovereigns were looked up to with reverence and obeyed with submission. Royal ornaments, numerous attendants, and a multitude of wives attested their royal power. Heroic songs, hymns of praise, public dances of honor, together with the notes of musical instruments made of shells, and the deafening noise of rude drums, formed a part of their funeral obsequies.

The Bahamas interested but did not satisfy the the Spaniards. They sought in vain in the coralline rocks for the golden ores that gilded their fevered dreams. The passion for

> "Gold! Gold! Gold! Gold!
> Bright and yellow, hard and cold,"

was all pervading, and so absorbing and intense that they seemed dead to every tender sentiment and ennobling impulse. For a time poverty did for the islanders more than the greatest riches could have accomplished—peace and security, and the strange visitors whom they were ready to worship as divine, departed.

Guileless, unsuspecting, generous and unselfish themselves, how could these aborigines understand the wonderful beings, who, from the vast solitudes of an illimitable ocean, had suddenly landed upon their picturesque shores? In the distant east from whence the strangers had come, only the morning sun, in golden effulgence, had ever before emerged. Were not these then, the children of the sun? Had they not all of the divine and none of the human? No wonder, that as Herrera states, they were at first never satisfied with looking at the Spaniards, but knelt, lifted up their hands and gave thanks to God, calling upon each other to admire the heavenly men!

Afterwards, a new and strange interest invested these islands

of perpetual and unfading verdure.   It was reported and believed
by Juan Ponce de Leon and other bold navigators, that upon one
of them existed water medicated and endowed by nature with
most wonderful potency.   In tangled wood or rocky cavern, bub-
bled in the shadows or sparkled in the sunlight, that old dream
of the ages—the fountain of perpetual youth; and men toiled,
suffered, sickened and died in the vain search for the wonderful
waters of immortality.   It is indeed fortunate for the world, considering the infamous character of many of those Spanish adventurers, that this pleasing dream had no basis of fact upon which
to rest.

It has not been considered very strange, in an age which teemed
with marvels of fact which far transcended in interest, novelty
and importance, the wildest conceptions of the imagination, that
men of intelligence implicitly believed in the existence of

> "A bright floral isle,
> The jewel of a smooth and silver sea,
>   With springs in which perennial summers smile,
> A power of causing immortality;"

and that some were willing to risk their money and their lives in
efforts to discover it.   But the thread of life upon which these
dreamers were suspended, continued to weaken as it shortened,
and they soon found, as a practical fact, that the rejuvenating
spring is situated upon the other side of the dark turbid waters
of the river of death.

Bay Street, west end of Nassau.

CHAPTER XX.

> "O nature! what hadst thou to do in hell,
> When thou didst bower the spirit of a fiend
> In such a paradise?"—SHAKESPEARE.

> "I do not give you to Posterity as a pattern to imitate, but an
> example to deter."—JUNIUS.

COLUMBUS was a zealous member of the Church of Rome, and his mind seemed ever imbued with a strong religious sentiment. Religious zeal did much to encourage him to undertake and prosecute with tireless energy and unwavering faith his voyages of discovery. He believed himself raised up by Divine Providence for the purpose of communicating to the heathen a knowledge of the true God. But his royal master, Ferdinand of Spain, saw in the amiable, credulous and confiding Bahama Indians not men having immortal souls to be saved, but only living mechanisms capable of being stolen and utilized in money making. He did not merely tarnish his reputation, but he earned for himself eternal infamy, and the scorn and contempt of good men in all future times, by a royal order under which the entire native population of the Bahamas were conveyed to Hispaniola, and forced to labor in its mines. The removal was brought about by the grossest fraud. The "children of the sun" promised to take them to those Elysian isles where they could enjoy the society of their dead ancestors, and revel with them in supreme and never ending delights. Subjected to tasks to which they were unaccustomed, and for which they were unfitted, disappointed and broken hearted, it did not require many years for death to do for them all that the Spaniards had promised;

> "The whole race sank beneath the oppressor's rod,
> And left a blank among the works of God."

The "heavenly men" proved to be greater demons than any those unfortunate islanders had ever, by prayer and sacrifice, endeavored to appease and conciliate.

For a time the Bahamas were without human inhabitants;

> "Still nature spread her fruitful sweetness round,
> Breathed on the air, and brooded on the ground."

The fairy isles lost nothing of their charming loveliness; the soft, perfumed, and medicated air retained all its healing and attractive qualities; while the ocean kissed with its crested waves the white beaches and honey-combed shores, and ceaselessly uttered its regretful murmurs.

Capt. William Sayle, an English navigator, entered the harbor of Nassau in the year 1607, and gave to the island of New Providence its present name, in commemoration of his escape from threatened shipwreck. England claimed the Bahamas as an appendage of the British crown, upon the ground of his discovery, although more than a hundred years before Columbus had made the acquaintance of some of them. sailed through the group, and claimed all for Ferdinand and Isabella. Soon after this alleged discovery by Capt. Sayle, Charles the Second of England made a royal grant of all the Bahamas, including the islands which Columbus visited in 1492, to the Duke of Albemarle, Lord Craven, Sir John Caterel, Lord Berkley, Lord Sibley, and Sir Peter Coleton—the proprietors of Carolina; who did very little for the islands which was of any service to England or to themselves.

Afterwards, the outlaws of civilization and savages of the sea, frequented the islands, and made them the center of their hostile operations against the commerce of the world. With vessels of light draft, they mastered the intricacies of the tortuous channels, and made themselves familiar with the points of special danger, the safest lines of approach and retreat, the harbors of refuge, the best places for concealment, and the strongholds of defense. No light-houses, buoys or reliable charts warned the mariner, or guided him in his course over the perilous waters. Countless rocks and reefs, extensive shoals and banks, intricate currents and cross-currents, severe storms, and an occasional hurricane, would seem to have been sufficient without the still more fearful peril of armed and demoniac brigands of the sea.

The pirates who succeeded the original inhabitants must have been lineally descended from the early inhabitants of England, if the following description of the latter by Greene is to be credited: " From the first, the daring of the English race broke out in the secrecy and suddenness of the pirate's swoop, in the fierceness of their onset, in the careless glee with which they seized either sword or oar. 'Foes are they,' sang a Roman poet of the time, 'fierce beyond other foes, and cunning as they are fierce; the sea is their school of war, and the storm their friend; they are sea-wolves that prey on the pillage of the world.' "

The most violent of the sea-wolves that infested the waters of the Bahamas, and the neighboring seas, was a native of Bristol, England, by the name of Edward Tench. The historic name of Black Beard was conferred upon him by his cotemporaries on account of the color and quantity of hair which helped so much to give him a wild and savage appearance. He first made himself felt and feared as a privateer. Sailing in that capacity in the early part of the eighteenth century, from the island of Jamaica, he soon distinguished himself by his daring intrepidity and reckless courage. Between privateering and piracy there is but a single short step. A little practice in capturing, robbing and destroying the merchant ships of one nation, is a good preparatory and training school, in which an apt scholar, like Tench, is soon prepared for the business of waging merciless war on the commerce of the world.

Black Beard soon had a piratical fleet well manned and powerfully armed, which, for a short time, was a terror to all honest men who frequented the West India Islands or the neighboring shores of the main land. His audacity and power are indicated by the fact that the city of Charleston was once coerced into furnishing him with a valuable supply of medical stores, by the assurance that if his demands were refused, he would burn the vessels and kill the prisoners then in his possession which he had captured, and send the heads of the latter to the Governor of South Carolina. He was finally hunted down and killed in a bloody hand to hand fight among the inlets of North Carolina.

It is difficult at the present day to realize the extent and character of the peril from pirates to which a century and a-half ago persons were subjected who sailed in the waters which penetrate or surround the Bahamas. The black flag with its death's head and cross-bones, is a thing of the past. A marine police, mounted upon powerful and fast sailing steamers, and armed with breech-loading cannon, have driven the freebooters from the sea. But while history and tradition still preserve their memory, their blood, to some extent, courses down to our times in the channels of descent. The motto upon the Bahama Coat of Arms, and which is engraved upon its Great Seal—"*Expulsis Piratis, Restitutia Commercia*"—is an official and durable testimonial of the power which the pirates possessed, and the terror they inspired in former times.

The proprietors in 1670, appointed one Collingworth (or Chillingworth), Governor of the Bahamas, but the inhabitants concluded they had no need of him, and therefore took forcible possession of his person, and shipped him off to Jamaica.

In 1677 the proprietors conferred the vacant gubernatorial crown upon one Clark, whose great exaltation was purchased at the price of his life. His piratical subjects, by their filibustering excursions, had so exasperated their Spanish neighbors, that the latter invaded New Providence, destroyed the houses upon it by fire, took all the inhabitants captive who did not find refuge in the woods, carried Governor Clark to Cuba, and, it is said, tortured him to death and roasted him.

In 1684, the Spaniards again surprised the people upon the island, and, after destroying the improvements which had been made, they carried off some of the inhabitants. After the invaders left, such of the inhabitants as survived, emerged from their hiding places in a forlorn and necessitous condition, again started a settlement, and in 1687 chose a Presbyterian minister by the name of Bridge, their governor—a rather heavy and cumbrous title considering the limited number and poverty of the people. He held his high office three years.

In 1690 the proprietors sent out one Jones to be Governor " in and over " the Bahamas. He tyranized over the people with a high and unscrupulous hand, being aided by the pirate Avery who commanded a ship with 42 guns. When the latter was away, the outraged people put the Governor in prison, and chose Ashley, one of their number, President. The pirates returned and set Jones at liberty, who in turn imprisoned all whom he suspected of hostility to himself, and desired the pirates to carry them off the island and make way with them.

In 1694, Jones was superceded by one Trott, whom the proprietors appointed in his place. He liberated the imprisoned inhabitants, but allowed Jones to depart without a trial. Cowed by his fears, he also permitted the pirates to land with their plunder upon the island. The inhabitants fraternized with the freebooters, who remained unmolested. To protect themselves from the Spaniards, the inhabitants built a small fort upon which they mounted twenty-two cannon. "They also built a town of 160 houses which they called Nassau."

In 1697 Webb was appointed Governor. After holding that office two years, the discretion of his excellency got the better of his valor, and he left for Pennsylvania.

In 1699, while away, he, without the knowledge of the proprietors, installed in his place a mulatto by the name of Eldridge, a man of most infamous character, who secured the pirates for his protectors and patrons, and thus was enabled to retain his title and his power for two years.

In 1701 the proprietary "lords" conferred the office of Governor upon one Haskel, who put his immediate predecessor into prison, and also some of the inhabitants, whom he caused to be prosecuted for abetting the pirates. His zeal proved to be greater than his power, for in five weeks after his arrival upon the island, his turbulent subjects seized and ironed him, and after keeping him a close prisoner for six weeks, shipped him back to England.

These practical believers in self-government appointed one of their associates named Lichtwood, (or Lightfoot,) president and

deputy Governor, who held his office for two years, when the
French and Spaniards surprised, captured, and burned Nassau,
plundered its inhabitants, destroyed the fort, and carried the
president and a number of prisoners to Havana. Shortly afterwards these formidable enemies returned to Nassau and captured
and carried away all the inhabitants and negroes they could find.

The few who remained fled to Carolina and Virginia, and the
island for a short period was uninhabited. The pirates then for
a number of years made it their general place of rendezvous, and,
it is said, buried their booty in its woods.

Soon after the last invasion, Burch was appointed Governor
by the proprietors, but, upon his arrival at Providence, he discovered that subjects and ruler were all consolidated in his own
person. Like a horseless rider, he could perambulate his capital
on foot and alone, with the useless and unused whip and spurs
of his high office, but a few thousands of subjects would have
been extremely handy and desirable as a source of supply for his
empty exchequer, for even upon small islands a man cannot get
fat or exist long upon his titles, although, as in this instance,
they may enable him to live in history. So this Governor without subjects, pocketed his formidable credentials, packed his
trunks with the gilded insignia and baubles of his high office,
and soon exchanged the new world for the old—a wiser if not a
better man. He appears to have had no desire to play the part
of Robinson Crusoe, and possessed so little of the ambition that
inspired poor Sancho Panza, that he was not satisfied to be the
Governor even of a whole archipelago of unoccupied islands.

The lord proprietors became fully satisfied at last, that they
had upon their hands a good sized Bahama elephant. Had their
royal master been pleased to have given them, in lieu of the Isles
of Summer, an equal number of square miles of volcanic mountains in the moon, which some English astronomer had falsely

claimed to have first discovered, they would have occupied a more enviable position, for while the grant would have added nothing to their income, it could not possibly have impoverished or annoyed them. This pestiferous nest of pirates had only served as a burial place for their money and their hopes.

The British government finally, in the interest and for the security of commerce, bought the title of the legal representatives of the six proprietary interests, giving for each £2,000.

Upon the petition of the merchants of London and Bristol, interested in the security of commerce, King George I appointed Mr. Ward Rogers Governor, and sent him with a force of one hundred men and an ample supply of all necessary stores to fortify New Providence. He arrived out in 1717, and an act of indemnity having been passed, the pirates accepted of its terms, surrendered without a struggle, and became, thereafter, down to 1742, when Bruce wrote, "*the principal inhabitants of the island.*"

According to Mr. Mosely, the gubernatorial office was filled by Mr. Rogers from 1717 to 1721, and from 1728 to 1733; George Phenny or Finney was Governor during the intervening years. The population did not exceed 1,000 persons.

During this period of sixteen years the executive office seems to have been well filled, and peace, security and confidence prevailed, so that many families, besides many Palatines, settled and made improvements upon the islands.

In 1733 Richard Fitz Williams was appointed Governor, and with ample stores, a force of fifty men, and an engineer named Thomas Moore, arrived at New Providence, with special directions to fortify the place. This new colonial Governor was arbitrary and tyrannical, and so abused his power that "the best of the inhabitants and all the Palatines abandoned their improvements and left the island." The engineer died suddenly before he had made much progress in his work. In the bad business of oppressing the people, the Governor had the assistance and active co-operation of a member of the council, the judge of the court of admiralty, and one Archibald, ("his excellency's" servant,) who silenced opposition by knocking its authors down. The British sovereigns appear to have generally made their Bahama Governors out of very bad material. It was difficult as well as expensive for the oppressed islanders to make their complaints heard across the wide and stormy Atlantic, but three prominent inhabitants succeeded in reaching London, and preferred "charges of a very extraordinary nature against the Governor," who, after much delay, was ordered to meet his accusers, and defend himself against their formidable indictment. After a long and expensive trial, the charges were sustained and the Governor removed.

In 1738 John Tinker was appointed Governor, and made the people happy in the commencement of his administration by his removals and administrative reforms, but he appears, from Bruce's account founded upon personal knowledge, to have developed some of the worst qualities of his predecessors. In the most arbitrary, unjust and illegal manner, he made a variety of orders for the disposal of very valuable prize property captured by a privateer, for the purpose of enriching himself, and benefitting certain people of Nassau.

Peter-Henry Bruce, in April, 1741, arrived in Nassau, and and commenced work upon its fortifications under a commission from the British government. An old fort, very much out of repair, called Fort Nassau, within which were wooden barracks in a tumble-down condition, then stood on the north side of what is now known as Flemish Square, where the present stone barracks are situated. It had sixteen badly-mounted guns; the remainder of its armament consisted of guns in part spiked, in part charged with stones and sand, in part buried below high-water mark, and in part scattered about the place; and of gun carriages, trucks and shells, each of which appeared to have started out upon its own account to explore the island. Many of the guns had been used as ballast for vessels. Mr. Bruce, after collecting and testing the guns, found he had sixty-four six, nine, twelve and eighteen pounders fit for service.

In repairing and building fortifications at Nassau, Mr. Bruce labored under great and peculiar difficulties, which we mention because they indicate the destitution and condition of Nassau at that time. There was but one mason, and not a wheeled vehicle of any kind in the place. He imported two brick-layers from Philadelphia, and taught them how to cut and lay stone. No laborers could be hired unless they were furnished with provisions, supplies of which he procured from New York, for "the natives lived principally upon tortoise and fish, any kind of flesh meat being a great rarity."

Rumors of another Spanish invasion secured for Mr. Bruce the co-operation of the Bahama legislature in his efforts to suitably fortify the place. The east entrance, or "back door" of Nassau, required to be guarded, and the present Fort Montague was at that time erected. The Governor laid its foundation stone on the 10th day of June, A. D. 1741, in the presence of the principal inhabitants of the island. A sea-battery was erected near it at the same time. Necessary building stone would have been brought from the woods upon the heads of the negroes, had not the alarmed local authorities furnished the necessary boats for its transportation. Pallisades were made of mastic wood, which Mr. Bruce states, "is as hard and heavy as iron, and musket balls make no impression upon it." The inhabitants informed him that it would last a century, and was proof against swivel shot. The pallisades could be cut and worked only when green.

Then, as now, the rocks were soft below the surface, and easily cut, but hardened when exposed to the air. Cannon balls, when fired into the soft stone, were buried as in sand banks.

Mr. Bruce found sufficient leisure time while at Nassau to collect much historical information which he published in his "Memoirs." Most of the facts contained in the foregoing historical summary are collated from his book. So far as we have been able to learn, no other writer either preceded or followed him in sketching the history of the Bahamas. The historic pen which Bruce laid down in 1742, when he left Nassau to make good the defenses of Charleston, S. C., no one has taken up. The soothing air of the Isles of Summer is not favorable to the making or writing of history. We have gleaned but a few items with which to fill the intervening historical chasm measured by the past one hundred and thirty-seven years.

When the independence of the United States was confirmed, and established by the treaty of peace in 1782, there were many inhabitants of the Carolinas and Georgia, who, during the revolutionary war, retained their affection for the mother country, and their loyalty to its government. These people lacked faith in the republic, and the same spirit which induced them or their ancestors to emigrate to the American colonies, caused them to abandon their new homes and seek their fortunes elsewhere. Many of them removed with their slaves to the Bahamas, and commenced new plantations upon a number of the islands. The virgin soil for a few seasons yielded large harvests; but its fertility was soon exhausted. Deprived of trees and bushes, the fields were scorched by the hot sun, while swarms of destructive insects consumed and otherwise destroyed the scanty harvests. It required but a few years to complete the financial ruin of the new settlers. Their improvements and negroes were of little value in the absence of paying crops. What had been saved of their fortunes in the States speedily disappeared, and they were left destitute even of the means of removal from the little islands in which their courage and hopes were entombed.

During the war of the American revolution the island of New Providence was for a brief time a part of the young American republic, and the starry flag floated in triumph from all the forts and flag staffs of Nassau, and decorated the governor's house on the crest of its hill. The bold and intrepid Commodore Hopkins, with a small body of men, accomplished this result. The American commander very soon made up his mind, as did Columbus before him, that he could do much better elsewhere. In fact, there were no lofty mountain crags upon the Bahamas, where the great American eagle could build its nest, and no sufficient room upon the island of New Providence for the national bird to fully and comfortably spread its wings. The island seemed designed by Divine Providence for parrots and birds that were satisfied to spend their lives in the hot sun, admiring the beautiful plumage which the brackish waters of the still and shallow lagoons reflected. So the Commodore furled the stars and stripes, and abandoned as worthless the island he had so gallantly captured.

In the year 1781, a Spanish force made up in part of some American volunteers, took military possession of Nassau, and garrisoned it with six hundred troops. A short time previous to the notification of the treaty of peace, Lieut. Col. Deveaux, of the loyal militia of South Carolina, planned, organized and led an expedition against Nassau, in which great boldness, ingenuity, address and ability were displayed. With two armed brigantines and only fifty volunteers, he sailed from St. Augustine, and, after obtaining some recruits, (principally negroes,) from Eleuthera and the neighboring islands, he landed with his little handful of adventurers upon the island of New Providence a little to the eastward of Fort Montague. The officers of that fort were completely taken unawares, and when the column of attack reached the ramparts, only one solitary sentinel was in

sight to receive them. He had a lighted match in his hand,
ready to blow up the fortress if the exigencies of the case should
require it, but the intrepidity of Col. Deveaux who headed the
assailants, thwarted his design; springing upon the bewildered
and astonished sentinel, Col. Deveaux made him his prisoner,
and immediately afterwards, without a struggle or even a parley,
the fort, with its garrison, armament and military stores was
surrendered.   The Colonel, quickly, and without opposition,
proceeded with an attacking column to the crest of the hill and
to the grounds upon which the Governor's house was situated,
overlooking the town.   McKinnen says:

"Every artifice was used to deceive the Spaniards, both as to
the number and description of the enemy they had to contend
with.   A show of boats was made, continually rowing from the
vessels, filled with men, who apparently landed, but in fact concealed themselves by lying down as they returned to the vessels,
and afterwards made their appearance, as a fresh supply of troops
proceeding to disembark.   Men of straw, it is said, were dressed
out to increase the apparent number on the heights; and some
of the troops, to intimidate the Spaniards, were painted and disguised as their inveterate foes, the Indians.   One or two galleys
in the harbor had been captured, and, trusting to the circumstances in his favor, Colonel Deveaux summoned the Governor
to surrender, with a pompous description of his formidable force.
Some hesitation being at first discovered, the Colonel seconded
his overtures with a well-directed shot at the Governor's house
from a field-piece, during his deliberation, which produced an
immediate capitulation.   The Spanish troops, in laying down
their arms, it is said, could not refrain from expressing the utmost mortification and confusion as they surveyed their con-
querors, not only so inferior in point of numbers, but ludicrous
in their dress and military appearance."

28

By the terms of the treaty of peace, the title of the king of Great Britain to the Bahamas was established. Since that time, for nearly a hundred years, the islands have remained one of the out-lying portions of the British Empire. Situated at one of the gates of entrance to the Gulf of Mexico, near to our shores, and in the path of our commerce, nothing prevents Britain's possession from being a menace but their insignificance and weakness in a military point of view.

The late war of the rebellion demonstrated the capabilities of Nassau and its harbor for mischief when occupied in time of war by a professedly neutral, but covertly hostile power. Except during the period covered by our late war—1861 to 1865—the history of Nassau from 1783 to the present time, has been as dull and devoid of interest (outside of that which accompanies wrecks and hurricanes,) as the still and shallow waters of a mangrove lake. But, as has been well said, a nation is most prosperous when it furnishes the least for the historian to record;

> "And noiseless falls the foot of time
> Which only treads on flowers."

One event, of an extremely radical and revolutionary character, should not, however, be passed by unnoticed—the abolition of slavery. This result was accomplished without the loss of a life, the firing of a gun, or disturbance of any kind. By the silent operation of a law enacted upon an island some four thousand miles away, upon the other side of the wide and stormy Atlantic, all of the enslaved Bahama negroes were changed from chattels into men, and became at once free citizens of that great empire which circles the world, and upon which the sun never sets.

CHAPTER XXI.

Nassau Revisited. Lack of Confidence in the Northern March. Missing Trunks—Man and His Clothes. The New York and Nassau Steamboat Line. The Western Texas. Notable Passengers. The Fountain of Youth on Litchfield Hill. Fernandina, Picturesque Shores. Sea-birds. The Mouth of the St. John's—its Bar and Breakers. A Visit to St. Nicholas. Incidents and Scenes in the Gulf of Florida. "Bank Sharks." Porpoises. Crossing the Gulf Stream. Dolphins. Sun-set Views. Arrival at Nassau.

> "Once more upon the water! yet once more!
> And the waves roll beneath me like a steed
> That knows its rider—welcome to their roar!"—BYRON.

WHEN we awoke Thursday morning, March 4th, 1880, the air was filled with the melody of the birds of early spring, and the soft sweet notes of the blue birds were especially noticeable. The air was as warm and genial as that of a pleasant morning in May. Gentle zephyrs sported with the leafless branches of the orchard and forest trees, and lovingly kissed and quickened with a new energy the arbutus, the crocus, the daffodil and other flowers, that were courageously pushing their long buried heads out of the ground to see if winter, their natural enemy, had retreated to its arctic home. What folly, we exclaimed, to leave the shores of Connecticut and encounter the perils of an ocean voyage in search of a summer that is already here! But we had good reason to mistrust appearances. The northern March has an established reputation. Its record is as old as the centuries that have passed away. Though it approached concealed in the

327

gay mantle of spring, and greeted us with sunny smiles, we knew that more disease and discomfort lay ambushed within its thirty-one days than can be found in any three of the remaining months of the year. It might deceive the flowers—they have perished in its frosts before; and the birds that have more melody and beauty than mind and brains; and tempt the fish back to their old spawning grounds—a shad cannot be expected to know any better—but as for us, we said, we would seek for summer where summer lives and reigns throughout the entire circle of the revolving year, where the northern March is unknown.

Our arrangements were soon made, and the steamer Elm City landed us safely in New York, after a refreshing night's sleep. Before the break of day, while we skirted the eastern shore of Manhattan Island, we looked out of our stateroom window, through the murky and humid air, upon the sleeping city, and mused and marveled at the wondrous changes which an hour or two of daylight would produce. Its shipping and great business arteries were but dimly revealed in the gas-light and lamp-light, while gloomy vapors concealed from view its dome of stars. The fevered and mad pulses that so wildly beat and throb by day, were soothed and quieted by kind nature's grand opiate and restorative, sleep. Day and night work wondrous changes in our country's great commercial capital. Ocean in calm and storm is not more unlike than a great city at mid-day and mid-night. O, how we abominate the horrid noises of its crowded streets— the awful solitude of its thoroughfares!

It was between eight and nine o'clock in the morning when the astonishing fact was discovered that our trunks had not accompanied us to New York, they having been left unchecked at the steamboat dock at New Haven! Our stateroom in the Western Texas was engaged, and the steamer was advertised to sail at 3 P. M. of the same day. Had we lost our money we could have drawn for more, or borrowed or got trusted, perhaps. If we had even lost our reputation or character we might get along among strangers by leading a virtuous life in the future, and we knew that God forgives us if man does not. Even the loss of reason may prove to be a temporary affair which the quiet and medicated air of the ocean has power to sometimes restore. But to lose one's clothes—to leave behind one's wardrobe, just as the ship that is to carry you to distant countries is getting up steam to take you away, is a calamity so crushing and overwhelming that one would hardly desire such a misfortune to befall his bitterest enemy. Why, character and respectability, social position, civilization, everything that makes a man among men and a lady among women, is involved in one's personal dry goods. When one begins to wear clothes he ceases to be a savage, and is indeed almost a Christian. It is true we were bound for the isles of perpetual summer, where clothes are not required to meet any physical want, and are only worn to indicate that man is not a brute beast; but still we, and especially the female half of us, were really horrified at the idea of leaving New York upon a long journey, almost as naked as we were born.

A young and efficient officer of the New Haven Steamboat Company came to our relief, utilized the telegraph, and thus endeavored to secure for our trunks a place on board the Continental, which was to leave New Haven for New York at 10 A. M. A delay in the sailing time of the Western Texas was promised us, and we waited in a state of mingled hope and fear the slow creeping of the languid hours. O, how much depended on the result! Whether we should leave our native land decent, respectable people, or otherwise, all depended upon the arrival or non-arrival on time of those ill-starred and sad-fated trunks. We sat upon the deck of the Western Texas and closely scrutinized every approaching steamer. How beautifully, like gigan-

tic white-feathered water fowls, they unceasingly cut and skimmed the dimpled waters which constitute that grand navigable
highway that separates and yet makes one two great cities! At
half-past three o'clock, a steamer more beautiful than the rest,
with a proud air of conscious superiority, made her appearance,
and as she changed her course to enter Peck's slip, the name
"Continental" was plainly discernable. The next twenty minutes were the longest and most anxious ones we ever experienced.
Stars may wander from their spheres and be lost forever, and
not affect us in the least—but to lose all one's wardrobe, including one's newest and best "store-clothes"—ah! that was altogether more than our equanimity could endure; there was no
relief or palliation for it in the philosophical reflections and teach-
ings of a life time. There is an end to all things, and we devoutly thank God that suspense and fear have their limits. The
last one of at least fifty baggage wagons that we examined contained the missing objects of our heart's then fondest affections.
The countenance of that old Jew who welcomed back the returning prodigal son, was certainly less wreathed with smiles, and less
illumined with the light of a new joy, than was ours at beholding
at that auspicious but late hour, those missing trunks; and, after
seeing that they were properly checked and shipped, we went
again on board and were soon employed in reading Milton's great
work—so evidently composed for such an occasion as this—"Paradise Regained."

The sea treated us tenderly. For a time it foamed, hissed,
howled and shook us up, but only, by giving us a slight taste and
token of its powers, to make us more appreciate the greatness
and goodness of its forbearance. For perhaps a hundred miles
each side of Hatteras, we crossed the great ocean storm belt, and
the sky lowered upon us as if in anger, but we soon sped away
from the impending danger and basked on deck in the warm rays

of a more southerly sun. Although out of sight of land, we skirted sufficiently near the Atlantic's western shore to have the constant company of large white gulls, who, to some extent, depended upon our ship for their supplies. The occasional appearance of steamers and vessels with sails spread to the wind, clearly indicated that we were traversing one of the great frequented but trackless paths of the sea. We passed the entrance to Charleston harbor, and if we could only have prolonged the daylight for a few hours, we would have reached Port Royal, our first stopping place, the third night after leaving New York. A gentleman with a sea-glass reported that he saw trees upon the Carolina shore, but we suspected he was somewhat aided by his imagination.

The Western Texas is one of a line of steamers which runs between New York and Nassau, touching at one or more of our southern ports going and returning. They are owned by C. H. Mallory & Co., and carry the mail under a long contract with the Bahama government, which pays the company a handsome subsidy for the service. From the position and nearness of the Bahamas to our coast, intimate and close commercial intercourse between them and the United States is inevitable.

The Texas is a new boat, about three years old, and has superior passenger accommodations. Its main saloon, "social hall" and staterooms, are roomy, very handsomely finished and furnished, and uncommonly pleasant. Neatness, cleanliness, order and efficiency are marked characteristics, and comfort and confidence are the result. The table, during our voyage, was supplied with an abundance of well-cooked food, including all the substantials and many of the delicacies that are to be met with in a good hotel. She registers 1250 tons, and is one of the largest of the line; the freight and passenger business is not sufficient to warrant the use of larger vessels.

While our passenger list was small, we were remarkably favored in respect to the general good character of all, and the exceptionally high character of some of our passengers. Among them were included the venerable ex-Chief Justice of Connecticut, the Honorable Origen S. Seymour, of Litchfield, and his wife; the Honorable George C. Woodruff, a veteran of the bar of Litchfield county, for legal ability probably second to no lawyer in our State, and formerly a member of Congress, and his wife; Mrs. Sanford, the widow of the late Judge Sanford, formerly of the Connecticut Supreme Court, and several members of her family, and an old sea captain who had spent the greater part of some forty years upon the ocean. We never looked upon the Litchfield delegation without feeling a strong sentiment of state pride, and personal veneration and admiration. What a grand stock! What a place is old Litchfield for mental, moral and physical development! At the ripe age of seventy-six, with what an elastic step our old judicial chieftain trod the steamer's deck! How keen his intellect! How bright and sparkling his soul-lit eye! How youthful, ever green and sunny his spirits! The great leader of judicial reform, there was not a fossil or a barnacle about him. But, towering high and strong above all, was his tender devotion, his unremitting care and watchfulness, his devoted and unflagging affection and love for his aged and sea sick wife, the mother of his stalwart and able sons! Turning from him to the hale, hearty, rugged Woodruff, full of the learned lore of the law, we inwardly exclaimed that the dream of the past is a veritable fact—there is a "fountain of perpetual youth," and it bubbles up on the top of Litchfield hill, and these are they who have drank of its wonderful waters. May their shadows never grow less, nor their blood cease to circulate in the veins and arteries of the men of the future!

Having freight on board for Fernandina, it was necessary for us to go up for a short distance the St. Mary's—a river that constitutes in part the line of division between Georgia and Florida. We remained outside all one night, and in the early morning cautiously proceeded towards the city, here and there feeling our way with the sounding line. Nearly all the day was consumed in discharging freight. The weather was so threatening that we were content to simply view the city from the upper deck. One colored policeman, black and dirty, was on duty at the wharf. He much needed a new uniform, but his "billy," and the revolver that protruded conspicuously out of one of his pockets, looked as if capable of doing good service. We must confess that we were not very favorably impressed with this specimen of the right arm of Florida's civil power. A big negro boy, who, in our presence horsewhipped a little one, and boldly returned the blows of a colored man who undertook to avenge the small boy's wrongs, was allowed to escape.

A smart, pretty white boy, only four years of age, smoked three cigars in the course of a few hours, and was reported to have received in the morning at the hands of his father—who had charge of the men who unloaded the freight—his morning glass of brandy and water! Fernandina, apparently, is a place of some three thousand inhabitants, white and colored. It has a pleasant look, resting upon a gentle elevation above its harbor. In leaving it, we steamed along nearly the whole line of its water front, and noticed that its streets seemed grass grown, being green with a low vegetable growth of some kind. As it is connected with the Gulf of Mexico by railroad, it is the center of considerable freighting business. St. Mary's river, like the St. John's, seeks the ocean through several channels, by which means a number of islands are formed—low, green savannahs, here and there diversified with forest growths, the trees and bushes giving no indications of having ever felt the noiseless, killing touch of the great northern frost king, who so quietly and thoroughly paves our roads and bridges, our lakes and rivers in a single night.

Our passengers thronged the bow of our boat and feasted eye and mind upon scenery of unusual loveliness. The shore lines, with their white beaches and dark backgrounds, were constantly changing in their forms and outlines. Amelia beach reminded us as we passed of the pleasure we experienced when driving over it a little more than a year before. Our water-way was marked by buoys, while several lighthouses proclaimed the fostering care of a wise, paternal government, in lighting at night the watery highways. We passed within a few feet of a warning bell, so hung that the play of the ceaseless tides causes it to constantly rise and fall, and, unattended, to ring out upon the waters in calm and storm, during the long hours of the day and the darker and longer hours of the night, in musical tones, "Ho! mariners, this is the only true way! As ye value your lives, heed me and obey my voice!"

In vain the sun struggled to look down upon this charming picture of sea and land. Cold looking clouds veiled the sky. Beautiful pelicans sported in the air, amused, perhaps, at the frolicsome play of the porpoises in the waters below. Wild ducks, obeying some great social law, were seen associating together in large flocks, observing the most perfect order, and giving to man examples worthy of imitation of mutual forbearance, domestic peace, and freedom from family jars and internal dissensions. Our old friends, the sea-gulls, held not each with the rest so close a communion, and seemed to have more individual liberty with their unity; but they kept sufficiently near to each other to avoid the crushing loneliness of a solitary life.

Danger ever hovers above and around us, and unseen peril often most suddenly and unexpectedly darts out upon us from its ambush. But thus far only two petty annoyances had interfered with the deep, strong, and steady current of our joys.

One occurred at Port Royal, where our steamer was tied up all night to the wharf close to a freight house in which a thousand bags of Peruvian guano were stored, the intolerable stench of which invaded our ship, entered the saloons, took possession of every stateroom and remained with us all night. For pungency and power it certainly surpassed the fifty-nine distinct and independent bad smells that formerly regaled the traveler at one and the same instant of time in the streets of Cologne. We carried away from the Palmetto State only a vivid memory of a horrible odor that will last us a life time.

The other was a plague of insects at Fernandina, where our ship was taken captive by great swarms of little gnats, who were so glad to see us that it really seemed as if they were determined to literally eat us up. Some hid away in sheltered nooks out of the wind when we left, and seized every opportunity to renew their acquaintance with the northern strangers.

Our steamer took the outside route from Fernandina, and for some time before we reached the mouth of the St. John's our attention was called to the fact that the water of the river is carried to the north in a well defined stream, strongly distinguished by its color from that of the sea with which it refuses to assimilate. Fed by vast wooded swamps, great lakes and unnumbered tributary streams, the noble St. John's, after rolling in solemn majesty through low but picturesque banks for hundreds of miles, becomes at last a river of the ocean, scooping out for itself, like the Gulf Stream, a channel in the heavier waters of the sea.

The great rivers of the south are constantly and persistently endeavoring to barricade their mouths, as if principled against intercourse with the outside world. Channels for commerce are no sooner made and buoyed through the great bars and banks than they are closed again. The bold navigator is perplexed and confounded by changes which are constantly taking place, and the soundings of one day are no sure guide for the next.

At the mouth of the St. John's the breakers, foaming over vast submerged sand fields, please the eye, but are strongly suggestive of danger. The tortuous channel was said to be only six weeks old. It certainly differed greatly from the one through which we were piloted the previous year. Without the aid of steam-tugs, sailing vessels must find it very difficult and decidedly dangerous to make their way along the submerged banks and over the bar. The remains of two wrecks—one that of a steamer —which we passed, bore silent testimony to the perils which navigators are here called upon to encounter. A large number of pilots live at the mouth of the St. John's and study its constant mutations. They have built up a village on its left bank, which bears the appropiate name of "Pilot Town." Opposite this is the village of Mayport, which is inhabited mostly by fishermen, whose fishing nets, boats and reels gave variety and interest to the view.

Soon after we entered the river, a cloudy night deprived us of the pleasure we had hoped to experience in viewing for twenty-five miles the St. John's below Jacksonville. We tied up to the wharf at about 8 P. M.

The next day we took passage in the little steamboat that daily makes frequent trips to "The Home" (stopping at intermediate landings) upon a beautiful bank at the junction of Arlington creek and the river St. John's. We landed at St. Nicholas, and for a few brief but happy hours observed and tasted the sweets of plantation life. A re-union with some old and highly esteemed friends "refined the pure gold" of smiling, verdant, blooming nature's welcome.

The river bank where we landed is about twenty-five feet high, the top of which we reached by a winding path through a wild tangle of bushes and vines, covered with verdure and adorned with buds and blossoms. Once more upon the land—not in the

man-made city, but, to our great joy, in the God-made country—
how fresh and beautiful everything appeared! We bade the rest
speed on and leave us to enjoy in silence and solitude the delights
of the place and hour. Here a little nameless shrub, with its
curious leaves and fragrant blossoms, called to us from the thicket,
and climbing vines reached out their tendrils as if to lovingly
clasp and detain us as we passed. The mocking birds sang their
varied songs from unseen coverts; high-vine blackberry bushes,
loaded with green fruit, recalled many a familiar spot a thousand miles away, and faces we desired so much to see again. The
beautiful and spacious river, with its winding shores and low
green banks, its little skiffs and occasional steamers, compelled
us often to stop and look back. In full view, some four or five
miles away, was the city that we had just left; over our heads
was a smiling sky, and a sun glowing with a heat that was, at 80°
in the shade, made agreeable by a steady breeze from over the
water. Upon the top of the bank large, tall pines, with tops
crowned with green tasseled leaves, huge live oaks and water
oaks, some with great clustered stems, one with a spread of over
ninety feet, and all drooped and festooned with gray moss,
adorned and shaded the private carriage way that runs between
beautiful villas and the top of the river's bank. Occasionally we
rested on the seats which thoughtful hands had placed between
the trunks of the noble trees, and more deliberately studied our
novel and fascinating surroundings. Near the dwellings which
we passed were groves of orange trees, with their waxen, polished
leaves and opening and exquisitely sweet flowers, from one of
which alone 2,500 oranges had been recently taken. We saw
no alligators, but we learned that they were only just awakening
from their usual three months winter's sleep. Like other reptiles during this long season of torpor they take no food—thus,
with them, does sleep anticipate and closely resemble death.

Beneath a friendly and hospitable roof we slaked our thirst with cool and delicious orangeade—a drink differing from lemonade in that it is made of the juice of the sour orange instead of the lemon. We were regaled at lunch with oranges such as only Florida can produce, and with strawberries of large size and delicious flavor, taken from vines which were said to yield fruit continuously from January to June. From an orange orchard near by we were informed that 70,000 oranges had been taken within a few weeks. Before the crop was gathered, the trees, loaded with golden fruit, were said to have been marvelously beautiful. After a few hours of very great enjoyment, we steamed back to the city, where during the evening, in the saloon of the Texas, we were honored by a call from Gov. Brown, of Georgia, an old friend and Yale Law School classmate, some members of his family, and his brother, Col. Brown. The Governor, not only by his eminent success in political life, but more especially by the judicial laurels he has won and worn (having filled with distinguished ability the office of Chief Justice of the State of Georgia), has reflected honor upon the institution in which in part he received his education for the bar.* Col. Brown also studied law at Yale, and both gentlemen will be pleasantly remembered by all those who then enjoyed their acquaintance and friendship. Having introduced the Governor to our honored and venerable ex-Chief Justice Seymour, to whom by reputation he was well known, it was pleasant to witness the play and mingling of the intellectual light of these two justly distinguished men. As a young man, the author saw in Gov. Brown the promise which has been fulfilled in the golden maturity of later years.

After another night spent at the wharf on ship board, we con-

---

* The author has learned with pleasure since this was written, that Gov. Brown has been appointed by the present Governor of Georgia, to fill a vacancy, a United States Senator.

tinued our voyage in the early morning following, down and out of the river into the broad Atlantic.

The deep solitude of the sky-bound sea was relieved by occasional white-winged but lonely wanderers, bearing the varied products of distant and invisible lands. Dark, graceful smoke plumes, at first but dimly seen, revealed the presence of approaching steamers, and furnished welcome food for speculation. A German barque, looking as if it had wrestled with the elements, raised its flag to indicate that it desired to communicate with us. Having sighted the land after a voyage across the Atlantic of more than three thousand miles, its captain wished to ascertain as accurately as possible, his whereabouts, and to test the correctness of his reckoning. Upon a large blackboard, each vessel marked and exhibited to the other, first the latitude and then the longitude of the place where they met, as indicated by their respective logs or records, from which it appeared that the barque was fifty miles removed from the position its officers supposed it occupied.

In the neighborhood of Jupiter lighthouse, well down on the Florida coast, we met a schooner, one of whose officers inquired of us if we were going to Key West. It had no name in sight and was in ballast. As it sailed, after parting company with us, first towards the east, and soon, without any apparent good reason, changed its course to the south, our experienced passenger captain, having watched her closely, quickly made up his mind as to her character and business. He explained how easily but fraudulently a few thousand dollars could be made. "Depend upon it," said the captain, "she's a bank shark. She hails from Key West, no doubt, and very likely has a Key West license. She may have English papers, or both English and American papers. Nassau wreckers can't come here—our wreckers would drive them off. So at the Bahamas they will not allow our wreckers to interfere with their trade. They pay sometimes to pilot a vessel, and pilot her ashore—then they come in for salvage. "See," said he "she has no cargo aboard, and her boat is on her davits ready to be launched. You can't keep any account of goods taken from a wreck, and, running into Jupiter inlet, it is an easy matter to secure the plunder. Depend on't, them fellows are wide awake and watching for business. Their vessel shows no name and can't be reported."

An old resident of Nassau informed us that formerly there were persons doing business in that city, who were well known to be in collusion with certain ship owners who desired to sell their vessel property and cargoes to the insurance companies. When one of these men visited New York, very soon afterwards New York vessels would be wrecked in the Bahama waters. The masters of vessels purposely wrecked their vessels, an arrangement having been previously made with the wreckers, and a certain division of the salvage money agreed upon. It is believed and hoped that such cases do not often now occur.

Having no communication with the silent man at the wheel who held in his hands our lives upon the sea, we seldom knew precisely where we were, while we "floated like bubbles onward." Our steamer's prow still persistently pointed to the south, and we skirted the eastern shore of the Peninsula of Florida, in what is called "the Florida Gulf." A long sand beach gave to the blue sea a fringe of snowy whiteness. Beyond this, and between it and the sky, Southern Florida was sandwiched. A low, narrow, monotonous belt of green was all that we could see of the wet, wooded and flowery land, with its luscious fruits, beautiful birds and loathsome reptiles. As we approached the latitude of St. Augustine, our course was so far to the east that "the shining shore" was with more difficulty discerned. We almost envied the few long-sighted passengers who seemed to see and professed to describe the landmarks which our less gifted eyes failed to discern; and we thought of the holy seers who peer into the invisible world, and challenge our doubting faith with stories of spirit realms. A delicate blush, like that which lingers where the sun has set, curtained with rosy light the vanished land. Floating in and above this radiant air, as far as we could see along the western hem of the bending sky, were soft pearly clouds, most beautifully configured and colored, in which seemed to flit the happy and viewless spirits of the air. Around us the sea rolled in gentle ripples. Low, soothing sounds came to us as our beautiful ship cleaved the slumbering waters. The wind god breathed softly upon us from the south. So profound was the calm repose, all the mighty forces of nature, that at times in these latitudes make themselves felt and feared in the hurricane, seemed to have been chloroformed to insure for us a safe and pleasant voyage. None of our passengers were sick. A musing, dreamy spirit rested upon all. Most of the passengers were during the day upon the main deck, sitting upon folding-chairs under the awnings. Many mused in silence. Those who conversed spoke in low tones. Not the slightest excitement was manifested. The repose was profound; the rest was perfect. The pulses throbbed gently, and the gentlest ripples masked the tides of varied thought. In indolent repose, lulled by the softest sounds, slightly rocked by the gentle undulations of the slumbering sea, we passed the happy hours. The thermometer registered 80° in the shade, but the heat was far from being oppressive. The author took out his stylographic pen, placed it upon the white paper, and watched it while it ran.

The porpoises, whose gambols had given a pleasing variety to our quiet enjoyments, no longer raced with our steamer or leaped out of the water to challenge our admiration, and extort involuntary and loud applause. But near the close of day they came to the surface, leaving the deeper and cooler waters as the sun approached his setting, and like a dog before a flying horse, they raced with our ship. Directly ahead of and close to its sharp iron prow, with unmistakable evidences of pride and joy, they led the way, and seemed to challenge us to overtake them if we could. It was exceedingly interesting and somewhat exciting to observe them at such times. They frequently leaped bodily out of the water, and seemed to indulge in a competitive race with each other while testing their locomotive powers with those of the strange, man-made monster that had invaded their watery realm. The sport was continued for many a mile, but like the great golden god of day, they retired to depths we could not see, and to realms we had no capacity fully to explore.

We were told by an eye witness in Florida, of sanguinary fights between the porpoises and the sharks. Our lady informant on one occasion saw three or four of the former mercilessly attack one of the latter at the mouth of the St. John's, and the contest was continued until the surrounding water was colored with their blood.

In the Florida Gulf we soon parted company with the sea-birds. Not a single gull looked to us for supplies. The river St. John's probably teems with a larger quantity of food suited to their taste and adapted to their wants.

We missed them much. The ocean was more lonely. It had been exceedingly pleasant to watch them while they followed our ship, and as some of the more venturesome hovered over us, the undulations of their white wide-spread wings seemed like silent benedictions. The persistent waving of the unspotted feathery arms we gladly welcomed as favorable omens. We were not disposed to disregard the favorable augury of the beautiful birds who so persistently followed us over such wide spaces of ocean solitudes. Certain it is that clear skies, smooth seas and fair winds came with the gentle white-robed birds. As a natural consequence, mind and heart were pervaded with the dead faith of old and buried nations. Messages of love and peace seemed winged from heaven to earth. Give us, we inwardly exclaimed, the old dream of the past, in exchange for some of the fresher and more orthodox superstitions of modern times. It certainly affords a temporary pleasure to diversify hackneyed beliefs with a little of the antique.

We passed within ten or twelve miles of Jupiter Inlet and Jupiter Lighthouse, both being plainly in view. Soon after, the course of our ship was altered, and, steaming a little south of east, all traces of the Western Continent were lost to view, but low, light-colored clouds still curtained the vanished land.

Nearly all our passengers were upon the upper deck, musing in grateful shadows, and, with the thermometer at 80°, feeling only an agreeable warmth in the cooling wind. A marked change was soon observed in the color of the water. Its deep, rich, beautiful blue was unlike anything we had observed before or since we left New York. It attracted and riveted all eyes, and loosened every tongue. Gentlemen vied with the ladies in expressing the pleasure caused by this new sensation. One passenger, of a domestic turn of mind, inferred that it was Neptune's washing day, and that he had made a liberal use of his indigo bag. The mystery was soon explained. We were crossing the Gulf Stream; unconsciously we had entered the great ocean river. It had gathered up the equatorial heats, and, impelled by great natural laws which man has not been able as yet to fully discover and satisfactorily explain, it was executing its great beneficent mission, and materially aiding in equalizing the temperature of regions widely separated. How unlike it seemed to the Gulf Stream we crossed a year before! Then we brought with us from the frozen north opposing winds—and a just resentment was felt and seen in billows that hissed and howled, foaming in anger. Now, gentle winds, born in the warm tropics, traveled with the rolling tide, and hand in hand, air and water were bearing their thermal blessings onward. It is theirs to loosen the icy bands, and quicken into life the slumbering energies of northern climes.

At times dolphins played about our ship, and flying fish, like flocks of small birds, traversed considerable spaces of air, just clearing the waves. "The dolphin," said our passenger captain, "is the swiftest fish that swims the sea; where there are flying fish there are usually dolphins; the dolphins feed upon them, and the flying fish jump into the air and try to get away." Vague memories of ancient fables came dimly back to us as we watched the quick and playful movements of this interesting mammal of the sea. The dolphin was a sacred fish in Grecian mythology, and gave name if not inspiration to the famous Delphic Oracle that made known to mortals the decrees of the invisible and immortal gods. Modern scientists, upon observing the relative size and character of its brain, are disposed to entertain with more favor the belief of the ancients in its superior intelligence. As with the sea-birds, so with the fish, they stirred our souls with the quickening spirit of creeds that flourished in earth's fresh green spring time, and our voiceless thoughts declared—surely, these dolphins, which appear to be doing pilot and escort duty for our ship, are the lineal descendents of those which, in the old days of the old world, were the friends and benefactors of our race, almoners of divine favors and the bearers of messages from a world real but invisible; for with them came most delicious air, charming skies, and a quiet sea most beautifully colored.

Some of our sun-sets were exceptionally brilliant and beautiful. On one occasion, when a vast shoreless sea had received the day-god in its engulfing waters, great golden columns of brilliant light, radiating from the place of its burial, lighted up the western sky, and illumined the ocean's surface with their reflected light. At other times the zodiacal light, for several hours after the sun had set, rose like a monument, a huge pyramid of beauty, delicate, spirituelle, but well defined, upon the lofty apex of which rested the Pleiades. It was first observed by our venerable ex-Chief Justice, who seemed delighted to watch it during the early evening hours; he appeared to be very much at home among the beautiful stars of the southern sky, and to derive great pleasure in viewing the heavenly hosts, as, arranged in familiar constellations, they in solemn, silent majesty passed slowly by. The beauty of such skies is closely allied to the spiritual; their grandeur and solemnity is indeed divine; the undevout gazer upon such heavens is mad. But how dwarfed everything appeared when we looked down!

While still at sea, a beautiful silver crescent, like the visible eye of some invisible god, gazed from the western sky upon the setting sun. It added a new element of beauty to the night, but, as it increased in size, many a star retired, and the mysterious zodiacal light was unrevealed. It, like the ghosts, exists only in shadows.

On Saturday evening, the 13th day of March, we made "Isaac's Light" upon Isaac's Island, one of the Bahama Archipelago, and knew that the crossing of the gulf of Florida was, with us, an accomplished fact, and that a run during the night of about one hundred and twenty miles in the somewhat sheltered "New Providence Channel," among the islands, and towards the center of the group, would complete our voyage. We left the upper deck, with its brilliant canopy of gleaming stars, and retired early to our stateroom, that we might secure a good night's sleep and be able, at the break of day, to greet the rising sun and watch for the first indications of the lovely isle upon which Nassau, in the shade of its palms and other tropical trees, reposes.

The early Sabbath morn found a large number of our fellow voyagers intently scanning the eastern horizon from the good ship's upper deck. The usual speculations, inseparable from such an occasion, as to the time when we would reach our haven of rest, afforded fit material for the interchange of thought and a comparison of views. It was a subject in which all were deeply interested, but the weather had been so fine, and the voyage so pleasant, that we felt that in landing we should only exchange one form of happiness for another. Our ship was new, scrupulously neat and clean, staunch and steady, admirably officered and manned, and all its appointments were decidedly first-class, so that a sentiment akin to that which one entertains for a beautiful, spirited and intelligent horse, that has carried him safely and ministered to his happiness, sprang up and took firm root in the minds of the fortunate passengers in reference to the Steam Screw Ship Western Texas. The Texas we felt was our ship, and to it we seemed to owe a kind of fealty and true allegiance.

As the morning wore away, our passenger captain, with his trained, long-sighted sea-eyes, detected a faint trace of curling smoke upon the background of delicate low clouds rising from the eastern horizon. This, he assured us, was smoke from a fire on the island of New Providence. Soon after, his telescopic eyes discerned in a white, perpendicular line, about as big around as a spider's thread, the coralline lighthouse at the eastern end of Hog Island, at the entrance of Nassau harbor. Very soon the less visually gifted were able to verify assertions which, to their more narrow vision, seemed to be prophetic—and their faith was soon supplemented by actual knowledge. Thus is it often with hidden truths and mysteries profound!

Between 9 and 10 o'clock in the forenoon we crossed the bar, and once more revelled in the picturesque beauty of the winding shores, the honey-combed rocks, the stretches of white sand beaches, the low green islets, the tropical verdure, and the sparkling and gleaming waters, dotted and striped with colors which no pen can adequately describe. We seemed to feel their welcome in the soft and soothing wind. For men and their works we cared little—they were so dwarfed by those which we had left behind us. But for the coral isles and keys, and for the elements above and around them—the handiwork of the world's great Architect—we entertained a genuine affection, and our hearts experienced a thrill of pleasure as we gazed upon the beautiful panorama which was gradually disclosed as we neared the place of our landing.

It being Sunday, a much smaller crowd than usual awaited our arrival upon the neighboring streets and adjacent wharfs. A few young negroes, black and glossy, nearly nude, were perched like great frogs upon the dock, and soon amused the new-comers by diving for pennies and other coin. The first on shore to recognize us, as we scanned the dusky upturned faces, were those little black dots of children—Moody and Sankey. They bowed and smiled and waved their hands, while eyes and teeth gleamed with unmistakable pleasure at seeing once more those who had listened to and taken an interest in their songs. The tall, manly form of our old yachtsman, Capt. Sampson, with his neat nautical blue uniform and "Triton" hat, was a very noticeable landmark, and, when he discovered us, he triumphantly exclaimed, as one of his hearers informed us—"Dere's a gentleman who's consigned to me; he knows de Trident; he ken tell you about her; he sailed with Sampson when der Trident was first built; he's consigned to Sampson—sure!" He was not long in finding us, and, with a hearty shake of the hands, interlarded his speech of welcome with those graceful, courtly airs and diplomatic phrases which, unstudied, he knows so well how to employ. Seizing our bundles he escorted us to the best and largest carriage at the landing, and loaded us up. Soon a man appeared who claimed ours was his carriage, and that from the bows of the steamer he had engaged it before any one had a chance to put a foot on the dock, and had put his bundles in it while he went for the other members of his party. "Can't help dat," said Sampson; "dis carriage belongs to dis gentleman—why, he spoke for dis carriage las' year! Driver, you take dis gentleman and dese yere ladies to der hotel,"—and he did so before we had fully time to consider and decide the doubtful question of our right to keep possession of the vehicle.

CHAPTER XXII.

> "Where'er I roam, whatever lands I see,
> My heart, untraveled, fondly turns to thee."—GOLDSMITH.

HAVING embodied in the preceding chapters all the information we obtained concerning Nassau and the Bahamas during our visits in 1879 and 1880, which we deemed would be useful or interesting to our readers, but little remains to be added before we lay down a pen which we have found it a difficult matter to stop.

After returning to Jacksonville in April, 1879, we spent several weeks in Florida enjoying its climate, and waiting for the time to come when summer at the north should be firmly established. We soon learned to love the dreamy lakes and languid rivers; the deep solitude of the pine forests; the wild, weird beauty of the cypress swamps; the gracefulness of the palms and palmettos; the grand old water-oaks and live-oaks, all profusely draped, festooned and decorated, from largest branch to smallest twig, with Spanish moss, so gray and sombre; the stately magnolias, royally adorned with dark waxen leaves, and large, white, floral incense cups; the orange orchards, whose leaves, and flowers, and fruit seemed intended to minister to the happiness rather of gods than men; the floral treasures everywhere scattered with lavish hand; and the birds, unsurpassed in plumage and un-equaled in song. We lingered for a while, reluctant to leave, after many of the larger hotels were closed. At last our time to depart came, and we made a part of the extreme rear of a great, but generally intelligent and cultivated army, which, having in the previous fall and winter fled from frost, was now being driven and scattered by a nearly tropical sun.

Dimpled all over with smiles, and reposing in calm and quiet majesty under an atmosphere that glowed with the genial warmth of May, the ocean, like a good foster mother, rocked us gently upon its bosom, tenderly floated us hundreds of miles homeward, and at last landed us safely upon old familiar shores, that had, in our absence, exchanged their robes and wrappings of ice and snow for beautiful carpets of verdure of the purest and brightest emerald.

Our second visit to the Isles of Summer was less pleasant than the first by reason of the heat, for the same causes which pro-duced the remarkably mild winter of 1879-80 at the north, gave to Florida and the Bahamas weather exceptionally warm. As we had anticipated when we turned our backs upon the northern March in the manner which we in our last chapter described, we escaped a great deal of exceedingly disagreeable weather, for winter and summer, as in other years, struggled for the mastery upon the neutral domain of spring, while fortune favored both sides with characteristic fickleness. But when in Florida and Nassau, both upon land and water, the thermometer during the greater part of every day stood at eighty and upwards in the shade, and hot, sultry, southerly winds were more than usually prevalent, we were at times led to exclaim, O, for a cool puff of northern wind, and carpets of beautiful snow; and mountains lofty and snow-capped! O, for an exchange of lazy and indolent air for an atmosphere that vitalizes the blood, stimulates the nerves, gives birth to noble purposes, and inspires with a laudable ambition!

Afterwards, when the weekly mail arrived, with letters and newspapers from home, and we learned how badly both March and April had conducted themselves at the north in our absence, we immediately rushed out from beneath the grateful shade of tropical trees, and, with heads bowed but well protected, we made to the hot sun, and to the beautiful lands that panted in its fierce and scorching rays, our most humble and sincere apologies.

At the conclusion of our second visit to the Bahamas, we had a most delightful voyage in the Western Texas, of the C. II. Mallory & Co.'s line, from Nassau to Fernandina. We were favored with clear skies, while beneath and around us the Atlantic was at rest. All the storm gods of the sea were indulging in deep, profound, voluptuous sleep. Our ship rivaled the ducks upon sheltered lakes in the quiet grace with which it passed over the smooth waters. We spent much of the time during the day dreamily watching the sky, the birds, the murmuring waves, the fish, the sea weed, and passing vessels. The glory of the stars and of the Southern Cross added brilliancy and gladness to the night.

> "New stars all night above the brim
>   Of waters lightened into view;
> They climb'd as quickly, for the rim
>   Changed every moment as we flew."

There are often among the passengers on shipboard "late birds," sometimes, upon the land, called "larks," who linger behind after the staid, prudent, and conservative have retired, and, with songs and stories, and fragrant Havanas, endeavor to get more than the average amount of enjoyment out of hours generally devoted to sleep. But the passengers who sailed with us to and from the Isles of Summer were so far homogeneous, that none had occasion to complain that the hilarity and good fellowship of a few were carried so far into the night as to encroach upon hours generally devoted to sleep.

Sailing in the path of an ocean current which furnished our ship with a part of its motive power, and aided by a wind that, while it warmed, wafted us on our way, we were not long in reaching the Florida coast. The trip was also materially shortened because health and happiness winged the flying hours.

About four weeks after our last arrival in Florida, we proceeded by rail from Jacksonville to Fernandina, and intercepted the steamship City of Austin, Capt. Stevens, of the C. H. Mallory & Co.'s New York and Nassau line, which, on its way to New York, had stopped there for passengers and freight. We found it a good ship, well officered, manned and equipped, though the closing of the Royal Victoria Hotel caused it to be crowded with passengers, but as during the voyage the weather was pleasant, little inconvenience was experienced from that cause, the cases of sea sickness being very few in number and mild in type. The passengers spent the days upon deck, and many of the evenings also, notwithstanding the heavy dews. The profound mystery which seems ever to brood over the ocean and penetrate its profound depths, is greatly intensified at night. We were much impressed with it as our gallant ship tore and leaped into the dark, leaving behind a brilliant but troubled path of foam and fire. Around it the phosphorescent light gleamed in the waves and sparkled in the spray. A halo of white and luminous foam girdled the ship, which, with its long and brilliant train, made it seem, prehaps, to the marine monsters miles below under its keel, like a strange comet of the sea.

While sitting in the evening upon one of the camp stools with which the deck of the Austin was supplied, Captain Stevens occasionally favored us with his presence, and we succeeded in obtaining from him some interesting stories of the sea, founded upon his personal experience. He is a medium sized, strongly built, calm, cool-headed, self-possessed man, on whose judgment and discretion we think one may safely rely in time of danger. His hair is perfectly white, but not with age, as he is only some forty-two or forty-three years old. Having spent most of his life upon the water, and been a number of times shipwrecked, the hardships he has endured have left their record upon his hair.

One evening while the captain was making a tour of inspection of the ship, he stopped for awhile and occupied a seat on deck beside us. We were between Capes Lookout and Hatteras, and sailing over what the sailors call, on account of the foul weather often experienced there, "the ragged edge of the ocean." The perils incident to and inseparable from the navigation of the ocean by steam having been referred to, Captain Stevens, in illustration of the subject, said: "Disasters occur upon the water sometimes from unexpected and inexplicable causes. A few years ago I commanded a steamer which foundered and went to the bottom when the weather was fair and the sea smooth. It occurred at a place very near where we are now. She had not been, so far as I knew or was informed, weakened by storms, or damaged by any of those accidents to which steamers and other vessels are sometimes exposed. In the night, some two hours or more before daybreak, the engineer sent me word that the ship was leaking, and the water steadily gaining upon the pumps. I found that the entire loss of the ship was only a matter of a few hours time. I gave directions to have a report sent to me every fifteen minutes of the progress of the water, and commenced at once making arrangements for abandoning the vessel. The second officer asked if he should not awaken the passengers. I replied, no; let them sleep on—and they did.

They no doubt would have had less pleasant dreams if they had known or suspected that the ship all the time was gradually set- tling down deeper and deeper in the water. I sent up signal rockets of distress, and kept the crew busy. All the life boats were made ready for immediate use, and when every practicable measure to ensure the preservation of life had been taken, the passengers were awakened and informed of the condition of the ship, and of the steps I had taken to prevent any loss of life. Although greatly surprised, and somewhat excited, there was no panic, and all behaved well. In the dim morning light, a steamer, that had noticed our signals, was seen in the distance approaching. Her captain, upon learning our condition, agreed to receive us on board, and did so. The transfer was quietly and safely effect- ed. No boat was swamped, and everything passed off as quietly as a military dress parade. After the personal safety of all the passengers and crew was assured, I proposed, as my ship was still afloat, to make an effort to save the baggage. This I succeeded in doing; but I had no sooner returned with the last boat-load of trunks, when the abandoned steamer sank out of sight."

The quiet, modest way in which Captain Stevens described this thrilling episode in his life upon the ocean, in connection with the facts of the case as he had described them, very favorably impressed us. Coolness and courage in time of peril must accom- pany and supplement sagacity, prudence and a thorough knowl- edge of one's business, in order to qualify a man to properly fill the responsible position which he occupied.

Little Sankey was included among our passengers. He was the protegé of the captain, who, having been attracted by his shining qualities, concluded to transplant the little tropical negro, and see what effect cultivation upon American soil would produce. Good citizens are sometimes made out of less promising materials. Having become acquainted with many of the passengers in the court of the Royal Victoria Hotel, he received, particularly from the ladies, attentions which helped to palliate the heart-aches incident to a sudden sundering of all the tendrils of affection that had bound him to the small coral island upon which he was born and reared. Words of kindness were mingled with the small coin given him from time to time, partly as a reward for such services as he was able to render. Sometimes he was seen reclining upon packages of freight, taciturn and sober, apparently the victim of two maladies—sea-sickness and sickness of the heart. He, however, manifested as much fortitude and cheerfulness as could be expected under the peculiar circumstances in which he was placed.

Although during our absence new scenes had afforded us much enjoyment, while relaxation from business and a change of air had been of substantial benefit in a sanitary point of view, our hearts throbbed with no small degree of pleasurable excitement as we approached the city of New York, through shores which art and nature have done so much to adorn. Long Island and the Island of Manhattan, as seen from the deck of the Austin, belted with forests of masts, enlivened by numberless steamers, each with passengers enough to make a good sized town, and covered with the immense warehouses and palaces of merchant princes, together with the constantly increasing evidences that we were in close proximity to vast, swift, and ever changing eddies and currents of human life, strangely and sharply contrasted with all that we had seen and experienced among the Isles of Summer, upon the peninsular of Florida, and in ocean solitudes.

Our return to the north was well-timed. The morning was lovely; the air of a most agreeable temperature; the sky cloudless. Nature, with smiling face, welcomed us home. The little dimpled waves glistened and gleefully danced in the sun-light.

Brooklyn from her heights, Jersey City from her lowly position upon the shore, and New York from behind her shipping, seemed to waft us pleasant greetings. Our fellow passengers thronged the deck of the Austin, and exchanged cards and congratulations. We again found that the love of native land is intensified by absence. Exile hallows and makes home more sacred. The earthly home suggested the heavenly, and we repeated the poet's appropriate and tuneful numbers—

> "Lone voyager on time's sea!
> When my dull night of being shall be past,
> O may I waken in a land at last,
>   Welcome as this to me!"

www.ingramcontent.com/pod-product-compliance
Lightning Source LLC
Chambersburg PA
CBHW021337110726
47900CB00005B/1512